Award-winning jou....................................iminal Börge Hellström are Sweden's most acclaimed fiction duo. Their unique ability to combine inside knowledge of the brutal reality of criminal life with searing social criticism in complex, intelligent plots has put them at the forefront of modern Scandinavian crime writing. Visit them at www.roslund-hellstrom.com.

Kari Dickson was born in Edinburgh, but grew up bilingually as her mother is Norwegian. She has a BA in Scandinavian Studies and an MA in Translation. She currently teaches in the Scandinavian department at the University of Edinburgh.

## Also by Roslund and Hellström

# TWO SOLDIERS

## ROSLUND & HELLSTRÖM

*Translated from the original Swedish*
*by Kari Dickson*

Quercus

First published in Great Britain in 2013 by Quercus Editions Ltd
This paperback edition published in 2014 by

Quercus Editions Ltd
55 Baker Street
7th Floor, South Block
London
W1U 8EW

First published in Swedish under the title *Två Soldater*

Published by agreement with the Salomonsson Agency.

A CIP catalogue record for this book is available
from the British Library

ISBN 978 0 85738 685 4
ISBN 978 0 85738 686 1 (EBOOK)

10 9 8 7 6 5 4 3 2 1

Typeset by e-type, Liverpool

Printed and bound in Great Britain by Clays Ltd, St Ives plc

We want to be loved; failing that, admired; failing that, feared; failing that, hated and despised. At all costs we want to stir up some sort of feeling in others. Our soul abhors a vacuum. At all costs it longs for contact.

(Hjalmar Söderberg, Doktor Glas, 1905)

Ur brutha is like ur own body,
Lives 4 u and dies 4 u,
There in the morning and the evening,
In pain and in pleasure. But then dosnt
Listen 2 orders. Finds Bazz, Raha, Jamba.
Respect. U know deja. Wallah rules:
A BULLET IN THE KNEECAP. We r
bruthas. We r power. We r fighters and
famly 2 death.

(Evidence 2012-0221-BG2219 p. 41,<br>found in Adidas bag 120207)

much

earlier

SHE'S BEEN LIVING here for so long.

It's mostly voices.

Maybe footsteps.

When they pass outside in the long corridor, the fast ones and ones that seem to shuffle along; sometimes they stop by the metal door, as if they're listening, and she wants to call out to them, ask them to come in and hold her hand. They never do. They carry on down the corridor, steps that drown in the regular beep of the machine and the ticking of the bright lights – beep tick beep tick – she closes her eyes but doesn't dare to cover her ears – beep tick beep tick – she's on her own and doesn't want to be.

---

Her face, so strange.

She's sixteen, maybe seventeen, or even eighteen.

But she looks old. Whether it's the pain, fear, or whatever, how the body encapsulates time, lets it settle.

She seems to be lying comfortably, the stretcher she's been rolled onto is wide and her body is thin. The room is much bigger than the others, the bed and cupboard and table and chair and shower and it's – even though someone is breathing close by – almost empty. The green overall by her feet, a hand rubbing up and down on the coarse material to warm it up before moving to her young thighs, carefully touching her genitals, fingertips against the head of her uterus, while the other hand keeps a firm hold of the needle, thirty centimetres of plastic tubing against the membrane that is so soft, a clear balloon of water flying, bouncing away. The needle again, again, again, it gives up, breaks.

———

Footsteps that stop and then vanish.

Someone opens a door further up. Someone else screams, or cries, it's hard to make out.

She doesn't have her eyes closed any more. It's white, everything she sees, white, almost glossy, the naked lights and the machine with its digits and green lines and thin tubes. It'll take a while, and then a bit more, before her eyes get used to it.

It doesn't hurt as much anyway. Or she's just coping with it. Like her period. Exactly the same. But more, more often, longer.

Two of the people in the room, both women, are wearing green overalls. The others, three women and three men, are wearing white overalls that cover dark trousers, dark shoes.

The green ones are standing nearest, the white ones further away, nearly by the wall.

She doesn't know any of them, at least she doesn't think she does, or maybe, that woman, she recognises her, she works here, and him, the one who broke down the door and screamed at her, held her to the floor, put her in an armlock.

———

It's easier to see now. She turns towards the window. It's dark outside, cold, the snow is deep; only a few days ago she made an angel out there, lay down on the ground and swept her arms and legs back and forth, back and forth until they shouted at her, came over and grabbed her hands and carried her in. Now there's an ambulance out there beside her angel, in the middle of the big yard. She tries to get up so she can go over to the window and wave down at the guard who's waiting by the front of the car, a thick cloud where his breath meets the cold air.

'Come on.'

The green overall sighs; the thin body on the stretcher looks so vulnerable, so wrong.

'Come on, you have to lie down.'

Sweetie. Not here.

The room the corridor the metal door the bars.

Sweet, sweet, sweetie.

'Did you hear me? You *have* to lie down.'

The green overall's hands on her arms, chest, thighs, they pull at the hard, brown strap down her back, point the electronic arm at exactly the spot on her stomach where the heartbeat can be heard loudest, one hundred and forty-seven beats per minute, racing, speeding.

She's almost completely dilated now, nine centimetres, not long now.

———

Like waves. Like fire.

Something hitting, pressing, forcing. It's happening inside her body. But she has no control.

———

She tries to look over at the window again, the bars that are in the way, the round black steel poles across the great sheet of glass. Out there – inside the fence and sharp barbed wire – the searchlights brush the white snow, such a different light compared to ordinary street lamps. The ambulance is still there by the snow angel and the guard is slapping his arms to his sides to keep warm, and if she raises her head a bit more and lets go of the rough edge of the bed, she can see the other car as well, small, grey and completely dark.

'The waters?'

'Clear.'

'Head?'

'Engaged.'

The people in green overalls are constantly touching her, talking to her. The people in white overalls are standing still with their backs to the wall.

She's lying here for security reasons.
That's what they said.
A risk that she might try to escape.

———————

The waves. The fire. The pressure. The pounding. The force.
She screams.
The ribcage that is squeezed together as it passes through the birth canal and the water that is forced out and the lungs that are filled with air – the first breath.
It's not her. She realises now. It's not her who's screaming.

———————

Something wet, warm on her stomach. A baby. Her baby. She sees it as the two hands that quickly become four hands lift it up, carry it across the room, through the door, out into the corridor, away.

———————

The woman and the man – the ones holding the baby, who went away with it and then came back without it – are taking off their white coats now, jeans and a jacket underneath, and the woman reaches over for a briefcase, fills in one sheet of paper, then another and another. The others – who've been standing farthest away, almost blocking the door, who haven't spoken at all – are wearing blue under the white. The course material of the prison service uniform, oblong name tags in hard plastic just over their left breast. The men beside them have normal suits on underneath, they're not wearing uniforms, but she still knows that they're police; the big one in his forties is a detective inspector and the other one's a police trainee and not much older than her.
She doesn't know them, and yet they've seen her naked, being emptied.

———————

It had been lying on her stomach, breathing close, a wet mouth.

They should have put a blanket over the red and white skin that was soft and smooth and that no one had touched.

————

She looks out of the barred window again. The midwife and the nurse open the doors to the white ambulance, a mobile incubator held like a basket between them. The grey private car immediately behind, the couple in jeans and jackets open the front doors and get in, the vehicles drive in convoy down the asphalt strip across the yard to the high fence and sharp barbed wire, the gate slowly slides open, then one carries on towards the hospital in Örebro, whereas the other has farther to go, to the family unit in Botkyrka.

She wonders whether the shiny road is slippery, if it's difficult to drive so far at night.

————

She's not said anything for a while now.

Not when they took the baby that was resting on her tummy, not when the two vehicles left Sweden's top security prison for women.

And it's as if she can't bear it any more, the silence.

She turns towards the only person still in the room, the one that's a policeman in his forties, who held her to the floor, forced her out of her home.

'Did you see?'

He starts, lost in his own thoughts, or maybe he's just forgotten what her voice sounds like.

'See what?'

She points to her tummy, which is still wet, she should maybe wipe away the clear stuff and the other stuff that's a bit bloody.

'If it was a boy or a girl?'

# now

## first part

### (twenty-eight days)

Light outside.

The blanket that was red with a touch of yellow and perhaps a thin white stripe round the edge, didn't cover the whole of the dirty window.

He could see that now.

They normally lived in the dark and slept through the light, only waking when the evening and night had returned, but in August – and with that bloody blanket that wasn't as big as it should be – the day ambushed them around about this time; no matter how tightly he shut his eyes, the transparent square on the inside of his eyelids got bigger, it grew and wormed its way slowly in, into his brain, into his chest.

He punched the wall and sat up in the low bed, a thick mattress that had been in one of the big houses at Hägersten, the sort that costs about twenty thousand, a thick square on the shiny linoleum floor.

She was naked, asleep.

Her pale, soft skin; she was lying so still, her back towards him and he carefully ran his hand down her hip, behind, thigh, she moved uneasily, turned over, maybe she was dreaming – it looked like it – her face tense and rubbing her feet together, as she often did.

He was just as naked. He sometimes forgot. How incredible that was. Another person who could see his skin and didn't laugh. Sometimes he wondered if it was all in his head. He had been so fucking certain that he knew what they saw. He wasn't any more. It had started with Leon, they were eleven and one day they had ended up in the same room, watching each other take their clothes off and his eyes – no repulsion, scorn, or even surprise. Until now, only Leon, no one else. Not even the mirrors. He had smashed all the ones at his mum's and turned away every time he went past the wide, rectangular one at his gran's, every time he went down the hall, he knew exactly when it was looking at him and exactly when to look away.

He looked at her.

Never a woman. Not before her. She hadn't said anything either, hadn't been frightened, or evasive, or even asked questions.

His hand was still on her hip, she opened her eyes, squinted at him, with small pupils that focused on the light shining in through the gap between the blanket and the window frame. Her gentle fingertips on his back, over the skin that was thick with uneven edges, pieces of a jigsaw puzzle lying in a heap instead of laid out flat, he had lain on top of her for a long time after, she had her period and they both smelled pretty potent. It was hard to lie there without moving, sweat slipping on sweat.

He wasn't tired. He should be. Early morning and they never usually got up before late afternoon; if he was to guess, they'd been asleep for about three hours, couldn't be helped sometimes.

He dried himself with the sheet, then smoothed on the cream from the white tube that was always close to the bed, his feet legs balls back stomach neck, but never his face, never there.

'Give it to me.'

He looked at her.

'What?'

'Gabriel, give it to me. The tube. I'll rub it in, you can't reach everywhere properly, like on your shoulders, your back.'

She held out her hand for the sticky, broken tube and he rapped her hard, the palm of his hand against her fingers, a red mark across some of them. He stared at her and she looked down; he turned away and rubbed cream onto his chest and thighs.

They left the bedroom, out into the sitting room; fully clothed bodies in the corner sofa and armchair and further away on the floor – Jon, Big Ali, Javad Hangaround, Bruno – stoned, sleeping, breathing.

He nudged, shook . . .'

He slapped Javad in the face.

*She shouldn't have reached for the cream.*

'You gotta wake up, brother.'

'Why?'

*She shouldn't have asked to put cream on his back.*

'Because *I'm* awake.'

Fags ends, bottles, needles, cans on the table top that was covered in yellowish swill, spat-out peanuts and leftover pizza salad. They were awake now, but just lying there, exhausted as you are after only a couple of hours' sleep, and he leaned over towards the new TV screen, searching for the purring high pitch that had accompanied the night and still reverberated in the walls of the room. They all stirred when he turned it off, even the stack of DVDs wobbled, fell forwards.

The hallway had always been empty.

No furniture, no rugs, no lamps.

Only one thing leaning up against the wall, long and shiny with rows of tiny, tiny white pearls around the edge. He really liked it, often straightened it – it was important that it could be seen when he and she came in the front door. A shoehorn. From when they'd burgled that enormous fucking pile outside Södertälje. They'd sold the rest to that guy in Nacka, but the shoehorn, he didn't sell it.

She was still naked.

He kissed her tits and handed her her jeans and a cropped T-shirt with shiny writing on it; his own clothes were still on the chair out on the balcony, the black joggers with white stripes, grey hoodie, red baseball cap.

He was hungry. He wasn't usually hungry in the morning.

The top shelf in the fridge – what was left of a big bottle of Coke.

On a narrow shelf in the larder, an unopened packet of wine gums, he picked out the red and green ones.

It was blowing a bit outside, easy to breathe.

They walked side by side, he thought she was beautiful, he knew that he wasn't. They passed the first parking place and she headed towards a silver BMW, eight hundred and fifty thousand in cash, but he caught her hand, not that one, not today. They walked slowly through his past, present and future. He knew every concrete block, every asphalt path, listened to what no one else could hear, could distinguish the smells, the one from a burnt-out rubbish room and the one from the deserted kiosk where he'd bought sweets, porn, hash when he was a kid, even the smell that wasn't there any more, the sweet smell that came from the fruit stall on the square, the bastards should have paid more.

The whole of Råby was empty.

The concrete tower blocks so silent, desolate, not even the curtains in the windows twitched. He turned to Wanda, her face and eyes, and he wondered what she really saw, she who hadn't seen what others saw, who came from another world further away, this was the Råby she could see, no other images, not like the ones from before, when there were more people outside.

The metro, like a living, reliable blue vein running through something that didn't exist.

The image, maybe the smell he liked best.

The way in. The way out.

The steps down; they walked past a skinny little guy, might have been ten but was actually twelve, gold chain round his neck, hair greased back.

'Gabriel.'

The runt had said his name. He didn't turn round.

'Gabriel!'

He stopped. Four fast steps back.

The little guy smiled proudly and held out his hand.

'*Sho*, bro.'

Ran his other hand through his slickback, stood a little taller.

A hard slap.

The one cheek.

An obvious mark left by one of his rings.

'You know . . .'

Gabriel looked at the runt. Not a flicker. Just as proud, just as tall. His voice just as jarring when he held out his skinny hand again, didn't give in.

'. . . Eddie's the name. One love, brother.'

Gabriel didn't hit him again.

He carried on down the stairs and past the old tart in the ticket office and she said nothing, not even when he turned round and nodded at Wanda, she was with him and she wasn't going to pay and no one was going to make a fuss.

They leaned against the window, the glass cold against their foreheads, past stations that all looked the same.

The same concrete blocks, the same people on their way home, on their way out.

Hallunda, Alby, Fittja, Vårby gård, Vårberg, Skärholmen. Twelve and a half minutes.

They got off, went through a shopping centre that with every revamp got more like a gallery and less of a hub, the shiny glass walls of the elevator, down to three thousand parking spaces. They went as far back as they could – new signs and new colours, but it smelt the same, damp and exhaust.

He asked for the Adidas bag and picked out a Mercedes. A slightly older model. They were the easiest.

He started the clock on his mobile phone and 00.00 lay down on his back on the mucky asphalt and with bent legs pushed his torso back under the car, arms above his head 00.05 in the small space behind the grille, looking for the red cable that was thin and obvious and attached to the car alarm. As was his habit, he used a small pair of hairdresser's scissors to cut through the red plastic, then wriggled back out and stood up, the newly sharpened end of a screwdriver into the petrol tank lock 00.11, then a wrench round the screwdriver handle, he turned, could almost hear the air pressure drop, and all the doors opened simultaneously.

He glanced over towards the exit, raised an arm and got a raised arm back, she was standing there and she was reliable and they were still the only ones there.

He got into the leather-clad driver's seat and took out 00.15 a feeler gauge from his bag, held it against the cigarette lighter filament, then put it into the ignition and turned, turned, turned, heated it up again, turned again, quickly melted down 00.24 the small sharp plastic pegs that would catch, the actual locking mechanism.

She raised her arm.

Voices.

Steps.

He felt inside 00.28 the ignition with a biro, nothing catching now, took out another car key – any of the ones lying at the bottom of the bag, because older Mercedes generally started once the plastic pegs were gone – and checked the clock, 00.32.

They didn't talk much. They never did.

He had nothing to say to her.

Gabriel drove out of the shopping centre car park, slowly through the southern suburbs of Stockholm in the middle lane. You could see the city behind them and he accelerated into the outside lane, they were heading north, another forty kilometres to go. They normally stopped at the Shell station by the Täby exit, in front of the square glass cabinet for air and water; Wanda normally went into the dirty toilet round the back and prepared herself for the visit and he went into the shop and got his two bottles of Coke from the chiller and stared at the woman behind the counter who looked away as he walked out, who never said anything, who knew his sort, had seen too many young men like him, knew that it wasn't worth risking that arrogant and superior look, to challenge him and ask for eighteen kronor for the drinks in his hand.

He was sitting in the driver's seat, radio on full blast, half a bottle of Coke on the dashboard, when she came back from the toilet after twenty minutes. He always tried to check her walking first, see if her movements were normal, then if she had a dirty back from the hard floor – there should be no signs.

They left the motorway and from the exit to Aspsås you could already see the church, the small town, the prison. The almost deserted prison car park, he always went as far in as he could, close to the high wall.

He was eighteen. She was seventeen.

They didn't go many places, didn't often go far, but here, obviously they came here.

She straightened her jeans, top, looked for the mirror on the back of the sun visor that wasn't there, changed the angle of the one on the door instead and smiled into it, then walked towards the grey concrete building as he drove towards the church that loomed a couple of kilometres away – he would wait there until she was ready, by the carefully raked gravel path in front of the rows of headstones in the churchyard.

The gate in the wall, the intercom by the handle, she turned towards the camera and microphone.

'Yes?'

It crackled, in the way that all loudspeakers by all prison gates crackle.

'Visitor.'

'Who for?'

'Leon Jensen.'

Someone in a blue uniform ran a nimble finger through a list of registered visitors.

'And you are?'

'Wanda.'

'Surname?'

'Wanda Svensson.'

She was freezing.

There was no wind, bright sunshine bouncing on the concrete, she was sweating and freezing.

There was a click. The door was open.

Heavy steps over to central security and the window and the uniform that belonged to the hands that looked at her.

'ID.'

It was colder. She was even colder, shaking.

'Have you been here before?'

'Yes.'

'Then you know what to do. Go in there. Take off your coat.'

A stuffy room.

Just one window, with bars.

The wall over there, from the inside.

One two three four ten-kronor coins, both mobile phones and her key ring in one of the small lockers. She locked it, walked slowly over to the grey metal detector, through it, clutching the key to the locker in her hand.

The piercing, monotone noise around her, inside her.

*You have to be heard.*

Two uniforms stepped forwards, checked the red light that was flashing in the middle of the arch, the one that indicated waist level.

'Your pockets.'

Freezing, sweating, freezing.

She made a show of searching her front pockets, back pockets, still clutching the locker key in her hand and then went through the metal detector again. The same piercing noise.

Leon's orders.

*You have to be searched.*

'Still waist level.'

One of the uniforms positioned two blocks about half a metre apart, the other held out a long plastic stick; she had to step up onto the blocks, she had to stand still with her legs apart while the plastic stick slid over her hips, the outside of her thighs, the inside of her thighs.

'Your belt.'

She took it off and put it in a plastic container.

'Oh . . . sorry.'

Her hand up in the air, the key inside it, as if she had forgotten it, she looked at them and smiled sheepishly and they stared at her until she had put it in the plastic container beside the belt.

'Go through again.'

Her chest, a small point slightly to the left, just there, it hurt so much.

She was sure they would see that she was trembling.

She walked through.

*But only that.*

Not a peep. Not any other sound.

*This time only, you have to be heard, you have to be searched, that's all.*

She waited while the uniform that had been standing furthest away let the dog finish sniffing the belt, then she was given it back and pulled it through the loops on her jeans, tried to meet their eyes and then hurried over the concrete floor towards the visiting room that was in the middle, and a bit brighter than the others.

They locked the door from the outside.

She had sat on the chair before. She looked around.

It wasn't a kind room.

She often did that, divided rooms and flats and houses into kind ones and mean ones. This one was mean. There was plastic under the sheet on the bed and no one would ever sleep there. The yellowed porcelain sink and tap only had cold water. The window was barred and looked out over a strip of grass that led to a seven-metre high wall and unpainted administration buildings.

She wasn't as cold any more, was barely sweating.

She washed her hands and dried them with some sheets of toilet paper from the roll at the end of the bed. She looked in the mirror, smiled as she always did – her little brother called it her mirror face – checked her lips, eyebrows, hair.

A metal door in a prison has heavy locks that make a very particular sound. When someone unlocks it, there's a kind of clunking, quiet at first, then louder.

'One hour.'

He came in.

'We'll come for you first, then her. OK?'

The two guards who'd walked in front of and behind him stopped in the doorway, nodded to her and waited until she nodded back – they could go, they could lock the door again.

He pointed to the bed. She sat down, he pointed again, she lay down on her back, the pillow was hard and the plastic chafed her neck when the sheet slipped down.

He looked at her.

She knew how she had to lie when his hands undid her belt, pulled down her zip, pulled off her trousers.

Leon's hand on her skin, just above the knee, her thigh, it pulled her knickers to the side and made her open her legs wider, his index finger and thumb against her labia.

———

Around the outside.

'Relax.'

Inside.

———

He found it, held it, pulled it out.
    A plastic bag, hard to see through.
    He weighed it in his hand.
    Two hundred grams.

Leon smiled at her, the slippery, shiny plastic bag in his hand, but maybe not enough for her to dare to smile back.

'You'll come back. Here. In exactly fourteen days.'

Was he pleased, had she done well? She breathed in carefully, hesitated, and again. Then smiled.

'Put it up. Put it up again, but then *dump* it before you come. You have to smell. But have nothing up there.'

They were standing close. He wasn't much taller than she was.

She shouldn't have smiled.

Leon's voice, raised again.

'Whore, d'you understand?'

His movements, angry.

'*Whore*, with your stupid fucking smile, you're to smell but be empty, get it?'

His breath. She nodded.

'I get it.'

He looked at her. *I get it.* You don't get fuck all.

Throughout the week, he'd made sure to mention that he was getting a visit, who was coming to visit, when she was coming again.

Two hundred grams in two-gram capsules.

Within a couple of days, every screw in every unit in Block D would know that a new and strong supply had got into D1 Left and they would all guess that this was how it got in.

He stared at her until she looked away and then put a hand on his own stomach, there was pressure on the sides.

He had taken eight condoms out of the packet that always lay beside the toilet roll at the head of the bed and filled each one with capsules, then swallowed them with cold water from the tap on the yellowing sink, and in a while he would throw up in another sink, in another cell.

'Reza.'

Österåker prison. One hundred grams.

'Uros.'

Storboda prison. One hundred grams.

'Go there now.'

Aspsås, Österåker, Storboda.

A visit to three prisons, every second week.

'I'm going there now.'

'They've got fines. Both of them. Five thousand in cash.'

'Five thousand?'

'Yes. Give them what they're expecting first. Then tell them that they've got fines. You understand, whore?'

'I understand.'

Leon went over to the metal plate on the wall between the doorframe and the mirror, and touched the red button without pressing it.

'And Gabriel?'

'Yeah?'

'His report.'

He was still very close, his breath just as hot.

'The kids have sold everything. Ninety thousand. And there's more from Södertälje and maybe from Märsta.'

Her voice almost a whisper, as if she was reading to herself, it was important to get it right.

'Twelve houses in Salem and Tullinge. A hundred and forty-six thousand. Two debt enforcements in Vasastan. Fifty-five thousand. Two big barrels of petrol from the Shell station in Alby. Nine thousand. A computer shop tomorrow, I think.'

He nodded. She didn't know if it was good enough. She hoped so.

'And . . . one more thing. It's important.'

'Right?'

'Gabriel said it was important to tell you that your phone's being tapped.'

Leon had kept his hand by the red button, but now he let it drop, looked at her.

'Which one?'

'He said . . . Gabriel, he said . . .'

'*Which one*, whore?'

'He said . . . the one you share with Mihailovic.'

She had remembered. She closed her eyes. His eyes, she didn't like them.

'And you are sure, *whore*, are you sure that's what he said?'

'Yes.'

She didn't want to be near him, his face was so tense. Instead of lashing out, as he turned back to the metal plate between the door and the mirror, he leaned towards the microphone and pressed the red button.

'We're done.'

That crackling again.

'Central security.'

'Jensen. We're done.'

'Five minutes.'

He was finding it hard to stand still, his breathing was irregular and his voice was raised.

'Are you living there?'

'Where?'

'*There.*'

Every time they were done, when they were standing there waiting, the same question.

'Yes.'

'In his room?'

'Yes.'

'All the time?'

'Yes.'

He was standing so close. She was so scared.

'I moved here. You moved there.'

She waited in the room when he left, one prison warden in front of him and one behind him, down the spiral staircase, into the passage. They stopped in the first room on the right-hand side; he had to be naked when plastic-gloved fingers ran through his hair, felt under his arms, up his arse when he leaned forwards. *I'm going to kill them all.* A new set of clothes and they carried on down the straight, wide passage several metres under the prison yard, through the locked doors with small cameras that stirred into action as they approached, the corridor to Block D, one floor up, the unit on the left.

————————

He hadn't eaten all the day, and while the screws got ready for evening lock-up, he'd emptied himself in one of the shower room sinks, handed out the first supplies in the unit and then broken and emptied three two-gram capsules into a mug, stirred the cloudy water for a long time with his pinkie and drunk it before the powder had completely dissolved, then rinsed it down with more water so that it wouldn't stick to his tongue or throat. He would hand out the rest tomorrow, it wouldn't cost them anything this time and every prisoner in the corridor would take too much and for too long over the next few days.

*This time you're to be heard, you'll be searched, that's all.*

He looked out of the window.

*You'll come back. Here. In exactly fourteen days.*

It was already light outside.

*Put it up again. But then dump it before you come. You have to smell and they'll stand there with their dogs, doctors and signed documents from the Prosecution Authority. You'll be searched. But you'll be empty.*

It had been dawn before, but now it was daylight.

As soon as the door had been locked, Leon turned on the lamp that had no shade and gave off a hard, white light that stayed on all night. He had sat down at the simple wooden table against the wall by the window in each cell, had taken out some fine felt-tip pens and white A4 paper – real writing paper that you could buy in the prison shop, with thin blue stripes marking out each line, and started to write, and

*One love best brutha!*

after four fucking words had thrown the pens against the wall, stood up and screamed *I'm going to kill them all* at the barred window and metal door and

*Miss u so fucking much.*

screamed *I'm going to kill them all* again at the walls and ceiling and floor and bed and wardrobe and table and chair and

*But hope alls good with u bro. Aspsås is soft. And brutha Alex gives love an respct.*

just after midnight he'd taken another four g and it had been difficult to get the black felt pen to do what he wanted, as if his mind couldn't catch his thoughts any more because they were racing so fast and when they did stop for a moment, they could-n't be held for long. He had read through the eleven pages

*Its night deja an its summer an I make it 4 inside an 4 outside. An we cant fight 2gether brutha but soon brutha soon.*

and realised that what had seemed so good when he wrote about dark and light and the difference between a seven-metre wall and a see-through wall was just bollocks and

*Bro, u know I make the rite decision for the famly. RW is buried and GS will b seriously armed and a tight unit*

when the first rush had passed he had written more, counted on his fingers, twenty-seven days, that's when it would start, *they* would start.

Eleven pages.

Leon put down the pen and stood up, looked at the bedside lamp and turned it off, but never before it was light outside.

Out there, beyond the bars, sun already, it was a nice day.

The first floor of Block D.

D1 Left.

Cell 2.

He could see nearly the whole prison yard from here: the cracked asphalt, the small squares of brown grass, then the wall, maybe sixty metres away, so grey, so heavy. He knew that he had to hate it, that it was important. But he'd never managed. Not back then, long ago, when it had been more of a fence, nor later when it became more of a barrier with great rolls of barbed wire on top, nor even later when the first concrete wall, which had been three metres high, grew into this one, which was seven metres. He had tried to hate them, to spit on them, but it was as if they were just standing there, protecting, waiting, embracing.

Leon got up from the rickety table, looked out beyond the edge of the wall at the sun hitting a church tower in the distance, the tree tops that moved slowly, as if hesitating, and the white fluffiness that was presumably a cloud in the blue sky. Gabriel, *one love best brutha*, had been over there yesterday, the neatly raked path in front of the churchyard fence where they always waited in the driver's seat while the bitch who was carrying smiled at the screws. His best brother. The only one he trusted. The only one he needed. They'd said hello the first time one day in grade three, Gabriel had been sitting at the front of class with his track marks, punctures in his veins the size of craters, nine years old and a drug addict, his body had been caught in a house that burnt down – Leon had never understood how or maybe Gabriel had just never told him – and white coats had treated the skin that screamed for morphine for nearly eight months, and then when he left the big hospital, he carried on collecting his prescription and injecting and when his skin no longer screamed so much, they got together to sell what he didn't need, and then when they started middle school they'd added amphetamines, which earned them more, and soon the two of them had a third of Råby covered.

He turned away from the view and the table and lay down on the bed; the ceiling was yellow and changed to white by the wardrobe and grey by the sink and door. He swallowed, cleared his throat, carefully gathered the saliva with his tongue, rubbing in what he could find with slow movements; they stung, the big ulcers on the top of his tongue and the slightly smaller ones at the back of his throat. He had tried to knock back the amphetamine water without touching too much, but hadn't been very successful; the ulcers itched and would continue to do so for another day or two.

The rattle of metal. The door opened. It was seven o'clock.
'Good morning.'
She popped her head round the door, tried to catch his eye.
He didn't answer.
'*Good morning.*'
The female screw wasn't going to give up, so he raised a hand to show that he'd heard and was alive, that was all she wanted to know and what with the ulcers, he was going to talk as little as possible.

Leon got up, the letter on the table,

Brutha seriously ARMED and very TIGHT unit!!!
200% love respect pride bruthahood duty belonging honor.

he turned the eleven pages over and pulled a pair of underpants out from a pile under the chair and then a towel from the shelf in the narrow wardrobe. He left the seven-metre-square cell and strolled down the corridor that was waking up, past eight open cell doors on either side, past the TV corner, the billiard table, the kitchen and stopped just in front of the fish tank, the screws' room with its big glass window. He stared at the screw bitch who had opened his door and demanded a *good morning* and she stared back and he pretended he was fucking her so she would look away or down, but she carried on holding his gaze and he chose the grey door with the steamed-up window, went into the shower room and the one in the middle with water that burned your neck, shoulders, chest. When Alex came in, pale, tall, nine-teen and almost trustworthy, Leon nodded. Neither of them said anything, their tongues and throats were as sore as each other and Leon sneaked a look at his dick – Alex didn't write letters when he was wasted, he wanked, tired pupils that had been open all night and a fiery red foreskin that was shrivelled and loose, the shaking hand that had held it, tugged it relentlessly. They'd met for the first time at a secure training centre in Örkelljunga; a sharpened knuckleduster had left three round marks on the right of his chest that were still visible, the bastard had been so in his face. A few years later at Bärby prison, from high up on his left shoulder all the way down to his hip, a long, wide scar with lighter edges, Alex had tried again and Leon had held him by the left arm and dragged him across the asphalt in the prison yard.

The hot water, he closed his eyes.

The metal door groaned when the older man came in, prob-ably thirty or maybe even forty-something, some said fifty; it was always hard to count time when chemicals had broken down the years. He was so skinny and moved with a kind of rolling gait, a face that was distorted by eyes that wanted to close and eyebrows that shot up, several missing teeth, the sort who does ten months at a time for some crap hold-up with a bread-knife and without a balaclava in some video shop or 7-Eleven, whatever is nearest. Almost shuffling the final steps into the shower at the far end, his arms potted with big holes like the ones Gabriel had had, but that carried on down the back of his hands and up his throat, needles that had obliterated the same veins, hollows that had turned into cartilage, so that every time more pressure was needed to get through. Leon watched him, the shuffling, he knew that the soles of his feet were the same, that was why he walked like that, only using the ball.

Leon nodded to Alex and they left the warm water at the same time and the old bugger had just enough time to turn round, his naked body almost transparent, his lips apart. Leon kept his hand open and the impact was hard when he hit him on the cheek; the man collapsed, lay still on the floor, fingertips covering the redness and lips even wider apart.

'What are you smiling at, you bastard?'

'I'm . . . not smiling.'

'You're smiling.'

The hand again, the same force, the other cheek.

'*Stop fucking smiling.*'

There were people like Smackhead who smiled every time they finished a sentence, tense, ritualised, maybe because they were uncertain, maybe frightened, most of them didn't even realise, just stood grinning and wanting to be liked.

He hated that grin.

'When will you be ready?'

Even bigger grin, the body that was at cross purposes with itself moved uneasily as the water continued to run over it, the twitches between the eyes and cheeks and eyes and forehead more frequent, more exaggerated. Leon grabbed hold of his straggly hair and held it tight, the only thing there was, if you wanted to pull up a wet and naked body with a wet and naked hand.

'I said, *when will you be ready*, Smackhead?'

That smile.

The spasms in his cheek.

The body that tried to hide.

'Soon. Soon. My gs?'

Leon's fingers even tighter round the long straggles.

'Soon?'

'Fuck's sake, I've got everything, except the ink! And I want my ten gs.'

The other hand on the skinny shoulder, thumb and index finger round the collarbone that stuck out.

Smackhead screamed like they always did.

'*Soon?*'

'Today. Today, for fuck's sake. After lunch. A screw who—'

The fingers and the collarbone in, around, again.

'I don't give a toss who. It's ready, isn't it? It'll be ready when I come tomorrow.'

He shoved the frail body down in front of him, pressed it against the tiles until it started to bleed and that bastard grin disappeared.

# twenty-five days to go

AFTERNOON.

He was certain of it.

The sun was no longer forcing its way further in through the gap between the red, yellow and white blanket and the window frame; he guessed it was about half past two – three, maybe even half three. He was woken by the dog's foul-smelling tongue on his cheek and neck, he didn't like it, black and white and much heavier than it looked; a couple of times he'd tried to get hold of it and push it away, but each time forgot that a body barely half a metre long could be as heavy as a sack of stones that refuses to leave the floor.

Gabriel pushed away the tongue and snout, a knife-like pain in his shoulder; the wound had turned into a wide, swollen gash overnight, on top of old scar tissue – despite two stones and a long metal pole, the window at the back of the shop had still had sharp teeth that were hard to see in the half light and sank into the flesh of those who tried to pass. He had pulled himself into a small, tight ball on his way into the shelves of goodies, but had still managed to get caught and only freed himself on the third attempt. They'd sat in the kitchen afterwards, Jon had held a short needle over a lighter flame until it glowed and then doused both the needle and the wound with Finnish vodka; he'd sewn eleven stitches through the already partially dead skin with nylon thread. Gabriel gingerly touched the wound, which had stopped bleeding, and lifted his arm up and down – the pain eased with the slow movements but was replaced by a dull, silent ache.

Wanda was still asleep.

He yawned, sat up on the edge of the bed, looked at her naked back and bum and thighs, his cock swelled and

*BTW brutha, ur whore. She seems to have plenty of room for everything, hahaha brutha.*

clenched his eyes tight until things calmed down, looked at the clock, nearly three, half an hour to go. The white tube, he quickly rubbed the cream on his skin all the way up to his neck, his clothes were lying on the red carpet that was so thick and soft, his hoodie stained dark brown from the right shoulder to halfway down the back by dried blood, he picked it up and pulled it over his head then scraped off what he could reach with his nails, couldn't find his pants and one of his socks, two pairs of joggers and bare feet in his trainers.

Her ears. He leaned over, his fingertip gently touching the soft skin and her earrings, two crosses with a small diamond in the middle. From the jewellers on Kungsgatan. He'd emptied the binliner on the floor and let her choose two things before they sold the rest to the Chinamen down by Odenplan – one hundred and ninety-four thousand for a window and five display cases. She had chosen the earrings and a ring with a red pearl that was too big really, but fitted if she wore it by the knuckle on her middle finger.

He looked at her naked body, she moved uneasily when he opened the door, said something he didn't catch and then turned over.

Big Ali was lying on the sofa in the sitting room, the cut on his forehead from when he'd smashed the window with his fist wrapped in a jacket then leaned in to reach the lock on the door, was now a straight, dark gash from his eyebrow to his hairline. Gabriel shook his sleeping shoulders hard, rapped Jon's feet at the other end of the sofa and punched Javad Hangaround, who was asleep in the armchair with his mouth open, in the chest.

The red – or maybe it was orange – front door was unlocked, this was Råby after all, no one would ever come into their flat without permission.

The air was afternoon warm and without smells and seemed to kind of pack itself into the space between the concrete wall of the balcony and the railings, through the door onto the main stairwell and the lift down to the basement and the metal door, heavy key in the lock. They went into the garage that had been dug out under the six-storey concrete building that constituted Råby Allé 1 to Råby Allé 214, past the rows of cars, down round the bend to the next level and the two shiny cars at the far end, one silver and one black. Gabriel carried on when the others stopped, waited, watched while he walked slowly round each one in turn, *Mercedes CLK 500, cabriolet, eight cylinder*, no scratches, no damage, *Audi R8, four-by-four, six gears*, he opened the driver's door, *three hundred and six horsepower*, started the engine, listened, *four hundred and twenty horsepower*, checked the boot, the tyres, the lights, the wheel rims. Two parking spaces away was a rental trailer from OKQ8. He looked around, then opened two padlocks and lifted off the plastic hood. Twelve small cardboard boxes with pictures of laptops on the sides and two considerably larger ones with eighty-inch screens and four yellow oblong boxes with something in them that looked like loudspeakers.

Gabriel calculated, one hundred and twenty thousand, a quarter of that if they sold it to the man in Tumba.

He could feel the nylon thread pulling in his shoulder – eleven stitches and Big Ali's forehead, thirty thousand, it hadn't been worth it.

They walked towards the automatic doors which opened without a sound and marked the end of the underground concrete space, carried on across the square to the metro, passed the station manager and ticket attendant, who turned their heads and looked the other way as the four young men with no tickets went straight through the barrier and up the steps and onto the 3.25 train to Norsborg, the next and final station on the line.

They got off, had a smoke, waited.

Ten dead minutes while a short man in a Stockholm transport uniform walked down through the eight carriages to change driver seat, from one end of the train to the other, and the journey back along the red line through the southern suburbs to stations in central and northern Stockholm. Gabriel stood on the platform by one of the middle carriages as the driver passed through, a rollie still between his fingers, while Jon, Big Ali and Javad Hangaround went in and out the open carriage doors, checking who was sitting where, explaining to those necessary who had chosen the wrong places and how long they had to switch seats.

They caught his attention, gave a thumbs up and disappeared into their planned carriages.

He stayed where he was. Waiting.

Any minute, there, *there*, he heard feet rushing up the steps and crossing the platform, jeans, a jacket, twenty-five, the sort who stuck out when he sat down at the back of the now empty carriage.

Gabriel got on.

A minute from Norsborg to Råby.

Plenty of time, they'd done it so many times before.

*Love respect pride bruthahood duty belonging honor don't forget that brutha.*

The doors slid shut, the train started to roll, he sat on one side right at the back, the Jacket sat opposite, looked at someone who looked back. Gabriel took off his hoodie, opened the window, then closed it again with his top caught in it. They were now hidden between the grey concrete wall and the grey top.

*The new GS will b led by the command. The command will be 2 people.*

The guy sitting opposite took two white ICA supermarket bags from his inner pockets, and placed them on the empty seat. Gabriel put his hand on the thin plastic-wrapped metal shapes, hard and angular; he lifted them up and weighed them with small movements, close to his body. *Lahti.* They contained what they were supposed to contain. *Glock.* He raised his arm and watched Big Ali in the carriage in front and Jon in the carriage behind open the end doors into his carriage with their allen keys, hurry in and pick up a plastic bag each, then disappear out again the way they came.

*Only 2, bro! Seriously ARMED, very TIGHT unit!!*

One minute. Plenty of time. When the metro train stopped at Råby station, they all stepped out from their carriages and walked towards the exit and a deserted centre with the eerie glow of fluorescent lighting. They passed two empty shops and waited as a young boy stood up from a bench some distance away, gold chain round his neck and slicked-back hair, he looked for acknowledgement from Gabriel – *Eddie's the name* – and nearly caught his eye, that was enough, he grew, the mark from a ring still visible on his cheek. He took one of the white ICA bags and carried it to the supermarket and the lockers just inside the main entrance where you could pay five kronor and store your bags while you were shopping. They watched the wee guy put in a coin and stuff the bag in, then lock it, and Gabriel knew that he was perfect – twelve years old, illegal possession of a weapon, a minor.

*No more president, vice president, prospect. Now its commander, soldier, private.*

The sun was shining when four boys, teenagers, young men, left an empty shopping centre and walked through a summer slightly warmer than the last. Råby was seldom beautiful to anyone who didn't belong there and on days like this the bright light peeled the last layer of colour from the high structures and the concrete buildings became, even for Gabriel, Jon, Big Ali and Javad Hangaround, a grey, airless place and none of them said anything as there was nothing much to say. The automatic door into the underground garage opened as silently as it had thirty minutes earlier and they walked into the cool darkness, a vast cavity that stretched the length of Råby Allé, to an exit in the middle of the garage, a door that said number 34, and then took the lift to the third floor, the door by the rubbish chute.

She looked about thirty-five, dark hair that had been dyed even darker when grey wisps had displaced time, quite beautiful really, but a pale face, a mouth that didn't want to smile and eyes that were older than her years.

'You're to keep this.'

She looked at the other white plastic bag with an ICA logo on it, which had recently been on an empty train seat.

She didn't answer.

She pulled the door hard to, but a foot was in the way, she couldn't close it as long as the one they called Big Ali, who was tall and square, was stopping her with his foot.

'Five hundred a day. You've to keep it for twenty-five. Until he comes to get it.'

'Go to hell!'

*The commanders have the power. The commanders deside the jobs. Soldiers and privates can never refuse.*

She pushed his shoulder with one hand and pulled the door with the other.

He stayed where he was.

She looked at the others, half a step behind, the same clothes, the same arrogant tilt as they glared at her.

She met Gabriel's eyes. He would look away. And he did.

*A fucking order is never refused.*

'Gabriel?'

It wasn't long, but he looked at the floor for a moment which triggered more words, louder.

'Gabriel? Listen. Him, get him . . .'

*Never refused. Or else they'll have 2 pay.*

Then the moment was gone, he looked up, met her eyes, he wasn't going to look away again.

'You'll keep it, bitch, because we want you to keep it.'

She took a step forwards, he didn't move, her open hand struck his cheek.

'Don't you threaten me.'

They were standing close looking into each other's eyes without blinking and they knew each other so well and not at all.

She had struck his cheek.

He wasn't quite sure why it was to be kept here, Leon must have his reasons, but he hadn't moved, hadn't looked away, hadn't answered.

'Don't you threaten me, Gabriel, you—'

'*Keep it.*'

He caught her arm and pulled it, not hard, but enough for her to move so that Big Ali could get into her flat and leave the white plastic bag on the hat shelf.

HE STOOD AS he normally did, by the window next to his desk and the armchairs and the photograph of a daughter who had flown the nest, who he never saw any more. If he stood on his toes, he could see the upstairs and a tiny bit of one of the bedrooms in the house where he'd lived for the greater part of his life. Lennart Oscarsson spent his days in alternate worlds that were separated by a brisk two-minute walk and he had never wanted to be anywhere else. The town of Aspsås, with its low white- and slightly higher red-terraced houses, and the big detached houses up by the woods, had two thousand six hundred and forty-seven inhabitants and Aspsås prison, with its twelve three-storey concrete buildings inside a fence inside a wall inside two protective barriers had two hundred and nineteen inhabitants and it felt like he knew every face out there and in here. He still woke up every morning with the realisation that he was someone who would rather be big in a small world than small in a big one.

The windowpane caught the sun; he moved so he could better see the people sitting down there in the warmth, waiting, groups of inmates, sentenced to days, months, years. They never thought about time, never allowed themselves to, they knew that anyone who counted their breaths in prison could not bear to draw air for much longer.

This morning – three were leaving. At around five o'clock, transfers, 0342 Gorgis and 2415 Lang from Block F, on their way to Kumla prison and Tidaholm prison, respectively. Around seven o'clock, a release, 0221 Jacobs from Block C, on his way to the Bommen hostel in Gothenburg.

Part of life. That would continue elsewhere.

This morning – three who were due to arrive. From Härnösand prison, six and a half years, aggravated rape, A3 Right. From Huddinge remand, four and a half years, armed robbery, F2 Left. From Kumla, transferred because he was a bad influence on other inmates, life for murder, segregation unit, Block H.

Part of life. That would continue here. And could not be counted.

But he did it himself.

Counted.

Four and a half years plus six and a half plus life, expected to be the full twenty-five years. Thirty-six years more in a morning.

Half an average life to long away.

He studied the dusty prison yard again, looked at the men sitting on a simple wooden bench just inside the concrete wall, who were so different from those who had sat there when he started; they were younger, angrier, more broken, more violent – what once had been a life of crime that petered out when exhaustion replaced energy, was now conscious career choice: *I will be successful, I will be someone, I will be a criminal, and you know, if I'm really good, I'll even go to prison.* He had walked back and forth between the terraced house and the wall all his working life and somewhere along the way he had failed to see the change and no longer had any idea of how he would recognise it. In Aspsås there had been the community inside that you could long to leave and a community outside where you could long to be, but now there was a third one and he had never been there because he had no idea where it was.

There was a knock on the door.

He waited, turned towards the other window, which was wider with a view of the main gate, which opened just then, and the roof of the white prison service transport bus that drove in and parked near the central security entrance.

The door again, harder, longer.

He opened.

'Have you got a minute?'

'Come in.'

An older man, tall, slim, a friendly face, lines that had lived. Martin Jacobson. Lennart Oscarsson looked at one of his few friends. Both here and out there. A friend whom he had nearly lost following an ill-judged decision during a hostage drama some years earlier, but who had survived and asked to be transferred to the isolation unit – greater security for staff, two guards present on each visit, no physical contact between outsiders and inmates who could only mix with other inmates on the basis of drawing lots, not by request.

'We've got a problem.'

'We do?'

'Him.'

The prison governor turned back to the wide window. A young man, no more than a teenager really, was being led out of the side door of the white bus.

Handcuffs. Body cuff.

Four prison guards, in front and beside and behind.

'From Mariefred prison. Six years and four months. Relocated following threats to the staff and suspected of beating up two other prisoners, crime classification perverting the course of justice.'

One more.

Six years and four months.

A morning with thirty-six years had become a morning with forty-two years and four months. More time not to be counted.

'Marko Bendik. He's on his way over to me. But I can't have him.'

'Why not?'

'Sentenced in the same case as someone who's already there. Aggravated assault and attempted murder in central Stockholm.

Plus the public prosecutor is preparing another case for *other* crimes that the two of them have committed together.'

The prison service bus had red stripes running along the white. The young man pulled forwards for a moment, hit his handcuffs against one of the side windows; it sounded and looked like it broke.

'Never two accomplices at the same time. Never in isolation.'

Lennart Oscarsson nodded and sat down at his desk, straightened the keyboard, looked at the screen.

'Block D.'

He changed his glasses; it was difficult to differentiate the letters and boxes when the sunlight reflected his own face on the dusty glass.

'D1 Left. Cell 12. It's been empty since yesterday.'

One careful step at a time down the spiral staircase to Administration and the reception area. Lennart Oscarsson kept his eyes on his friend's neck until their ways parted, Martin Jacobson carried on down the passage towards the isolation unit and Oscarsson opened the door and stepped into a bright and cramped space that was the first place to greet newly arrived prisoners. In the middle of the floor, surrounded by the four uniformed guards, stood a muscular and extremely pale boy who had been a child until very recently. Eyes that looked past him, through him, over him, anywhere other than at the person who held out his hand and wished him welcome.

'Lennart Oscarsson.'

And that didn't answer.

'I'm the governor here.'

The eyes that neither saw nor answered, narrowed.

'Good for you.'

Recently strip-searched, now with new clothes.

Recently a child, now a man with a long sentence.

Oscarsson turned towards the prison guard who was standing closest, lowered his voice.

'He's to go to Block D.'

'But it says here—'

'I know. It was me who wrote it.'

It wasn't very often that he went through the underground passage, a square concrete body that stretched the length of the prison yard, with straight arms and legs that headed off in different directions and then turned into locked doors and security cameras, the way in when days were no longer to be counted and the way out when there was less of life left. He glanced at the prisoner who had lived only one adult year in freedom and would now live the next six years and four months inside these walls. He looked like all the others, hated like all the others. He was about to be let into the unit and would sit on the bunk in his cell and immediately get stuck in the quagmire of antisocial behaviour. They always came from another time zone, they had committed crimes and filled their veins with drugs at night and slept and mustered strength during the day, and now the metal door they sat staring at would be locked at half past seven every evening and opened again at seven every morning, they would wake up, get up, piss, shower and then either walk to the workshop to make red wooden blocks or to the classroom to read out loud.

'Screw in the unit!'

Oscarsson hadn't even opened the door yet.

The child, who only had a matter of minutes to prove that he was a man with a long sentence who knew exactly where he was at and so should be treated with respect, yelled at the sleepy unit in the way that he'd learnt to yell, from now on one of thirty young people who were placed in various units at Aspsås alongside the older prisoners. Never more than that. Because the group then grew into a gang. And then the gang grew in power. And the prison governor had several times recognised only too late the moment when a group no longer needed to be fed recognition from the outside as an enemy and a threat, but had simply become an enemy and a threat, the moment when it was sufficiently big and sufficiently strong to feed itself.

Lennart Oscarsson stayed standing in the doorway, *screw in the unit*, saw the first peer approach the new inmate and hold out his hand.

'*Ey.*'

Then another, and another.

'*Ey.*'

Always the same. The youngsters always knew each other. It didn't matter whether they came from Fittja or Råby or Södertälje or Gävle. They *always* knew each other. Every time a young man took his first steps into one of the prison units, the others were standing there in a row ready to welcome him.

Lennart Oscarsson was just about to leave when he saw one of them approach – he couldn't remember his name, tall, short hair, long sentence for a serious crime – hand in the air.

His eyes, darting restlessly here, there and everywhere.

His mouth, dry lips, smacking sound.

'Marko.'

Oscarsson was certain. The boy who said hello was seriously under the influence.

'Leon.'

First the hand, then the embrace; they smiled at each other.

'Welcome, my friend.'

———

Leon watched the older man who was standing there in the doorway, who he knew was the governor. The uniform stayed watching for slightly too long, he'd seen that they were high and Leon had made sure to smack with his lips in the way people do when speed has stolen their saliva. He raised a hand to Marko, then embraced him, they'd known each other since he was twelve and Marko was thirteen – Örkelljunga secure children's home, Sirius Paragraph 12 home, and then Bärby juvenile detention centre. Marko from Rotebro was one of the ones who had always been there and who wanted to belong, and maybe he would one day.

They walked down the corridor, past the TV corner, past the cells with low numbers towards the one that had been empty since the day before, the guy who'd hanged himself in the narrow space between the wardrobe and the sink, Cell 12. Marko had his stuff, washed-out prison clothes and towels and bed linen in his arms, and Leon left him sitting on an unmade bunk in a bare room with pockmarked walls.

'Cell 2.'

The face that nodded to him.

It was older now, nineteen, but just there just then, the look of abandonment, he'd seen it before.

In Vemyra.

Fourteen years old. Secure training centre.

They had lain on their backs on a desk each in the classroom, it was night and they had been sniffing strong glue and were off their faces, and had smashed the reinforced glass – a pot of boiling water and a cross scratched with a coin in a corner of the window – which they'd only ever come across before at a child psychology unit; they had forced their way into the teachers' corridor, to the head's wife who was on duty that night, and they had fractured her skull and broken her right thumb and stolen the keys.

Forty-eight hours. Then they were back again.

Marko had sat there just like he was sitting there now, when they were separated and forced into their rooms, his face, that expression, abandonment.

'Cell 2, if there's anything.'

On the opposite side of the corridor, the cells with uneven numbers, number 9. Leon knocked.

'One love, brother.'

'One love.'

Alex had waited, someone who already belonged; for so long it had only been Leon and Gabriel, Leon and Gabriel, then with Alex there was one more, and then one more with Bruno and one more with Jon and Reza and Uros and Big Ali and now there were eight of them and there weren't going to be many more, a core that was hard, and that fucking longing to be part of it was for those who were outside, who were prepared to do anything to get in.

He looked at Alex, dropped his hand as they walked over to Cell 10.

They stood side by side in front of the closed door.

Never open a door and go into a cell on any corridor in any prison without knocking.

Because it's not just a door. Because it's not just a cell.

Because most of them had lived longer here than they'd lived there, outside.

He didn't knock.

This wasn't a home. It was a junky den.

'Oi.'

The skinny bugger was sitting on the only chair by the only table, with his back to the door, looking out of the window. He hadn't heard him come in, started and turned round.

The smile.

Stiff lips, slightly apart.

'Smackhead.'

A hard fist to his shoulder.

'Don't *ever* smile at me.'

Leon couldn't understand why, he never had, but that bastard smile still annoyed him, it kind of got hold of you and was ugly and exposed all those yellow dirty teeth that somehow sank into the feeling of being in the way, that fucking drawn-out apology, a reflex that stared at whoever was staring.

Another fist, the other shoulder, knuckles on skin and bones.

'D'you understand?'

'My deal.'

'Later. *Do you understand?*

The scrawny body got up.

'I want my hit.'

'When you're done, Smackhead.'

'My name's Sonny. And you can hit me as much as you like. Whenever you like.'

Desperation. A surprising strength.

'But I want my payment. *Before*. I want my ten grams.'

He pointed at the table, at what was lying there, all lined up.

*Electric shaver, ballpoint pen, spoon, needle, sellotape, pipe cleaner, nail clippers, cotton thread, piece of metal.*

His high voice, his stammer, it was worse now.

'I've got everything. Even the ink. But I'm not going to put it together. Not until I get my pay.'

Leon saw the punctured feet that couldn't stay still on the hard floor, cheeks that twitched around the eyelid, his tongue constantly running over his yellow teeth trying to wash them clean.

But the lips. They weren't open any more, weren't smiling.

Leon opened the cell door, nodded to Alex who was standing outside, keeping an eye on the whole corridor.

'Ten g.'

He went in again, closed the door, looked at the skinny old bastard who must be around thirty, maybe even forty.

'But you're not to touch it. Not until you're done.'

They didn't say anything while they waited. They had nothing in common, didn't know each other, had never met before, would never meet again anywhere else once their days of living locked up together were done. They were the same height and looked straight into each other's eyes, one who had already lived a life of crime and was now simply trying to survive the slow slippery downwards slope and one who was still on the way up, taking up more space, who had energy and hate and no idea that the older man in front of him had until very recently been him.

The door opened, Alex, five capsules in his hand, up close to the thin face that looked at them, felt them, took them.

'You're not to touch it. Not until you're done.'

That smile again, lips apart as the scrawny hands picked up the sellotape and then stood by the table and stuck the five capsules to the wall just where the curtain rail was widest, they were his now and he had hidden them, so he sat down again, his back turned as before.

*The tattoo brutha. Only on right thigh. ONLY THERE!!!*

First the *electric shaver*. Always a Braun. With the kind of blade that moves horizontally back and forth.

Grinning, Smackhead held the shaver in one hand and with the other lifted up the *piece of metal* from the table that he had sharpened little by little over the past week, whenever he was certain that the screws were looking the other way, while he did his morning stint in the workshop, sharp enough to cut a bare throat, to cut off the locked rounded head on the shaver and take out the blades.

He put the shaver to one side, picked up the *ballpoint pen*, cut it carefully across the middle and pulled out the plastic tube with ink, then cut off the ballpoint at the end with the *nail clippers*. Then he picked up the *spoon* and pressed it hard against the table, twisted it round until the shallow hollow that he'd eaten his buttermilk with only this morning fell off and his skinny fingers were left holding a straight rust-free handle, and when he then pressed this against the table for a second time, it became a metal hook, bent at ninety degrees.

*I trust a new tattoo 200 %.*

The *needle*. The wires he'd pulled out of one of the metal brushes in the workshop with pliers.

The *pipe cleaner*. That he had bought in the prison shop.

The *cotton thread*. That he'd just pulled out of his trousers.

He positioned the needle right next to the pipe cleaner and wound the thread round them, hard, the end of the needle only a few millimetres longer than the pipe cleaner, then pushed them carefully into the empty shaft of the ballpoint pen, and when the pipe cleaner was too big and got caught and couldn't go in any further, the needle point came out through the opening, the hole which had been made for a plastic ink tube had now become the holder for a needle that was sufficiently sharp to puncture and colour skin.

Only on the right thigh. An order! Otherwise, punishment.

Then he taped the bent spoon handle to one side of the shaver, checked that the needle moved without touching anything, positioned the pen shaft on the spoon handle and finally attached the end of the pipe cleaner to the head that had until recently secured the blades, and taped it up again.

'Right.'

Plug in the socket on the wall. Smackhead smiled. Almost properly.

The noise was loud, a humming that took over when he held the machine out in front of him, the sharp needle that had once been a wire in a metal brush was now the essential component of a tattoo machine that moved back and forth at high speed. Leon unbuttoned his trousers and lay down on his side on the foul-smelling bed. White, shapeless cotton underpants and on his left thigh, a big square scab. Leon picked at it with his index finger nail, broke up what had already begun to heal until the fresh scab fell off and the opened wound started to bleed again.

'Looks OK.'

Infected. Bleeding.

Smackhead leaned closer, nodded.

'Looking pretty good. A few more weeks. Pick at it once a day.'

Leon looked at the bleeding rectangle.

*An old name. A name that no longer existed and was going to be replaced.*

With a needle, he had injected old sour milk into the skin around the long-since tattooed letters, waited until the infection took hold and when the first scab started to form, he had scraped it off and when the second scab had started to form, he scraped that off too; he had scraped off one after the other and with each scab that came off a little more colour disappeared, with every new drop of blood the past had been washed away a little more.

'The Bollnäs Butt, when I was in Skåltjärnshyttan in Filipstad, he taught me. I've made over a hundred of these, done eight hundred and forty-four tattoos. I've—'

'Shut the fuck up.'

'I—'

The young man who'd pulled down his trousers and lain down on a stinking bed got up and punched the bony cheek with his fist, the electric shaver fell to the floor, the tape around the bent spoon slipped.

'Keep your mouth shut. And get on with it. And write what you've got to write on my thigh, *here*, from the knee to the edge of my pants.'

ONLY THERE!!!

The skinny guy who was maybe around forty said nothing, looked over at where the curtain rail was fixed to the wall and the five capsules that were taped there, spat on his hands three times like he always did and put the plug into the socket. It worked, as it had before, the sharpened needle going back and forth at high speed in the air. He smiled as he dipped it in the dish with ink that was called Rotring and could be stolen from well-stocked stationery shops and this time had been smuggled in up the arse of one of the long-termers who had been out on leave, only one g in return for ink that with any luck would be enough for three or even four tattoos.

ANA STOOD ON the red and white rag rug out in the narrow hall, looking at a plastic bag she would never open. If she had nothing to do with it, it had nothing to do with her. She made the decisions round here. She was the one looking at the plastic bag, the plastic bag wasn't looking at her.

She would throw it away.

She would go out onto the landing and over to the rubbish chute and throw it down into the dark.

But she knew things didn't work like that. *You're to keep this.* If it disappeared, she disappeared. *You're to keep this until he comes to get it.*

She had twenty-five days. They had twenty-five days.

To start again.

She closed her eyes, another time, other eighteen-year-olds outside another door with another plastic bag.

The same words. The same warning.

*Until he comes to get it.*

He hadn't come. He hadn't collected it. Not that day. Not ever.

It just seemed to carry on, further in, further away.

And they had nowhere to go as there was nothing to leave.

Ana looked at it again, plastic wrapped around hard metal edges on the ugly hat shelf in front of her; the next visitor of normal height would be able to stand here and see exactly what she was seeing . . . it was so hard to breathe and swallow, to draw in new air when an entire life lay in the way and took up all the space.

Not any more. Not again. Not ever.

*She had done her time for others.*

She was absolutely certain that she was still standing up but her legs buckled and the floor came closer and she hit her head on the wall, so it would seem that she had slowly collapsed and maybe even shed a tear or two. Someone who can't go forwards and can't go back and can't bear to sit still either doesn't have much choice other than to cry. She cried and shook and looked up at the fucking plastic bag that just lay there and looked back at her.

She stood up.

She reached her hand up towards it and got hold of it between her finger and thumb; if she held it as close to the edge as possible, maybe it wouldn't cut so deep into her hand and wouldn't be so heavy. She picked it up and started to walk and was immediately back at Hinseberg prison for women, locked up and waiting, and she couldn't understand why the heavy metal door was locked and she lay down again in the narrow cell and slept for four years, and had reached the front door when she dropped the bag and went back into the flat, she needed tape, heavy grey packing tape. She lifted the bag up with two fingers again and went out onto the stair and down to the next floor, opened the rubbish chute and held the bag in the middle of the cement cylinder and felt her hand spasm. She was crying, other plastic bags flashed in front of her, when he was younger and when he got older and she hated them all as much as she hated this one because nothing ever changed, time clung on with sharp edges and hurt. *You'll keep it, bitch, because we want you to keep it.* She was shaking as she pulled her hand back out and put the bag down on the hard floor, took out the roll of packing tape and cut off four pieces of equal length, attached them to her arm, then picked the bag up again, into the chute, one piece over, one piece behind, she pressed it hard against the cement wall inside the rubbish chute, then another across the top, and a piece of tape across that, and another, and another, and another until it was secured and she closed the cover.

SHE WASN'T CRYING any more. But she was still sitting on the rag rug with her eyes shut. She had no idea how long, if it was just now, hours ago, days, years.

Then she heard them, the sirens, she got up, stretched herself, that was familiar, home.

She hated them.

Faint at first, a couple of kilometres away she guessed, then louder, then a demanding, insistent sound that bounded and echoed from building to building.

She had been counting.

Five times so far today.

Six yesterday.

The day before, nine. The day before that, five. And the day before that, fourteen.

A quick glance at the hat shelf, which was empty, but even so, the stupid bloody fucking plastic bag was lying there, staring at her.

Ana made her way to the kitchen and the noise pounding on her window, forcing its way in, taking over. Outside, the back-yards and houses were pressing in, yards and houses that she loved and protected in a way that only a woman can love and protect someone who abuses her until she no longer has a choice, to be beaten and broken or to fight back. The conversations that had died, the stalls and shops that had closed down, a life that had been dismantled bit by bit by people who threatened them and stole from them while the outside world looked on, other people who had no idea how to recognise the boy or girl who's so far gone they'll burn their own house down.

The hooting, the noise, there it was, she wondered if it was the same truck, the same fireman as before, the one who usually came.

———————

He sat on the right at the front of the fire engine. *Officer In Charge Front Passenger Seat*. He checked the outside rear-view mirror, glanced over at the driver, turned round and looked at the lead firefighter, then at Number One, Number Two, they were all ready. They had responded to the call-out within eighty-two seconds, never more than ninety and they were proud of it – that they could call themselves the ninety-second crew every day, every time. And the journey hadn't even taken a minute, fifteen hundred metres from Eriksberg station to Råby Allé, one of four addresses that required police contact or an escort on any call-out. And today they'd been to all four – Råbygången, Råby Backe, Albyvägen, Råby Allé.

Thom sighed.

For every real alarm, he reckoned on sixteen like this. Cars, bikes, mopeds, rubbish bins, fences, waste-paper baskets. Sixteen. And then *one* serious call-out.

He had just gone for a lie-down, it had been a long morning, he had put on his equipment and helmet five times and the smoke and strange feeling that you're chasing shadows made his legs weak these days. He'd lain down but not been able to sleep in the fire station that he'd walked into twenty-two years earlier and was his security; eight weeks' training as a firefighter had led to seven weeks' training as an ambulanceman, a few years working one day with the ambulance service, two days with handicabs and two days with the fire brigade, then an offer from the fire service college and a permanent position and the bed he'd just left and the corridor he'd just run down and the locker from where he'd just grabbed his helmet, uniform and bullet-proof vest.

Black smoke.

He wound down the side window.

It smelt of metal, oil, petrol.

The first call-out, early that morning, Råby Allé 17 – a moped. The second, a few hours later, Råby Allé 128 – a container and two piles of tyres. Now Råby Allé 46 – it smelt and looked like a car.

He opened the door and the flames seemed to grow, the smoke get blacker. He could see faces, hear voices.

He couldn't understand it.

They were burning their own environment.

He checked the straps of the bulletproof vest that he'd refused to wear for so long, and was about to climb down from the cab when a dull thud shuddered by his cheek, forehead, temple. The heavy, square paving stone had hit the reinforced side window with force; the thick glass, covered with some kind of protective plastic, had been installed when the hate had tipped over into violence a few years back.

He looked at the window that was still intact, leaned forwards – the paving stone, the one that had been intended for his head, was lying down by the front tyre.

'Abort.'

The driver, a young, shy man who had driven backwards and forwards between the fire station on the Eriksberg industrial estate and the Stockholm suburb of Råby five times since dawn, looked as if he hadn't heard or understood the officer in charge's order.

Thom raised his voice.

'Abort. *Now.*'

The large vehicle had just started to reverse when it suddenly stopped.

Thom saw the young face, red, flushed.

Then one behind, in front.

The fire engine was surrounded. He guessed around thirty,

maybe even forty, young bodies in trackies and hoodies and faces that were hard to distinguish as they were blotted out by the smoke and burning petrol.

They stood completely still and watched the car change colour as it turned into a metal corpse.

When something hit the front screen they didn't have time to react; the hard and sharp edges shattered the unprotected glass into snowflakes on the floor, the seat, the dashboard, drifts on his knees. The axe looked new and was quite short, maybe thirty centimetres, it had impacted in the metal frame, just above the driver's head, a big gash in all the red.

'Drive.'

The threats. The hate.

But not this.

He had never been aggressive back, not once in all these years had he hated back. He had chosen not to see them – the few hundred who disrupted the lives of twelve thousand.

A gob of spit.

'Drive.'

He had leaned forwards through the window that was no longer there and the gob landed on his neck, one of them standing nearby, the spit now running down his chest.

The next one landed on the face, dribbled down his nose, cheek, chin.

A boy.

He was just . . . a boy.

Twelve, maybe thirteen years old, the slicked-back hair, the heavy gold chain, a child dressed up like the adult he wasn't and would never live long enough to be, and his boy's mouth grinned as he pointed to the axe and then turned to the thirty or forty others who were guarding the fire engine, then spat again. Thom wasn't sure what, but something burst deep, deep inside and he didn't look at the driver with the tense, youthful face, but heard his own voice, loud and clear.

'*Drive.*'

'Drive?'

'They'll move on. Let it burn.'

---

Cheek and forehead against the windowpane.

Was she imagining it? Though the flames were long gone, it felt warmer now, as if the heat from a burning car had risen on the black smoke and was now washing over the building and the people who lived there.

Ana recognised him.

She had seen him many times before. He never shouted. Not like the others. He looked straight through them, just carried on with his work, putting out the fire, not a word, never.

This time, he'd been scared.

His abrupt, agitated movements, his eyes, he had looked at them, studied them.

First the stone. Then the axe.

But probably most of all the gob of spit, saliva hit harder, cut deeper than metal.

The car was still burning when the large, red vehicle reversed out of the car park and the ring of tracksuit bottoms and hoodies dispersed. She recognised the sudden, loud bang of a petrol tank exploding, a sound as shattering as the recent sirens.

She sat down on the narrow wooden window sill and looked out at the metal that was turning black and the flames that had been given new life, rubbed her forehead and cheek against the windowpane and felt sure that it was getting hotter.

A world within the world.

Identical concrete buildings that faced the E4 like a wall and everyone driving past at a hundred and ten kilometres an hour.

They had nowhere to go as there was nothing to leave.

THEY HAD NOWHERE to go as there was nothing to leave.

Identical concrete buildings inside a wall that kept the rest out.

A world within the world.

Lennart Oscarsson stood at his window, stretched. Aspsås over there with identical roofs and deserted playgrounds in a tiny town, Aspsås in here with gravel yards and rectangular football pitches in an even smaller space. He wanted security, he spent his nights in an idyll but would never understand why he had chosen to spend his days in a high security prison, one of three Swedish maximum security prisons for only the most dangerous criminals with long prison sentences.

He stretched again, swallowed a persistent yawn and walked over to the door as someone had knocked, a timid hand on the boss's closed door. Martin Jacobson. And a very young woman whom Oscarsson had only met briefly at an interview and vaguely recognised, but had never really spoken to.

'Julia. Julia Bozsik. I work in Block D. D1 Left.'

With a friendly gesture, he showed her over to the new sofa and they sat down with their arms first on, and then around, a square cushion each. Lennart Oscarsson had consciously worked to recruit more women into what was a traditional and sometimes stale male domain and he was glad, almost proud, to see the young person in front of him, who wasn't much older than the youngest inmates in some of the units.

'Now, how can I help you?'

Julia turned towards the prison governor, whom she'd barely met, let alone spoken to. He seemed friendlier than his office, which was far too big and far too formal, and she could look at him without feeling she was being studied, assessed.

'A couple of nights ago . . .'

A sofa in the prison governor's office.

She looked around, she felt uncertain, sometimes . . . it wasn't always easy to work out where you were heading or why.

*Jesus . . . a prison?*

Three years doing science at high school. Unemployed for a few days in summer and an appointment with the job centre.

She had never seen a prison before.

She had never spoken to, known or even met a criminal before.

Three days later – after three days' training – she had signed for her uniform and done her first day and was supposed to be responsible for them.

'A couple of nights ago, the nightshift was . . . sorry, pure hell. Nine cells, nine inmates who didn't sleep, who started . . . it sounded, I can't explain it any other way, like they were constantly moving, noisy and aggressive, tidying their cells, making their beds, pulling off the sheets, making them again, pulling them off, pulling them off.'

After three days' training, she had put on her uniform and taken responsibility for them, but for the most part she'd been scared. Of the young guys. Their aggression, their hate was tangible and overwhelming. Not that the older ones were any better, they sized her up and commented on her body but never triggered the same feelings – the uneasiness, discomfort, the young guys could lose it at any moment and their hate was different, so potent.

'Last night was the same. Awake, restless. And since I opened up this morning, they've all been complaining about headaches and done just about anything to get a sick note and some sleep. The ones who didn't get one, the ones we forced to go to work, are confused – one managed to knock over four pallets on his first attempt to pick them up with the forklift, and then drove straight into one of the workshop walls – another one hid in one of the toilets in the laundry, turned off the light and stayed there for three hours, he'd jammed the lock and door handle with two rubbish bins.'

The uneasiness, the fear, from the first day she'd walked the locked corridors prepared for a fist in her face or a piece of sharpened metal in her back at any time, she'd been so tense, so terrified of these men who didn't for a moment care about the consequences – the men who hated, exploded, lashed out – and soon she realised that she was creeping along the grey concrete walls and had tried to deal with it, was trying to deal with it, she looked straight ahead so she would never show how frightened she really was, always looked people in the eye, laughed too loud for too long, talk, talk, she knew that the fear only existed if she didn't hide it well enough.

*Jesus . . . a prison?*

'Thank you . . .'

Martin Jacobson, who was sitting at the other end of the new sofa, nodded to his young colleague.

'. . . no one sleeping, confused, unpredictable. You don't need to hear any more, do you, Lennart?'

The governor gave a light shrug, maybe he sighed, remembered the smacking lips and darting eyes.

He had seen it and guessed correctly.

'No, you don't need to explain any more.'

He looked at his colleague, friend. They had worked there for so long, seen it time and again.

'I've looked into it.'

Martin Jacobson was unaware that he leaned forwards, hands on the coffee table.

'And I'm quite certain that the drugs were smuggled in by a visitor three days ago. Nine zero two two, Jensen. D1 Left, Cell 2.'

He flicked through a small notebook, spiral-bound with thin red lines.

'The visitor – a young woman, seventeen years old, registered at an address in Råby, Botkyrka municipality. She's called . . . hold on a moment . . . Wanda Svensson.'

Oscarsson was responsible for a prison with two hundred and nineteen inmates. All serving long sentences. He had the time and opportunity and always made sure that he greeted each one individually, shook their hand at least once before reading about their past.

'Jensen? Came here about four, max five months ago?'

'Råby. Father from Botkyrka. Mother from Zagreb.'

'Aggravated assault, armed robbery, blackmail?'

'Four and a half years.'

'Gang related?'

'Correct.'

He got up, was heading towards the window when he suddenly stopped. Not yet. He liked to stand there alone.

'And her?'

'Like most of them. No convictions. A bit of flesh and a container.'

They looked at each other again, they had also seen this so many times: young, easily manipulated girlfriends with no criminal record who first opened their legs for boys who wanted to be what they thought men were like and then wider for those who wanted to be what they thought high status criminals were like.

'I want to get an extra dog here, from Hall prison.'

Her voice was calm and matter-of-fact and sounded much older than twenty-one, it was easy to like.

'Search every cell with a dog after lock-up. D1 Left and D2 Right. Every cell, common rooms and the wardens' room.'

The prison governor was still standing in the middle of the floor, halfway over to the window; it looked like it would rain.

Dogs.

The prison service had increased the number of dogs from two to twenty-five. It wouldn't make any difference if they increased it to one hundred and twenty-five. Someone who needed drugs, who screamed for more methamphetamine or heroin or subutex, always found new ways to get it.

'And tomorrow, general UA.'

UA.

Piss analysis.

Lennart Oscarsson knew, just as Martin Jacobson knew, just as anyone who had spent their life in a blue uniform in a Swedish prison knew, that an inmate who pissed positive would have problems when the eyes and ears of the authority focused on his unit and he would be punished harshly by his fellow inmates who wanted to take drugs in peace. They knew that inmates would therefore rather refuse to piss and accept the prison punishment of more days behind bars, than test positive and end up with a broken arm.

She wanted something. She believed in something.

'Dogs. UA.'

He wasn't going to destroy it. Time would do that.

'Of course. We'll organise that.'

He'd stopped halfway over to the window. Now, as they closed the door behind them, he went over and looked out at the grey, heavy clouds that were thicker, darker.

Jensen.

Block D. D1 Left.

He remembered the face that had stared at him two days ago, the wild, darting eyes, the dry lips, the persistent smacking sound.

Like all the others. Like every other young man in every other high security prison. No father in the picture. Serious crime from the age of twelve. Like all the others who knew nothing about the society they didn't belong to.

*Like all the others who knew nothing about the society they didn't belong to.*

He had read every file, compared all their stories and every time been astounded by the very simple knowledge test that they were asked to take on arrival.

None of them had ever been able to answer even one question. Not one.

They knew nothing about the Swedish state and Europe and the world. They had no knowledge of anything outside their own community, which would never become too big.

He couldn't understand it. They were eighteen years old. And going nowhere.

```
Criminal network of young men who have
grown up in different Stockholm suburbs,
with Råby as the hub.
```

Down there – through the glass and light rain, on the benches by the fence in the middle of the prison yard – they always sat there, right now he counted four, five, six, seven of them from different places and various groups, but each with a cigarette in hand, the same age, the same pose, part of a posse that protected, shut out everything else.

```
Fraternity, family, bound together by
loyalty, friendship. Commit crimes
together or with other criminals.
```

He crossed over to his desk and the pile of white A4 sheets that were lying stapled together, two by two, on the brown, empty surface, pulled the top one over.

```
Eight, maybe nine full members. All
previously convicted of serious crimes.
```

```
Four, possibly five are currently in
prison serving long sentences.
```

He held the two sheets of paper firmly in his hand, one of several regular reports from the *Prison Service Intelligence Unit*, prepared when a number of serious incidents inside the prison walls were confirmed to be gang-related.

This report, one gang, one of many.

```
Dramatic developments in the group. New
rules, new members, new name. Now moved
to the target list for priority serious
organised crime.
```

Lennart Oscarsson should have sighed, but he didn't even do that any more. He knew that this was just the start. The gap which had become a chasm was now a huge fucking hole, which people fell into headlong and which would be one of the great mysteries of Swedish and European society today, tomorrow, and for evermore.

He turned his gaze to Aspsås again and the red terraced house, so close, so unbelievably far away.

He picked up the phone, the number some way down one of the two white sheets of A4.

'Hello?'

He recognised Pereira's cautious voice, the kind that doesn't fit the face.

'It's Oscarsson.'

'What can I do for you?'

The prison governor was still holding one of many reports from the PSIU.

'You were looking for a reason.'

'Yes?'

'Well, Pereira. *Now* we've got a reason.'

A ROOM LIKE no other.

Small, square pictures of staring men.

José Pereira rocked back and forth, his black shoes light on the floor. He often stood like this. He went closer, paused by a cheek, a nose, a pair of eyes, face by face.

On the back wall – the shorter one closest to the corridor – all in a row, green and yellow drawing pins in the corners of each grainy photograph of passport size, small notes underneath them, gang connection, ID number, address.

*Target list Alcatraz.*

On the first of the two long walls further into the room and behind four identical desks with computers, files, folders, photos of the same men pinned up in the same way, but organised by group – *Hell's Angels MC* (twenty-two staring faces), *Bandidos* (eighteen staring faces), *Red & White Crew* (fourteen staring faces), *X-Team* (twelve staring faces), *Outlaws MC* (nine staring faces). On the second of the long walls, if he took another step forwards and stretched out his arm, he could pull them all down – *Wolfpack Brotherhood* (eleven staring faces), *Syrian Brotherhood* (thirteen staring faces), *BFL Uppsala* (seven staring faces), *OG* (ten staring faces), *WYG* (six staring faces), *Råby Warriors* (eight staring faces), *ASIR* (thirty-seven staring faces), *Chosen Ones* (twelve staring faces).

José Pereira drank some of the black coffee from the new machine that had been installed in one of the corridors of Råby police station only yesterday. There wasn't any noticeable difference – the same bitterness, the same bite – and he did the same as everyone else, swallowed and waited for the caffeine to kick in in his chest and stomach. He looked at the walls and the faces staring at him, his everyday. When he had been allocated to the new police station in the south of Stockholm nineteen years ago, he was convinced that serious organised crime divided up among gangs with silly English names was something that belonged to the cinema and popcorn and Los Angeles. How quickly that had changed. The men who stared so aggressively from the first long wall – the ones who were most dangerous, most violent right now. The men on the other long wall – they were nearly as dangerous and therefore perhaps even more violent, trying to get ahead, so they had to be more visible more often in order to position themselves in a rank they hadn't yet achieved. The ones on his desk, he ran his finger along the edges of the files that were stacked in blue and green piles, another seventeen organisations, more terrible names that would soon strike with as much force. Right here, in the southern suburbs. The growth was faster and stronger than anyone could understand; he turned, looked around, there was no wall space left.

'Now?'

'Yes.'

He nodded to two men in civvies who were each sitting on a chair drinking the bitter, pungent coffee, drug squad, surveillance, his pretext. They got up and hurried through the police station that had been built in the mid-nineties for twenty-two policemen in north Botkyrka, of which only four remained three years later. He had seen his colleagues redeployed, one after another, as all the letter boxes, windows and chimneys in the building were doused with flammable liquid which then turned into flames, when the threat grew with every intervention, when the tyres on private cars were slashed so many times that they didn't bother to change them any more and just watched the seats and engine burn.

'Left through the door. Four minutes' walk. Råby Allé 67.'

The buildings, the asphalt, the smell of smoke. All part of a place that had become as much his as theirs. He knew and recognised the voices, faces, he knew which buildings were hottest in summer and where the wind blew coldest in winter.

They had only scraped the surface back then.

Identified open drug-dealing, emptied vehicles of guns, sawn-off shotguns, automatic guns, confiscated knives, axes, nunchucks and batons from young men.

At the time, there had been more criminal groups in this concrete wilderness of high-rise blocks to the south of Stockholm than ever before in the entire country. It was a national issue. Which resulted in the Fittja Commission, the Special Gang Unit, the Section Against Gang Crime. Their patch started as Råby, then grew into Botkyrka, which expanded into Södertörn.

After three years only four were still there. And now, for a long time there had been just one, one person gathering information and building up a new police force with the sole aim of breaking up criminal networks in the southern suburbs of Stockholm.

José Pereira walked half a step ahead of the drug squad officers, past a burnt-out rubbish room, two new piles of burnt tyres, the car that the fire brigade had abandoned in the morning, the moped that had so recently been in flames.

He no longer noticed it, in the way that we no longer see what's always been there.

'There. The stairs in the middle. Second floor.'

The building looked like all the others. Seven storeys, access balconies, colours that varied from grey to worn-thin grey, and orange doors that screamed from afar.

'Three windows without curtains, blankets over the two to the left, kitchen and bedroom.'

He had learnt their names between the ages when they started to walk and later ride a bicycle. He had read through red files in social welfare offices, exchanged information with the principals of secure training centres and homes, had already had a clear picture of Leon Jensen and Gabriel Milton's criminal activities by the time they were nine, without being able to do anything except wait. Until they reached fifteen and could be sentenced. Until they had developed so much in their criminal career that the only thing to do was to lock them up.

The stairwell smelt of steam and food. The steps were too short and too close. The door out onto the balcony whined as it had the last time.

'Second on the left. Says SANTOS on the letter box.'

He had watched them grow up, grow together. When they were twelve, someone had whispered Råby Warriors for the first time and he had listened and thought *what kind of nonsense is that*, but then watched them expand, Leon Jensen and Gabriel Milton had become Alexander Eriksson and Bruno Viani, and others, Reza Noori and Ali Abdulahi and Jon Lindh and Uros Koren – he had started to monitor the twelve-year-old boys and discovered multi-criminal men: drugs, robbery, assault, contempt of court. He had watched them commit crimes together and that moment, he was sure of it, when they had somehow decided.

He closed in on the front door, checked the handwritten name, SANTOS, nodded to the two officers who were standing with their legs apart, hands to holsters.

He rang the bell.

Nothing.

José Pereira studied the flaking orange door, for a couple of months now the meeting place for the four who weren't in prison serving sentences right now, who were holding the fort and controlling the drugs in Råby, or rather, controlling the whole of Råby. He knew they were on their way and that they were about to succeed, that they would soon boast their own criminal halo. In recent weeks, several of his credible sources had reported the same, as had the prison service intelligence unit, that after six years they had now changed name, structure, rules – Ghetto Soldiers, *Jesus, another ridiculous name* – which meant more hate, violence, death.

He pressed the black plastic bell again. It wasn't working. Or maybe it was being drowned out by the volume of the TV set.

He knew they were on the move, but not where to, or why, or how.

He had been looking for a reason. Oscarsson's phone call – Pereira turned back from the two drugs officers with their feet firmly on the ground, and thumped the orange surface hard with his hand – the reason, he'd got it now.

———

He was sweaty, her soft fingers on his uneven skin, she almost dared to look him in the eye.

*Gabriel, never forget who u r, bro.*

He'd heard the doorbell ring twice and when they hammered on the door he'd seen them through the gap between the blanket and the window frame. Three of them. They were like the guys in prison. They would stand there ringing the bell until someone opened. They could do that. It didn't matter, whatever there was to find was in the trailer down in the garage, hired in someone else's name, or in the supermarket lockers at ICA and Konsum, and the changing rooms at the pool, and a couple of lockers at school, in several lift shafts and under the freezers in shops, but most of it was with people who stored it for them because they wanted to, or those who kept it because they had to.

*We r the power, brutha.*

Her fingers were gentlest furthest down, just where his back met his arse, his skin was less folded there.

He looked at her.

She had taken off her earrings, they were lying on the floor and he didn't like it, he picked them up, *you're to wear them*, and waited while she put them on, where they were supposed to be, she'd chosen them herself and he hadn't sold them and so she had to wear them.

*And we've got soldiers who'll do exactly what we ask them to do brutha.*

When they hammered on the door, *open up*, for the second time, he shouted even louder than the TV in the sitting room, he *fucking open it* shouted until he was sure that someone had heard and hauled themselves up.

———

'Pig bastard.'

The one they called Big Ali was a good few centimetres taller than the three men he glowered down at, his head nearly touching the top of the doorframe, the eyes that had so recently been staring at them from a wall in the police station were now two big and obviously drugged-up pupils, his arm movements spiky, his voice aggressive – amphetamines.

'I want to talk to Gabriel.'

José Pereira was standing in front of someone he'd questioned every month since he was fifteen – three years, thirty-six times – someone he'd talked to for hours but didn't know at all.

'And behind the fucking pig, two more.'

Big Ali made a smacking sound with his mouth, pointed at the two police officers who were standing there half a step behind.

'I want to talk to Gabriel. Not you.'

A violent film on the telly, Pereira was certain. The volume was turned up, loud music, loud shouting.

'I'm gonna get you, *you fucking pig*.'

His plate-sized pupils and body that couldn't stand still, Big Ali had managed to punch the air in front of him several times before a considerably shorter, muscular young man took hold of his arm, *go into the bitch*, and pushed him away, stood there in his place by the front door, erect penis, bare chest, bare feet.

'Pereira.'

'Gabriel.'

José Pereira had seen the badly disfigured body so many times before, the needle tracks, craters in his veins, but still couldn't get used to it. Eighty-five per cent burns didn't allow your eyes to see anything other than what they saw.

'A woman, Pereira.'

His groin only a couple of metres away, stirred, a couple of pelvic thrusts back and forth, as if this boy in the doorway was pointing at something with his hard-on.

'Råby cock needs a woman. And I rolled off her. So what the fuck do you want, eh?'

His legs, the skin, it was different.

On one thigh an infected, oblong sore; on the other a new tattoo that started by the groin, every black, powerful line bulging out from the skin, letters that were difficult to read from where Pereira was standing right now.

'These are my colleagues from the drug squad. We have a search warrant.'

The boy who was naked looked at the piece of paper in the policeman's hand.

'You know what . . . this isn't my flat.'

'We have the prosecutor's permission to search *the flat where you stay on a regular basis.*'

'Forget it.'

'I'd appreciate it if you moved to one side.'

A hand grabbed the piece of paper, it rustled slightly as he rapped it.

'You know you're not going to find anything here, you bastard.'

José Pereira knew that. He knew that this was the only place where they definitely *didn't* keep anything. That wasn't why he was standing here looking at an eighteen-year-old dick.

They were on the move.

It was his responsibility to find out where.

'*I'm gonna get you, you fucking pigs.*'

A voice further into the flat, Big Ali's voice, maybe he was punching the air in front of him again with his fists.

'He's shouting very loud. Unlawful threats. Not so smart.'

Gabriel Milton's organ had flagged somewhat and was no longer pointing at the three policemen.

'Not my problem. Did you want anything apart from to get in?'

'My colleagues . . .'

'Do they suck you off?'

'My colleagues have got some questions about your visit to Aspsås prison the other day.'

The eighteen-year-old smiled, at least, that's what it looked like.

'Maybe you misunderstood.'

'Your girlfriend.'

'What about her?'

'She was there.'

'And what the fuck's that got to do with me?'

'She—'

'Did you see me in Aspsås or did you not see me in Aspsås?'

'Your girlfriend was there. A few hours later, D1 Left was full of speed. We think there's a connection. That you were the supplier, that you provided her with the drugs.'

Gabriel Milton really did smile this time, it was obvious now when he looked at the two guys behind Pereira.

'Do they give a good blow job?'

Even broader grin.

'Or is it you that sucks off them?'

———

Four in prison. Four at large.

Half in, half out, like all the others, like every other gang.

They were following the same pattern, showing the same signs, treading the same path. Little boys who turned into reports and briefs and investigations, who, after a couple of years had got themselves a name and started to commit crimes together, were moved to a blue or green file on one of the Section Against Gang Crime desks to be monitored and reported on regularly, who a couple of years later were given a position at the bottom of the first long wall, the one for groups that were dangerous and violent, the position for staring faces which, in the police's own ranking system, belonged to those who ruled, who right now were deemed to be the most dangerous, most violent, at the forefront of organised crime.

José Pereira clutched the now slightly crinkled piece of paper hard, a search warrant from the public prosecutor.

'So, we want to come in.'

The eighteen-year-old smiled again, a partially erect penis that was thrust back and forth a couple of times, turned around and closed the door.

———

They were on the move.

It was his responsibility to find out where.

———

He clutched the search warrant in one hand and pushed open the orange, unlocked door and stormed into the empty hall, which was where he heard the voice again, Big Ali's voice from what he presumed was the kitchen, the hulking body holding the harness and collar of a black and white, almost square, dog, which he released and then shouted something as it moved silently through the sitting room, past the TV, past the sofa, towards the hall and the front door and the colleague who was already further in. José Pereira had never shot a dog before. The first shot hit the dog mid-jump, right-hand back leg, as the beast launched itself, jaws wide, at an unprotected neck and the unprepared and civvy-clad drugs officer put up his left arm in defence, sharp teeth straight through the black sleeve of his jacket and the skin of his forearm, muscles, sinews. The dog didn't even notice. The adrenalin smothered the pain and it continued to pull and tear when the policeman fell to the floor. Pereira shot at it again and his colleague behind him fired as well, both aiming at a point just behind the ear, the most effective way to kill a dog, and despite the powerful body moving all the time, despite the risk of hitting the man now lying in agony on the floor, they continued to fire – eight, nine, ten times. The animal gradually loosened its grip, fell heavily to the floor, then José Pereira took a step forwards and fired another two shots into the lifeless body.

'You stay bloody still.'

His colleague had slipped past him and gone into the flat, his gun pointing into the sitting room at the one they called Big Ali who was screaming *fucking pig cunts* and punching the air.

José Pereira aimed *his* gun at the one standing closest, in front of him, the one called Gabriel Milton.

'Fucking get down on the floor.'

The naked body looked at him with a sneer as he lay down on the linoleum floor. Twelve shots had been fired only metres away. The man next to him had a mauled arm and was still screaming. It was as if the young face didn't register any of it. He wasn't frightened. He wasn't upset. And when he lay as he did now – on his stomach with his right leg out for comfort – the tattoo that had been difficult to read became clear. It started on the hip and went the whole way down the thigh to knee; José Pereira had never seen the legend before, fourteen letters in the hall light, **GHETTO SOLDIERS**, across the burn scars.

They were on the move and now he knew where.

# twenty-two days to go

HE WAS STILL TIRED.

Eight grams the first day, eight grams the second day and he'd forgotten to count on the third. It was a couple of days ago now, but it was still in his body, spasms around the eyes, mouth smacking, chin that went back and forth of its own accord that gave him this weird look, but most of all the fucking sweat on his forehead and temples and scalp. He leaned closer to the mirror above the sink, he looked like fucking Smackhead.

It would last a while yet, he knew that. The voices were the worst. He had to be able to deal with them outside the cell, they were always there when he'd done two nights in a row, so real and they talked shit about him, almost as if they really existed and he couldn't pretend they weren't there even though they talked about things he didn't want anyone to know.

Leon adjusted the bedside lamp, it had to be on full.

He had written a bit, tidied, had a wank, made his bed, taken down the curtain rail, unscrewed the wardrobe, screwed the wardrobe back together again, put back the curtain rail, written a bit more, wanked again, tidied, made his bed. In every cell, D1 Left, the same. The whole unit was wired, awake twenty-four seven, refusing to work, inmates who locked themselves in.

He had dished it out for free and the suspicious looks and questions had disappeared after the first gram, they had consumed it until it was gone in the way that druggies in prison always do, and the whore mule was known to those who needed to know, prison management. And the next time they would check, they would get a search warrant and she would stand there, empty.

Until then, until he got what he really needed.

*U get what u deserve.*

He turned the bedside lamp a bit, the light hit the concrete wall and was brighter, his grandmother had often done that, chased off the dark with light that protected. And sometimes, but only for a second, he was sure that the woman who was his mother had done it too, the one who'd stopped coming to visit when he went to Bärby or maybe it was him who'd asked her to stop coming, probably was.

The light from the bedside lamp dissolved into the light coming from the window.

He stayed lying on the bed, but turned towards the bars, a sky, some clouds, the only things he could see from here.

In twenty-two days.

He knew what was needed, *the first wall*, how it worked, what separated one wall from another.

*Until they were there, until they were at the top, until it was gone.*

'I'm going to kill them all!'

He shouted it again and again, until the rattling outside the door stopped, a key was turned and the door opened.

The screw whore.

'What's . . . going on?'

He didn't answer.

'You were shouting, what . . .'

'Close the door, will you.'

She stayed standing where she was, not much older than him. She stood there and pretended that she didn't feel uncomfortable.

'UA.'

*It had worked.*

'You think so?'

*UA today. And next time, the dogs and a search warrant and she'd be empty.*

*It had worked.*

'Urine test, now. Test room.'

He took his time getting undressed and then turned round to face her when he left the cell naked and walked down the corridor.

'If you're wanting to see it, you can have a look now.'

She followed half a step behind and noticed that one of his thighs looked septic, bloody, and the other had a tattoo that looked completely new, a name of some sort, difficult to read.

A small room that wasn't much bigger than a cell, opposite the TV corner and beside the fish tank. One of the mirrors was on the floor in front of the toilet, two others on either side of it where the screws could see his penis, not taking their eyes off it for a moment, it was to be his piss and completely fresh.

Julia Bozsik wore latex gloves when she handed over the white jug and met his eyes when he thrust his pelvis at her several times.

Scared.

She was so scared.

And she mustn't be, mustn't, mustn't show it.

'And what if I . . . don't piss? If I . . . think that people like you should die?'

'If you refuse to take a urine test, I will report you and you will have your sentence extended by ten days. And then next time, ten more.'

Scared. She was so scared.

He thrust his pelvis at her one more time, then smiled, held the jug up to his penis for the first few drops. He had pissed in Eknäs and Bärby and several times in Mariefred, but always in a special hospital unit, with nurses in white uniforms handing out and collecting the plastic jugs. This fucking piss parlour inside the unit, it already stank.

'You want to see more?'

The plastic mug in his hand as he filled it all the way up to the rim, held the yellow liquid out towards her and then just as she was about to take it, turned it upside down, poured the contents down right in front of her feet, making sure that nothing got on her shoes, never risk the possibility of being accused of assault.

'You wanted me to take a piss. Otherwise you were obviously going to give me time. So I did what you said, I pissed.'

A queue outside the door when he left, Smackhead and Alex and Virtanen and Västerås and Marko and the Count. He stopped briefly at the front of the queue, the old skinny guy who was always fucking smiling.

'You know what to do, Smackhead.'

He was to take the jug, fill it with piss while they watched and then he was to pour it out, close, but not on their feet.

*A whole unit that refused. If they had been in any doubt, they now knew, there was plenty of drugs.*

Leon walked away, he still didn't understand it, that fucking smile, he wanted to punch him, hated those parted lips, it was as if . . . but here, not with the screws here, and he carried on, naked, back to his cell.

———

He didn't even see the bars any more. And the wall was transparent. And there, the sun, the sky, the other life.

Twenty-two days.

'I'm going to kill them all!'

He and Alex were in Aspsås – maximum security, class 1.

Reza was in Österåker and Uros in Storboda – high security, class 2.

Locked up and watched for years, because people who shouldn't have talked had talked.

The truth, isnt it brutha, a soldiers with us or against us.

This time she knocked. The screw bitch. And he'd got dressed.

'You asked for visitation rights.'

'Yes.'

'Visitors' room 2.'

Down the unit corridor, the long passage under the yard and the stairs up to central security and the visitors' room on the right, where he'd undressed that whore a week earlier and emptied her of two hundred grams of amphetamine.

The narrow bed with its sticky plastic cover over the mattress, the toilet rolls by the condoms at the end, the dripping tap on the sink, the small table in the middle of the room and the view between the bars on the window.

And the lawyer.

On the chair, with his briefcase on his knees, fat and bald, he couldn't remember his name, something beginning with P maybe. He'd actually used up all his visitation rights for the period, but with lawyers it was all right. They were like pigs and priests, came when you called on them and you could do it as often as you liked.

Leon sat down on the other chair, waited while the lawyer opened his briefcase and put a pile of papers on the table.

'I've got what you asked for.'

**SÖDERTÖRN DISTRICT COURT    JUDGEMENT    CASE No. 211-1**

**ACCUSED** Jensen, Leon
**CRIME COMMITTED** Aggravated robbery
**SECTION OF THE LAW** chapter 8, § 6 Swedish Penal Code
**SENTENCE,** etc
Imprisonment four (4) years, six (6) months
Probation is hereby declared forfeited.

'So, I've been hearing things.'

Leon pulled the papers over.

'Someone thought I should read these. He said "If you're changing walls, you should read".'

Stockholm. Central Station. The Forex office. Quite late. It was dark outside.

He had been holding a gun. Alex with one Kalashnikov replica, Reza with the other. Uros had been sitting waiting in the car outside, engine running.

'I've been hearing things. People have been saying things they shouldn't say.'

The short, stocky lawyer shifted position, the wooden chair was uncomfortable, they always were in prison visiting rooms; the higher the level of security, the more uncomfortable the chairs, as if the punishment included the visitors.

'What do you want?'

*The genrals have power over the lawyers.*

The lawyer felt very uneasy.

He knew what the young man in front of him wanted, why he had called for a meeting with his legal representative. He knew where it would lead.

He could feel it in his stomach, he always felt tension and discomfort there – some people felt it in their chest, others across their brow, but for him, always in the pit of his stomach.

'The interviews.'

The lawyer had his hand on another pile of papers, his fingers were sweaty and didn't want to let go.

'I want to read the interviews.'

*Lawyers do what we say they should do.*

He was obviously pressing harder with his right index finger and the metal splint under the white bandage snagged the paper. Until he saw that Jensen was looking at it, then he pulled it back, as if it had been broken again.

*Or they'll pay.*

'You want to read them?'

The lawyer had witnessed this sort of thing several times before. Gang members who demanded to see their judgements, the whole investigation – the basis of what became a prison sentence – to find out who'd blabbed, who would have to pay later.

'Do you want me to say it again? What exactly is it that you don't understand?'

Then, the same story every time. Once he's read the papers, the gang leader flushes out those who can't be trusted any more, makes his organisation stronger, protects it.

'I want to see the interviews with Daniel Wall and Javad Kittu.'

A client who normally doesn't read anything, not a book, not a paper, but after the judgement has been pronounced requests the interviews, tapping transcripts, technical evidence and then studies every single word, interprets every single comma.

'All of them?'

'It's my right.'

Leon followed the bandaged finger as it leafed through hundreds of pages. The Central Station and Forex office, how they'd howled like dogs in the car afterwards, they had owned the world as they always did, he'd wound down the window on the bridge outside the parliament and screamed even louder and Reza had taken off his top and leant his whole naked torso out, and Uros had swung from the cars on the right to the cars on the left and then the right again, and Alex had sat in the back singing a bloody marathon, they had headed out of the city and off the motorway into Råby, hooting like fuck, they had laughed like fuck and all the dollar bills were stuffed into a wardrobe in Danny Hangaround's flat, and the other foreign money under the bed in Javad Hangaround's flat, they had divvied up the Swedish money in a café in the centre and each bought a new car that would be parked in the garage in the basement and a new TV with white varnished loudspeakers and for six nights in a row had sat at the best table in the club, nearest the window with a view over Stureplan.

'Yes, you do have a right to read it.'

The lawyer turned towards the barred window and wall, his back to the prisoner and the papers that he didn't want anything to do with right now.

'And it's my right not to know why.'

Sometimes, when he didn't feel like he did in the pit of his stomach, he could laugh at their pseudo-morals, pseudo-honour, pseudo-respect. All those big words for all those little boys.

'These ones, this file, the interview with Daniel Wall.'

**Reference number 0211-K166723-11**

**INTERVIEW LEADER JAN ZANDER (IL):** I want an answer to my question.
**DANIEL WALL (DW):** You mean . . . Central Station?
**IL:** Yes.
**DW:** Well . . . we've . . . well, maybe I know.
**IL:** Do you know who?
**DW:** But just a little.
**IL:** A little?
**DW:** I mean, fuck! A little!
**IL:** On that particular day? Did you meet Leon Jensen – on that particular day?

But with the boy sitting on the other side of the table, it was more. More than just flushing out, punishing, protecting, strengthening.

That was what he felt in his stomach. Someone who didn't know himself.

'And there, the final interview with Javad Kittu.'

**Reference number 0211-K166729-11**

**INTERVIEW LEADER LEIF LUNDH (IL):** Good.
**JAVAD KITTU (JK):** What the fuck's good?
**IL:** That you remember what he was wearing.
**JK:** You said it, pig bastard.
**IL:** His clothes?
**JK:** Normal.
**IL:** And what are normal clothes?
**JK:** A hoodie, like. Trackies.
**IL:** What colour?
**JK:** Dark, I think. Reza's were lighter.
**IL:** And Jensen? What clothes did he have on?

The lawyer who had been sitting with his back to him while he read now got up and walked over to the window, looked at the unmoving concrete wall.

*We r famly.*

Now and then he turned round, looked over at the table and the eighteen-year-old turning the pages, reading, turning the pages, reading,

*We r bruthas unto death*

at the determined aggression that was looking for the answer that wasn't just staring at the floor or keeping your mouth shut with a smile or shouting *fucking pig*, an answer that would always mean punishment later.

*And u always get wot u deserve.*

When the eighteen-year-old with a tense face had finished reading and in silence pushed the large pile of paper back towards the lawyer's empty chair, when the brown briefcase was packed and closed, when the female, and very young, prison warden had opened the door to let the inmate who was serving a long sentence return to his cell, the lawyer looked her in the eyes, not for long but long enough to see the fear she tried to hide with her determined movements and firm voice, you could see it and feel it and he felt sorry for her, he would be *outside* the walls very shortly.

'By the way . . .'

Leon Jensen had been sure to shake his hand hard afterwards, squeezed the bandaged index finger, before he walked away.

'I was asked to tell you that your dog died a few days ago.'

Now he stopped and turned round, waiting to hear the continuation.

'An American Staffordshire terrier attacked a civilian-clad policeman in a flat on the second floor of Råby Allé 67 and so was shot to death by a total of twelve bullets.'

His client just stood there, listening, but didn't react.

'Did you hear what I said?'

'I heard what you said.'

The lawyer hadn't known how he would express his pain, and so had waited until he had to and now was uncertain how to carry on.

'And?'

'And what?'

'The dog, you, I'm . . .'

He probably hadn't heard. So the lawyer who thought the metal splint round his finger was uncomfortable, now hurried to add, in an even louder voice: 'But the good news is . . . your friend . . . the one who was being held for unlawful threats and causing bodily harm has been released due to lack of evidence – the prosecutor couldn't prove that the dog had been unleashed with intent.'

He had been running, but stopped when he got to the spiral staircase down to the underground passage and locked doors. He didn't think that the person he was talking to had heard. So he'd gone even closer, was almost shouting, when his client suddenly turned round. *You get what you deserve.* For a while, the lawyer stood looking at the door he couldn't see through and felt that the security camera by the ceiling was a bit too close when it zoomed in on his face; he was almost certain that was what his client had said.

José Pereira was close to the town with its proud, white church and rows of terraced houses, the sort of place he knew he could never live in himself, but still envied the people who did, who lived close together, had contact with each other. He had a wife whom, in one week's time, he had loved for exactly fifteen years and they had two girls together, born fourteen minutes apart and he still hadn't found a good enough word to describe what he felt for them, because *love* wasn't even a start. Every now and then he was struck by guilt because he was the one who kept them in a small flat in a part of the city called Södermalm; he loved the cafés, the restaurants, the crowds of people, bumping into him or her, watching them for a while and knowing they would probably never meet again, everything that wasn't Aspsås, the town he was now driving into.

A dog had been shot twelve times.

The square, dumb, slavering dog had remained clamped onto the policeman's arm and continued to tear it apart.

He had been looking for an answer. He had found his answer. He had seen the skin on a thigh that was otherwise covered in eighty-five per cent burns that had healed long ago, but was now an infected wound where a name had once been that now had to disappear. A name he had known of for so long and tried so hard to counteract. And then on the other thigh, a new name to show that they had left something behind, that they were on their way, wanting more room.

José Pereira had called an ambulance. His colleagues from drug squad left the building at high speed, the ambulance's blue lights flashing. One sat beside the gurney with his hand on the

93

shiny, wet forehead of the man lying on it, who was in deep shock, trying to calm him.

He had never experienced anything like it before, a life that carried on even after several lethal shots that should have killed it had been fired. And he had never seen an arm so mauled before either.

He had walked on his own back to the police station on the edge of Råby and gone into the large room that was the hub of all the work with gang crime in south Stockholm; he had stood silently by the two long walls and then moved the eight faces, who until now had called themselves Råby Warriors, from their position at the top of the second wall, to a new position at the bottom of the first, and given them a new sign – Ghetto Soldiers.

They were established.

They had grown out of the social services' files into police files on a desk, into faces on the second wall and now into faces on the first.

They had succeeded.

He turned off the motorway exit, passed the church and headed for a gate in the enormous wall, waited with the engine running while it opened and then carried on over to central security, where only those who visited frequently enough to be recognised were allowed to park. He stayed in the car, as he sometimes did, preferring to finish listening to a song on the radio that he liked but didn't know the name of. It was also normally when he tried to understand just how long a person could take it. And if, in the end, it really mattered. Nineteen years at the heart of the battle against organised crime. And he'd seen it increase, not decrease – more frequent, not less; more violent, more fierce – and soon, they already knew, another five thousand young Swedish lads would work their way into the criminal network, as many as all of those who were now in prison.

He recognised the prison warden who was sitting behind the glass in central security, one of the older ones, who waved him through with a friendly smile before he'd even managed to find something that resembled ID, and he walked on towards the stairs to the first floor and Oscarsson's office, a trolley with tea and coffee by the sofa, steam rising as the prison governor chose his brew.

'Green?'

'Black.'

Two cups, one green, one black.

'And Martha?'

'She's fine. She sends her greetings.'

'And the girls?'

'Growing up.'

José Pereira smiled and Lennart Oscarsson smiled cautiously back, as if he didn't really dare, afraid that what was between them might hurt. Pereira knew the prison governor had also had a family once, but he'd let them go and so lived ever more lonely in the house you could see from his desk, if you leaned over slightly. And every time the question arose, because it always did – *And the girls?* – it was as if he didn't really want an answer, didn't want to know that the other person still had their children close and that everything was fine, and José Pereira always felt a little awkward when he answered, as though by telling the truth he made someone who was missing something miss it even more.

'You were right.' Pereira put down his cup of black tea. 'I've upgraded them. They're on the move. And I want to know where.'

The tight smile had vanished and Pereira was grateful for it, he'd done the right thing, getting straight to the point rather than elaborating on the two girls that he cared for more than anything else in the world.

'I wondered if you'd seen this anywhere in the prison?'

He'd carried the sketch in a plastic sleeve in his hand, afraid to fold it.

'The most recent and clear indication that the group is expanding.'

He put the piece of paper down on the table between them. A sketch of the new tattoo that had been on Gabriel Milton's right thigh.

'Ghetto Soldiers?'

'Until very recently, Råby Warriors. First a local name, then something more ... philosophical. Tumba Lords became Fucked For Life. Bredäng Legion changed to Red Generation. Hallunda Boys ...'

'A prison organisation.'

'Have you seen it?'

'Never. But the name ... we've come across it here several times in recent years. One of the ones that you only hear *inside*, an organisation that protects you when you're doing time. But the fact that it also exists outside ...'

'Leon Jensen, Alexander Eriksson. Full-blown members. Daniel Wall, some kind of hangaround. I've also got information about another person who's about to become a full member. That would make it nine. The sources I've been talking to have mentioned some kind of ... initiation.'

'Who?'

'I don't know yet. I don't know who's being tested. Nor on whom.'

Lennart Oscarsson picked up the sheet of paper, closely studied a good sketch of a thigh, and words obviously drawn by a handmade machine, then he got up. There were some shelves behind his desk, and on the top one was a plastic bag. He opened it and took out an electric shaver.

'We confiscated this yesterday. D1 Left. Jensen and Eriksson's unit.'

José Pereira looked at the Braun electric shaver; he also saw a bent spoon handle, a pen that had been emptied of its contents and a pipe cleaner.

'Where? Who?'

He'd seen a couple of similar things before. But this was unusually well made.

'In the cell and bed of a man who's done a lot of time and who's pretty notorious thanks to his combination of unpleasant aggression and astonishing technical skills in the classroom, but who looks like a . . . wreck. His name is Sonny Steen. But he's usually just called Smackhead.'

Pereira looked at the prison governor.

'Sonny Steen?'

'Yes.'

He didn't say any more, but Lennart Oscarsson noticed something akin to irritation, perhaps confusion, when Pereira got up and walked around the room. His face was still agitated, or was it confused, when he picked up the machine from the table and carefully poked at the various parts.

'A shaver. A ballpoint pen. A needle from a wire brush. A spoon. A bit of tape. Each thing separately, each part allowed in a maximum security prison. But only in parts. *Not* together.'

He turned it over, opened it, looked for a socket and plugged it in, a needle that whirred and punctured the air with a regular beat.

'I want to go in.'

'Go in?'

'D1 Left. To Jensen. Alone.'

'You know you can't do that.'

'And you know that I've done it before.'

The governor of Aspsås prison took the whirring electric shaver, turned it off, put it back in the plastic bag.

And shook his head.

'I would strongly advise you not to do that.'

'I have to.'

'Your safety. In there . . . I can't guarantee anything.'

'If I'm going to get the answer I need . . . I have to be alone. You know that. Too much face to lose.'

Oscarsson gave an exasperated shrug, pointed at his desk, at the chair where he'd recently been sitting.

'I'll sort out an interview room. If none of the visitors' rooms are available, you can use my office, here, my chair, sit down.'

José Pereira didn't sit down. He stayed standing where he was and would continue to do so.

'I have to challenge him. His authority. And to do that, I have to go in on my own, when I want to, show that I'm not afraid. Challenge him.'

They looked at each other in silence. One who wanted a confrontation, and one who could refuse him the chance.

'Excuse me.'

Neither Pereira nor Oscarsson had heard her knock.

'You wanted a report.'

The door was half open and Julia Bozsik stood on the threshold until the governor waved to her to come in.

'Well?'

'D1 Left. General UA.'

'And?'

'We . . . we couldn't analyse anything. As they all poured it out. One after the other.'

On the floor.

'Good.'

And then stood there looking at her, waiting for a reaction.

'Good?'

'Then we know. They'd test positive, every single one of them. And I'll make sure we get a search warrant. OK?'

She nodded and was pulling the door closed behind her just as Oscarsson called after her.

'Bozsik?'

Her head appeared in the gap.

'Yes?'

'Can you take our guest down into the unit?'

Pereira turned to Oscarsson, gave a brief nod, thank you, then turned to the young prison warden.

'José Pereira. Section Against Gang Crime.'

Julia studied the man in civilian clothes.

'You're a policeman?'

'Yes.'

'With all due respect – I don't think it would be a good idea for you to visit the unit. Or . . . any other unit in the prison, for that matter.'

He had already started to walk.

'I need information. And in fact that's precisely what I want them to know, that I'm looking for information.'

He stopped, waited for her to catch up.

'And I take full responsibility for my own safety.'

Down the stairs and into the underground passage. The first camera by the first locked door; he glanced over at her, a very young prison officer who had just advised a considerably older policeman against visiting the place where she spent eight hours a day.

'You're frightened.'

Her eyes. And her manner of speaking, almost *too* self-assured.

She stood facing the locked door and didn't answer.

'You're frightened of them.'

The door made the clicking sound they were waiting for, she pushed it open and they walked in silence along the concrete corridor to the next locked door, the next camera.

He didn't say any more. She still didn't look at him.

Until she suddenly turned.

'Yes.'

The clicking sound again. But they stayed standing where they were.

'I *am* frightened.'

The door clicked again, and the camera zoomed in on the two people who didn't seem to hear it.

'Every time they look at me.'

Now they opened the door, carried on towards the final locked door in the underground passage, then turned right, up the stairs to Block D. She stopped, halfway.

'They don't care what happens. Do you understand?'

He looked into the eyes that were trying so hard to be professional and to cope, but couldn't face doing it much longer.

'Yes.'

He hoped that she would realise soon, look for another life.

'I understand.'

One flight up. The unit called D1 Left.

'I go on my own from here.'

She looked at him for slightly too long, as if she wanted to talk more about what she couldn't mention to anyone else there, as she had to be strong.

'In that case, wait here.'

She was perhaps only nine, ten years older than his two girls. And he didn't even know what her first name was. But she had still trusted him, revealed what she otherwise kept hidden. He waited while she disappeared into the wardens' office and then came back with a rectangular piece of plastic in her hand, grey with a red button on the side.

An alarm.

'*Just in case.*'

He smiled at her, accepted it and put it in the front pocket of his trousers.

A long corridor. TV corner, kitchen, billiard table. Further down, sixteen cells, eight on each side.

Suddenly, as if everything had stopped. A peculiar silence.

The two who were playing billiards and were only concerned about their next shot had stopped playing, followed him with a concentrated frown, billiard balls demonstratively thrown up, down, up, down, in the air until they were sure he'd seen. The four playing cards at the round table had turned down the volume on the TV, and glared at him in silence. The ones standing in the kitchen, one by the fridge and one by the cooker, turned round and it was they who shouted, twice, three times, *pig in the pen.*

José Pereira carried on, but not so fast, looked around, recognised at least three of them. The one to the left at the card table, one of the faces that had been moved from the second to the first wall this morning – Alexander Eriksson, full member. The one beside him, cards in hand, one of those so-called hangarounds, prepared to do whatever it took to be accepted – Marko Bendik. And the one in the kitchen by the fridge, the one who'd made the tattooing machine that was lying between the tea cups on Oscarsson's desk – Sonny Steen, Pereira was sure it was him, even though it was a long time ago now and he'd aged in the way that only junkies do.

'I'm looking for Leon.'

José Pereira peered down the corridor, while they stood or sat and looked at him and didn't answer. He closed his hand round the rectangular piece of plastic in his pocket, and felt what she felt, fear.

'I'm looking for Leon Jensen.'

But if you so much as showed it, they only got more aggressive.

One of the guys who'd been throwing billiard balls up and down was maybe throwing faster and higher and the guy beside him had a cue in his hand now and was slicing it through the air, a swishing twitching sound, but nothing more than that for the moment.

'Pereira.'

The voice came from one of the open cells further down the corridor.

One of the first cells on the left.

Cell 2. Or maybe Cell 4.

'I don't think you should be here. I think you must be lost.'

It was him. Jensen. And he came closer. Conscious of the faces watching his every step, the others listening to them through open cell doors.

'I'm pretty sure that I've come to the right place.'

José Pereira didn't see the billiard ball, but he heard it.

It passed only centimetres from his forehead and slammed into the corridor wall.

'I'm sure that I've come to the right place as it was you I wanted to talk to.'

'And I don't talk to pigs.'

A civilian-clad policeman on his own in a place that policemen otherwise only visited in flocks, with protection. The billiard ball was just the start. They were standing there watching carefully, waiting for the man who showed no fear to do just that.

'I've come to ask you to roll up the right leg of your trousers. And as soon as you've done it, I'll leave again.'

That peculiar silence. Eyes that were watching. The four around the card table stood up almost simultaneously but stayed where they were when Jensen raised his hand.

'You can see my arse if you want.'

The door to the wardens' office was closed. He had asked to be alone and they had done as he asked, retreated out of sight for a coffee.

José Pereira gripped the rectangular piece of plastic in his pocket even harder, his thumb on the red button.

'Right trouser leg. Your choice. Either you roll it up now – or later in an examination room with your favourite screws and me watching.'

Pereira looked Jensen in the eye. And he could see that he knew.

That the policeman he'd known for as long as he could remember was standing in front of him and was not going to back down. That the staring faces around them were waiting for a show of power. That he couldn't lose face.

'Right?'

Every step he'd taken. That fucking pig had been there.

And he'd been a nuisance, been in the way with his reports and questions, his meetings with his mum.

And then, the morning he turned fifteen, the pig bastard had rung the bell and his mum had opened the door and they had done all the things they couldn't do earlier, taken his finger-prints, photo, DNA and in a column for special features, a description of a tattoo drawn with soot and needles that was no longer there.

And the pig just went at it. Knew what he wanted.

'You can see the left.' Leon Jensen laughed out loud and looked at the others, who also laughed.

Then he slowly and with a great flourish rolled up his left trouser leg to the middle of his thigh. The large wound was infected, the scab was fresh.

He didn't lose face. But had answered the question.

José Pereira met his eyes again, nodded briefly, and left.

THE CAR IN the middle lane was careful to keep to the speed limit despite the fact that the warm August evening had emptied the wide motorway of traffic. It came from the south, a light grey Mazda, stolen from a parking place in central Södertälje just over an hour before.

It had passed Rönninge and Salem church and changed lane as it approached Råby and the exit, slowly, but not too slowly, into the area called Råby Allé and the entrance to a garage, a vast concrete underground space that linked thousands of flats. A short and extremely overweight man in his thirties had great difficulty getting out of the confines of the passenger seat, but managed on the third attempt by putting his hand on the gearstick and levering himself out. He punched in a code and nodded to the driver as the door slowly slid up, then followed the car on foot as it drove down into the garage before stopping.

Night, silent, not a sound.

Except for a faint clatter, a loose steel blade that fluttered in the warm air blowing out of one of the many ventilators.

The driver closed the car door without locking it and they walked together towards one of the many exits, and as they continued towards the metro station, one of them got out a mobile phone and whispered '*PSW 656*', then hung up.

———

Gabriel snapped shut his phone. *PSW 656*. And he had the whole wide world in his hand. A feeling he recognised, the rush, as if it grabbed hold of something inside, all the anger and all the tears and all the hate at the same time, and he almost laughed, he who never laughed, who couldn't laugh, had once so long ago, but he remembered it was a bit like this, as if everything deep inside was released and he was light.

He got up from the bench on Råby Torg and walked towards the garage entrance, feeling the rush, the power, the whole fucking world. He took a gun out of the front pouch on his hoodie, he'd had it a long time and loved it and when he saw the car standing there exactly where it should be, he opened the cylinder and took out the six bullets and let them rest in the palm of his hand before putting only one back. He held the butt tight in one hand and spun the cylinder with the other, lifted the gun to his temple and pulled the trigger, a clicking sound that was brittle but could have been an almighty bang, he nearly laughed again, opened the cylinder and put the other bullets back in.

They all came at the same time.

Jon from Råby Allé 6, Bruno from Råby Allé 36, Big Ali and Javad from Råby Allé 77. Identical metal doors into the garage, and over to a light grey Mazda with the registration number PSW 656.

They waited there in a random circle while Gabriel took out his phone again and dialled a number that only he had.

To a phone that right then was lying on a bed, close to a hand under a lit lamp.

––––––––––

He had switched it to silent, but was lying awake, waiting.

Now it vibrated and flashed.

The one that was just his, the one he'd collected in between the lawyer and Pereira coming to the unit, the one he kept in the kitchen, inside the fridge door, where he'd made a hole.

'Brother?'

Gabriel's voice. He almost felt a warmth in his chest.

'Best brother.'

He'd never trusted any bastard, ever. And he knew that Gabriel hadn't trusted anyone, ever. Two people who didn't trust anyone, but did trust each other.

'It's here.'

'Registration?'

'PSW 656.'

'Left-hand front wheel. Back of the driver's seat.'

Leon straightened the bedside lamp, it was crooked and the cell was darker than normal.

'The judgement.'

'Yeah?'

'I read it.'

'And?'

'They talked, brother.'

A lawyer had stood with his back to him and known that every court case against a gang member was built on someone grassing on his brothers, his colleagues.

'Who?'

'Javad.'

**IL:** Which colour?

**JK:** Dark, I think. Reza's were lighter.

'You take care of him. In Masmo. Mum's flat.'

'Who else?'

'Danny.'

**IL:** So you met Leon Jensen that day?

A lawyer who knew that the consequences for someone who cooperated were always sufficient violence to punish them, tidy up, prevent any repetition.

'And I'll take care of him here. In his cell. One floor up.'

Leon didn't want to hang up, it was almost like being with him out there and he wanted to stay there as long as possible.

'One love, man.'

'One love, brother.'

———

He missed Leon so much, emptying the car, they should be doing it together.

His mobile phone beside the revolver in the pouch of his hoodie when he opened the boot: empty apart from a wheel wrench in a side pocket, which he handed to Bruno who was already on his way round to the front left-hand wheel.

Big Ali and Jon got into the back seat of the car and cut through the fabric of the driver's seat and took out four plastic packages that were in there. They were done at about the same time that Bruno loosened the five nuts on the hubcap and lifted off the wheel.

Through the door to Råby Allé 85, and the lift up to the fourth floor.

Gabriel opened the door to the empty flat with one of the keys on his heavy key ring and chose the living room. Bruno whooped loudly as he threw the wheel down onto the floor, it rolled away towards the far wall before bouncing and spinning and then lying still in the middle of the parquet. He used the same knife that Jon had just used to slash the driver's seat, and cut deep into the tyre and then waited for the rushing sound when the knife flew out releasing two kilos of air in just a couple of seconds. Now he went for the lightly glued edges, mustered his energy, jumped, landing with all his body weight, and on the third time it started to come away from the shiny rim, the fifth time even more and he turned the wheel over, carried on jumping on it until it came away on that side too. Big Ali and Jon took over and each jammed the end of a crowbar in under the rubber edge, four eighteen-year-old arms pushing up, centimetre by centimetre until the whole thing was free and Bruno could cut loose several thin packages that were taped to the rim.

————————

A large piece of tin foil like a rug on the parquet floor. And a pile of yellow and white capsules growing in the middle.

First the four round packages that had been in the back of the driver's seat – six hundred yellow methamphetamine capsules from Thailand for one hundred and twenty weekly customers.

Then the four flat packages from the rim of the front wheel – two hundred white heroin capsules from Russia for seventy weekly customers.

Altogether, eight hundred capsules that were immediately repackaged and divided into four plastic bags.

————————

When the doorbell rings in an empty flat there's an echo.

And when it's the middle of the night and there are no other sounds to compete, the doorbell becomes a jangling clamour.

They were so eager. Their thin hands pressing and pressing until they heard footsteps inside the flat bouncing off the walls and Gabriel opened the door. They all stretched up as far as they could. But it didn't make them any taller.

Four of them, the youngest eleven years old, the oldest thirteen.

He gave them each a plastic bag with two hundred capsules. He recognised the one furthest to the right, *Eddie's the name*, gold chain and slicked-back hair and still a mark on one cheek from his ring.

# fourteen days to go

HE HADN'T SLEPT. He had never slept at night in the dark.

Leon screwed in the bulb that must have come loose sometime after lock-up.

It didn't matter where.

Örkelljunga secure training centre or the foster home in Västervik or Liljanskolans independent training centre or the foster home in Arvidsjaur, or that place in Jönköping – he had never really understood what it was – or Eknäs secure home or Vemyra secure home or Mariefred prison or Aspsås prison, not even the months in the Barnbyn Skå family hostel where he and his mum had stayed when she was released from Hinseberg prison for women, so they could learn to be a family, not even then.

A strange night.

He'd had a call from Gabriel and listened to the sound of a tyre being dismantled and a car seat being slashed.

Then he'd banged on the wall to Cell 4 but the bastard was asleep.

He'd banged again and again and when he finally got a reaction, he'd pressed his lips to the flaking paint and shouted *Marko Bendik will be sick tomorrow* and then listened to the banging pass from Cell 4 to Cell 6 and from Cell 6 to Cell 8 and on to Cell 10 and Cell 12 where Marko got the message.

There was a knock on the door.

'Good morning.'

The screw whore.

'Good morning. Time to get up.'

He didn't answer.

'If you don't get up, you'll be reported. You were warned the last time.'

He turned over, but stayed lying where he was until she gave up and left.

He'd got some information from the cleaner yesterday, the one they used to beat up and now paid, that they'd changed position on the bastard pig's walls, from the second to the first. And today, he was going to prepare the way for them to move even higher up.

*The Whore* was going to visit him and this time she'd just carry the smell and have dumped it and the screws would use all their papers and dogs, then wouldn't be able to do it next time round.

*The Kids* would sell another load and settle up and that should give enough for both guns and flats.

*Marko* would be given an initiation test that would equal cleaning up in here and a new full member and at the same time Gabriel would do his bit on the outside.

It was going to be a long day, a big day.

He almost smiled.

He might even have a fuck, might even make someone pay a fine.

And the next time the cleaner reported to him, they'd be even higher up.

HE HAD STAYED lying on his bed and listened to them go to the showers and have breakfast, then some went to the workshop and some went to the classroom and there was only one screw left who hid in the fish tank with a cup of coffee; only then had he left his cell, with a number 2, and hurried down to number 12 and gone in.

'You look ill.'

'Strangley, it started during the night.'

Marko was up and about in his cell, waiting, his large frame filled with longing. The first time, at the secure training centre in Örkelljunga, he'd gone on every day about being part of it, and Leon had finally let him in on it and got him to help steal the four Mercedes that were needed for the escape. The second time at rehab, at the Sirius Paragraph 12 home; Marko had been nagging again to be in on it, and they'd made him a prospect. The third time they were both in Klockbacka; Marko's desire to belong was so strong they'd made him their runner, and he'd been forced to make his friends stash drugs, break a pinkie or a ring finger as a debt enforcer, the fingers that were least important so as not to attract too much attention, and to start disturbances when needed by smashing all the furniture in his room. Six years of longing and Leon knew that Marko would never even get close, but sometimes gangs needed particular qualities and right now, they needed someone who was prepared to do anything.

'You wanted an initiation test.'

There were eight of them.

'Yes.'

Soon there would be nine.

'Danny Hangaround.'

Marko was already on his feet and Leon pointed at the ceiling, the floor above.

'D2 Left. Cell 12.'

———————

Wanda felt the hand on her breast and pulled back, they were tender around the nipple. Gabriel stretched after her, his hand on her skin and she felt the fever, or whatever it was that felt like fever, like pressure or a burn, the tension in her body.

She kept her eyes shut when he pressed against her pelvis, demanding.

She pretended she was asleep.

He often sat and looked at her. Sometimes she squinted up when he wouldn't notice and his face was different, he looked kind, almost as if he liked her. If she woke up, his face changed, and if she looked at him and he noticed, it was like he'd been caught red-handed and his cheeks became pointed, his lips tight and eyes narrowed, chasing off what they were looking at.

'Not today.'

The hand was demanding, the fingers, she pushed them away.

'What the fuck . . .'

'Not yesterday, not today, not tomorrow. You know that. But after . . .'

Gabriel stared at her for a long time but didn't force her, didn't try to give her a bad conscience or convince her. He respected her. He'd never done that before, respected a woman. And sometimes he realised, but only sometimes and very briefly, he felt something akin to what he felt for Leon; he recognised it and was ashamed.

She rolled over to the side and got out of bed, left the bedroom with the sun shining on her face through the gap between the blanket and the window, walked down the hall into the sitting room and it was empty. Jon wasn't there, Bruno wasn't there, nor was Big Ali or even Javad Hangaround. She smiled, it was a relief, Gabriel was always nicer to her when they weren't there, the way they stared and *bitch come here* and *bitch piss off*, she smiled again and headed for the shower.

———————

Leon stood in the unit corridor. It was silent, deserted.

He had just left Marko in his cell, on the edge of his bed.

An initiation test. Marko should have laughed and given him a hug, *one love, brother*, he'd been wanting this for so long. But Leon knew he wouldn't react like that, in the same way that he wouldn't react like that, to laugh out loud with joy – guys like him just didn't do that, to be so fucking happy, if he ever was; there was sure to be some bastard who would take it away, run off with it, hide it.

He walked down the corridor, empty of people, and opened the wooden door with a small square of glass in the middle, the telephone cubicle for approved numbers, left it ajar and carried on to the kitchen. Perfect. If he stood here, at just this angle, the reflection in the glass showed the screws' fish tank, he could even see them, the bitch who insisted on *good morning*, and the one further in. Leon watched them move between the desk and the coffee machine.

Another door, this time to the cleaning cupboard.

First he checked the reflection in the glass, they were sitting comfortably, drinking their coffee, so he could open the cleaning cupboard door without being disturbed, move the cleaning trolley and vacuum cleaner and take out the metal bucket. Which just fitted in the sink and he filled it almost all the way up with warm water. He opened the food cupboard and took out three slices of bread from the bread box, the sort that tasted of syrup and stuck to your teeth, broke each one into five pieces and put them in the water. Some bags of apples, red and sweet, from a shelf higher up, twenty of them, quartered, and dropped in the water. A couple of bags of stale cinnamon buns in the water, half a box of sugar lumps in the water. A quick glance over at the precisely angled door to the telephone cubicle and the bucket went back into the cleaning cupboard, behind the trolley and the vacuum cleaner and two mops, a black binliner over the top.

Fourteen days. It would be ready then. When he needed it.

————

Back in his cell, Leon had lain down again to wait for the lunch break from books in the classroom and drills in the workshop. They'd come back one by one from their various places to the wooden table, the best place in the yard, as far from the watchful eyes in security as from the dusty gravel on the football pitch. They sat there with their faces to the sun and five cards in their hands and if he closed his eyes, if he couldn't see the seven-metre-high wall that kept them in – Alex beside him on one side and Marko on the other, they could have been sitting on the other side.

'Oi, you.'

At the next table, Smackhead and two guys from Denmark, or Skåne or wherever, who were just as fucked, were playing poker and holding the cards hard in their skinny, scabby hands, playing as if their lives depended on it, half a gram in the pot for every deal.

'*Oi, YOU.*'

Smackhead looked up and turned round, scrawny thirty-five-year-old body and twitching face.

'Come over here.'

Leon used his whole arm to wave him over and the guy at the next table dropped his cards and practically ran over, smiling as he got nearer, stiff lips, slightly open.

'This guy.'

Leon put his arm round Marko.

'Very soon. The same.'

The rag-and-bones cast a glance at Leon's right thigh, what he had written there only a few days ago, then at Marko, and at Alex, and Leon again. It was as if he only now fully understood and was overcome with fear.

'Who?'

He knew what was about to happen. If someone was going to carry the same emblem. There was only one way to become a full member.

'You don't need to fucking know.'

An initiation test. A murder.

He didn't want to die.

'But—'

'Not you.'

Over the twenty years that he'd spent in prison, he had regularly tattooed new full members and there was a strange feeling, the way they always shone, like they'd just left a mouse on the sitting room floor and expected payment and praise, so proud of having just taken away someone's breath.

'Not me?'

'Not you, Smackhead.'

The smile softened.

'The name's Sonny. I want—'

'One like that.'

A smiling skeleton that could barely stand on his feet, eyes switching between Leon's thigh and Marko's thigh. They couldn't care less what he was called. It made no fucking difference, he didn't care and he couldn't remember what they were called, always some new little shit who he didn't know, who told him what he was going to do, and then lashed out if he didn't do it.

'Then I want more. Fifteen g.'

'What the fuck, you—'

'They confiscated it. The searches. But . . . I can still do it. Needles. It'll take longer. And then I want more. Fifteen g.'

'We're not getting any in today.'

'And I want it up front.'

Leon leaned closer.

'You . . . I don't think you've understood how it works.'

Smackhead's smile, his mouth that smelt putrid.

'If you . . . if we haven't got any use for you, we'll kill you too.'

———

Lennart Oscarsson stood between the table stacked with sixteen TV monitors and the small fan that circulated warm, stuffy air round the cramped central security office. He looked out through the window at the prison yard, the gravel, the inmates. If he turned round, he could see through the other window: the wall, the church, the sky.

His world. He had only questioned it once.

The time when Martin had been lying there on the monitor in the middle, curled up with a gun to his head.

Maybe that was why he came in here so often, stepped out of the governor's office for a while to look at the TV screens that flicked through the images from sixty-four security cameras. He focused on one of them, a black and white picture from a warm prison yard and a thin man getting up from a game of cards, rolling in the way that people with sore feet do – his name was Sonny Steen and he'd had a handmade tattoo machine hidden under his mattress, *a bloody electric shaver*.

And he knew the prisoner who Steen was talking to right now, Leon Jensen, serving a long sentence, confirmed gang member, the one that José Pereira had first asked questions about and then asked to see, *inside* the unit. The picture was unclear, no colour or sound, but it was still obvious that the older guy was frightened of the younger guy, constantly moving from one foot to the other, as if he wanted to run away.

'The day's catch?'

Martin Jacobson had come into the office without knocking and sat down on the only chair, automatically reading the images from the yard, the wall, the corridors.

'Right. The day's catch.'

'Plus or minus?'

They smiled at each other. A strange game. Counting time.

'Plus.'

'Lunch?'

'Yep.'

Martin Jacobson checked his papers.

'Two that left. This morning just before eight – an inmate with seven and a half years to go was moved abruptly from solitary confinement to Karsudden hospital and a closed psychiatric ward. Barely an hour later – an inmate in Block C with two years and seven months left, was taken by the police to Kronoberg remand on suspicion of assaulting a fellow prisoner in the prison library.'

Ten more years of longing, somewhere else.

'And in exactly . . . twelve minutes, two new prisoners will be registered at reception. From Gothenburg remand – eight and a half years, serious drug crime, allocation G2 Right. From Huddinge remand – fourteen years, murder, allocation B3 Left.'

Twenty-two and half years of longing, here.

'Minus eight years. Plus twenty-two and a half. You're paying for lunch.'

Martin Jacobson nodded to the governor, smiled and went on to the next document.

'There will be twelve visitors this afternoon. Five first-time visitors who will be observed. Four lawyers. And three where dogs have been ordered – Lundgren, Block B, Jensen, Block D, Syrjämäki, Block K.'

Lennart Oscarsson studied the TV screen again, three young men who were shouting at an older man on his way back to another table. And he thought about the equally young female prison warden, and the chaos she had told him about that indicated amphetamines, about Jensen smacking his lips, obviously high, that it wasn't often someone was so obvious about being wired. And he was expecting a visitor today – he had registered a visit from a young woman called Wanda Svensson and they were certain that she was the one who had supplied the whole unit on her last visit and that this time she was going to get a different reception.

'Sniffer dog. And if there's the slightest indication, a full body search. Everything's clear: doctors, female police officers and a search warrant.'

The older guy with the rolling gait had reached his table, and the youths had turned away, cards on the table, their faces to the sun, and it looked like they had their eyes closed to the summer warmth.

———

Leon almost relaxed. The strong sun burned on his skin, it was so good, like the bedside lamp when he pointed it directly onto his face.

'You talked to the screws this morning.'

He still had his eyes closed, but had turned towards Alex.

'I was in bed. Listening. And you . . . *you talked to the screw bitch.*'

'Fuck, brother . . .'

'Fine. Two thousand.'

'Brother, I just answered back . . .'

Alex fell silent, cleared his throat, paused a bit before he carried on.

'One love, brother.'

'One love.'

Sun and no wind, it was easy to hear the heavy gate opening and a car that started, rolled in and stopped again. Leon got up from the table, careful to walk alone across the prison yard towards the place where you could see through a gap into central security. He'd heard correctly. It *was* the grey Volkswagen bus. And when the doors opened, three uniformed police *did* get out. And when they gave the all-clear, a black Labrador *did* jump out of the back.

They had been given the information that she was coming soon. And they had done exactly what *he* wanted them to do.

Leon ran across the yard towards the unit and the screw opened the door for him when he said he needed a piss, and when he was sure that he was on his own, he put down the toilet seat and stood on it, just reaching the strip lights and the mobile phone that lay hidden there, the one he shared with Frank and that he knew was not tapped.

He dialled the number; they should be in Täby now.

---

He had reached over to touch her breasts and her sex and she had turned away – *not today, not tomorrow, you know that, but after* – and now they were sitting in the front of the car and Gabriel handed her the bag and plastic-wrapped package. They said nothing, had already said what they needed to, and she got out of the car, walked past the petrol pumps and the water and air, towards the back of the building and the toilets.

Every fortnight, same routine.

The walk through Råby to the metro, twelve minutes to Skärholmens Centrum, bottom level of the car park. A green Mercedes today – 00.31 – pretty good going. Then north on the E4 and Essingeleden and past the city in the middle lane all the way to the Shell station by the Täby exit.

Wanda turned round the moment she was inside and locked the toilet door. She was anxious, wished that he was with her, but knew that she had to do it and that Gabriel was sitting right outside in the car, and he'd still be there when she went back.

*She had to do what she normally did.*

She wiped the floor around the toilet with some wet toilet paper, a couple of times, maybe that made it a bit cleaner. She unbuttoned her jeans and pulled them down, along with her knickers, to her knees. She lay down, back on the floor and feet on the toilet seat.

*And yet not quite.*

She sat up, put the plastic-wrapped package on one side of the sink. She opened the plastic bag and carefully sprinkled the contents over it, ten grams of loose amphetamine, careful not to get any of it stuck on her fingers. She leaned forwards and sniffed the package, a strong smell of acetone that should be enough.

She lay back down, back on the floor, jeans around her knees.

From her jacket pocket, some baby oil, a few drops in her palms and around the package until it was completely covered, then her oily fingers into her vagina to lubricate the outside, inside, then the flat plastic package in bit by bit, a bit further until the first pain and then she stopped.

She had to lie there for ten minutes and she thought about Gabriel's face again, so good when she pretended to be asleep, the only part of his body with no burn scars. He had glanced over at her in the car as well, on the way, when he thought she wasn't looking, and it had been the same, his face had been good, relaxed.

Ten minutes. Until the strong acetone smell was locked to her insides.

Two fingers in and she felt the plastic, took hold of it, then it got stuck and she tried to get hold of it again, pulled it and it got stuck and then pulled it a bit more and it slipped out.

It was good to stand up again as the stone floor was always so hard and everywhere stank of urine.

She had to do what she always did. And yet not quite.

She put the plastic package in the toilet, hesitated, then flushed and it disappeared.

Soft paper towels and liquid soap from the dispenser on the wall, she washed the sink and the toilet seat and rinsed her hands again, a quick look in the mirror as she went out, her mirror face.

––––––––––

Gabriel was sitting in the driver's seat, mobile phone in his hand. He was waiting for her to come back, for his precious brother to call.

She'd been in the station toilet for more than ten minutes. He'd got himself a Coke, then when she didn't come, another Coke, the same woman as two weeks ago, he'd walked from the chiller straight out of the door and she'd stood there looking down at her feet.

Wanda and Leon.

If he thought about them. If he *tried* to think about them.

There wasn't enough room. Not for both of them at once. His mind couldn't stretch to both of them, as if he could only think of them one at a time.

There she was. He looked at her with a critical eye, the walk from the toilet door to the car, it looked like she was walking normally.

'You put it in, then dumped it?'

'Yes.'

'Dumped everything?'

Wanda and Leon. The whore and his precious brother. They'd both seen him without turning their faces away.

'Answer me, whore!'

'Yes.'

'Yes, what?'

'Everything.'

He tried to put his hand on her cheek, she was upset, he could see it, he shouldn't have shouted at her, shouldn't have called her whore, she didn't like it.

It was ringing now, his mobile phone, the number he knew was secure.

'Where are you?'

'Just leaving the Shell station by the Täby exit.'

'And the whore . . .'

*The Whore.*

'And the whore . . . does she smell?'

*She's called Wanda.*

'She smells.'

'Carry on then. The dogs will notice. The pigs will body-search her.'

Back to the middle lane of the motorway, twenty kilometres north.

'Bro?'

'Yeah?'

Leon should have hung up and was breathing in that way that Gabriel knew meant he was agitated.

'When's she moving out?'

Gabriel looked at her in the windscreen, just where it was shiny and he could see her reflection and he pressed the phone harder to his ear.

*Wanda. And Leon.*

'When you come.'

'One love, brother.'

'One love.'

———

The grey Volkswagen van was still there. Two of the uniforms – a man and a woman – were on their way in. The third one hung around outside central security with the black dog on a lead, he was talking to someone, the screw from the unit, the one who pretended she wasn't scared.

Leon waited by the window on the stairs between the two floors, D2 and D3. The best place for keeping an eye on the prison gate and the road in from the motorway past the church.

A green Mercedes.

They were driving slowly. He had a clear view of them stopping some distance away at the parking place on the hill by the field that separated the prison wall from the churchyard.

She got out and walked across the asphalt towards the wall, normal movements, she was completely empty.

———

Freezing, sweating, freezing.

She had never been arrested, apprehended or held in custody. She didn't have a criminal record, wasn't in any of the police registers, anywhere. She had never even seen a prison until Gabriel asked her to visit Leon, Reza, Uros once every fortnight.

*The dogs will notice. The pigs will body-search her.*

The bell by the prison gate, ID at central security, keys and money and mobile in the locker in the room to the left. She was freezing and sweating. Not less, but more. She had no idea why she did it, but suddenly she stopped in the changing room by the two waste-paper bins, stood there and looked at them instead of going out into the entrance hall and the metal detector and the uniforms and the fucking dog, and after a while she took out both her contact lenses and dropped them. She was shaking so much and sometimes it was just such a relief to be in fog for a while, to keep a distance, and maybe then she'd freeze and sweat a bit less too.

'Wanda?'

She was barely out of the room, hadn't even closed the door behind her, when they called her name for the first time.

'Wanda Svensson?'

She turned around. A fuzzy uniformed policewoman. And a fuzzy big black dog. And further behind, two more fuzzy uniforms.

'My name's Lena.' She waved her arm at the other two. 'These are my colleagues. And we have to give you a full body search.'

They were fuzzy. But it didn't help. She was shaking just as much as before. And it was freezing.

But she knew what she had to do. She had to protest.

She wasn't sure why, she had asked once when Gabriel had his nice face on and it had quickly changed.

'You can't. No way are your hands going to touch my body, feel inside me.'

The black dog came closer.

'And that, it can't sniff me.'

Even closer.

'We know the ground rules.'

'Take it away then!'

The woman called Lena pulled out a chair.

'I'll take it away when you sit down here.'

*Do you remember last time? I'm frightened, Gabriel. Do you remember or don't you? I remember. Good, because you have to make sure you're heard, just like you did then.*

'No.'

'Is that one of the rules as well? That we can't order you to sit down?'

She sat down.

'Good. Then you can get up again.'

She stood up and everything was fuzzy when the uniform pointed to the chair and the dog jumped up eagerly and sniffed around, scratched.

'It's showing us. You smell. This way, please.'

Another door, like a room in a hospital. A bed in the middle and pipes and machines on the floor and walls.

'I want you to pee,' the policewoman held out a white cup, 'in this.'

Wanda sat down in front of her on a big potty, the plastic cup underneath her to catch the urine, like when she went to the school nurse when she was little. Once it was half full she held it up to the policewoman's fuzzy hand.

'Please get undressed.'

She was freezing from before. But more from the inside. Now she really was shivering.

'Hands behind your head.'

Rubber gloves that searched her armpits, her scalp.

'Legs wide, feet further apart.'

The warmth near her vagina without touching it.

'Your mouth, open wide, lift your tongue.'

*It's important that you're heard.*

Rubber finger under her tongue, the back of her teeth, down her throat.

Until she pretended to gag, then the policewoman quickly took a step back and Wanda laughed scornfully as Gabriel had said she should.

'Did that frighten you?'

'Lie down there, please, and lift up your legs.'

A bed and the policewoman popped up two metal rails that were secured to the frame.

*You have to make a noise!*

'So you want to see more, do you? Maybe touch me up?'

The fuzzy arm opened the fuzzy door. A fuzzy doctor in a fuzzy white coat was waiting outside.

'Not me. *And then, Gabriel, what then?* But someone who has the right to do it. *You have to let them search you.* We have a warrant for a full body search. *I'm scared, Gabriel, d'you hear?* So, it's your choice. *There's nothing to be scared of, because you'll be empty this time.* Either you put your legs up and let the doctor examine you. *And I'm so cold, like I'll never be warm again.* Or you don't, and I will be forced to call in my two colleagues who are waiting outside and we'll hold you down while the doctor examines you.'

———————

She closed her eyes. Even the fuzziness was too clear. And didn't open them again until she was dressed and being escorted by two wardens to the visitors' room.

He was already sitting there waiting for her.

———————

She wasn't freezing any more.

She didn't feel the tube going up her rectum, a camera lens on the tip, nor the rubber-gloved hand that poked around in her vagina.

She had done what she was supposed to do. And when she sank into the chair opposite Leon she was as frightened as she always was, but didn't need to strip her clothes off and he wasn't going to touch her as she didn't have anything for him to take. So they sat there looking at each other, they'd never really spoken before.

———————

He was angry with her.

He didn't know why.

She was sitting in front of him and had to sit there for fifty minutes for the visit to look normal. She had done exactly what had been asked of her. And yet, the rage, like he wanted to hit her.

'Gabriel?'

And when she looked down, it just made it worse.

'Yes?'

'His report.'

They'd only ever met like this. Once a fortnight for three months and two hundred grams of amphetamine each time. That was all. A fucking whore. Whatever it was that made him want to lean forwards and hit her, hit and hit, he didn't understand it.

———————

He looked angry. She didn't know why. She'd done exactly what they'd asked her to.

'The kids sold everything, one hundred and eighty-two thousand kronor. And they . . .'

Wanda tried to remember what she'd repeated, Gabriel had said it was important to get it right.

'. . . they'll settle today, tomorrow at the latest.'

She looked down, if she looked down it was still there.

'The jewellers in Solna and Huddinge Centrum. Two hundred and sixty-four thousand. Enforcement in Sundbyberg. Twenty thousand. The newsagent by Slussen. Four thousand.'

His eyes. They were like Gabriel's when he was shouting, only worse.

'What else?'

When he stared at her like that, it was so intense and she forgot, she tried to remember, it was there, it . . .

'*What else?*'

She swallowed, looked down again, at her shoes, glanced over at his.

'Gabriel . . . he said . . . he said to tell you that the phone . . . it's still tapped.'

———————

Leon raised his hand.

But he didn't hit her, he took hold of her face and pressed into her cheeks, forced it up from the floor; she was to look at him.

'You still live there?'

'Yes.'

'*Still*, all the time?'

'Yes.'

'*Still*, in Gabriel's room?'

'Yes.'

Gabriel's room. *My* room.

He leaned closer, whispered that she was good, that they'd searched her and found nothing and couldn't do it again next time, when it really counted, in fourteen days, she would be here again in exactly fourteen days, and now, as she had to stay for half an hour more, she might as well lie down on the bunk while they passed the time, Gabriel wouldn't mind, he knew what it was like to be locked up and a brother's a brother.

———

Gabriel's room. *My* room.

That fucking tension in his chest and stomach and now in his cock.

Leon wasn't sure. If that was why he asked her to strip and open her legs. That he had to have a bit of what was there instead of him, someone who lived there all the time.

She didn't know – that there was only one love.

———

Leon held her.

And wanted her to hold him.

He didn't look so angry any more. And when he held her, he did it gently.

The tattoo on his thigh, the same as Gabriel's.

But his back was different, when she ran her hand over it, it was smooth, not pitted like Gabriel's, which she loved so much.

And when she lay here like this, the plastic sticking to her skin, she could see the barred window and the grey wall outside.

EDDIE SAT ON the bed and did nothing. That's to say, he was waiting. If that's doing nothing. But it wasn't boring, like waiting can sometimes be. It was exciting. He was about to sell some more. And every time it felt like he got a little closer. Gabriel had still not said his name, but had looked at him more than once over the past few weeks.

His room. He wasn't often here. It was so small, and out there, out there was so big. He liked the large mirror with the gold frame that hung by his bed. And the poster the same size, of Gabriel's favourite film the one called *A Clockwork Orange* and was made forever ago and that he'd never actually seen but maybe would one day. And his tag on the wall beside it, straight on the white wallpaper; his mum had been so angry when he sprayed it with that stuff, the spray he'd nicked from the paint shop down by Globen, she hadn't realised that it was *his* tag, *his* name, *Eddie's the name.* He didn't think much of the computer and the small TV that she'd saved up for and bought second-hand and given to him for Christmas, he'd get new ones when he got paid for what he was storing in the locker at the ICA supermarket in Råby, and the locker at the Coop Extra supermarket in Skärholmen and the locker at school, three hundred a week per gun. And he hated the fucking duvet cover he was sitting on, Donald Duck and Huey, Dewey and Louie, and that fucking pillowcase with a picture of Mickey Mouse – next time they torched a car or even a moped, he'd take them with him, burn them up too.

He closed the door to the hall and lay down on the floor, shuffled in under the bed next to a black Puma bag. Inside, if he opened the zip on the side pocket that tended to get stuck, were twenty small packets wrapped in plastic, ten capsules and half a gram of heroin in each. Last week, white and yellow capsules, this week, brown and red, but with the same content.

A jacket like the one Gabriel wore, and under it, a bumbag where he stashed seven of the little plastic packages. Wax from the shelf under the mirror on his short hair until it was completely rigid and shiny. Gold chain carefully clipped round his neck.

He stood in front of the mirror for a while, as he always did. One point five metres tall. Slim. No facial hair, no spots.

He knew that he'd look different in a few years and he couldn't wait. The laughter in his body when he thought about it was such a good feeling, and it was connected to Gabriel and Bruno and Jon and Big Ali who left their cars near the stairs to number 67, and with Leon and Alex and Uros and Reza who were doing time in a real prison right now. And it was also connected to the fact that he was one of the first to know that they'd changed names, and that he was allowed to look after the Puma bag once a week. The laughter came from somewhere deep inside, and he loved it.

He pulled down the zip on his hoodie until the heavy gold chain was as visible as he wanted it to be. He left the room; his mum had set out a snack on the table but he didn't pay any attention, he just wanted to get away, out.

Early afternoon and it was quiet down at the centre, not many people, first stop Konsum supermarket. He went in and made his way over to the bread counter that was behind the cakes and biscuits. He was on his own. A few people over by the fruit counter, he could hear them, some others by the cheese and eggs, no one else. He chose the shelf furthest to the left, the one with white bread, looked around, still on his own. One of the seven packages from his bumbag, the plastic caught the light, stuck to his hand a bit. He went down on his knees and fixed it with enough tape so that he was sure it would stay there, a bit in under the bread shelf.

Then he went over to the coolers, chose the green milk cartons, in the middle, down on his knees again, and fixed the next package with tape as far in as his fingers could reach. Then by one of the long freezers, where a woman the same age as his mother with a child in a pushchair trundled past, and he pretended to be reading something on the packaging until he was on his own again, then chose the corner with the blue boxes of frozen fish – the third package from his bumbag just fitted in the gap between the bottom of the freezer and the stone floor. He carried on toward the tills, paid for a Daim bar and a packet of sweets, some sickly chocolate and a few bits of foam so the woman at the till would keep quiet and take his fifty-kronor note. She noticed his gold chain, he saw that, and he puffed up his chest a little more. Four packages left in the bumbag, next shop, ICA.

———

He had stood on the steps by the train platform for half an hour and only had three customers. Things were maybe slower today. Or was it the two cops who had passed by in the middle of it all – it usually took a while then before anyone else dared approach him. No one could see him here either. Apart from the ticket attendant, but she was busy talking to people on her mobile phone and just waved anyone who wanted to buy or show a ticket past in irritation.

Eddie smiled. This was where he'd been standing when Gabriel hit him on the cheek and his ring left a mark.

A punter.

He hadn't seen him before, but could recognise them straight away, skinny, sweating, stressed-looking, he came up from the subway from the other side. They looked at each other, the boy who had just turned twelve and the man who was thirty-seven, gave each other a hard handshake, the slight boy's hand in the skinny adult hand.

'Eight.'

'Five. Or ten.'

'I want eight.'

The older man raised his voice, tried to dominate. So the one-point-five-metre-tall boy leaned forwards and waited until the one-point-eight-three-metre-tall adult automatically did the same, close up when the considerably shorter one raised his hand and slapped the other's cheek.

'I said five. Or ten. *Eddie's the name.*'

The taller, older man shuddered, stepped back, his hand to the red mark on his cheek that was burning.

He bit his underlip when he spoke.

'Five.'

'Eight hundred per gram. That's four thousand.'

The bigger guy with the red cheek pulled some crumpled notes out of his trouser pocket, twenty-kronor notes and fifty-kronor notes and hundred-kronor notes and a couple of five-hundred-kronor notes and a handful of coins. Eddie counted them, gave back what he didn't need, and put the rest straight in his own pocket.

'Konsum. Milk chiller. At the bottom of the one with the green cartons.'

Eddie hadn't even finished speaking.

The man who had just bought five grams of Russian heroin was already on his way.

———

After that, things picked up. The last three had all come within fifteen minutes.

When he walked into the lift in Råby Allé 67, he was shaking, not from fear, but rather from anticipation and when he checked his chain and hair in the mirror, he had a good feeling in his stomach, not lonely, not empty, the laughter inside again.

Second floor and traces of blood on the balcony that hadn't been there the last time, but he knew they were the dog's, twelve fucking bullets. He knocked on the door that said SANTOS and adjusted his chain, which he could see in the shiny door handle, the one he'd got when he strolled into Tumba Centre, to the jewellery shop on the ground floor, he was to see where the two Securitas guards were and then go back out to the car without looking at the three masked people who came in right then with guns in their hands, and smashed all the glass display cases, filled their rucksacks. As payment, Eddie had chosen the chain that had shone in the middle of the display window, and on the way back to Råby, squashed in the middle of the back seat, he had felt it caressing his neck.

He knocked again, then rang the bell, Gabriel opened with a bare chest, burned skin everywhere.

*Gabriel's hall.*

Eddie had stood there nine times before, accounted for a total of 227,000 kronor, his cut 11,350, he knew exactly.

*In Gabriel's flat.*

He clutched the banknotes in one hand and ran the other through his shiny hair, it was like his feet were moving of their own accord, the rush inside, he was on his way into the sitting room.

'Stop right there!'

The hard voice, he wanted to avoid it, took out the money.

'Sorry, I . . . seven packets, thirty-five gs, twenty-eight thousand.'

Gabriel took it, weighed it, but didn't count it.

'Thirty-five gs. Sixty-five left.'

'On Friday.'

Gabriel almost smiled, at least, that's what it felt like, sat down on the hall carpet and indicated to Eddie he should do the same. Some tobacco from the worn, brown leather pouch in one hand while he opened a small round glass bottle that hung round his neck with the other, a couple of drops in the tobacco.

Eddie watched carefully as Gabriel used his fingertips to mix the tobacco and fill the Rizla paper, roll it with one hand, light it and take the first toke then hand it over.

*Cannabis oil from Gabriel's leather pouch in Gabriel's hall.*

Eddie took it and inhaled, one more and then he coughed, as if his tongue was stuck to the top of his mouth, words that were too big.

'One love, brother.'

The blow to his right cheek was hard.

'You're not my brother.'

Gabriel was sitting close by and pointed towards what Eddie knew was the sitting room.

'Jon is my brother. Bruno is my brother. They're my brothers because Leon and I made them members. Maybe, if you carry on, if for example you run now and get the plastic bag from the locker in Vivo supermarket for me and look after it until I'm ready – and if you help me in a couple of days with a little something that I want taken to the police station, if you carry on doing things like that for me, then maybe one day, you might be my brother.'

AFTERNOON. EARLY EVENING.

The whore had been. The kids were done.

But the good, long day wasn't over yet.

Marko still hadn't completed his initiation test and Gabriel, who was back in Råby, was still waiting; they would clean up inside and outside, at the same time.

Leon lay on his bed, listening, voices always had the same echo in institutions. Every place surrounded by a barbed-wire fence or a wall had special acoustics, a scale that only existed there and that was hollow. Emptiness for anyone who opened the door from the outside and listened, hopelessness for anyone who had just come in and sat down, security for anyone who went to sleep and woke up in it.

He had taken off her clothes – taken from her – and felt nothing. He wasn't as relaxed as he normally was afterwards, not worried that Gabriel had anything against it. He didn't know why. Except that he'd wanted to hit her. And that this was better.

He turned on the light. Turned it off. Turned it on.

He listened to the different-sounding footsteps. The ones that were softer, the muffled sound of slippers, always inmates. The ones that were harder, the clacking sound of black boots with heels, always screws. He was waiting for footsteps from the cell further down, for them to open the cell door, come down the corridor, pass him, the ones that were even softer and more muffled – Marko was the only one in the unit who wore the prison-issue plimsolls, thin and ugly and free . . . when those steps went past, a good day would have a good finish.

Leon turned the light on. Off.

A couple of weeks ago he'd told the lawyer he was to be there in the visitors' room and the stupid fuck hadn't come, *you have a legally binding judgement*, they had smashed up his car and he still hadn't come, *I no longer have any obligations to you as a client*, Bruno had put one of the kid's bloody canaries under his pillow in his bed and he still hadn't come, *and you and I therefore need have nothing more to do with each other*, it wasn't until Jon had broken his right index finger a week later that he'd understood, booked a meeting, taken the papers with him.

**INTERVIEW LEADER JAN ZANDER (IL):** I want an answer to my question.
**DANIEL WALL (DW):** You mean . . . Central Station?

The footsteps from Cell 12 went past, Marko's footsteps.

They should be by the kitchen now, nearly at the door, going out onto the stairs and up to the first floor, D2 Left.

**INTERVIEW LEADER LEIF LUNDH (IL):** What colour?
**JAVAD KITTU (JK):** Dark, I think. Reza's were lighter.

The lawyer had stood with his back to Leon while he read the judgement, the interviews, the technical evidence. The material that had helped to convict him and Alex and Reza and Uros, four and a half years.

Leon turned on the light, off, on, off.

Danny Hangaround had talked. Javad Hangaround had talked. And they knew, they all knew, that anyone who talks won't talk again.

———

Gabriel was sitting on one of the benches in Råby Torg, Bruno on the next bench, warm sun on their faces. Then he appeared, the youngster who was twelve and had greased hair and a thick gold chain, the one who'd given his earnings in exchange for some cannabis oil and the promise of belonging, and had then run off to get one of the bags, the one in the locker in Vivo, between the entrance and the shopping trolleys. The plastic bag in Gabriel's hand as they walked towards the metro, through the barriers and up onto the platform for trains to Hallunda, Fittja, Masmo. They knew that Javad would come on the 17.14 train, they had agreed to meet him, explained that he was to collect a package and keep it for the family. Bruno stayed by the exit from Masmo station, behind the kiosk where he had a good overview of everyone who came and went, Gabriel carried on through the suburb, which was just like Råby, the same asphalt, the same buildings, to the door of Masmo Allé 23, first floor, where he sat down one of the steps to wait – this was where Javad's mum lived and this was where he was coming.

\*

Marko slowed down as he passed Leon's cell, wanted to make sure that he could be heard and that the brother lying in there would be proud. He'd been given his initiation test. He was going to do it, had longed to switch from nothing to something, from him to them. Out of D1 unit, up the stairs, into D2. Five minutes without screws. Past the fish tank, a quick glance over at the glass, no blue uniforms, past the cards corner where everyone was careful to keep their backs turned, past the bogs and the showers, past Cell 2 and 4 and 6 and 8, opened the door to Cell 10 and took the chair leg that was just inside that had been unscrewed from one of the chairs in the kitchen at lunchtime, Cell 12, he knocked on the door.

---

Javad walked fast, he was late and didn't want to keep Gabriel waiting, maybe he'd make it if he ran the last bit from the metro to his mum's. Gabriel had phoned and said that they would meet there. Felt a bit weird at first as they'd never met there before, but then Gabriel had talked about a package that was to be kept for the family. Javad ran even faster and got to the door, but no one was there. Not until he turned round and saw Bruno coming up behind him, and then Gabriel coming down the stairs where he'd obviously been sitting waiting.

*

Danny heard the knocking on the door.

Marko Bendik?

And he'd come to see him?

He'd heard that Marko Bendik was in D1 Left, the floor below, and he knew that it wasn't usual for anyone from down there or any other unit for that matter to come in here and risk the consequences, so it must be important. Danny smiled, flattered and proud, and they gripped each other by the hand, he opened the door wide and waved him in. He knew who Marko was, what he was doing time for, why he'd been transferred here from Mariefred prison, it wasn't often that one of them talked to someone like him.

———

Javad turned to Bruno, then to Gabriel, whatever it was that had felt weird didn't any more – he could see the plastic bag in Gabriel's hand, the one he was going to look after and that Gabriel was opening now, a black gun and a full magazine.

'Glock. Seventeen bullets.'

Javad held his hand out but wasn't given anything. Gabriel pushed the magazine into the butt, pulled back the slide with his thumb and index finger, it was loaded. Javad couldn't understand why they were standing there showing it to him, put his hand out again for what he was supposed to be looking after.

'You got a fag?'

Gabriel looked at him, he didn't actually smoke, certainly not Camels, but he'd asked for one and now got two and a lighter.

He was glad he'd taken the knock-off Rohypnol. He always did, take a few grams when he didn't want to feel anything, it was easier then.

He dropped the cigarettes he didn't want onto the floor and threw the first blows to Javad's nose and cheek. Javad tried to make a break, but Gabriel and Bruno helped each other to hold him down and throw more punches and when he crumpled and lay there, they both kicked him in the stomach and then Gabriel held the pistol up high enough for him to see, aimed it at his head, then lowered it to his chest, to his stomach, his groin, his thigh.

\*

Marko looked at Danny, who seemed pleased and asked him to come in, and it was when he turned round to sit down and talk to his visitor that Marko whacked him on the back of the neck as hard as he could with the chair leg. Danny fell forwards onto the bed – it was important that he landed softly, there would be other marks on the back of his neck from the noose anyway, but nothing should be visible on the front.

He was pretty sure that Danny was already unconscious when he landed.

———

Gabriel couldn't help looking Javad in the eye when he aimed at him. He knew he shouldn't do it and the Rohypnol should have stopped him. Never look in the eye of someone who's going to pay.

He actually liked the guy. Javad Hangaround had done so much for the family.

But he should have said *I'm not going to answer that question.*

Gabriel was almost standing over him, one foot on either

side, with a metre at most from the barrel to his left knee when he took the first shot – you could normally hear them crack as they exploded – and then another shot, to the right knee.

*

In every cell there was a space between the head of the bed and the heavy table next to it, and it was across this space that Marko lay one of Danny Hangaround's books. He'd taken the cable from the TV on the table in the corner where they played cards, and tied it around the book, and with the other end – which was hanging down in the space – he now knotted a noose. He positioned Danny on his knees and placed the noose around his neck.

With the book jammed as an anchor at the other end, taking Danny's weight, he would stop breathing pretty soon.

---

There had been two loud explosions which were amplified by the stairwell. A couple of tenants on the same floor cautiously opened their doors a crack but then closed them again when they saw who was out there, looking at them, only a couple of metres away. Gabriel and Bruno each took a phone out of Javad's pockets and then walked away, and just as they were about to get on a train at the metro station, they heard the first sirens.

*

Marko closed the cell door and walked back through D2 Left, backs still carefully turned and still no screws, then hurried down the stairs to the floor below and his own unit and own cell, slowing down as he passed number 2, a light tap on the door, Leon would hear it, Leon would know that he was now one of them.

---

Eddie was standing where he was supposed to when Gabriel and Bruno got off the train at Råby station, to the right of the exit and a bit further down along the track.

'Clean it.'

The plastic bag switched from Gabriel's hand to Eddie's eager, waiting hand.

'And then look after it.'

Eddie's heart was pounding as he ran off with the plastic bag in his arms, not stopping until he opened the main door to the school and was standing in front of his locker.

Not many people about, the school day was over and those who were there were the sort who did football, or who just hung around and played cards, or some with guitar cases who normally stayed in the auditorium.

He opened his locker, took out the other plastic bag that was lying there under a couple of books and then went into the toilets, checked twice that the door couldn't be opened.

First the white plastic bag that he'd just got from Gabriel. A gun, a Glock, seventeen bullets. He pressed the button on the side of the butt to release the magazine, pulled back the slide so that the bullet that was still in the chamber came out, then bent down under the sink to pick it up from the floor. The second bag was always in his locker: two towels and a bottle of degreasing solvent. He turned the magazine upside down and pushed out one bullet at a time with his thumb; there were fifteen in all, so they'd used two. He sprayed them and then the gun, dried it all with a towel and put the bullets back into the magazine, one by one.

Voices outside. Someone tried the door. He sat on one of the toilet seats, completely still, waiting, he recognised the voices, some people from seventh grade, he could have shot them if he wanted.

Then footsteps died away, silence.

Towel round the gun and into the plastic bag, he opened

the door to the toilets and then to his locker, looked around, there was just enough room for it under the maths book and the geography book.

LEON TURNED THE light on, off, on.

He had just heard the muffled sound of prison-issue grey plimsolls come back down the unit.

*Marko was done.*

In a couple of hours, the staff at Aspsås would find a dead person and confirm that an inmate had hanged himself in his cell, by lying down in the space between his bed and the wall, with a book holding one end of a cable that was tied round his neck. Yet another suicide, one of those tragic incidents in Swedish prisons that would lead to a dead-end inquiry because no one had seen or heard anything.

*Gabriel was done.*

A short while ago, a young man was taken by ambulance from the first floor of a tower block in Masmo to A & E in Huddinge hospital, both legs in agony after a presumed shooting, according to one witness.

He turned the light on, off.

*The whore had dumped her load and reeked of it and the screws had wasted their papers and their doctor and couldn't do it again next time.*

*The kids had sold everything and settled for what they were supposed to settle.*

*And now – they had flushed out two.*

Leon looked out through the barred window as he normally did in the evening when the sun was still there, the wall and the church spire and the sky and the white clouds that he followed for a while across the blue, on their way south towards Stockholm, towards Råby.

It had been a good day.

# thirteen days to go

IT WAS DIFFICULT to get used to the coarse, bitter coffee from the machine that stood in the corridor at Råby police station. José Pereira closed his eyes and gulped it down – alone in the room that was the heart of the Section Against Gang Crime, he had to stay awake for a few more hours as the evening, night, dawn hadn't been enough to digest it.

The faces on the wall stared down at him. The desk was full of files about gangs and networks that were at the start of their criminal career; they lay in the way. He moved them from the desk down onto the floor and instead spread out some photos of a splintered knee.

```
X-ray department admission note: young
man, seventeen years old.
```

The officer on duty had put in a call from the County Communications Centre at 17.37 to report a shooting in west Masmo that was presumed to be gang-related.

```
Shot in both left and right knees.
Circulation stable.
```

He had sat in the car, called home and Martha had answered. She told him she missed him and he said that he wouldn't be able to pick up the girls who were exactly the same age and this evening were wearing green football socks that went well above their knees and white football shorts that would only be white until the first tackle and green and white football strips with the numbers eight and nine on the back; two girls who looked identical to anyone who wasn't family, who had been born on the same night eleven years ago and were now standing side by side on a football pitch near Nynäsvägen waiting for the referee and the whistle and the week's match that was in two thirty-minute halves.

He had arrived at Masmo Allé 23 at 17.52, at the very moment when the back doors of the yellow ambulance closed and it sped off. An initial sweep of the crime scene, then knocking on all the doors on all the six floors, talking to neighbours who'd been there at the time of the shooting but were adamant that it had been a normal evening, no strange noises, no unusual visitors. He had learnt to understand that fear never talks.

He had then driven to Huddinge hospital, called Martha again, who was at Tallkrogen playing fields. One of the twins in the green and white team had made the match 2–2 just before half time, and as he put the phone down he could hear the coach shouting in the background, so it was with a lighter heart that he had parked outside the hospital entrance and made his way to the surgical ward with another reality crowding his chest.

José Pereira leaned closer to the desk, adjusted the reading light slightly, used a magnifying glass. `X-ray report.` He had seen black and white pictures of shattered kneecaps before. `Multiple fractures to the patella, distal femur, proximal tibia and proximal fibula.` And yet still couldn't grasp what he was looking at, or perhaps quite simply didn't want to. `Multiple bone fragments and extreme soft tissue swelling.` But he knew what it meant and how it should be interpreted, a clear message: don't talk to the pigs.

He had sat and waited in the corridor during the operation that was intended to get the body functioning again, but not to make it perfect; the seventeen-year-old boy who was rolled into a room of his own on a shiny hospital bed would never walk normally again. The woman sitting there beside him, Javad Kittu's mother, had stood up and followed the sleeping boy who had once had two older brothers, who had both turned into criminal youths and who had both been shot with two bullets each, in different parts of the body. The weeping, waiting woman had several times tugged at his jacket sleeve and begged him to reassure her that the one son she had left would not die before he was nineteen as well.

An hour and twenty minutes later Javad had come to, had looked at Pereira and answered all of his questions in the same way, which, with the exception of the swear words and hate and threats of a frightened seventeen-year-old, could basically be interpreted as *You know just as well as I do that if I do the same thing again, if I even consider answering, they won't aim at my knees.* Pereira had left the room, then come back, sat down again and reformulated his questions, but had been forced to stop when the mother had screamed at him and hit him, *I won't let you ask my son all those questions,* and then leant over the bed with an ashen face, *Don't answer, never answer anything ever again.*

He moved the pictures of the shattered knees and scene of the crime, splashes of blood on the stone floor in a cold stairwell, and replaced them with one of the files from the low bookshelf by the desk, leafing through until he got to GHETTO SOLDIERS and ASSOCIATED and the fourteen staring faces defined as *hangarounds*, seventeen defined as *prospects* and sixteen defined as *kids with no criminal record*; a total of forty-seven very young people who burned with a desire to belong and who were prepared to do anything at any time if it meant that they might at some point become a full member. He had used plastic sleeves that were slightly too small and too thin and the photo paper stuck to the sides when he pulled out three of the photos – profile left, full face, profile right – held them briefly over the waste-paper basket, then let go; Javad Kittu's face settled at the bottom, upside down, no longer relevant.

'Leon Jensen.'

He hadn't even closed the file and put it back before the phone rang. Lennart Oscarsson. He was already in his office at Aspsås prison, even though it was barely morning.

'What about him?'

'The criminal network that previously called itself Råby Warriors.'

'Yes?'

'When you were here . . . you asked me to contact you if there was any suspicious behaviour.'

'Carry on.'

'Yesterday, sometime between five and six o'clock.'

José Pereira gave the waste-paper basket a gentle kick and one of the three photos at the bottom turned the right way round.

'There was a . . . hmm, for the moment let's just call it an . . . incident involving one of our inmates who, according to the report from the prison service intelligence unit is associated with the group you're investigating. An inmate in the same building as Jensen, the floor above, D2 Left. And I've just read in the Prison Service records that he was sentenced – albeit a shorter sentence – for his part in the armed robbery for which both Jensen and Eriksson are doing time.'

Pereira listened, without knowing where the prison governor was going, only that it was a direction that neither of them wanted.

'Wait a moment.'

He bent down and picked up the photographs of someone who had two holes in his knees, turned them round at different angles, dropped them on the floor again.

Between five and six yesterday evening.

*The same time.*

'I'm listening.'

Lennart Oscarsson cleared his throat and it sounded like it was in some way constricted, as if he was looking down and reading from a piece of paper.

'An inmate called Daniel Wall. Who was found dead in his cell.'

José Pereira was breathing heavily.

'Hang on a moment again.'

He opened the same file, pulled out the paper with GHETTO SOLDIERS and ASSOCIATED – the three pictures were in the fourth row, the one known as Danny Hangaround.

'Dead?'

'Yes.'

'Murder?'

'We don't have murders here. There will of course be an inquiry, based on the usual assumptions, probable suicide.'

Pereira held the receiver in his hand even though the conversation was long since over, he didn't have the energy to put it down.

Javad Kittu had answered some questions in the investigation that led to a prison sentence for four full members. Daniel Wall had answered some questions in the investigation that led to a prison sentence for four full members.

Javad Kittu was shot in both knees yesterday sometime after five. Daniel Wall was found dead in his cell yesterday sometime after five.

A murder and two shattered kneecaps that were linked to nothing.

Because no one saw anything, no one heard anything.

Because fear never speaks.

José Pereira took out another three photos, dropped them into the basket where they ended up beside the other face. A frustrated foot rammed the waste-paper basket, which toppled over and rolled around the room. He wanted to ring Martha again. He wanted to go back to the other reality, to his two daughters in oversized football socks, it had been 2–2 at half time and the next time he looked at the clock it was suddenly too late to call and he didn't know if the two tired and sweaty girls in the back of the car had talked and talked and talked, as they always did after winning, or if they had sat silently in a corner each as they always did after losing.

He looked at the phone: not yet, they'd be awake soon.

He went over to the first wall and the faces he'd moved over only two days ago. Eight pairs of staring eyes. Reliable sources had mentioned a ninth full member. An initiation test. He drew an oval on a piece of paper with a marker and pinned the empty face beside the others.

They had increased their criminal activities, become more violent. They had spun a bigger net of hangarounds, prospects and minors. They had changed name.

Now they had also committed bodily harm, murder, to flush out bad blood.

A hard core had become even harder and was on the move.

Higher up.

# eleven days to go

Sixty-eight seconds.

He had run to his shelf when the alarm went, overalls, helmet, pack on his back, twenty-five kilos and then the heavy bloody tactical body armour they'd borrowed from the army because some health and safety advisor wasn't happy about axes being thrown around.

He hated it, still didn't understand it. Eleven thousand eight hundred people who loved their homes, who were proud of them and lived and breathed in a world that two hundred other people held captive.

The body armour was to protect him from them; he took it off and threw it on the floor, kicked it – not today.

Thom looked at the big clock in the changing room. Seventy-seven seconds. He'd make it.

The third fire in Råby this evening, a container and a moped and a climbing frame, and every time stones and hate. And out there, further afield, Råby's fires had spread to the other suburbs in southern Stockholm, Hallunda and Alby and Vårberg, in the same way that a few years ago Rosengård in Malmö had set light to Oxie and Hermodsdal, and Backa in Gothenburg had engulfed Tynnered and Biskopsgården, and it wasn't going out, it just kept moving, growing.

He ran to the truck and his place at the front right, a look at the young driver and another at the crew manager whom he'd worked with for so long, and the Number One and Number Two who were both quite new but solid. A nod towards the exit, siren on and off, they sped to an address that was in fact a level two, which required an escort, police cars that were always busy elsewhere.

'Råby Allé. About twenty-five onlookers.'

They had seen the smoke some way off, and as they got closer to the block it was obvious that it was concentrated in one particular stair.

'Black smoke coming out main door. Over and out.'

Thom turned off the walkie-talkie, opened the door and ran towards the intense heat.

———

Ana was standing where she usually did, by the kitchen window on the third floor with a view over the greater part of Råby Allé, a half-drunk cup of coffee in her hand, and in a while, maybe another cigarette. She had seen them sneak into the entrance a few hours ago, down into the cellar, seven of them in hoodies and joggers, ten years old, maybe twelve. She had stood there waiting for the first signs of smoke and the sound, faint at first and then getting stronger.

———

The Number One and Number Two had got out the small hose and metal pipe *turn on the water* and rolled it out to twenty-five metres *more length* and turned on the pump *we need more hose* and when it wasn't enough had rolled out the bigger hose and then, armed with a crowbar, they ran towards the locked door to the cellar.

Thom adjusted his earpiece and moved closer to get a better overview. 'Less water.' A metal door, ten seconds. A security door, one and half minutes. They were in. 'Tyres. Mattresses. Clothes.' He turned up the volume on the earpiece. 'Still mainly smoke.' Two voices, breathing heavily in nine hundred degrees, a concrete cellar without ventilation and with water that quickly became steam, six minutes in there, no more.

They were in control.

The whole cellar was drenched in water. He moved closer and prodded the remains of a bicycle tyre with the toe of his boot, he wouldn't need to post someone here to make sure it was out. A strange feeling of relief. Not a single threat. No stones or bottles. He looked around, it was a long time since they'd extinguished a fire in peace.

'Thom?'

They had dismantled the pump and rolled up both hoses. He had just sat down in his place when the call came.

'Yes?'

'Car fire. Råby Allé. The garage, basement.'

———————

She leaned her forehead against the glass that felt warmer. Every day a little closer, a little more. Seven years ago, five years ago, the fire had always been a bit further away, a rubbish bin, a park bench, and one time a fence. In more recent years, cars, the school, a couple of nurseries, and now the buildings, our homes.

Ana stretched up, standing on her toes while the basement burned, black smoke, something with oil that oozed into the flat.

She needed fresh air.

She went into the hall then out into the stairwell, slapped the cover of the rubbish chute on the floor below hard, opened it to remove the damn fucking plastic bag that she should throw to the bottom, but a cry started in her chest and erupted into her throat and she slammed it shut, a bang that echoed as she carried on down the stairs. She pushed open the front door onto a beautiful summer evening, a gentle warm breeze, but walking towards the smoke was like going back to another time when the kids who wore trackies and set fire to things had been other ten-year-olds and twelve-year-olds; she had run out every time and screamed at them, grabbed hold of them, held them, and tried to understand. And she hadn't understood, and they had heard her screams.

The black cloud. Oil smoke. Burning cars indoors were the worst. The last time, a couple of weeks ago, the same garage, and they had had to evacuate ninety-one flats when the poisonous smoke belched into three stairwells via the lift shaft. Thom jumped down from the truck that had moved two hundred metres and opened the big garage door.

The smoke hit them like a wall.

The attack hose, the supply hose, metal pipes, pump, connection, foam.

He went to where he should stand as the firefighters rushed towards the source of the fire which was parked by a concrete wall: a grey Mazda.

He didn't see them before it was too late.

Four of them with something oblong in their hands as they ran towards the unrolled hoses, stabbing at them, once, twice, three times.

'Turn off the water.'

The driver, who was looking after the pump, had heard, and a few seconds later the water and foam that was pushed out in fountains had dried up, as more of them approached – Thom counted up to thirty kids around the damaged hose. And that feeling he had had for the first time only a couple of weeks ago – something that had snapped somewhere deep inside when a paving stone and an axe had morphed into saliva that dribbled from his neck down to his chest – he felt it again now, only stronger. He realised that this was what it was all about, this was why they'd been able to put out the fire in the cellar in peace, the feeling of relief had just been a distraction when this was where they would be lured, and then attacked. And it burst again right there, despite the fact that he'd sworn it would never happen, he lunged into the midst of the arms that were stabbing at the hoses, caught a glimpse of a gold chain and the slicked-back hair, grabbed the thin boy's arm, forced it back until the knife fell on the ground.

Thom was panting, eased his grip.

It was only a kid.

He'd been so close to lashing out.

'I'm going kill you.'

The boy's face that had spat at him last time gathered ammunition and spat again. Then smiled, swept the now empty hand in front of Thom's face, aimed his fingers at his head, looked him in the eye, pretended to cock a gun, fire.

'Eddie's the name.'

The fingers again, the fingers that shot.

'Next time I'll kill you.'

Thom faced what was being aimed at his temple, he was shaking like he used to a long time ago when he sometimes went too far, he looked into the black smoke and then over at the tower block and the sky, then turned around.

———

She didn't push to the front. She'd thought about it, about talking to him, the fireman she needed to help her in order not to kill or injure anyone, but decided to wait, maybe he would be more accessible next time. Instead she had watched, near enough to feel the threat and frustration and yet far enough away not to be part of it.

Ana started to walk slowly through the dark and the Råby where she'd lived all her life, except for the four and a half years behind barbed wire in Hinseberg prison for women, the Råby that she loved and hated and that had been her starting point for the years at college and studying social work and her driving force as a newly employed social worker in the social welfare office that no one else wanted to work in; the Råby she had searched for and carried and decided to keep.

When she left Råby Allé and headed towards the buildings at the lower end of Råby Backe, the smoke disappeared, the taste of oil.

It hadn't been possible to reach them. Not at home. They had sat at her kitchen table, nine years old and part of Råby's amphetamine market, separately they had been strong and rebelled, but it had still been possible to talk to them, they gave each other strength, protected each other, united like a wall that just sat there, in the way.

Not even the two at her kitchen table. Not even the one she had carried in her arms.

And then when two had become three, four, five, six, seven, eight, when she had moved them from the kitchen table to the social services desk, when she had threatened and cried and forced her colleagues to recognise these children who behaved like criminal men and the bulk of the social services' work had involved eight boys who had called themselves Råby Warriors, nothing had changed.

*One love.*

She and her colleagues had offered tailor-made solutions, employment, good financial terms and conditions. They didn't have a chance. There were other employers, recruitment officers who knocked on the door and said one love and brother and came from agencies with names that weren't Manpower or any other temping agency, networks that offered simple solutions and lots of money.

*Another love.*

Råby Backe and Västra Ringen and the smell of smoke had vanished, the warm summer breeze was undisturbed where she sat on one of the benches overlooking Råby Torg.

It had once been so full of life.

Her gaze rested on a bench in the middle of the square. That boy was sitting there, the one who had just shot the fireman with his fingers. She'd seen him around for a while now, Deniz's son, and he was becoming more and more like her own son, it was already too late.

He didn't notice her, was waiting for someone, maybe something. Maybe the guy who just walked past, who went over to him and greeted him and took some papers out of his pocket and then left again, twice his age but obviously submissive, frightened of a twelve-year-old boy.

She looked at him through the dark that hid her and wanted to go over too.

She wanted to hold him, pick him up, carry him away and not let go until he'd understood.

It was dark.

But not completely dark, like it can be in summer. And quiet. He didn't like it at all, like everything was empty and hollow, like nothing existed. There wasn't much he could do about it on a bench in the middle of Råby Torg, but at home he always had the bedside lamp on all night. He hoped Leon and Gabriel would never find out.

There was the bastard. He nodded to him and the skinny fuck stuck out his hand and said hello, gave him some crumpled notes that had nestled in his pocket and in return he told him about the place in ICA, under the shelf for chocolate and sweets; he had put the plastic package there just before the supermarket had closed and an eager hand would tear it away as soon as they opened in the morning.

He would sit on the bench a little longer; it wasn't time yet.

He tried to think about something other than the dark and started to laugh when his thoughts focused on the car they had set alight, his fingers against the old man's head and pretending to shoot him, saying I'm going to kill you. The feeling that he sometimes had in his stomach, like a great cloud drifting around, disappeared, and the other feeling that was more like bubbles came back, fingers in the air again, and he fired at an imaginary head and thought about a towel in a locker in a school and what was wrapped inside it and that he would have one like that one day.

Eddie checked the time on his mobile phone, got up, and only spotted her after he'd gone a few steps, the woman standing over there, watching him, whose hair was turning grey and was probably as old as his mum. The woman who never showed him any respect and was mean, a social worker who saw through him, as if she knew everything about him. She knew who he was, she did. And he knew who she was. And if it hadn't been *His* mother, he would have aimed and shot at her as well.

A couple of minutes' walk to Råby Allé 44, in through the main door and down to the basement – he was the first one – sat down on the step closest to the lift.

No windows. Not here, right at the bottom.

Compact darkness, a tapping sound from the door to the cellars, another when the lift clunked into action and then stopped. Dark. Silent. He had a towel in his locker at school, if he'd had it in his hands, been holding it, things wouldn't feel so fucking hollow, so fucking empty.

He couldn't turn on the light. They'd be here soon and they didn't like it when he did that.

Soon.

Soon.

He knew why he was sitting here. It was connected to the fact that he'd sold more drugs than normal in the past month. And that he had a gun in his locker that was missing two bullets. And that there were only eleven days left.

The front door opened.

Footsteps coming in and down into the basement towards him.

Things weren't hollow any more. It wasn't empty.

'One love, brother.'

He said it, and got a slap on the ear. A punch on the shoulder. He'd said it and they'd seen him. Maybe he should say it again?

A torch in his face. Bruno. And Jon. They each had a shoebox with them.

He looked around.

'Gabriel?'

'Later.'

He swallowed his disappointment, tried not to show it.

Bruno gave him a shoebox before he went back up the stairs, pressed the lift button, waited, opened the door, pressed the button and they went back down. He took a ten-centimetre-long piece of metal from his pocket, unscrewed the small screw above the door handle of the lift shaft with his finger, put the piece of metal in the square hole that was left and turned it, opened the door onto nothing.

There was a faint light above their heads from the lift, standing one floor up. They carefully lowered themselves into the lift shaft one at a time and jumped the last metre or so down to the floor. The torch shone on the big black blanket that Bruno pulled away and the beam hit an unopened twenty-five kilo hessian sack and two boxes. First the sack and what looked like small round balls, like rabbit shit, like the ones the dwarf rabbit that Eddie and his sister had begged for used to leave in a pile on the rug in the hall. The small round balls would fill both the shoeboxes. Then the two boxes, long rows of little tubes in one, about a centimetre in diameter and ten centimetres long, and some longer, wider tubes in the other. Bruno picked up one of each sort and put them in his back pocket.

Bulk industrial explosives. Detonators. Sticks of dynamite.

One of six lift shafts in Råby Allé that was being used as a storage space.

Eddie had seen them for the first time only a couple of weeks ago, someone from the lift company was going to inspect and quality-assure all the lifts in the area and they had managed, with less than half an hour's warning, to shift everything into the cars in the garage, seven twenty-five kilo sacks of bulk industrial explosives and sixty-two sticks of dynamite and several thousand detonators. It had been stored in the cars for a few days until the lift company went on somewhere else, and then promptly moved back that night.

The black blanket back over the bag and boxes, they jumped
up from the bottom of the lift shaft, used the piece of metal in
the square hole to lock up, and hurried back up and out of the
door and over to Råby Allé 67 and the flat with the orange door
off the balcony on the second floor.

––––––––––

Eddie could smell it out in the hall. Marzipan. It smelt just like
marzipan. He looked at Bruno, at Jon, and they nodded. He
could carry on in. *That feeling in his stomach.* He'd been allowed
to sell more, to look after guns, move their explosives. *That bub-
bling feeling.* And now he was on his way into their kitchen and
would see them preparing it.

And maybe, but only maybe, he would be allowed to put it
out somewhere.

Wanda on the sofa in the sitting room. Big Ali beside her,
lying down, a film on the TV that Eddie recognised, which
looked good, he'd also have to watch it sometime.

Gabriel was standing by the table in the kitchen. Eddie
looked at him. And he almost looked back.

They had already laid out a thick plastic tube and a roll of
clingfilm on the table. Both shoeboxes with the bulk industrial
explosives, the detonators and the sticks of dynamite beside
them. Eddie went closer and caught the smell again, the smell of
marzipan. He put his nose up to it, it was the dynamite, he was
sure of it.

Gabriel waited until they were all quiet, tapped Bruno on the
shoulder with his fist when he wasn't. Then he turned the tube
upright and put it back down on the table. He pressed a detonator into a stick of dynamite and pushed them both through
the small hole at the bottom of the tube until they had disappeared except for the long wire that was left dangling. Then he
turned the tube upside down and poured in what Eddie still
thought looked like rabbit shit, but what he now knew was bulk

industrial explosives, the pressure of which squeezed the life out of human bodies more than ordinary explosives.

*Gabriel, best brutha. Remember The Rite way The Rite wall.*

He knew that it had to be pressed down hard into the tube, that was important. And that the top had to be firmly attached. And that the clingfilm had to be wound round, layer by layer, as it was to be stored near water for several days. Eddie followed Gabriel's hands as he made seven adhesive cushions on every side of the tube, took a recently stolen mobile phone from the charger on the worktop, and fixed it to the tube with even more clingfilm, opened a rucksack and put what was now ready at the bottom.

*Remember. No 1 has blown it up b4.*

'You look after it.'

Gabriel's hands opened one of the outer pockets on the rucksack and put in a pair of pliers and then handed the whole thing over to the twelve-year-old boy who was standing close, dying to be part of it.

'Keep it until I tell you we're going to use it.'

Two small hands reached out, took it, held it in his arms.

'Until next time one of us is hauled in by the pigs.'

Gabriel looked at the little boy who wanted so much. One point five metres tall, holding a red rucksack in his arms. Face of a child, eyes of a child.

That's what you are really, just a child.

If I was going to sell the amount of drugs that you do.

If I was going to keep a gun in a locker at ICA or at school, like you do.

If I was to stand there with a bomb in my arms like you are right now, if the police came, I'd get fucking five years.

But you, you're perfect, you'll get an appointment with a social worker and then be taken to the cinema by a support worker.

Eddie saw that Gabriel was looking. At him. He held the rucksack even harder and felt the laughter in his stomach again; it was the first time he'd been so far into Gabriel's flat, and he had seen them and they had seen him.

He didn't want to go, leave them, out into the dark that was hollow.

He didn't go home. Not yet. He walked along Råby Allé, then past Råby Backe to the school, which was totally empty.

He looked in through the window on the ground floor – all dark. He counted to three and then kicked his foot through it. If he bent down and twisted his body, he could get through without catching his clothes on the jaggedness.

Eight minutes. Before the security guys would get here. He had forgotten how loud the alarm was, it hurt deep into his ears.

It was always totally weird to walk down the school corridor alone in the dark like this. He went over to his locker and opened it, forced the red rucksack in with all the maths books and geography books and the gun, the locker was full now. As the alarm continued to wail loudly, he walked slowly back, the way he'd learnt to, back to Råby Allé 102 and a flat on the sixth floor and a door that was always open. His room was straight in to the left and he heard voices from the kitchen, his mum and someone else; he lay on the bed with his clothes on and turned on the light. He was tired and about to fall asleep and the lamp would be turned off in the morning when he woke up, it always was; his mum, when he was asleep.

# eight days to go

SHE SAT ON the sofa and watched the film and even though she'd seen more than an hour now, she still had no idea why everyone on the screen was running and why someone was shooting. She didn't feel well and it was hard to concentrate when her stomach was churning, it wasn't long since she'd thrown up and she was about to be sick again.

Wanda tried to lie down without touching Big Ali's feet; it eased off then, was easier to breathe. She had seen the kid with the gold chain leave the kitchen carrying a red rucksack at some point in the evening or night. He'd looked straight at her, seemed proud, she'd heard them laughing loudly out there, then someone had opened the fridge, more cans of beer, and they'd laughed even more.

She lit a cigarette, inhaled deeply.

She didn't want to. But she had to. Gabriel had looked at her as he went into the kitchen and the film had started – it wasn't his kind face, it was the one she didn't like as much, *you've got three flats left, bitch*. And then turned back, didn't expect an answer, didn't notice her swallow, look away.

She didn't like it when he called her bitch. But when Big Ali did the same, or Bruno or Jon, she didn't hear it, not really. Gabriel, it hurt more when he said it, she wanted to explain to him that it was like being stabbed in the chest every time.

One more cigarette, more deep drags, until she suddenly felt sick again and threw up in the bucket by her feet.

She had three flats left to go.

She had fixed two, Råby Allé 124, Råby Backe 4, as well as three cellar storerooms in Råby Allé 16, Råby Allé 143, Råby

Backe 192. They were all to be at different addresses in Råby, that was important, and no windows that anyone looked in on.

The first one was quite old, almost twenty-five, and her husband was doing twenty-two months for drugs; she'd screamed and spat at her and Wanda had raised the offer to five thousand a week, the old bird had screamed again but taken the money and left her the keys. The second one had been easier, nineteen and unemployed and her man was doing time for armed robbery, three thousand a week was a lot of money.

This one, Råby Allé 172, fifth floor, HOLMGREN on the door, she was twenty-one and her man was a lot older, sentenced to fourteen months for assault. They'd done some things together before, but after he'd gone to prison, they'd seen a lot more of each other, she was called Linn and Wanda knew her and liked her and had protested when Gabriel had said that they wanted her flat.

She didn't want to ring the bell.

She rang the bell.

It took a while – eye to the peephole – bare feet padding on the straw mat in the hall.

Linn was pleased, she always was when Wanda came to see her, smiled and they gave each other a hug and she asked her to come in.

Quite a small flat. But nice. Two small rooms, lots of white and quite a lot of glass on the big shelf beside the TV. Wanda had always felt comfortable here, with Linn, she was as warm as the flat.

She asked if she'd like some tea. And she knew that Wanda liked half milk, half tea, not even Gabriel knew that.

They drank two big cups, and it sloshed around in her empty stomach. It was easy to laugh here, she hadn't been in Linn's sofa for a while and had forgotten how much she missed it; it was a long time since she'd laughed like this.

Linn was just about to pour a third cup when she felt it was time to say something.

'We need your flat.'

At first Linn didn't understand.

'In eight days.'

Wanda was forced to explain more.

'For four, maybe six weeks.'

When Linn finally did understand, she just sat there and didn't say a word, didn't even look at her. *But it's me that lives here*. She didn't ask any questions, didn't protest. *But I don't want to*. They rarely did, they knew who Gabriel was and who Leon was, how it worked.

Linn just looked down at the table, then out of the window, Råby at night.

'But you'll get three thousand a week.'

Wanda got up from the white sofa.

'And you'll get it back, after.'

The third cup of tea stood there, untouched.

'In eight days, don't forget.'

She had fixed another one. Only two to go. And only one more cellar room.

She opened the door, looked at Linn and the flat that she'd always liked to visit, Linn who had lived here for quite a while, Linn who was always warm and friendly. Wanda gave her a hug, held her tight like she always did.

# six days to go

No ONE ELSE in the unit.

Leon was sitting in the TV corner, cigarette in his hand, the screw in the fish tank hadn't seen him or couldn't be bothered. Some programme on TV, probably the news, it was the sound he wanted, anything to drown out the silence.

The first of September. Soon autumn. But still warm outside, summer if he sat in a sheltered spot out in the yard, near one of the walls.

Five months since he came here.

The last snow had just melted, it was nearly spring. It was easy to forget – that there were seasons out there.

He'd been alone in the unit all week, still refusing to work and being reported every day as being on strike. But not tomorrow, he'd go to work again, go to the workshop and make red wooden bricks for toy cars and oblong metal doors for lampposts. If he refused to work again he'd be moved to solitary confinement and he had to be here, for exactly six more days.

As the phone he shared with Mihailovic was still tapped, he'd used the one that he paid a screw in Block E two thousand kronor in cash for every call, to phone Gabriel a few times to talk about Javad Hangaround who wouldn't be able to stand up for a long time and about double deliveries from Afghanistan via Russia and Torneå that would pay for the flats for as long as they needed them and the bags and boxes in the lift shafts that were to become something that no one had ever done before, and he'd spoken to Reza about the wall at Österåker prison and to Uros about the gate at Storboda prison and it felt like all the waiting was unbearable.

*Ur brutha is the same as ur own body.*

But they never talked about the inmate that the staff in D2 Left had found on his knees with his head in the space between the end of the bed and the table that was attached to the wall, nor about the TV cable that was tied around a large book at one end and around his neck at the other.

*He lives 4 u an dies 4 u.*

He no longer existed. He had talked. And would never become the ninth.

*He's there in the morning and in the evening, 4 better or 4 worse.*

But the one who came over now, just as Leon lit up another cigarette, the one who was in the greatest rush of the men returning from a day in the workshop or doing the cleaning and laundry, or the visitors' flats or classrooms or even on the grass between the walls and the inner fence that was looked after by trustworthy prisoners, the one who came almost flying into the unit, he soon would be.

You can trust someone who kills for his brothers.

'We've got the wire brush.'

Alex pointed to his right pocket, Marko stood a few steps behind, his face flushed with expectation and joy.

'And Smackhead's sorting it out right now.'

They opened the door to Cell 10 without knocking, and the bastard smiled and Leon wanted to smash the parted lips, but it was Marko's day and he unfurled his clenched fist, he'd punch him tomorrow.

'You can go and lie down on the bed then.'

Marko unbuttoned his trousers and pulled them off; even his white thighs were flushed.

'No fucking lights.'

Leon stretched over to the bedside light and switched it off.
'I like having it on.'
*At night.*
'But it's the day.'
'I always have it on when I work, I can see better.'
*I have it on at night.*
He couldn't help himself, the clenched fist right in the middle of that fucking smile, bleeding parted lips.
'Bedside lights are always off during the day.'
The thin fingers belonged to a thirty-five-year-old man who was about to turn on the light again, but stopped himself and instead fiddled with five bristles from a wire brush and a glass bottle of ink beside an empty glass tube on the small table. The proper one he'd made a few weeks ago had been confiscated after a cell search. But he still had the ink, immersed in a milk carton in the fridge, and what he was about to do always worked well; it took a while longer and it was maybe more difficult to get even edges, but he'd done it so many times before – the sharp bristles from the brush were like needles, the glass tube was the body – he normally put one wire at a time in the tube, let each new wire stick out a bit further than the previous one, like steps, and then secured them by winding round some cotton thread.

Remember, I trust a new tattoo 200%.

Marko lay with his bare right leg stretched out on the bed and Leon looked at his face. Marko's eyes shone as they had never done before, his cheeks still flushed, a restless tongue constantly licking his lips, and Leon recognised his own longing from way back, to belong to something that was greater than himself. Then the boy who would soon carry their name closed his eyes, those gleaming eyes didn't want to watch when Smackhead's hand stretched out the skin on his thigh and the other dipped the needles attached to a glass tube in tattoo ink and then stabbed hard with great control – two needles lifted the skin and three pressed in the ink.

*Remember, with each job they grow to b better soldiers.*

Marko opened his eyes, looked at Leon and smiled even though Smackhead was puncturing him again and again, to print **GHETTO** drop by drop with the improvised needles and write **SOLDIERS** what was going to be his life from now on. Six years of running errands in secure homes and young offenders' institutions and then the initiation test and he had done it and he was no longer lonely.

––––––

They had been eight.
  Now they were nine.

––––––

Someone who kills for his brothers can be trusted.

# four days to go

Photographs from a school yearbook.

José Pereira absent-mindedly ran his finger over one face at a time. To break the law and secretly cut out pictures of pupils in grades five and six – children – in order to investigate serious organised crime was not something anyone had mentioned at police college all those years ago.

More than a week had passed. And what he did know was that two bullets in the knees and a TV cable tied around a neck were in some way connected with the group that had changed names and were on the move. He knew nothing more about them. He had nothing – door-to-door inquiries, questioning, information sources – fear kept a rein on those who hadn't heard or seen anything.

He carried the open file with both hands as he wandered aimlessly around his office in the Section Against Gang Crime, between the two walls of staring eyes. The plastic sleeve with Ghetto Soldiers and Associated, he leafed through the faces, past the hangarounds, past the prospects to the category he had created himself, *no criminal record* and *kids*, photographs from the local primary school yearbooks of boys who couldn't yet be IDed, or found in official police registers. He knew, and yet didn't know, and so had to look further afield. If you called it a chat rather than questioning, if you let a guardian or social worker sit in, Pereira could talk to them one at a time. He'd begin with the one in the blurred picture down on the left, the one who had already been called to this room on several occasions before, with his slicked-back hair and thick gold chain.

---

Eddie was in the common room with his feet up on the rectangular table that bore deep wounds from his knife, the corner near the locker that was home to several kids in grade six, where they sometimes played cards. They hadn't put a new window in yet – the one that he'd kicked in and then wriggled through – it was covered with a piece of plywood and layers of brown tape, so you couldn't see out.

Afternoon and only two classes to go.

He'd been sitting here since the morning and he felt lonely. It was totally quiet. He didn't like it when it was so quiet, it clawed at his throat and chest. The others had classes, but he didn't go any more – being lonely in there with all his classmates was worse than being lonely out here.

He heard the main door opening. And footsteps. An adult's footstep.

'Pig bastard.'

He wasn't sitting with his feet on the table any more, he got up and stood too close to the man who was at least forty and was wearing jeans and a jacket, trying to look young.

'I'm going to kill you.'

---

The boy stood up and came close to him, like they always did.

José Pereira never allowed himself to be part of it – to stand in front of them, measuring them up – colleagues who unwittingly fell for it had already lost.

'You're going to come and see me. To talk about things that you and I need to talk about.'

He had looked through the file for *no criminal record* and *kids* linked to the group who now called themselves Ghetto Soldiers and a twelve-year-old who was registered as living in a two-bedroom flat with his mother and little five-year-old sister in

Råby Allé caught his eye. He'd seen his face around for a while, it looked like the ones who had been Jensen and Milton six years ago and were now serving long sentences in high security prisons, *observed boy, eleven–twelve years old, in conversation with Leon Jensen and Gabriel Milton at Råby metro station, southern exit,* a face that had increased its activity over the past two years, *usual mini-gangsta outfit, thick gold chain, on his way to the flat in Råby Allé 67 used by Gabriel Milton,* the face that had gone furthest among the kids and took the greatest risks.

The face he was now looking at.

'I'm not going to answer your questions, pig bastard.'

'I've already spoken to your mother. And told her to come with you.'

The boy came even closer, stared at the policeman, held up his hand in front of the grown man's eyes, screamed when Pereira grabbed hold of it and gripped it firmly.

'Don't you touch me!'

He didn't let go, maybe held even tighter.

'On Wednesday, you'll sit beside your mum in my office and we'll talk about what happened to Javad Kittu.'

Eddie stood still, swallowed.

'What the fuck are you talking about?'

'Someone shot him. Twice in the knees. You know who. And I want to know too.'

'Javad?'

'Yes.'

'Who's that?'

José Pereira didn't smile, didn't sigh. He might still be only a child. But he was already someone who without hesitation would harm another person if it helped his standing in the group.

'Wednesday.'

'You can't question me.'

You're standing there and just don't *want* to. Just like you're sitting here because you don't *want* to go into that classroom over there.

'You're twelve years old. I can talk to you if your mother is present.'

I've regularly picked you up, at home to begin with, when the school reported you, and when your social worker asked for a hand. She doesn't often do that any more. Even though that makes you not *want* to even more.

'Pigs who shoot dogs deserve to die! D'you understand? I'm not coming.'

'It's your choice. That or be taken into care.'

'Fucking pig bastard . . . then I want a lawyer.'

'Lawyer?'

'Yes.'

'You can have a nanny, if you like.'

———

You run errands. You hide guns. You sell methamphetamines and heroin. You keep watch during the armed robbery of a jeweller's shop, you take money from your classmates to threaten the teachers and abuse the teachers' children, you fix a getaway car and burn it afterwards, you carry the tools for burgling a villa in Nacka and help take the goods away, you tell shop owners in Råby that rates have gone up and collect fees for protection that they never get. You will be exploited every morning and evening until you're fifteen, until it's you that's doing the exploiting.

———

The fucking pig was holding him and he couldn't get free. Then he managed. And ran towards his locker, opened it, *I'm going to kill you*, the towel was lying there under his maths book and he wanted to get it out and use what was inside it, he held the gun in his hand and then let go again, he mustn't touch it, mustn't, Gabriel had said.

------------

He tried to shut the locker door when the pig came over, but he couldn't, not with the gun in the towel and the rucksack with explosives, maybe if he moved one of the files, if he pushed hard with his shoulder. The pig just stood there and watched him, and didn't realise there was more than books in the way and then he left and Eddie shouted after the bastard coward, but louder now, *I'm going to kill you.*

He only realised afterwards. He hadn't thought about it when it was all happening.

The deserted common room wasn't as empty any more.

He was alone again, but it didn't feel it, the cop had been here, they had shouted at each other, and it wasn't quiet any more.

He walked out of the school building into the air that was not scheduled into timetables or classrooms, walked across the playground quickly into Råby, out of breath when he started to run along the asphalt walkways to the flat with the orange door.

------------

'What the fuck are you doing here?'

It was Jon who opened the door.

'I need to talk to Gabriel.'

*You'll keep it.*

He was still out of breath, he hadn't had time to wait for the lift so his words were stuttered.

'It's . . . important . . .'

'You're not supposed to report before tonight.'

*And you'll keep it until I tell you that it's time for us to use it.*

'The rucksack, I . . .'

Jon opened the door a crack more and pointed to the doormat.

'You wait here.'

*Until next time one of us is hauled in by the pigs.*

He stood exactly where Jon had pointed. The others were in the kitchen, he could hear them, all of them.

'Well . . . what's so important then?'

'Pereira.'

'What about him?'

'I've to go and see him.'

Jon almost smiled, gave a clear nod towards the sitting room. He was allowed to go in. He could go further in. The sofa and films and TV that was on with the volume turned up, but no one was there and he followed Jon's back into the kitchen.

Gabriel was standing in the same place as the last time when he'd been making the bomb, alone by the short end of the table and in front of the fridge and sink. Big Ali opposite, Bruno to his right. They were all looking at something lying on the table. A pile of what looked like jackets. Eddie knew what they were. Bulletproof vests. Gabriel lifted up the one that was on top and put it down in front of him, then opened the boxes that were there, a big needle and a thick square bit of cloth; he positioned the piece of material on the chest of the vest and started to sew; the needle was thick and it was difficult to get through both the vest material and the badge.

'Ballistic neck protection. Ballistic shoulder protection. Kevlar protection plates. The police don't have anything like these.'

Four stitches along each side, sixteen in total. Gabriel tried the badge, it was pretty secure. Then he put the vest on for the first time. And Eddie stood there in the doorway and was allowed to watch, it looked so good with their new name.

'Hold out your arms.'

Gabriel had seen him and was pointing at his arms, showed him how he wanted Eddie to stand.

'And then put this on over your head.'

The bulletproof vest, Gabriel's new one. He seemed to want Eddie to put it on.

'Like this.'

Eddie was uncertain. Should he? Gabriel's bulletproof vest? With the new name on the right-hand breast?

He wasn't sure if he actually did it. Or whether he just thought that he did. Sometimes it's like that, your arms just go out of their own accord. But it felt like he was holding them out from his body and like Gabriel took the vest off and put it on him.

*Gabriel's bulletproof vest.*

That was probably why he didn't react until after it had happened. The gun looked like one that had previously been in his school locker, a Smith & Wesson .45 calibre, the kind that produced a flash at the muzzle with every shot, a flash as long as his hand.

Gabriel fired two shots.

The first bullet hit him on the chest, just beside the badge. The second hit him in the middle of the stomach. It hurt more than anything he'd ever experienced, but he didn't scream, you can't when you've been winded. He couldn't stay standing where he was either, his legs just crumpled, and he was on his knees facing the wall and there was still no sound, even though he was screaming and screaming.

They were laughing. Jon took several pictures on his mobile phone. Gabriel pulled the bulletproof vest off him and they all gathered round. You could barely see where the bullets had hit, the material was undamaged and when they felt it with their fingertips, the plate inside was dented, nothing more.

While Bruno sewed a badge on his new garment, Gabriel put his arm round Eddie's shoulders and started to walk towards the sitting room. His ears were sore, ached and ached – he only noticed now that the pain in his chest and stomach was easing – the explosions had been loud and had echoed in the bare kitchen.

Gabriel wanted him to sit down on the sofa. He did, sat

down on the sofa, he'd had tears in his eyes a moment ago and it had been difficult to breathe, but it was easier now, and the tears didn't spill over, not here, he'd just been allowed to wear their bulletproof vest.

Gabriel sat down beside him, took hold of his T-shirt and pulled it up, revealing the pale skin around two big round red marks. Eddie touched them gently with his finger, they were sore.

'They'll get bigger and softer and in a few days they'll go blue.'

Gabriel smiled and showed him his own stomach, the thickened, uneven, damaged skin.

'Fuck it, you look like me.'

Eddie couldn't stop touching the tender red circles, they went in and would soon turn blue.

Gabriel had shot at him. And he'd stayed standing.

It would be fun to go to the police.

'I'm to go to Pereira. Day after tomorrow.'

'Why?'

'Javad.'

Gabriel wasn't smiling any more. He looked at him. With eyes that sometimes hit you.

'And?'

'I don't talk to no pig cunts.'

Gabriel continued to look at him with eyes that sometimes lashed out, but didn't ask any more questions.

'You said . . . the rucksack. That I . . .'

'When you're done. When Pereira has asked his questions, which *you haven't answered.*'

The eyes again. Eddie nodded. Several times until Gabriel was satisfied.

'Then you say that you've got to go for a piss and choose the one just outside the room. Put the rucksack on the floor. Open the top of the cistern – the thing you lean your back against when you're having a shit – and lay it upside down on the sink. Take the plastic tube out of the rucksack, peel off the paper on the sticking pads and secure it to the underside of the cistern lid. And finally, before putting it back, cut off the wires that stick out from the end of the tube. Each one. It's important that they're as short as possible.'

*New name. New rules. Preparation. Escape. Kidnapping. Murder. Newspapers. TV. Bomb.*

Eddie watched Gabriel's hands as they cut an invisible wire in the air. And when they took out the Rizla papers and put them on the table, filled a skin with tobacco from the pouch and two drops from the triangular bottle that always hung on a gold chain round his neck, when they rolled the cigarette, lit it and put it to his mouth, inhaled, and then passed it over to Eddie.

A deep drag, he smiled.

Gabriel had offered him cannabis oil on the sofa.

He trusted him to do the right thing in an interview with Pereira. He'd explained to him about the rucksack.

Another toke, even broader grin.

He'd even shot at him.

# three days to go

EARLY MORNING. If it was even that. Maybe the tail end of the night. She lay back down on the bed and smoked a cigarette. There was still a strong smell of THC, the potent cannabis oil had saturated their pores, clothes, wallpaper. They had all been smoking when she got there, even the young kid was there, he'd looked really happy and laughed loudly when he tried on the bulletproof vests again and again and lifted his top several times and pointed at the two round marks that were as big as a five-kronor coin. She'd helped them carry all the new stuff down later, the things they'd been working on in the kitchen, the bulletproof vests and hoodies and T-shirts, with the new logo sewn or ironed on, their new name, they'd carried it all down into a storeroom in the cellar of Råby Allé 22.

She'd waited until the kid had gone and then asked Gabriel to get the others to do the same, but he'd refused, so she pointed to the bedroom and he'd followed her in and closed the door.

Now he was lying beside her just as naked as she was, and he was smoking as well. Soon they would hang up the blanket to keep out the sun, and she reached out a hand to stroke his cheek and he didn't move, didn't push it away, didn't shout at her, and she knew that the time was right.

She rolled onto her side, stretched over to get hold of the plastic stick that she'd put on the floor under the bed so it would be easy to get hold of and held it up for him to see; he seemed to be calm still.

'See this?'

He leaned forwards.

'Yes.'

'Can you see what it is?'

'A drugs test.'

He automatically looked for the red plus sign and saw it.

'A *positive* drugs test.'

He had pissed in public in every secure home, secure training centre and young offenders' institution.

'No.'

'But I can see it. It's red! Why the hell have you tested positive?'

Wanda gripped the stick even harder, her breathing laboured in a way that wasn't normal for her.

'It's a pregnancy test.'

He didn't move.

'Gabi?'

He didn't say anything.

'Feel.'

She took his hand and put it on her stomach.

'Here.'

And tried to keep it there while she spoke.

'If you . . . it's like a . . . sesame seed. Do you hear me, Gabriel? As big as a sesame seed! There's . . . there's a bulge in the middle . . . a heart. It's not beating yet. But it's there.'

She could normally tell what to expect from his eyes.

They were empty. She couldn't see anything.

Not even his movements, when he stood up and left the room without a word, told her anything.

GABRIEL HAD HEARD sesame seed and heart, but nothing more. He walked naked from the bedroom into the kitchen. Jon was sitting on a chair by the table drinking something and didn't even have enough time to turn round. Gabriel's fist hit him in the middle of the face. He carried on into the sitting room where Bruno was lying in the sofa, watching some film or other when Gabriel grabbed hold of his T-shirt and pulled until they were both looking at each other – his forehead hard against Bruno's nose and cheek, twice. His trousers were lying on the floor and he put them on, his hoodie and socks were somewhere else. He ran barefoot to the car, wearing nothing on top. Out of Råby, onto the motorway towards Södertälje, he drove past Botkyrka church at two hundred kilometres an hour and it was hard to see the road through his tears, but with one hand on the wheel he managed to open the glove compartment and nudge out a gun and check that there was still a bullet in it. He spun the cylinder that had room for six bullets and cocked the trigger as he normally did when he felt he ruled the world, but he didn't feel like that, in fact, he felt the complete opposite. He pulled the trigger again, the clicking sound, and he cocked the gun, and pulled the trigger again, and again, click, click.

He stopped the car, cocked the gun for the fourth time, he closed his eyes and it clicked, two bullet chambers left, one full, one empty.

He pulled the trigger again and his eyes stung and watered even more when he dropped the fucking gun on the seat beside him.

# two days to go

EDDIE HELD ON to the toilet door handle.

What had seemed easy at Gabriel's and when he lay in bed waiting for the morning, was no longer as easy. His sleep had been fitful, as if he wanted to wake up the whole time, the hours in the dark had been in the way, then suddenly he was part of the day again and this.

He took a couple of deep breaths as he sometimes did when he was about to do something his body didn't want to do, then pushed down the handle and opened the door, closed it behind him, locked it and put the rucksack down on the toilet seat.

**INTERVIEW LEADER JOSÉ PEREIRA (IL):** Now, let's talk about Gabriel Milton.
**EDDIE JOHNSON (EJ):** Who?
**IL:** I know that you know him.
**EJ:** Don't know who you're talking about.
**IL:** See this picture?
**EJ:** Yeah.
**IL:** Råby Allé 67. Gabriel Milton's flat. And this is Gabriel Milton. And this, the person going into the flat, is you.
**EJ:** Nope.
**IL:** No?
**EJ:** I've never been to that flat. And I've never seen this guy. And that, that's not me, I'm Eddie.

He'd jumped out of bed when the alarm clock finally went off, slicked his hair back with enough wax to make it shine, picked up his gold chain from the chest of drawers and clipped

194

it on round his neck, checked in the mirror and pulled down the zip on his jacket so he was sure the chain was visible. The evening before he'd kicked in another window on the ground floor of the school and taken the rucksack from his locker; he'd kept it beside him in the bed through the night and he'd held it in his arms while he waited for his mum to get ready so they could walk the five hundred metres from Råby Allé 102 to Råby police station.

**IL:** Do you know what this is?
**EJ:** Pig papers.
**IL:** A PIR.
**EJ:** I know what a PIR is. Pig papers.
**IL:** The preliminary investigation report where Javad Kittu talks about Leon Jensen, Alexander Eriksson, Reza Noori and Uros Koren.

Pereira had been waiting for them in reception, said hello and tried to be nice, then walked in front of them along the corridor and into the room where the Section Against Gang Crime sat. He'd been there twice before – at ten and eleven – and Pereira didn't have the authority to question him, it felt cool when the pig bastard drove him home in one of the police cars and parked outside his stair. It was after that he'd spoken to Leon and Gabriel for the first time, and they'd instructed him about the next time, about rights, about accusations, but mostly that you could lie as much as you wanted when you were suspected of a crime.

**IL:** Do you know which case I'm talking about then?
**EJ:** No.
**IL:** Do you know who Javad Kittu is?
**EJ:** No.
**IL:** This photo, two people, you're on the left, Javad Kittu on the right. You're standing by the entrance to the metro. I can

hold it closer if you like, so you can get a good look. I repeat, do you know who Javad Kittu is?

**EJ:** No.

He turned around and looked at his mum a couple of times while they sat on Pereira's sofa; he'd tried to catch her eye but she'd just looked down, she nearly always did when he looked at her, it was a long time since she'd looked him in the eye.

**IL:** What does two bullets to the knees mean?

**EJ:** Someone's talked.

**IL:** Here are two pictures of two knees. Can you describe them for me?

**EJ:** Blood. And skin.

**IL:** Anything else?

**EJ:** Holes.

**IL:** Javad Kittu's knees. And two bullet wounds.

**EJ:** So this guy, this Javad's the sort who talks?

He had sat across from Pereira just like he should. He had looked at him just like he should. He had sighed when the recorder was put on just like he should.

And he had answered just like he should.

**IL:** Look at the pictures again. Bullet holes in two knees. Do you know who fired?

**EJ:** You know that I can't answer that question.

**IL:** Why can't you answer?

**EJ:** I don't want to answer.

**IL:** You don't want to answer?

**EJ:** No.

**IL:** Why not?

**EJ:** Because I don't have to.

After a while he'd got up from the chair and walked around the room a couple of times, glanced over at the photos on the wall; he'd recognised so many of them, Leon and Gabriel and Alex and Bruno and Big Ali and Jon and Reza and Uros, and it had said Råby Warriors and Ghetto Soldiers above them, and maybe one day, later, he would be there too.

IL: What's your position?
EJ: What d'you mean by position?
IL: You must have some kind of hierarchy?
EJ: Says who?
IL: Is that not the case?
EJ: Says who?
IL: I'm asking.
EJ: And I'm asking too. Says who?

He had paused by the photos that would soon be moved to the left wall, at the top, looked at Leon and Alex who were doing time in a seriously high security prison, felt the soft bubbles in his belly whenever he thought about it. In a few years from now he would have done all that too, and maybe he'd even have done time in prison.

IL: OK, take a look here. The photos on the wall – do you know them?
EJ: Who?
IL: The guys on the wall. The ones you're stealing a peek at when you think I can't see.
EJ: I don't know.
IL: You don't know.
EJ: I can't answer that question.
IL: You can't answer that question?
EJ: I can't answer that question.

He'd given the right answer every time. And hoped that Leon would soon read the interview, that their lawyer would take it to him, that he would see that Eddie was the sort who didn't talk.

**IL:** When they talk . . . they always talk about the family.
**EJ:** Right.
**IL:** The family is called Ghetto Soldiers.
**EJ:** Right.
**IL:** What does family mean?
**EJ:** What does your question mean?
**IL:** Do you want to be part of the family?
**EJ:** Which family?

He sat on the plastic toilet seat and looked at the rucksack that was standing on the floor, looking back at him. *When you're done. When Pereira has asked his questions that you haven't answered.* In there, behind the white wall, he was sitting in there, the pig bastard, in his big office. *Say that you've got to go for a piss and choose the one just outside the room.* He took two deep breaths like he normally did, but it didn't make him feel any better, as if he was two people, one that had bubbles in his body and the other who just wanted to get up and walk out, beside his mum the whole way home. *Open the top of the cistern and lay it upside down on the sink.* He tried the door handle one more time, to check that it was locked, two more deep breaths and then he carefully unscrewed the flush-button, it got a bit stuck on the thread and he had to use a bit more pressure than he'd expected, but soon it loosened and clinked when he dropped it down onto the porcelain sink. *Take the plastic tube out of the rucksack.* Holding the filled container in one hand, he peeled off the paper from the seven adhesive cushions and attached the plastic tube to the underside of the cistern lid, feeling along the clingfilm that would protect the mobile phone; it was on and properly attached. *And finally, cut off the wires that stick out from the end of the tube.* He caught the long, thin worms that were sticking out of the bottom of the plastic tube and got hold of them with pliers that slipped in his sweaty hands. *Each one. It's important that they're as short as possible.* He cut, ran his hand over them, cut again, even closer.

From now on, the detonators were unstable.

From now on, the current from one single telephone signal could cause an explosion and a pressure wave that would kill everything in the near vicinity.

Eddie screwed the cistern top back on, flushed several times until he was certain they could hear it, put two toilet rolls and a pile of handtowels in his rucksack to fill it up, and then opened the door and went back to his mum, who was standing waiting for him by the coffee machine further down the corridor. She didn't look at him even now.

# tomorrow

HE COULDN'T SLEEP.

It wasn't possible.

If he just let his eyes disappear into the white light, if he didn't close his eyes, didn't even blink.

He didn't sleep.

He sometimes thought about a mother. Every now and then about a father.

Always and only at night, always and only when he looked into the bright light, as if he couldn't chase them away then and they were there with him in the cell, on the chair and on the floor and by the wardrobe and sometimes sitting on the sink, but mostly in the bed beside him and he lay perfectly still so he wouldn't touch them.

Sometimes he imagined that she touched him, carried him, a hand on his cheek or maybe it was his dad's hand, but it wasn't, because he'd never touched him, it just felt like that, and he did what he always did, stood up and shouted *I'm going to kill them all* and tried not to think about four sticky hands over his body. But tonight, when he lay down again, they came back and he even recognised their voices: his mother's from so long ago and his dad's that had never existed; voices that said something he couldn't hear.

Leon turned the light off, turned it on, turned it off, turned it on. And rolled over towards the barred window; if he lay on his side he could see out across the dark of the prison yard, the faint profile of the wall, even the church tower in the distance, but not the sky, not yet.

*The carbon rods. The mash. The car. The ladder. The grinder. The boat.*

He trusted them. Gabriel, Alex, Marko, Reza, Uros, Jon, Bruno, Big Ali. His brothers. But he didn't trust the whore, she was trying to take something from him, and he didn't trust Smackhead, he smiled too fucking much and had the light on during the day. But he had to, had to trust them. They were the only two who could do the most important things.

He turned the light off, on.

Everything had to happen in the right order. Everyone had to do the right thing. Everyone had to be in the right place.

He looked at his watch, five to twelve, nearly midnight.

today

GABRIEL LAY ON his back under a white and somewhat rusty Mercedes Benz in the middle of a multi-storey car park in Skärholmen Centrum. Asphalt and grit rubbed against his thin T-shirt. He cut the cable to the alarm, put his mobile phone down where he could see it, the stopwatch had already started 00.02 to measure his last day alone.

He had been incarcerated in secure homes in Småland and in Hälsingland and in locked units in Bärby and Eknäs, but had never voluntarily left Råby for several days in a row. She had shown him the plastic stick she'd pissed on – positive – it should have just been a drugs test, but it was a sesame seed instead and he'd run barefoot to the car in the garage a few miles out of Södertälje, one single 00.05 bullet in his gun and only one chamber that it could be in and for a long time he'd wondered whether to shoot or not, started the car again and carried on south along the E4, stopping for the first time after twenty minutes and seventy-five kilometres at a petrol station some-where outside Nyköping and he'd hit the woman behind the counter across the cheek, nose and neck with his open hand, she'd fallen to the floor and he'd eaten two hamburgers 00.10 that were nearly done and kicked her in the stomach when a man had come running in from the pumps and he'd pointed his gun at the bastard's head and fired a shot past his ear and into the middle of the window, two hundred kilometres an hour to Jönköping and he'd driven into the centre of the town, still dark, and the pub in the pedestrian precinct 00.14 had been empty and he'd ordered a beer, but the bartender idiot had refused to serve anyone who wasn't wearing a top and shoes, so he'd walked out and kicked in the display window at Åhléns department store and grabbed a fucking awful shirt and a pair of old-man's shoes and gone back to the pub, got a beer from the idiot who'd forced him to commit a crime, then carried on south without getting out of the car before Värnamo and Ljungby and 00.17 it had started to get light as he approached Helsingborg and the harbour, he had been hot and sweaty and jumped in the water by the big ferries that bounced about like sesame seeds, he'd felt dizzy and screamed at them and spat at them and then carried on to Malmö and the Öresund Bridge, it was morning 00.21 by the time he'd driven into Copenhagen and suddenly everything had become blurred and shiny and cold and warm and he was sure that he was bigger than ever before and smaller than ever before, that from all the faces he'd first recognised Leon, who was waiting for him, then Wanda 00.24 who had walked along the pavement with her back to him with an even bigger sesame seed in her arms and carried on lying, then he'd maybe fallen asleep or he'd wandered around as it got light and then dark and then light again, then driven back and not slowed down until he could see Södertälje Bridge and Salem and Råby, he'd picked up Jon and Bruno outside Skärholmen and the faces that he'd hit three days earlier had looked at him but not said a word because they knew there was nothing to say.

He looked at the stopwatch on his mobile phone.

He had cut the cable, broken the lock, melted down the plastic knobs, started the car.

00.29.

Today, he'd always known, he would be better than ever. He checked the mobile phone lying beside him on the asphalt again, this day, today.

Gabriel its time.

They'd heard that he'd got the car started and came running from two different doors, Bruno and Jon had both kept guard and now opened the door to the passenger seat and back seat at the same time and got into the car that would be theirs for twelve hours – until they were all together again.

2 go all the way.

He stopped for the first time by Skärholmen swimming pool, left the motor running, and went into the chlorine-impregnated brick building where they'd gone once a week in grade three to learn to swim; he still felt uncomfortable when he thought about it, he'd refused every time, would never show himself naked with his disfigured skin. He paid the attendant who just kept staring at him, seventy kronor, then went into the men's changing rooms, the locker in the middle of the middle row. The lock buckled and the key got stuck and he jiggled it backwards and forwards until it opened. The Sig Sauer was small and black and just fitted in the inner pocket of his jacket. Three months ago, they'd stopped and mugged a policeman at the Råby roundabout, he was still missing his service gun. The metal of the muzzle in his armpit as he walked out again and dropped the dry towel into one of the laundry baskets. They carried on to Kungens Kurva and the huge ICA Kvantum supermarket, the locker furthest to the right in the middle row, a Russian gun, a Tokarev 7.62 millimetre that they'd taken from the fat, pale beardies on bikes who'd tried to sell on their patch, he put that in the other inner pocket. On to Råby and Råby Backe 7, second floor, door nearest the lift, he rang the bell and she was at home like she was supposed to be and he tried to remember her name, down the hall to the first cupboard on the left, behind the suitcases, the real thing that was older and had been used for seventeen armed robberies and the replica that was brand new, she opened a black bin liner and held it while he put in the two Kalashnikovs and gave her three thousand-kronor notes, one for each week, then finally down into her cellar room, with the lady's bike that covered an arc torch and a closed aluminium stepladder stolen from the building suppliers in Masmo.

He'd dropped Bruno and Jon off at Råby Torg – they would move the boat at Slagsta Strand and sort out mattresses and food for the flats – when suddenly he couldn't bear it any longer, what was gnawing at him.

Inside.

The whole fucking time that he'd been sorting out the car, guns, arc torch, ladder. It had been gnawing at him. And he couldn't understand why. It had been gnawing at him since the sesame seed, something that was happening and no matter how much he tried not to think about it, it kept coming back.

He swallowed all the extra saliva he didn't have room for. *It was tearing at him.* He took a deep breath and air caught in his chest. *Inside.* He hit his stomach with his hands hard and again and again, until his damaged skin was red.

*It was eating him up inside.*

Gabriel had been on his way to the garage when he suddenly changed course, accelerated, headed towards the barrier that had its arm across the asphalt pathway, drove towards it, through it, metal that didn't break but rather bent backwards far enough for him to carry on over the bushes and rows of plants to the door of Råby Allé 67, left the keys in the car when he ran up the steps.

They were coming back to him. The past few days.

One bullet left in his gun and the ferry that turned into a fucking sesame seed and her positive piss, he was still running when he opened the door to the flat and went down the hall. Wanda was sitting on the sofa and he screamed at her to take off her clothes and lie down on the floor, and then he went to the kitchen and the oblong cupboard and he took out the vacuum cleaner. He started with her feet until the attachment got stuck on her ankle and he carried on up her shin instead, knees and thighs and cunt, he avoided the damned belly, spent more time on her tits, careful with the nipples, up her throat, cheeks and forehead, changed the attachment to the small round one when he got to her hair. Back down to the stomach, the attachment hard against her navel and maybe he was crying a bit but it was hard to tell because he was screaming all the time about whores and bitches and brothers and about the kind of whore who takes his brothers from him, her skin was red and clean when he turned off the vacuum and opened it in the middle, took out the bag and carried out the front door to the rubbish chute where he emptied it like it was dirt.

---

They sat side by side in the car. It wasn't gnawing inside as much any more. But he didn't say anything and she said nothing as they drove north in the middle lane of the E4, as they'd done every fortnight.

Not much further now, not much longer now.

Into the Shell station to the right of the Täby exit, and the spot near the air and water cabinet.

Wanda was to stay in the car while he went into the shop, past the woman at the till who looked down and away. But this time he didn't try to catch her eye from a distance, nor did he open the chiller and take out two cans of Coke and then go out again – suddenly he was standing in front of her and she jumped when she realised.

He had put down a packet of condoms next to a twin-pack of big batteries.

'This.'

She still didn't understand. He was going to pay. He wasn't threatening her.

'Yes?'

'How fucking much does it cost?'

She moved gingerly and without a sound when she read the prices and tapped them into the till, as if she wanted to be invisible.

'One hundred and fifteen kronor.'

He put the exact amount down on the counter, but she didn't dare to pick it up until he'd gone out the door and got back into the car that she could see clearly through the window, always a Mercedes, always different from the time before.

Wanda was still sitting in the passenger seat and he handed her the condoms as he opened the box of 1.5-volt batteries and took out a knife and a metal cutter.

With the knife, he cut a hole in the plastic covering of a battery and peeled it off bit by bit.

He cut the metal part in two with the metal cutter.

Inside the plastic, inside the metal, there was a carbon rod in each battery – he took great care, they mustn't break, handed them to Wanda.

Two oblong, black, weightless carbon rods in her hand. The only thing they needed today that couldn't be found in a prison, where every electrical apparatus accessible to the prisoners had batteries with either carbon in powder form or alkaline with no carbon content whatsoever.

She knew what she had to do.

She opened the door, her hand gently on his cheek.

'I love you.'

He stayed where he was and when she turned round, halfway across to the toilets and looked at him, he'd taken out his mobile phone and was pretending to talk on it, his back to her.

She had never said it before.

He had a brother, after all, he loved him.

He hated her.

———

The hard stone floor was cold. It smelt of urine and mould. She lay down and cried, the naked skin on her stomach and thighs was not red any more, but she felt dirty. Gabriel had thought she was. She got up and turned on the tap that only had cold water, and took off the rest of her clothes, she couldn't really get close enough to the sink, so she scrubbed her whole body hard with her hands, fingers on her skin until it was red again, like Gabriel with the vacuum cleaner, she cried and scrubbed until she couldn't scrub any more and then she lay down again, back on the floor, her feet resting on the toilet seat.

Amphetamines in plastic bags or carbon rods in condoms, it didn't matter, she still had to do the same – baby oil outside and inside her vagina, on the rubber surface, on her fingers, and then, bit by bit, until the pain took over.

———

They still hadn't spoken to each other, he couldn't and she didn't dare, not when they left the motorway, not for the last few kilometres on smaller roads past the small town and the church until they were in front of Aspsås prison. The words got stuck, Gabriel couldn't even look at her; they sat side by side staring straight ahead. He didn't know why, but felt that it might have something to do with the positive plastic stick that she'd shown him, and the fact that he'd disappeared for three days and that this was the last and the first and that it would all start in a minute when Wanda walked through the gate in the wall in front of them. The only thing he knew for sure was that what was gnawing at him had come back and was even stronger.

They didn't even look at each other when she got out of the car in the prison car park and he quickly reversed out again. He would park the car by the church and leave it there, then go to the bus stop and wait for her. He looked out of the window, she'd started to walk towards the prison gate and suddenly he slammed on the brakes, went back and wound down the window.

'Come here.'

No words for so long. It felt strange to be shouting after her.

'But visiting time . . . Leon, he'll—'

'Come.'

She walked back and sat down in the car beside him and he looked at her and didn't know what to say and she waited until he knew.

'Whore.'

He didn't say it loud. And his eyes weren't aggressive. She didn't understand.

'I'll never say that again. Your name is Wanda.'

She dared to look at him now, but still without saying anything, frightened, not of him, but of breaking the spell.

'This.'

A white tube in his hand. The one he rubbed on his eighty-five per cent burn scars every day. The house that burnt down, and the morphine that was the only thing that could still the pain, the body that rattled when he left the hospital, nine years old.

He handed her the cream that no one else had ever been allowed to rub into all that ugliness.

'This morning . . . I forgot . . . you put some cream on my back.'

She had tried a couple of times. But he'd screamed at her.

'I want you to do it.'

He turned around, back to her when he pulled up his shirt. They didn't say any more. She rubbed the cream into his skin in the way she'd seen him do it in the morning, smiling the whole time. He shivered a bit a first and perhaps turned away a fraction, but when she did it the second time, even though it wasn't needed, he stayed still.

Then they went their separate ways. He towards the church and bus stop, she towards the gate and central security.

*Now.*

The microphone in the wall, walking across asphalt, the blue uniform on a chair in central security with a finger on the list of registered visits.

*It was because of this you had to be heard and searched.*

She left the room that had one single barred window and walls full of small lockers, went out into the entrance hall and through the grey metal detector, the two guards studying her like they normally did when the beeping noise broke the silence.

'Waist height.'

*You need to talk to them now.*

'Same as last time? A stick up my arse while you have a look?'

'Can you go through again?'

*You need to talk to them, remind them about the last time.*

'Your fingers inside. You've been fantasizing about doing it again.'

She walked through the arch again, through the beeping noise.

'Waist height. Take off your belt.'

*They got their warrant, and they used it and they had no luck.*

'Soon, you can touch me up again, you can watch and you can wank. You lot probably have to pay for it otherwise.'

'Just stand where you are.'

*They'll search you. They'll get right up close, threaten you, frighten you. But this time they won't have permission to search you inside, no prosecutor would give out papers again without reasonable grounds.*

She took off her belt and stepped onto the two foot rests, the long plastic detector against her thighs and into her groin, over her hips. She got down again, waited while the dog sniffed her belt, smiled at the uniforms when she got it back and walked towards the visiting room that they had pointed out.

———

She undressed like he wanted her to and lay down on the bed as soon as they locked the door behind him. He would be the one to take it out, she had done it once herself, she wouldn't do it again. He squatted down close to her, it was lubricated and slipped between his fingertips when he pulled it out.

Twenty-eight days ago she'd taken something in and he had made sure that it was noticed. Fourteen days ago she'd smelt of it but dumped it, so they stood there with the papers that gave them the right to search something that was empty. She had just walked past some uniforms that didn't have a warrant and smuggled in the only thing they didn't have.

Leon looked at the condom encasing the two carbon rods lying in his hand, put it to his mouth, swallowed.

'We're done.'

He had pressed the red button by the door, bent down to the microphone.

'Already?'

'Visit over. I want to go back. Can you let me out?'

---

He leaned over the sink with the cell door shut and his fingers down his throat and threw up a condom with two carbon rods in it, then rinsed it and walked down the corridor towards door number 10.

He walked in without knocking. Smackhead was sitting at the small table in front of the window, his back to him.

'You got everything?'

The face that turned round, that Leon hated so much. So close he could hit it. But he couldn't, not today, he needed him, after all.

'Yes. I've got everything.'

He went closer – on the table, two glass *bottles* that you could buy in the prison shop and that had once contained carbonated orange fizz and then were soaked in water until the labels came off; the two *felt-tip pens* that had been beside a notebook in one of the class rooms in D3; the *electrical tape* that was always on one of the shelves in the workshop and was now hanging in long strips down the back of the chair; the *nail clippers* that had been at the bottom of his wet bag and were one of the few sharp instruments permitted in a cell.

'And the rest?'

Smackhead nodded towards the closed cell door.

'Out there.'

Leon got closer and at least bumped into the skinny body hard as he leant over and put the condom down on the table beside the bottles, the two carbon rods very obvious, and the grinning fucker gave a satisfied nod.

'And my price?'

'Two hundred and fifty gs.'

'I want half a kilo.'

'You want to be part of this? Or what?'

'Yes.'

'Then you'll get two hundred and fifty.'

'That's not enough.'

'That's what you'll get.'

Smackhead looked around the cell. A few square metres. Then he turned back to the barred window, looked out, towards the wall that was never-ending.

'Two hundred and fifty. If I'm in.'

You fucking bastard.

You'll be in for exactly as long as we need you.

'Right. You're in. How long?'

'The others . . . they took three hours.'

'You've got one and a half. Deliver it to my cell.'

Leon opened the cell door and Smackhead spoke in a low voice.

'I'll get started when you get started.'

———

Leon hurried towards the unit kitchen, filled a large pan with water and put it on a hotplate, opened the fridge and took out the mobile phone that he knew was still safe from the hole on the inside of the door, went back to his cell, careful that the door was well closed when he phoned.

'Brother?'

He listened.

People. Traffic. Cars.

His true brother and the whore were on the bus on their way back.

'Reza?'

'Yep.'

'Uros?'

'Yep.'

Both silent again, listening to the other's world.

'The car?'

'Yep.'

'The gun?'

'Yep.'

'The flats?'

'Yep.'

He wanted to say so much. He could do that later.

'One love, brother.'

'One love, brother.'

———

He left the mobile phone in the cell when he went back to the kitchen fridge to collect another one.

The square buttermilk carton furthest back behind the others.

He was in a hurry, wasn't as careful as he normally was, after all, he wasn't going to use it again.

He poured the old buttermilk out, tore off the whole top of the carton, and picked out the plastic-wrapped package.

The third mobile phone in the unit.

The one he shared with Mihailovic. The one he now knew was tapped.

A good place that had worked for years – he had wrapped the phone in plastic, split the bottom of the carton with a razor blade, emptied out the buttermilk and put the phone in, sealed the bottom again with the flame from a lighter that melted it together, then poured in new buttermilk – Swedish prisons were full of buttermilk cartons hiding mobile phones.

From now on he could use two mobile phones.

The one that he knew was safe and was free to call from. And this one, that he would only use when he wanted those listening to hear.

He put it in his pocket and turned round to look at the cooker, the big pan of water had just started to boil and he lifted it off the hotplate.

He was ready to begin.

––––––––––

He used both hands to move the pan of boiling water from the cooker out into the corridor and the glassed-in wardens' office. He could see them both in the inner room, the young female bitch and the older male jerk, sitting there drinking their fucking screw coffee. He put the pan down on the floor and took a five-kronor coin from his trouser pocket, pressed hard as he drew it across the reinforced glass from the lower right-hand corner to the upper left-hand corner, then from the lower left-hand corner to the upper right-hand corner, a cross scratched onto the pane of glass when he saw them both get up and run towards him.

'What the—'

Leon bent down and lifted up the pan, it was odd, he remembered another time – *a child shrink he didn't think about very often* – thoughts do that, suddenly they're there getting in the way – *he had been carrying another pan of boiling water, he had been violent and kept behind reinforced glass* – and he now did the same as he had back then: threw the boiling water at the glass, at the cross where the two lines met, then used all his might to hit the same point with the pan – *he had been so small, jumped down from the first floor and landed on the newly laid asphalt, ran away and kept away for nearly thirty-six hours* – now, like then, the glass fractured into a spider's web that turned to snowflakes which fell to the floor in small, small pieces. And then – a couple of steps back to be standing far enough away, he'd let the screw bastards do what it said they should do in the rules – press the alarm button on the piece of plastic, run out, lock the door to the unit and call for reinforcements. He stayed standing where he was and watched them until they disappeared, the plastic boxes on their belts flashing as they were on the belts of sixty-eight other screws who were on duty right now in Aspsås prison.

———

The door to Cell 10 opened at exactly the same time that Leon Jensen smashed the glass wall and set in motion a well-prepared sequence of events in Unit D1 Left. *The others . . . they've taken three hours.* Sonny Steen ran down the corridor towards the kitchen and the cleaning cupboard as fast as his feet that were tender from years of injections would carry him. *You've got one and a half.* The vacuum cleaner was standing beside the mop and he pulled the lead out as far as it would go and cut it with the nail clippers. As soon as he was back at the table in his cell, he would first cut off the plug, then cut two pieces half a metre long, peel off the plastic at either end and plait together the bared copper wires – *two* fifty-centimetre leads that ran in parallel to one and the same plug.

One that would be plugged into the wall in a couple of hours.

The first step to making a cutting torch.

———

The last pieces of glass from the big window in the wardens' office fell to the floor and settled in even smaller shards at Leon's feet. Both the screws had run out of the door to the unit and locked it behind them. Smackhead was now on his way back to his cell with the long vacuum cleaner lead in his hand. And the moment that he gave the all-clear, fourteen prisoners left their cells. Four went to the TV corner – the standard lamp with a wide blue shade gave off a strange light when the metal foot hit the TV screen and the round table where matchsticks worth two-thousand kronor were traded between various poker and casino players every day broke into pieces when it hit the concrete wall, three of them forced open the door to the wardens' office and tipped over the desk and shelves and the coffee machine and pulled out the telephone lines and all other leads, three others went to the kitchen to pull out and empty all the drawers on the floor and wrench off the oven door and the doors to all the cupboards and hurl all the plates and glasses and coffee cups against the wall, and four men got hold of the billiard table, lifted it and carried it on their shoulders over to the screws' room and heaved it through the empty glass window that had been shattered by a scratched cross and boiling water.

---

Sonny Steen sat at the table that was attached to the wall and looked out across the prison yard. His cell was number ten and was at the other end of the corridor, a good distance from the wardens' office, but he heard them kicking off out there and knew that he had one and a half hours from now. He felt stressed. He'd built around ten before but had always had plenty of time, now his bony hands were shaking, he wasn't used to trying to lengthen every minute that he normally dreamed away. He tried to think about the other machines, calm himself with the knowledge that they'd all worked, like the one that Jochum Lang had ordered in Hall prison, or the one he'd made years before which was still one of the great mysteries of the Swedish prison service: Popescu's escape from the bunker at Kumla prison. He'd been doing time himself in Block H, just under the bunker, and had hoisted the machine up through the window, bit by bit.

The two leads that were half a metre long and joined together in a single plug lay ready on the table – he now cut another two pieces from the vacuum cleaner lead, a couple of metres each, stripped the plastic off them and wound the shiny naked copper wires round and round the empty bottles.

He put them down on the table, looked at them.

This was how he had fooled the security system that existed in every prison and remand jail, the automatic fuse; no one could kill themselves with electricity, if the resistance was too great, the automatic fuse cut off the power.

Copper wires from a vacuum cleaner lead wrapped round two bottles.

He had just built his own resistors.

The lights would continue to shine as normal when Jensen turned on the cutting torch.

———

Once the fourteen inmates in D1 Left had destroyed the wardens' office, the TV corner and kitchen, they split into groups of three or four and went into one cell at a time brandishing chair legs, billiard cues and frying pans and smashed first the lamps, wardrobes, beds, tables and then the porcelain sinks until everything was in pieces all over the floor. Leon checked the time on his mobile phone: thirty minutes. He had said one and a half hours, sixty minutes left. When the final sink, his own, was broken and lay in pieces between the splinters of the wardrobe and the bed's disembowelled mattress, he walked towards the kitchen and cleaning cupboard and the bucket that had been left behind the cleaning trolley and a couple of mops fourteen days ago: a brown brew of sliced bread, apples, cinnamon buns and sugar cubes in water. He put the bucket down in the middle of the corridor and went to collect the fourteen plastic mugs that were still intact and filled them with twelve per cent mash which always guaranteed rage and aggression in connection with any prison disturbance – they would continue to wreak havoc until he no longer needed them.

---

He had recognised the smell, strong mash, and had been on his way out to get his share, but turned round again when he saw Leon Jensen. He had an hour before the people waiting outside the locked door to the unit would have back-up and would force the door open. The double lead and plug and the two resistors were ready. Now he wound them together, the ends of the copper wires from the two leads and those that were wrapped around the two bottles, and with his few remaining teeth, he bit off several pieces of electrical tape to hold them together even more securely.

He was ready with half the cutting torch.

To make the second half, he now took the carbon rods out of their protective condom, emptied the two felt-tip pens of their contents so that they were simply two hollow plastic containers, divided what was left of the vacuum cleaner lead into two equally long pieces and bent down to put it all together.

---

The broken tables, chairs, cupboards, sinks, plates and glasses and a smashed TV set, trashed billiard table, a fridge and a freezer in pieces and a tipped-up cooker. They sat in the middle of it all, fourteen prisoners on the corridor floor, dipping their plastic mugs into the big metal bucket and filling them, drinking it up, spitting out the apple cores, and filling them again. Two of them – both junkies who weren't used to alcohol – threw up several times and were punched hard *don't fucking waste our mash* by those who guarded every single drop. Leon stood at a distance, keeping an eye on the evil-smelling liquid and the door to Cell 10, where Smackhead was doing what he was supposed to do. Soon, when the bucket was empty, they would all get up on his command and, full of alcohol, would together drag all the debris and push it against the door to the unit that was locked from the outside, locking it from the inside with a barricade of broken furniture, a floor mop and two billiard cues rammed between the doorframe and door handle.

---

Half done. The other half – he peeled the plastic off either end of the two remaining lengths of the lead, threaded each through an empty felt-tip pen and used electrical tape to make two handles, his fingers got black as always when he taped the carbon rods to one end of each lead.

---

Drunk on moonshine and power and the fact that fucking something had happened that broke the silence and tedium, the fourteen inmates ripped to pieces the last remaining curtains, pulled off the wallpaper strip by strip, tore up the grey and yellow linoleum that covered the hard concrete floor. While they did this, Leon went over to the barricaded door, listened to the first members of the Aspsås task force arrive – he guessed about twenty of them with helmets, shields, batons – and heard them immediately start to take off the door's two hinges. And when he moved over to the kitchen window that looked out across the prison yard, there they were: four special police force vans drove in through the main gate and across the asphalt towards Block D and parked immediately outside the entrance. Eight fully equipped policemen jumped out of each van, armed with tasers and Sig Sauers. They ran into the building and up the stairs to the door where the prison's own task force made way, ten minutes, no more, then they'd be in.

————

Sonny Steen's hands weren't shaking any more. He'd make it. He'd always had a relatively good supply of amphetamines, anyone who made machines in a high security prison could regularly pick up his pay. But it was more about beating the system, so apart from the carbon rods, he made them from parts he could get from things inside the prison wall and that were permitted as individual items, but which together combined to make something powerful and forbidden. What had started as a welding course in Tidaholm prison had continued in Kumla prison with the Finn who claimed that you could make a cutting torch. He had experimented and worked out the rest over the years he'd been locked up inside.

Now he was going to put the two parts together.

The double lead – with the plug at one end and the two bottles with the copper wires wrapped round and round them at the other.

And then the two slightly longer leads, with the carbon rods at one end and nothing at the other.

That was where the two parts would be joined.

The copper wires from the empty end were twisted into the copper wires that were wrapped around the two bottles. And it was ready. A plug that became two leads, that became two bottles with copper wire wrapped round them, that become two new leads, that ended in two carbon rods.

He knew that it worked. But couldn't help himself.

The plug in the socket, the carbon rods held carefully against the bars on the window in front of him, a few seconds only, but you could already see an obvious cut where the flame had touched the metal that was supposed to lock them in.

He opened the cell door and ran through the broken porcelain and wood with the cutting torch in his arms to Cell 2, he put it down near the door and nodded as he walked down towards the other end of the corridor; Jensen was standing there.

———————

Leon saw Smackhead open the door to his cell, go in for a couple of seconds, then come out again straight away, a short nod before returning to his own cell.

It was ready. It was in there.

He had waited a while between the now empty mash bucket and the barricade of junk that blocked the door into the unit, until the persistent noise of a drill on metal stopped; the troops outside had worked their way through all the hinges and a new noise took over, loud and pulsing, an alarm had been triggered, the sniffer, the detector that smelt its way to dynamite.

'Back, *now*.'

He hurried towards the kitchen and the only thing that had remained untouched, the coffee machine, then the TV corner where he grabbed the extension lead from the trashed television set, and with the coffee machine in one hand and the extension lead in the other, *you have exactly ten seconds to move away from the door*, he ran down the corridor. The explosion that blasted open the locked door was powerful. The first boot-clad steps could be heard on the naked floor when he sat down in his cell where his bed had been, the cutting torch close at hand but hidden by the pile of porcelain that had once been a sink, he leaned back against the wall, waited.

LENNART OSCARSSON WAS standing in a prison unit that lacked furniture, floor covering, wallpaper, a kitchen, a wardens' office, lighting, toilets. A prison governor who, while watching forty fully armed riot police walk across the prison yard to their vans, ordered the task force of twenty fully armed prison guards to lock all the cell doors as the inmates had, on their own initiative, gone into their cells and sat down. He gave a light kick to the empty bucket surrounded by empty mugs and spat-out apple cores and fresh sick. Moonshine. He'd always found the smell nauseating.

Following an incident some years ago when a prisoner had been shot by a police sniper *at the same time* that he was ripped apart by an explosion, he had worked intensely to improve security – installed explosive detectors in the corridors and larger spaces, granted permission for more cameras, installed metal detectors in every entrance, and acquired more sniffer dogs.

It made no difference.

He kicked the bucket again and then wandered through the battered wood that had once been a table, doors and cupboards that sixteen prisoners had reduced to splinters over the past hour and a half, which had been scattered down the corridor when the riot police had forced open the door, even the dented cooker lay on its side and the heavy billiard table was broken in two, both pieces leaning against each other. In his first years as a young and newly qualified prison warden, who had had his temporary position extended by three months at a time, they'd had three, four, sometimes five disturbances a year, but that was to do with the times. The number had dropped later, due to increased security, with only the occasional disturbance most years – he made a quick calculation, thirty-seven disturbances, thirty-eight including this one. They never really disappeared. He would continue the work to increase security, but it made no difference; a prisoner who wanted to instigate a disturbance would always succeed in doing so.

This time the broken sinks and wardrobes were not just shards of porcelain and splinters of wood, he felt an underlying tension that prodded and shouted at him, something wasn't right, but he couldn't work out what or why.

Moonshine.

He nudged an apple core with the toe of his shoe, side-stepped some vomit.

Thirty-seven disturbances before this and not a single one had started without alcohol – someone in the unit who made moonshine and shared it out with drops of frustration and aggression and the need to lash out. This time, according to both wardens, the prisoner who had started it all, Leon Jensen, appeared not to be drunk or high when he attacked the wardens' office with boiling water, nor were there any signs that the other prisoners were either. This time, Lennart Oscarsson sank down onto his haunches by the now empty bucket and tried to see what wasn't there and could therefore not be understood, they had only started drinking *after* the disturbance had begun – in order to stoke it, not to start it – enough alcohol to fuel them for a couple of hours until tiredness or the police overwhelmed them.

'All this.'

He got up and went over to the only person moving around in the chaos of the corridor who wasn't wearing black overalls and a white helmet.

'I want you to tidy away anything out here that could be used as a weapon.'

The head of Aspsås prison task force nodded.

'And in two hours we'll do a search of all cells, one at a time. We have no idea of what we might find behind these doors, what they might have managed to take in with them, what they might use against us.'

The head of the task force should immediately inform his twenty colleagues that they would be going home late tonight.

'Empty each cell and question every inmate, then lock them in again. They'll stay in there until this has been fully investigated. I want to know what all this is *really* about.'

Lennart Oscarsson stood there longer than he needed to, waded through the mess, bending down every now and then to pick something up, to run his fingers over the paperless walls and deep holes in the concrete where only this morning there had been cupboards and doors. Their home, the only home they had for the foreseeable future, and they had chosen to wreck it. And it would stay like that for a while, neither he nor the director general of the prison service had any intention of rushing to acquire new furniture. If this was how they wanted it, this was how they could have it.

The soles of his shoes crunched with every step as the pieces became even smaller, slowly past the cell doors that remained silent, each one sitting inside in their own dross.

He stopped outside cell number 2, Leon Jensen's cell, staring at it as though he expected it to talk to him, give him an answer.

You started all this.

And I cannot fathom why.

LEON SAT ON the cell floor and looked at the lamp that was switched on above his bed. What had been a lamp above what had been a bed. Now it was a hole in the concrete wall that separated him from the other world.

*In two hours we'll do a search of all cells, one at a time.*

A voice outside, the prison governor's voice, and it was loud, almost piercing.

*I want to know what all this is really about.*

The cell door was locked and on the other side, only a few steps away, the uniforms had started to tidy up, he could hear irritated shouts, porcelain against glass and after a while, something that sounded like an engine, a forklift truck that carried away one broken piece of the corridor after another.

He had two hours left.

———

The cell window was constructed in layers. A grid of four horizontal and three vertical iron bars. Behind the bars a window, glass reinforced with plastic, behind that yet another window of pure glass.

In order to get out through the bars, he would have to cut the iron in six different places.

He'd done it before, his first time in Mariefred prison – each cut had taken fifteen minutes.

———

He used a sharpened piece of metal – that had been taped to the wooden boards on the bottom of his bed – to scrape the colouring off the iron exactly where he was going to make the cut. Then he put the plug of the cutting torch into the only socket in the cell, took hold of the handles that had once been the plastic tubes of felt-tip pens, pressed one carbon rod to the metal and brought the other as close as possible, almost jumped when the welding flame flared up.

———

It was amazing how easily the electricity flowed between a negative and a positive pole, between two carbon rods that had been in ordinary batteries, cutting through the metal.

———

Every now and then they talked amongst themselves outside the locked cell door, amongst the broken shards that tore at their fingers, or sharp points and parts of a billiard table that needed some back put into lifting it. The forklift drove backwards and forwards, and there was rattling, clinking, thumping as twenty prison guards carried bin bags and cardboard boxes down the bare corridor.

As long as he could hear them, they couldn't hear him.

———

He was sweating profusely, his breathing was laboured and he couldn't understand why, it wasn't hard work, wasn't demanding, but still he was shaking.

———

There was another layer of metal inside all the bars, a column of ball bearings that would turn when touched, in case anyone tried to cut into it. But it was perfectly possible to cut it with a welding flame. Leon also wrapped one of the bedsheets tightly round the bars to make sure that they didn't slip and they fell to the floor, one by one.

The grille had been cut at six points to create a hole forty centimetres wide.

That wasn't enough.

He tied the extension lead that he had taken from the TV corner first round his waist and then round one of the bars that was still in the window, loosened the sheet and stuffed it in between the lead and his skin so that he wouldn't bleed too much, and then lay down on his back.

He had never looked out of the cell window from the floor before, still sunny and perhaps a bit of wind, you could tell by the way the clouds scudded across the sky.

He closed his eyes until his breathing slowed, he wasn't sweating as much, droplets clinging to his forehead and hairline.

Both feet against the wall under the window.

And he pulled on the extension lead tied to his waist and the bars, dug his teeth into the material of his T-shirt so he wouldn't scream with pain when the plastic cut deep into his skin, pushing on both legs as, gradually, the bar bent back, enough to make the hole bigger, so that a body could squeeze through it and out.

––––––––

Leon lay on the floor without moving. The clouds were still small and didn't seem to hang together, but they were moving even faster across the blue, it was getting windier.

He didn't hear the forklift as much now, or shouting and steps outside his door, they were quieter, as was the tinkling and clattering.

He still had time, but no longer hours, it was minutes and seconds now, and they were running out fast.

*Gabriel, this is long, 11 pages.*

HE HAD MADE a hole in the bars that was big enough. He had boiled water in the coffee machine which was the last thing he'd grabbed with him as he ran back to his cell, to avoid the exploding door. He'd scratched a cross on the reinforced glass window with a five-kronor coin.

Now he threw the hot water at it and then smashed it with a chair leg at the point where the two lines met and when the glass reinforced with plastic crumpled, he punched the next pure glass pane with his fist.

It was open.

The wind was really blowing.

*We r there.*

The forklift truck wasn't running any more. *Searches*. The heavy footsteps had disappeared. *One cell at a time*.

*New name. New rules.*

There were other footsteps now, lighter, more determined. *Come out and show us your hands*. He heard the first door, the one opposite, opening.

*Riot.*

The next door, the next one would be him.

*Escape.*

He loosened the extension lead that was biting into his back,

232

fresh blood on his hands, *come out of your cell, I said*, then tiptoed over to the door to listen, *don't touch me you fucking pig bastard*; they weren't done yet, opposite.

Kidnapping. Murder.

Leon wanted to rest for a moment, his back to the cell door, he looked at the window with a hole in it and the wind blowing through.

They would change walls.

He knew what was needed, *the other wall*, he knew it.

Papers. TV.

Explosion.

He smashed the two bottles on the concrete floor, unwound the rings of copper wire and broke the plastic felt-pen tubes and the brittle carbon rods and knotted together the metres of vacuum cleaner lead.

No clues that anyone might understand.

Then he went slowly over to the window, as if he wanted to draw out those few metres, the wood and porcelain under his feet, and, as he got closer, more glass.

The wind got stronger and when he felt it against his face it was much warmer than he'd imagined.

C u soon. One love and all my heart.

Ur brutha 4 life.

Leon.

**now**

**part two**

**(ninety minutes)**

THE WARM WIND in his face.

A strange feeling, an open window in a locked cell.

———

He got snagged as he pressed his torso through a hole in the bars that he'd cut with tips of two carbon rods and the window he'd broken with boiling water. He had to bend his knees so he could stand on the ledge, half in, half out the window, that made it easier. He was sweating, shaking from his feet to his heart that was thumping, but the prison yard below him was empty so he had to wait a bit longer.

———

They had carried out the final wreckage from the cell opposite. The rattle as they undid the handcuffs and then the loud voice that ordered the prisoner back into his cell. They would lock it again any minute now and open the next one.

———

Footsteps.

Just what he was waiting for.

Someone walking across the asphalt below, gravel dust.

He was sure of it, just around the corner of the building and coming closer, he would see a head and uniformed shoulders only a few metres below.

———

A woman. The screw whore. The one that wasn't much older than him, who'd opened his cell door every fucking day and wouldn't leave until she'd got a good morning, the one he knew was called Julia.

She had no idea.

It was easy to jump. Leon landed just behind her, she didn't even have time to turn round before he was up again and had hit her hard on the back of the head with his hand. She fell to the ground, he pulled her up again by the hair, the sharp piece of metal against her throat.

'Three steps forward.'

She didn't move. She'd heard him, he knew. He pressed the hard sharpness against her skin, a superficial cut that started to bleed.

'Three steps forward!'

They were in exactly the right place. A bit further down, a bit further away, right in front of the cell window. The bastard screws would be able to see her clearly.

He pressed the piece of metal harder again, she had to feel it and do what he wanted her to do.

He whispered in her ear.

'You're not going die. Not yet.'

They both looked up at a cell window on the first floor, D1 Left, that didn't look like the others as it had a big hole in it.

A few minutes. Maybe one more.

Then they heard it, the voice that screamed *search* at them, followed by the rattling of keys and the creaking of the cell door being opened.

A few seconds of silence.

'Come out with your hands up!'

Silence again and *come out, for Christ's sake* feet running in and stopping and then carrying on over to the window.

'You up there! Stand fucking still!'

Two faces framed by the hole in the window, he took another step forwards, pushing her in front of him, pulling back her head so they could see the sharp metal against the delicate skin.

'Cell 9!'

More feet on their way into the cell, heavier than before.

'Get him to come here.'

Leon grabbed hold of Julia Bozsik's neck and hair, jolted her back as he moved the piece of metal from her throat to the back of her left thigh, stabbed hard and cut deep and then he put the bloody metal to her throat again.

'Cell 9! Now!'

———

He held the piece of metal to her throat and could feel with his thumb that her pulse was racing. His other hand was on her forehead and hairline and she was already wet with sweat, he felt the intoxication surge through him, the heat that became a flush, the lightness and air in his chest, his cock getting hard.

His hand was shaking and he couldn't control it even though that's exactly what he was, in control.

———

The bastard screw was still standing in the window.

'Now!'

And Leon drew yet another line across the already bloody throat.

'*Now!*'

And another one.

Then he saw it. Alex's face peering out through the square hole.

'He's coming out! He's coming here!'

Leon moved back a couple of steps – the metal still against her throat – so he could see better when Alex climbed up onto the window sill, gathering himself to jump, and then suddenly changed his mind, turned around and went back into the cell, grabbed the coffee pot from the machine and smashed it against the screw's face, a horizontal movement to the one cheek that was likely to slice through it. Suddenly you could see teeth and a bit of the tongue through the white slash in the skin and it took a few seconds before it started to bleed.

———

The screw with the gashed cheek was supposed to stand still in the window.

He didn't.

So Leon pressed the piece of metal harder and it cut from the inside when she gasped and then fainted, fell back head first. He lifted her up by the hair and when he looked up at the screw who was supposed to listen to him he was sure he could see his cheekbone sticking out through the wound and the white enamel of his back teeth reflecting the light from the bedside lamp.

'Cell 12!'

*If life was in danger.*

'Right now.'

The metal deep into the back of her thigh again.

'Cell 12!'

*If life was in danger – play along, not against.*

'He's on his way.'

The prison warden whose cheek was now red with blood moved over and Leon saw Marko's face in his stead – he jumped, as Alex had just done.

———

'I'll cut her throat if you even try!'

———

He was about to turn round and take the first steps towards central security when he heard something hammering against another window a few cells down, again and again, hard, desperate. That face. Smackhead and his fucking hands that were now waving around in the air.

*And my price?* Leon was reminded of something he intended to forget. *I want my half kilo.* The hands frantically banging on the bars and the window. *You want to be part of this? Or what?* And the lips that were trying to say something. *Two hundred and fifty. If I'm in.* The hands that hammered and the exaggerated lip movements of that fucking ugly mouth. *Right, you're in.* He could see it now, at least he thought he could, the lips forming the words, 'I'm supposed to be coming with you!'

He pressed the sharp edge harder in the screw whore's throat and turned around, pushing her in front of him, Alex and Marko right behind, he could almost hear the tossers running through the passageway underneath his feet, twenty members of the task force leaving the unit and heading to central security, trying to get there before him.

————

The door in the first inner wall was monitored by a camera at face height and Leon looked up into it, and made sure that the light from the two lamps shone on her throat, so that what was pressed against it would flash.

————

The door in the second internal wall was larger, wider, with a camera installed high up and it was already open by the time they got there, he pushed her in front of him, towards central security and the big main gate.

————

The young prison warden who was on duty in the central security glass box this afternoon had watched on monitor after monitor the four people move from Block D over the prison yard, through the two doors to the window in front of him, a face pressed up to it, with a throat bleeding from several deep cuts.

*If life is in danger.*

Her eyes, they looked straight at him, through him.

*If you believe that a hostage-taker is prepared to carry out his threats.*

She was so frightened, she could easily have been him.

*If the hostage-taker demands to be released, then you have to open the door, in order to save lives.*

It was hard to press the button, his trembling fingers had no strength and the prisoner standing behind her holding the metal to her throat banged her head against the glass several times until the warden put one hand on top of the other and pressed with both. He pressed and pressed until the main gate, which was several metres wide, slowly started to slide open. Then he sat completely still and watched them disappear out through the gate and across the parking place and along the road to the church, his colleague limping badly, and they pushed and shoved and pulled her, four bodies merging with the shadows, getting smaller and more blurred as they got closer to the other community, the one outside.

SHE WAS MISSING a word. She tried and tried to find the right word to make sense of what she was feeling but it didn't exist. She had never experienced such pain before. A burning, stabbing, breathless pain, at the back of her left thigh, where her uniform trousers were torn and bloody.

For so long, she had been frightened of the aggression that might explode at any moment. Now, with the piece of metal making small cuts on her throat, she wasn't frightened any more. She was furious. The feeling that she always had to hide in order to avoid seeing and feeling now suddenly turned to rage, she didn't even notice that her leg no longer held her, that she collapsed.

———————

The screw whore was suddenly heavier when he tried to straighten her up. She fell to the ground. He screamed *get up you screw whore* and she whispered *never call me screw whore again* and he looked at her leg and kicked her exactly where the metal had cut her.

———————

Julia wasn't sure whether she was awake or asleep, whether someone pulled her by the arms, dragged her over the asphalt road towards the churchyard and the small parking place there, whether someone opened the back door of a car and pushed her down onto the back seat.

If that was the case, then it wasn't her standing by, watching.

———————

Leon opened the boot and checked that what was supposed to be there was there – the stepladder, the arc torch, the rifle, the replica and the ones they needed now, each wrapped in a towel: a Sig Sauer and a Tokarev. He sat down beside the screw bitch in the back seat when the first police car sped by – sirens, blue lights, on its way to Aspsås prison – they waited in the seclusion of the church car park until it had passed, then started slowly to drive into the small town of Aspsås, finally accelerating when they left the last houses behind.

He'd taken a firm hold of one of her arms and taped it to the other after she managed to reach the handle on the back door and open it. His first blow hit her on the nose and mouth. She let go and he pulled the door shut, grabbed hold of her arms, held them and taped them together, hard. Her wrists and fingers, thighs and feet, and it was when he was going to put the first piece over her mouth that she bit him on the back of his hand, her teeth sinking in deep. He hit her for the second time, across the jaw and ear, a third punch to her forehead, a fourth on her chin and then he pulled off her shoes and socks, rolled the dark fabric into a ball and forced it into her mouth, taped over her bloody lips bit by bit.

'I'm done.'

A lay-by at the edge of a wood, overlooking a lake, they stopped but left the motor running, carried her round to the boot, closed it and swapped places, Leon now in the driver's seat as they set off again at high speed.

———

She lay on her side. Her head hit against the metal every time the car stopped or took a corner or accelerated. Julia kept her eyes closed at first, but opened them again, darkness, there wasn't any difference. The tape and the socks, but most of all fear, she retched when she tried to breathe in air.

They were all shouting at each other, three youthful voices that had been in the prison for about as long as she had, who had frightened her and made her long to get away. People who were close to her had warned her about what could happen – and now it had. Her mum had given her a lift on the first morning and still met her in the visitors' car park after every shift. At some point during the week her dad always managed to leave new four-colour brochures from universities and colleges on the kitchen table in her flat, Jocke held her hand a little tighter, lay a little closer when they slept.

The car braked more suddenly than before, lurched more violently and she hit her head against the wall of the boot; they had left the main road and were driving on a smaller one now.

She tried to see again but saw nothing, tried to smell but smelt nothing, she listened but they weren't shouting as loudly any more. The boot felt like a coffin and she was shaking and lost all feeling, first in her toes, then her feet, then her lower leg.

Her knees had gone to sleep when the car stopped.

She had tried to count, lost it twice when the pain took all her attention, but she reckoned nineteen right-hand turns, seventeen left-hand turns and forty-three slow-downs. They didn't say anything at all when they closed three doors at the same time, hurried footsteps, and her eyes, everything was brilliant white when they opened the boot, it was hard to see their faces, but she could see something red behind them, she was sure of it, the edge of *another* wall around *another* prison.

IT WAS GETTING darker, but still light when they parked the car by the corner of a seven-metre-high wall.

Leon opened the boot and looked into the eyes of the taped-up screw whore as he shoved her legs to one side so he could get the aluminium stepladder, the arc torch and two Kalashnikovs, one real and one replica. He handed the cutter to Alex, who ran with it in his arms to the metal shell protection fence by the first wall, got down on his knees, turned it on.

Forty-five minutes ago they had cut their way out.

Now they were going to cut their way in.

———

The prison warden, who was on duty that evening in the central security glass office and keeping an eye on sixteen monitors showing black and white sequences from thirty-three security cameras in Österåker prison, had just sat down with a cup of coffee when he saw something odd on the middle screen. Three dark shadows transformed into a flaring light by the first protection fence, then again by the next one. He didn't really understand what he was seeing until the shadows ran up to the wall, put up a stepladder and started to climb.

———

Marko had crawled through the holes in both fences, then extended the four-part stepladder to its full eight-metre height and put it up against the wall, Alex a couple of steps behind with the cutter, Leon last with the loaded rifle on his back.

The wind was stronger up there, it felt so good on their faces when they stood on the top of the wall, pulled the ladder up and then dropped it down on the other side.

———————

It had happened so fast.

He'd worked in central security for nearly two years. This was like nothing he'd ever seen before.

First, he pressed the blazing red button that was the direct line to the County Communication Centre in Stockholm, *three armed men, a break-out*, next the button right beside it that raised the alarm on six pagers in the breast pockets of six uniforms of the Österåker task force, *protective equipment, prison yard*, then on the keyboard in front of him formulated a silent alarm on each screen in each wardens' office in each unit, *escape attempt, secure from inside*. And then he turned back to the moving images on the screen again, two shadows climbing down the ladder on the inside of the wall that then started to run towards the metal cages in the prison yard.

———————

Leon stood on top of the wide wall and watched Alex getting down on his knees again with the petrol-fuelled arc torch and a few seconds later cutting out a rectangle in the corner of the metal cage as three inmates stormed over the yard. The first one, tall and broad with a shaved head, threw himself down towards the hole, forced his way through, the second one immediately behind.

'Only Reza! No one else!'

The two others had heard but didn't stop and Marko aimed his gun at the ground near them, then fired three shots.

'*No one else!*'

They looked so small to someone standing on the top of a concrete wall, seven metres up.

Alex, Marko and Reza ran towards the ladder and Leon breathed in and out and in and out and in and this was easy, no one in the way, it was just him and the wall and the wind that meant he had to stand a bit firmer on his feet. A Kalashnikov weighed four kilos and had a magazine of thirty bullets. He lifted it and aimed at them, he wanted to laugh and fired into the sky and then at the woods over there, five six seven shots, one for each breath. He swayed a bit as he tended to do when he was concentrating, and after a while looked straight into the security camera on one corner of the wall, straight at someone who right then was sitting in a security office looking straight at him. He felt a tickling from his legs up to his arms and he laughed into the camera, giggled, aimed, fired and the glass shattered and showered down, close to Alex and Marko and Reza who were almost up now; they helped to pull up the ladder and drop it down on the outside.

———————

The man in the blue prison service uniform who was sitting on his own in the central security fish tank had seen a face on the screen and through the air vent heard the sound of a Kalashnikov, counted eight shots.

*Alarm, secure from inside, lock.*

He knew the security regulations. And had done exactly what he was supposed to. But he was trembling all the same.

He knew that a total of eleven police units were now on their way from Stockholm and Arlanda and Norrtälje, that Österåker's own task force was already out in the prison yard, forcing the prisoners back in, including the two who had crawled through a square hole, only to stand still at the base of the wall, that the prison wardens in each unit had locked all the cell and unit doors and were in their secure office. It didn't help. He was still shaking as he, on the screen, saw the four men leave an eight-metre ladder and run towards a waiting car through two protective fences that had been cut open. He could still hear the unfamiliar sound of automatic gunfire in the late summer evening, and his colleagues were out there, and he hoped that none of them had been injured.

JULIA TRIED TO turn over, stretch out her legs, arms. If she put up with the tape cutting into her skin, if she made small, small movements, she could manage to kick the metal, but the sound was muffled; she heard it best in her head.

She would have been walking back from Slussen by now, slowly up Götgatsbacken, it was warm and that kind of evening – people, bicycles, cafés and friends laughing at tables outside restaurants. They'd meet at Medborgarplatsen by the hot-dog kiosk with the Danish-sounding name, like they usually did, she'd be a bit late and start to run and Jocke would be sitting on one of the benches waiting for her – he always was.

She kicked again. That bloody metal sound.

The car had been standing still for several minutes by the red thing that she was certain was *another* prison wall.

It had been a short drive. There was only one other prison nearby.

Österåker.

It was easier to breathe when there were no violent stops and sharp bends, when she could keep the socks away from her throat. A couple of times she imagined that someone had walked past, someone who might find her, she'd tried to shout but the words just got stuck on the tape and her lips and she had kicked the metal again that was still muffled.

She heard someone shooting. An automatic, she knew that. First seven shots in quick succession, then one more, she had identified the sound of splintered glass and maybe metal falling somewhere nearby.

Who were they aiming at? Who had they injured? Who wasn't alive any longer?

Footsteps running, coming closer, the doors were wrenched open, the engine started.

She curled up, it was difficult to get enough air again, the more she breathed in the less seemed to reach her lungs, she was dizzy and what had previously gone to sleep from her feet up, started again. There were more voices now, a new one that was higher than the others, but didn't sound as loud. And soon there were smaller roads with sharper bends and she felt even dizzier, and she tried to focus on the only thing that was important, counting, thirty-five right-hand turns and thirty-four left-hand turns and fifty-two slow-downs before they suddenly stopped.

Sirens.

She could hear them clearly.

She tried to scream, kick, police cars were nearby.

And then disappeared.

They were going to go to the cinema, have a glass of wine. Jocke would be sitting on the bench waiting, she was normally late, but not this late, she was seldom this late.

She guessed it was another ten minutes until they stopped the next time and left the road. She was thrown against the boot wall as the car drove over grass, maybe a field or a meadow. They opened the doors and jumped out and she recognised the voice, the one who had cut her throat, Jensen, he was the one who yelled *screw cunt* as he passed the boot and hit the metal hard with his hand.

---

The sun was setting. Half an hour until dark.

He aimed his gun at the third prison in ninety minutes, one of the low security ones with no wall, held the butt hard and aimed while Alex cut the first square out of Storboda prison's outer fence, twelve seconds, moved on to the next which was thinner, eight seconds, and that was precisely when Uros ran over the asphalted prison yard. Leon looked at his watch, 19.25, five minutes until lock-up.

———

They hadn't stayed there as long this time.

She had heard a machine, then running, tried to work out where she was.

The doors opened, closed.

Now there were five of them, shouting and laughing loudly, punching the roof and the windows, stopped suddenly, repeated shots from an automatic rifle, then drove on again, fast and on small roads with sudden movements and it was now that she heard for the first time that they were talking about her. At first she thought she was imagining it, but the voice was clear, it was explaining that they didn't need her any more and another one asked if they should kill her here or wait a while. She wondered if Jocke was still sitting there, if he was worried and had got up, maybe even walked around to look for her and then started to make phone calls. She could see him in the middle of Medborgarplatsen surrounded by men and women holding hands when her toes and feet and knees and thighs gradually left her body, she tried, she did, but couldn't get any air, great gulps of air and the socks got stuck in her throat and it was hard to swallow as she slipped away, gone.

# now

## part three

### (twenty-three hours)

SILENCE.

It sat in his chair, possibly bent forwards with its elbows on the wooden surface, looking at him. It stood over by the closed door, leaning back, looking at him. It lay beside him on the old corduroy sofa that was brown and had lost most of its stuffing and, what's more, was too short to accommodate his stiff leg. It lay there and snuggled closer, touched his shoulder.

Detective Superintendent Ewert Grens smiled at it, a nod of recognition.

He wasn't frightened any more.

He had been, to begin with, when the noise from Hantverkargatan and the cars accelerating at the bottom of the steep hill crowded in through the window, and the footsteps and voices that passed in the corridor didn't dissipate. He had started to hear things he had never heard before, because the music used to block them out, Siw Malmkvist's voice, so soft, and the songs from so long ago. It had taken a whole year and he had on several occasions rushed down the stairs to the City Police property store, run with the shadows looming in his chest, filled out the reclaim form in detail at the wooden counter and then regretted it, closed his eyes for a moment and turned his back to the shelves, breathing deeply until he could face leaving again – they were there, so close, waiting among the property confiscated during criminal investigations, the sealed cardboard boxes of cassettes and a cassette player and loud-speakers and a black and white photo of the singer that he'd taken himself and then mounted in a silver frame, the boxed-up music that had accompanied him every day for thirty years and had taken up all his space and thoughts.

And all the silence.

He started by managing to get through one day. The next morning, he had decided to try for one more day.

Then another day.

And then, some months ago, he'd fallen asleep and woken up on the sofa and felt what he had avoided for so long – he wasn't frightened, the silence could scream at him as much as it wanted, sitting leaning forwards or standing leaning back or squeezing onto the sofa that was his alone – what couldn't be heard was almost beautiful.

He got up and walked through the room at one end of the Homicide corridor, opened the window that faced out into the Kronoberg courtyard, the air pleasant and warm, looked at the buildings that housed various parts of the Swedish police force and dealt with a criminality that was growing by the hour. More and more. More frequent. More violent. It had also changed appearance and clothes in recent years, a widening gap between the small-time junkies who ran around wielding kitchen knives and the open executions that were intended to send messages about respect.

He left the window open, as warm outside as it was inside, went back to the desk and the files that were stacked one on top of the other, lifted them up one at time, looked through documents that described violations and lives that would never be the same. He wondered where it was all coming from, the contempt, the illusion of the right to injure.

And despite it all, he could hear the birds.

The ones sitting in the small trees that would soon turn yellow, which were planted here and there, too far apart, along the asphalt path that led from the City Police to Swedish National Police Board, sinewy trunks that seemed to lack branches, but there the birds sat, looking up at the thin moon and singing their hearts out.

He dropped the files down on the desk, filling the surface between the telephone and coffee cups. They would stay there and he wouldn't return to them for another couple of hours, other people's violence and lives where he always sought refuge, but not now, not today. He opened the white cupboard that was squeezed into a corner of the room with two full bookshelves and an unlocked safe. The training gear that he never used next to uniforms he had long since grown out of. In between them, still in its plastic covering, a jacket – he took it out, it smelt new.

Ewert Grens held it, lifted it up to the strong ceiling light. A beige colour that he liked a lot. The protective plastic covering clung to the arms; he pulled it off with great difficulty, bit by bit, filling the waste-paper basket. It fitted him just as well as it had in the shop. He looked at the small mirror on the inside of the cupboard door, turned around, his head craning to have a look. There was a comb on the small shelf under the mirror, he picked it up and pulled it through his thin hair that was more like a grey halo round his crown.

Someone walked past in the corridor.

The birds started up again, singing even louder; there seemed to be more of them.

Otherwise, silence.

Until the damn phone on his desk launched an attack, shrill signals, despite being covered by one of the files.

He let it ring.

Hand over the smooth fabric. It was a long time since he had worn a new jacket. Ten years. To the day. What if he did up two buttons? Maybe three. He angled the cupboard door slightly – it was hard to see from shoulder to shoulder in the narrow, rather dirty mirror.

The phone was still ringing. He counted twelve. Sixteen. Twenty-two.

'Yes?'

'Ewert?'

Erik Wilson. He talked louder than his predecessor, Göransson, had done. The younger they were, they more effort they had to make to sound as small as they didn't want to be.

'What do you want?'

'I know you're not on duty. But you're here.'

'I'm always here.'

'I need your help.'

Further down one of the jacket sleeves, a crease. If he rubbed his fingertips back and forth over it . . . it disappeared, slowly.

'When?'

'Now.'

The metal comb through his hair once more, like a whirlpool on the right-hand side, but it normally flattened after a while.

'I haven't got time. I was on my way out.'

'Now?'

'Yes.'

'It's the middle of the night.'

'Sometimes it is.'

The voice that was nearly twenty years younger, that was about to give an order, coughed, took a deep breath.

'I wouldn't be calling unless it was important.'

If he pulled the sleeves. That almost made them longer. Covered his wrists and part of his hand, and then the shirt, white, the cuff showing.

'What do you think, Wilson? A beige jacket?'

'I'm sorry?'

'At the start of September, do you think it works?'

He was still there. His breathing was audible. But the words, they took longer.

'Ewert?'

'Yes? Do you think it works? Or should it be something darker? Stripes, maybe?'

'Have you been drinking?'

'Jackets, Wilson! What colour are you wearing?'

'Grey.'

'Not beige?'

'No.'

Ewert lowered the receiver, looked in the cupboard mirror again. He had somehow imagined that today would be different.

If he'd wanted that, he would have slept at home.

He didn't sigh.

'How important?'

'Eighteen zero five hours. Aspsås prison. An eighteen-year-old, a nineteen-year-old and a twenty-year-old. Escape, hostage, knives.'

'I see.'

'Eighteen forty-five hours. Österåker prison. A nineteen-year-old. Escape, automatic weapon. We're certain of it. Same guys.'

'Right.'

'Nineteen twenty-five hours. Storboda prison. A twenty-year-old. Escape, automatic weapon. Same guys.'

'Right.'

'I want you to take over.'

'Take over?'

'Gold command.'

Ewert Grens slipped the shiny metal comb into a narrow plastic sleeve, pushed the training gear and uniform back in with one hand while he used the other to close the cupboard door, crossed the worn linoleum through the silence that was no longer music, to the large window and the courtyard that still refused to accept the dark completely.

He snorted.

'Gold command. I thought that sort of thing was for bureaucrats. Really senior police commanders. Like . . . you.'

'Ewert, I—'

'And . . . it's twenty to two in the morning. More than seven and a half hours have passed. Half the Swedish police must be running around in the woods and the other half will be at home watching it on TV. So why the hell are you phoning me in your *grey* jacket, Wilson, interrupting . . . now?'

A late summer's night with air that was almost warm. He opened the window a fraction more, followed the shadows that lengthened where the lamps along the asphalt met forgotten lights in offices here and there in the sleeping body of the building.

'Because I now know something I didn't know then.'

'Which is?'

'That you're the best suited.'

'Suited?'

'Yes.'

Four floors down. He leaned out. He was heavy, falling from here wouldn't take many seconds.

'Aspsås prison. The one we think planned it. His name is Leon.'

'And?'

'Leon Jensen.'

Grens straightened up and left the window, hobbled in agitation across the floor, his stiff leg resisting more than usual.

'Jensen?'

'Yes.'

'Youth unit?'

'Yes.'

'Born in nineteen hundred and ninety-two . . . three?'

'Yes.'

*Like the others.*

'I want you to be in charge from now on.'

*Like all the others.*

'Ewert?'

A short strip of plastic on one sleeve. Hard to get hold of. His nails kept slipping, he pulled it a couple of centimetres, and then again, uneven edges that were too small, he let it stay where it was.

'I'm going to hang up. I've got some phone calls to make.'

––––––––

It usually didn't take very long. He'd seen the telephone upstairs, on the small table with rounded legs, Anita's side.

'Sven?'

'Yes.'

'Sit up.'

Ewert Grens always wondered whether his colleague got out of bed and hurried round on the cold floor to the phone so as not to wake her and then went back so that he could lie down again. Or whether he carefully rolled closer and stretched out his arm.

'I'm sitting up.'

'*Sit up.*'

The telephone always makes an irritating scratching sound when someone holds it in one hand and presses it against wrinkled sheets as he tries to haul himself up and clear his throat to rouse a voice that has just gone to sleep.

'Sven?'

A terraced house in Gustavberg that resembled a home. One of the few, the only one, where Ewert Grens was a regular visitor and felt welcome.

'Are you sitting up properly and listening?'

Sixteen years, working together.

The telephone calls could come at any time. But mostly, any time of night. And the man sitting naked on the hard edge of a bed, fumbling for the light switch, had long since realised he had either to switch jobs or accept.

He had accepted.

'Ready.'

'Good. I want you sitting here. In half an hour.'

He didn't know many numbers off by heart. But dialled the next one as soon as he got the tone.

It kept ringing.

He looked at the clock. Ten to two. He let it ring.

Then he smiled, got up from the desk, went out into the dark Homicide corridor.

He could hear it. A few closed doors down.

Passed the coffee machine, the vending machine, the photocopier, towards the noise that got louder.

Her door was open. The desk lamp was on.

'You're not answering?'

She hadn't heard him coming. A quick glance at someone leaning a heavy body against the doorframe.

'Ewert?'

'It's ringing.'

'I haven't got time.'

'It's me that's calling.'

She looked at the mobile phone, then at her boss.

Now it was her turn to smile.

'It's you that's calling.'

His voice. Something about the tone. Like a pleased parent. If he'd had children, that was.

'Hermansson.'

'Yes?'

'It's the middle of the night.'

That voice again.

'And you're still here.'

'It just happened.'

He wasn't aware that it was noticeable. As it probably wasn't there. Whatever it was that sounded like he was proud.

'How's it going?'

She ran her index finger down the spines of the thick files.

'I've gone through fifty-two open cases with a fine-toothed comb. We can close twelve of them. *No conclusion.* All minor crimes. *Preliminary investigation closed.* We won't get any further.'

She was wearing a uniform, the black one that was more like a boiler suit and was still lying in a box in his office, he hadn't even bothered to unpack it.

'Put the rest to one side.'

He was still standing in the doorway, filling it, as if he'd put it on and it had got stuck.

'Hermansson?'

'You've got a new jacket.'

'*Hermansson?*'

'Yes?'

'Put them aside.'

He turned and was already walking away down the corridor, echoing in the emptiness.

'My office. In twenty-five minutes.'

———

He lay on the faded brown corduroy sofa, fingers against the stripy fabric that no longer ran the same way, as he stared at the ceiling, looking for the newest cracks, he couldn't remember them being so tangled. It had until very recently been a quiet weekend. Ten armed robberies and four rapes. Now he had a pain in the middle of his chest, he couldn't understand it, it was so long ago.

He looked at Sven and Hermansson. Each sitting on a chair, waiting. There was no music in the room, but her voice hung in the air, filled their weariness and confusion. Two more beats, then he would get up, lean in towards the computer, see what he couldn't face seeing.

'Ewert?'

A hand in the air.

'One moment.'

The last verse. She went up half a note. He was convinced he could hear her, there, the refrain one more time. He listened and then sat up.

'Could you open the window, Sven?'

'You've already opened it. Wide.'

'The air is so stuffy in here.'

The laptop was waiting in the middle of the rickety coffee table. Ewert Grens selected the file named ASPSÅS and double clicked, nineteen documents, moved the cursor to one on the top left called CAMERA 4. He clicked again and slid along the thin, black timeline to a sequence of pictures on the stretch that marked 18.10, which according to the governor was the exact time that the search patrol opened the heavy metal door and went into the empty cell with only half a window.

They studied the grainy, jumping image in silence.

A section of green grass. A slice of the asphalted yard.

And – Grens guessed around thirty, maybe even forty metres away – the rectangular, three-storey building that the prison staff called Block D.

He moved the cursor back an hour.

He let the recorded sequence of images age one second at a time, concentrated eyes watching from the corduroy sofa and the plain chairs, one after the other, grainy, jumpy, the grass, the asphalt, the concrete building, a bit later a bird flew past the camera, then another, otherwise all calm.

Perhaps it was a bit lighter, maybe the colours were stronger, or maybe it was just their imagination – a late afternoon should feel good in early September.

There. *There*.

A flash.

Like sparks, or even flames in a cell window, quite far to the left on the first floor of the grey building.

They all leaned closer to the screen without being aware of it.

Fifty-seven seconds.

The grey building, the rows of crossed bars, everything was calm.

*There.*

The same window. Sparks.

'Do you see what I see?'

Ewert Grens had turned his head, he hadn't got an answer, their faces, frozen.

They saw it a third time.

A flash.

Mariana Hermansson nodded, her voice a touch too loud.

'Like ... I don't know ... a welding flame, only more, bigger.'

The solid detective superintendent with a stiff neck and gammy leg threw himself back on the corduroy sofa, sinking deep into what was far too soft.

'So now we know *how*.'

He snorted.

'Now we'll check *when*.'

———

He moved the cursor closer to the long, thin black worm that went across the screen, a peculiar line that decided time and moved the viewer forwards, backwards, even further back, something that had happened recently could reoccur or never have happened.

Cell 2. Unit D1 Left.

It had been empty at 18.10.

There had been sparks from a window at 17.14.

The difference between being locked up and freedom. Prisoner and on the run. Violent, full of hate, classified as dangerous and monitored, or violent, full of hate, classified as dangerous and someone anyone could meet on the street at any moment.

He moved forwards through the seconds that became

minutes, first at normal speed, then twice that, four times, eight times.

Nothing.

No movement, no sparks, not even a bird.

He let time stop by the slightly broader line that marked 18.00, rubbed his bloodshot, tired eyes, then normal speed, second by second.

Just as empty, just as silent.

Perhaps not quite so light, slightly more wind if you looked carefully at the uncut grass that could be seen and the rebellious halyard on the bare flagpole.

A few minutes.

One more.

Now.

An obvious movement to the left of the picture. The same cell window. A head. A person.

Him. It is a man, gradually appearing from the graininess, the fuzz.

Then the movement stopped, the hunched body waits, presses against one side of the barred window.

*You're on your way.*

Ewert Grens looked at the two colleagues he trusted most in the building where he'd spent his entire adult life. Sven Sundkvist and Mariana Hermansson were sitting close together, faces watching a body that was half out, half in.

*You, who don't want to go anywhere, don't want anything.*

He looked at Sven's concentrated eyes, at Hermansson's concentrated eyes and wanted to explain to them that they were watching much more than a body with an unclear outline, that you could build a machine with a cursor that moved time back and forwards, but that what had happened had bloody well happened and that only someone who had been there from the start could know what and why.

*You're on your way, and I know where to.*

This damn unease that he couldn't shake off no matter how hard he tried.

He ran the cursor over the screen back to the folder with nineteen documents, CAMERA 9, the same time from a different angle, from above, installed on the roof of Block D, looking over the edge, straight down.

The empty asphalt.

A bird again, probably a seagull, flying close to the camera lens that watches the plaster façade from above.

*There.*

A blurred body that slowly gets bigger, forcing its way out. Feet in light-coloured shoes on the window sill, arms and hands and fingers around the metal bars, back pressed against the bars and grey concrete.

Thirty seconds. Sixty. Ninety.

Then the picture changes.

In the right hand corner – a warden in uniform, a woman, she's young and on her own, approaching the corner of the building, coming round it.

A strange feeling, watching him waiting while she knows nothing, to be there and not be able to shout, warn her.

He can clearly hear the footsteps that aren't there in the silent film.

He bends his legs, prepares himself.

She passes, doesn't look up, why would she?

So she doesn't notice someone landing behind her, taking two, maybe three steps and raising an arm, hitting her on the neck with great force.

———

Sven Sundkvist leaned back and looked at the older man who was sitting on the worn corduroy sofa, wearing a beige jacket that looked new, with small pieces of plastic still stuck to the top right sleeve and middle of the left shoulder.

Ewert Grens.

His boss, a colleague that few could bear to approach. His intoxicating quickness that so easily tipped over into anger, lashing out, sometimes into cruelty.

A large man who could look so small.

One of the informal powers of the police headquarters, who had spent his whole life with a crutch under each arm: Anni, Siw Malmkvist – an absent wife, a present voice; a past that had never ended but then abruptly did and once he had fallen, he had slowly got to his feet, started to walk on his own, still limping with a gammy leg, but under his own steam, there wasn't anyone to visit every Tuesday any more, no longer a wall of sixties music, not as much fear masked as aggression.

But this, he'd never seen this. Ewert's face – it could perhaps be rage.

Sven looked for the vein on his right temple that should be pulsing, for his mouth that should be twisted, eyes that should be narrowed.

But they weren't there.

This, this rage was like sorrow.

Sven Sundkvist had a sudden urge to lean forwards again, touch the cheek that he had never been near, the person that no one was allowed to touch.

———

'She's just a thing.'

The mouth that wasn't twisted had raised its voice.

'A pawn for negotiation, something to exert pressure with.'

The temple that wasn't pulsing was flushed red.

'Do you see? For him, from now on, there . . . *there* when he hits her . . . from now on she's just something he can harm, destroy, cast aside.'

The eyes that weren't narrowed, raged.

Ewert Grens had said nothing when the piece of metal was pressed against her throat and when it cut deep into the back of her thigh and when she fell to the ground in pain and was forced back up and used as a shield.

He had moved the cursor back, studied the sequence again, and now, now he screamed.

A hand slammed the coffee table.

Then he opened a new file on the screen – ÖSTERÅKER, twenty-two documents, CAMERA 2. Another prison and the security camera on the drive up to the main gate. He froze the picture when a large white car passed at high speed at 18.44.

'How many can you see?'

Sven studied the grainy faces.

'Three.'

'And you?'

Hermansson nodded.

'Three.'

He hit out again. The plastic casing on the computer. Sufficiently hard for a small, but obvious crack.

'One person is missing.'

Ewert Grens pointed at the picture.

'She's already lying there. In the boot.'

Finger pointing at the screen, at the back of the white car.

'Something that will soon be thrown away.'

———

Sven Sundkvist looked at it again. The face he didn't recognise.

That morning a year ago, when Ewert had crawled around, sweaty, on his knees on the hard office floor and packed away cassettes, photos, a cassette player, he had stood up and broken a thirty-year-long dance with his arms around nothing. He slept less often on the sofa, sometimes laughed in a way that was too loud but that sounded natural, and had in recent months even done something that no other detective superintendent had ever considered, he regularly squeezed himself into a seldom used uniform and, of his own choice, went on the beat with newly qualified policemen, through the intoxicated, dirty, frayed Stockholm nights. He occasionally swapped the private loneliness that had been his own for so long for conversations with young women and men whom he didn't know and who had just started out on the journey that he thought he had long since completed.

It was connected with this change.

The anger that was like sorrow.

––––––

'He assaulted and threatened someone.'

A young woman who faced the bastards every day so that others wouldn't need to.

'Stabbing and kidnapping.'

A young woman who took responsibility for those who didn't belong.

'He . . .'

Ewert Grens's voice cracked when he shouted, he lowered it to almost a whisper.

'. . . like a piece of meat. She's not a person. No one he knows. For Christ's sake, she could have been out there drinking caffè latte with all the others. Meat! Until he throws her aside and looks for someone else he doesn't know and for that very reason can tear them apart.'

––––––

Grens looked at the alarm clock standing on his desk between the telephone and one of the piles of ongoing investigations. The young woman who was called Julia Bozsik had been taken hostage at exactly eighteen oh five. Forty minutes later, she was lying locked in the boot when the escape car passed camera number two that was installed on the driveway up to Österåker prison.

If she was alive.

That was eight hours ago.

*If she was alive.*

---

His large body back and forth in the room that felt cramped without music to hide the sound of restless feet on a tired floor and open hands on ulcerated walls. He had continued to open document after document, different angles and distances and time intervals, then stopped at what was called CAMERA 7, Österåker prison's high red-painted wall seen at an angle from the front, clear focus on the upper corner.

A face that stared straight at him.

Ewert Grens had studied the neck and back standing on the concrete that was supposed to keep him in, far below the shadow of someone kneeling by the inner fence. The neck and back had been on guard, that was obvious, the powerful gun in his hands when he turned and aimed at the lens. Such a proud smile, as if he was posing, for a second like every picture of young gang members that filled every mobile phone seized in connection with every criminal investigation, always photographed by another gang member, with their logo on the front of a black hoodie, someone who was eighteen, waving one hand in the air while he held death in the other, every time the same weapon, the same hate.

Unmasked. Smiling.

Ewert Grens closed his eyes, took a deep breath, looked at the face on the screen one more time.

The gestures, stature, features.

He looked just the same.

He was even the same age.

As his father.

---

You're standing there laughing. Without a mask. You want to be seen, you've succeeded. When you rob an inner-city bank and drive around in a shiny BMW the next day. When you rob a jewellers' shop in one of the centres in one of the suburbs and then drive around in another one. If we can't prove it. If we know, but don't have the witnesses, the weapon. You drive slowly past the police station and you park in the wrong place and you're visible and you've succeeded. And when this image spreads in a few days' time, journalists, the prison service, the police, when you smile and shoot at the camera on a prison wall and some of us choose to show it, you will have succeeded a little bit more.

Because there is no yesterday and tomorrow.

Because you are not on your way, anywhere.

---

The obvious crack in the middle of the computer's casing, Ewert Grens had hit it hard and when he grabbed the screen and turned it, the gap seemed to grow, even longer.

The last file. The third and final prison.

STORBODA.

He selected two pictures.

CAMERA 14. The white car drives up to the prison that has a high fence with rolls of barbed wire on top, instead of a wall. Three men get out and start to run towards the fence when one of them, the driver, stops by the boot, punches it and shouts something.

Grens froze the picture, zoomed in, his mouth in close-up.

'She's lying in there.'

The detective superintendent rewound the sequence and they all saw the same hand once again, the other side of the boot, communicating with someone who not long ago opened his door if he wanted to piss and locked it again when it was time to go to bed, but was now lying there and had to listen.

'She's still alive.'

CAMERA 18. The white car leaving the driveway to the prison, accelerating and then stopping abruptly. *I hate you.* The one driving leans out of his window, turns to the camera and holds up the automatic in one hand, shoots at the building for five seconds. *I hate this fucking place.* Ewert Grens froze the picture again, paused on a face that was eighteen and had the sort of power that only those who have never had power can have. *I could have killed you.* And the sort of control only those who have never had control can have. *If I'd wanted.*

———

A frozen face.

He recognised it. He didn't recognise it.

Every step a person takes changes them. Every action, every thought has a consequence.

Whether what I do is right. Or wrong.

Ewert Grens scrolled down the picture on the screen, the mouth that was shouting something, the eyes that didn't see.

He knew it. He had always known it.

Every intervention a policeman makes will have consequences. Every intervention he himself had ever made, makes or would make, would have consequences.

It wasn't his job to assess them, to weigh them up, try to understand how long the consequences would last.

Not even now.

In front of a frozen face that he almost recognised.

———

'At eighteen twelve the duty guard called on all available units, twenty-three patrols, to come to Aspsås prison.'

He had seen it all before.

'Redirected them to Österåker prison at eighteen forty-six.'

Just as all of them had seen it all before.

'Redirected them again to Storboda prison at nineteen twenty-seven.'

The escape from a cell was reminiscent of Popescu's escape at the end of the eighties.

'Three break-outs, five prisoners.'

The escape from Österåker was a copy of Maiorana's escape from Kumla prison fifteen years before.

'All – and we're certain of this – members of what was previously called Råby Warriors and now is called Ghetto Soldiers. And apart from that . . .'

And this one, Grens looked at the frozen face that still filled the computer screen and the driveway up to Storboda prison, planned and executed step by step like the escape from Norrtälje prison a year or so ago.

'. . . we know nothing.'

He pointed at the paused picture sequence, leaned in towards the computer and pressed play again, STORBODA and CAMERA 18 and a young man laughing as he fired with a big black gun in his hand.

The last picture they had.

In a couple of hours they would have access to the traffic movements, moment to moment, through the evening and night from all the speed cameras in the area. And a couple of hours after that they would have the first general overview of observations of the older Mercedes and the five young men who had already been spotted all over half of Sweden as well as a couple of places in Finland and some others in Denmark and Norway.

Ewert Grens let the sequence of an empty road run for image after image, a bicycle that passed in the distance where it met a bigger road, several white or light-coloured birds, maybe a hare.

The last picture they had. He paused there and put the computer down on the floor.

A peculiar feeling.

Just over a year ago, he had chased another shadow. A criminal who had been recruited by the Swedish police to infiltrate organised crime and who as part of this work had prepared, down to the finest detail, for his arrest so that he could get *in* to Aspsås maximum security prison. And when he had done that, when he was *in*, he had an exact plan of what he wanted to do, his final destination.

This – the exact opposite.

Ewert Grens was going to chase shadows again. A criminal again. But this time, someone who had planned, down to the finest detail, how to get *out* of Aspsås maximum security prison. And once he had done that, once he was *out*, Grens was absolutely sure that he had no plan whatsoever and no idea of where he was going, other than back to where he had always been.

So alike.

So incredibly unlike.

'Aspsås prison, Österåker prison, Storboda prison.'

The detective superintendent had moved his cumbersome body over to the desk and the map he had taped onto the wall between the two windows.

'They're not here.'

His hand over a green and blue area to the north of Stockholm municipality.

'And they're not in Finland, Norway or Denmark. They're not in southern or northern Sweden.'

It was crooked, the map, as if he'd been in a hurry when he hung it up, as if he didn't care. He stood in front of it and looked at Sven Sundkvist and Mariana Hermansson with temples that weren't pulsing and a mouth that wasn't twisted.

'They won't even reach the forest or water.'

The hand moved in towards the grey area on the map that indicated inner city and roads, carried on down.

'They only know asphalt.'

His bent fingers over south Botkyrka: Tumba and Tullinge, over north Botkyrka: Norsborg, Alby, Fittja. And the small area squeezed between them, closest to the E4: Råby.

'And I know where they're heading.'

THE CAPITAL WAS always most beautiful at rest, a couple of hours into the dark and a few before daybreak. These days he seldom went to sleep before then, the voices in the Homicide corridor had to fall silent, the running around down in the courtyard between various parts of the building that housed the different police organisations had to die down, only then did he dare let loose the thoughts that were conducive to sleep. There had been another time, he had been young and she had been young and they had chosen to get up at this hour, she had forced him to walk close to her through the sleeping city streets that were waiting for first light, and her face had been soft and he had kissed her cheeks and she had laughed a lot and sometimes he had laughed too, a hollow sound that was more energy than anything else. Her hand, Anni's hand, he could still feel it – it wasn't bewildered and damp any more, but warm, and he knew that she wasn't there, he knew that.

'Hermansson?'

'Yes?'

'Drive faster.'

Detective Superintendent Ewert Grens was sitting in the back of one of City Police's civilian cars, Sven in front in the passenger seat, Hermansson in the driver's seat – they had their places and sat in silence in anticipation of what had always been filled by music, his music. They had listened to Siw Malmkvist's voice and lyrics from the sixties for so long that they had never really learnt how to talk to each other in a car and now it was too late to start. Grens glanced over at the glove compartment to the right of the dashboard – close to one of Sven's arms. He could ask him. In fact, he could even order him. It would be so easy. He knew that there were still two cassettes in there, alongside the ice scraper and the car manual. Right there. The two that had never been packed away and forgotten and that called to him every time they sat together in silence, compilations that he'd made himself, photos that he'd taken himself and cut out and glued on. It was as if they couldn't come out, as if they couldn't be stuffed into the boxes in the store that would never be opened again. Every journey in the car, he sat in the back seat leaning forwards and staring at the bloody compartment, didn't dare sit in the front, didn't trust his hand, itching to open it. Sven probably knew that they were in there and Hermansson probably knew that they were there too, but neither of them said anything, they could just lie there, as a part and confirmation of something he'd left behind.

'Hermansson, faster.'

Dark beyond the regularly spaced streetlights on the E4 and dazzling lights from the occasional car passing in the opposite direction, the girl who was called Julia Bozsik was out there, somewhere. She'd had a sharp object pressed into the back of her thigh and then her throat at 18.12 on the timeline. One and a half hours later she was locked in the white car boot, the last picture they had. Ewert Grens looked over at the dashboard, an avoidance tactic, the clock beside the glove compartment, more than nine hours had passed.

Västberga, Fruängen, Segeltorp, the sleeping southern suburbs.

Nine hours.

In his thirty-seven years in the police he'd been involved in eighteen kidnappings and hostage-takings – police cadet, police constable, detective sergeant, detective superintendent – and had learned that every hour lost between someone's freedom being snatched and someone else being caught was an hour closer to death. Every time they had failed, not found the hostage alive, more than twelve hours had passed from the time of the disappearance to finding them.

The dashboard clock again. Quarter past three. Two hours and fifty-five minutes left.

'Hermansson?'

'Yes?'

'*Even* faster.'

The eight-lane motorway, Bredäng, Sätra, Skärholmen, so familiar, he had driven along it every day, to and from, in those years at the start of the nineties. Someone had just opened the door to a world the police authorities had thus far only observed from the E4, one hand on the wheel and the other winding up the window after spitting at the ugly buildings that didn't belong. Opened it and discovered networks that were gang primers and weapon depots that were control and power, already greater than its counterweight, and a police station that had been built and then abandoned and was being built up again and he'd been more or less ordered there to create and establish a witness protection programme, the way out.

Hermansson drove faster until the streetlights seemed to blend together and he leaned back.

Witness protection.

The only solution for those who wanted to jump ship. The way out in exchange for a protected identity, a new environment, no contact.

He hadn't been there since. Eighteen years ago. He'd done the same as all the others, looked at the high-rise blocks that were so ugly from a distance as he accelerated, never stopped, never got out, gone back.

Strange. How everything just carries on. How everything always carries on.

He started.

That light.

He hadn't heard the noise of the helicopter three hundred

metres above, but the light, the bright search light that came from somewhere under the flying machine was now sweeping the ground and passing cars. And suddenly became another flashing blue light.

Hermansson braked as hard as she could. They rolled slowly onto a well-lit stage.

Ewert Grens glimpsed a metal barrier across four of the lanes, southbound, counted nine, ten, eleven uniformed police with automatic weapons in their hands and stun grenades and tear gas on the belts round their waists. One of them pointed the shiny muzzle of a gun at the car, another moved towards them, torch in hand.

'Pull into the side.'

Mariana Hermansson steered towards the only opening in the metal barrier, the right hard-shoulder.

'Drive through. Then stop.'

The rotating blue light.

Grens wiped away the condensation from the side window to see three cars and a police van in front of two motorbikes.

'Let us through.'

A hand had knocked on the window by the driver and Hermansson hadn't even had time to turn round. Ewert Grens had already wound his window half down.

'*Now.*'

The bulletproof vest, the overalls, the helmet, and even more light from under the long barrel of the gun.

'Don't you point that at me.'

'You'll have to wait your turn.'

'And please move to one side so we can get past. You're stand-ing in the way.'

The bulletproof vest and overalls and helmet remained close, in fact took another step forwards, shone the light in the detec-tive superintendent's face.

'Can I ask you to step out of the car?'

Sven Sundkvist stretched in the passenger seat, turned round and spoke for the first time since they left the garage at Kronoberg.

'Ewert . . .'

Just one word. There were no more. Grens pushed open the back door and was careful to stand directly opposite the policeman with the light and automatic weapon.

*If she's still alive.*

'We've got two hours and fifty minutes left.'

'Excuse me?'

'Let us through.'

'ID.'

The sharp beam of light in his face again. The detective superintendent who was gold command for the entire operation pulled a fat, almost defiant, wallet out of one of his new jacket's many inner pockets that were small and tight for his large, slightly bent fingers. The policeman in the bulletproof vest and helmet took it and rifled through the contents inside the brownish leather, then held the square plastic cards in the beam of the now lowered torch.

'Grens?'

'Yes.'

'Ewert Grens?'

The detective superintendent took great care not to look at him when he got back into the car, closed the door and asked Hermansson to start the engine, to leave the place.

Not until the vehicle started to move, and then he wound down the window again.

'It was in fact me who gave the orders for all this.'

He nodded at the bulletproof vest and helmet.

'And you . . . you're doing a good job.'

Hermansson picked up speed, Vårby Gård, Vårberg, Hallunda, Ewert Grens leaned forwards again.

'National alert. Road blocks. Two helicopters. Two boats. Six dog units. Fifty-eight cars.'

He waved his hand at the windscreen.

'But it doesn't matter.'

And he pointed towards the motorway exit and the high-rise flats looming out of the dark.

'They're already there.'

———

The road into Råby narrowed where the metro tracks met the first bus stop, a sharp right turn, a sharp left turn and the long walls of concrete on both sides, covered in graffiti, colours sprayed in layer upon layer to hide even more greyness.

'Here.'

A cycle path that became a pavement right beside the road.

'Park here. Hermansson, you and I will walk the rest. Fifteen minutes from here. And you, Sven, change places and get behind the wheel.'

Sven Sundkvist looked at his boss in the rear-view mirror.

'I'm not staying here.'

Grens had opened the door and started to get out, when he put a hand on Sven's shoulder.

'How old is Jonas?'

'Sorry?'

'Your son. How old is he?'

'Thirteen.'

'Right.'

'Right?'

'I don't have any children. Hermansson doesn't have any children.'

The hand on his shoulder, Sven Sundkvist felt the weight of it, it wasn't very often that Ewert Grens touched other people.

'So, you stay here, Sven.'

The face in the rear-view mirror, the wrinkles, the bald crown, moved to get out of the car for a second time.

'We're not to go in, Ewert. Not yet. Not anywhere in Råby.

And if and when we do . . . not without protection. That was an order.'

'I've lost all I can lose.'

Grens's hand left his shoulder, Sven Sundkvist felt lighter, the touch which had been so circumspect had held him, weighed him down.

'There's nothing a snotty-nosed eighteen-year-old can take from me.'

———

They walked side by side down the straight asphalt path, past the lower blocks that all looked identical and the slightly higher blocks that all looked identical, a few playgrounds with sleeping swings and climbing frames that had long since lost most of their blue colour, a football pitch, underfoot now gravel and earth, a school, a youth club, and over there advertisements for food shops in a small shopping centre and beyond that, even higher blocks that all looked identical.

'He's escaped fourteen times before.'

Maybe it was getting a bit lighter, late-summer warmth, Mariana Hermansson looked up at the large man who limped and sometimes lost his balance, but rather than slow down, he increased his stride and was therefore sweating profusely, uneven breath in the windless still.

'From foster homes, children's homes, young offenders' institutions, prison.'

The shiny face, the jacket that looked new, eyes that flashed a different kind of anger – she couldn't recall ever having seen him move this fast on foot.

'And every time . . . here. The only place he can bear to be.'

A sudden step to the left, his stiff leg lost its footing and he fell towards her. She raised her arm, ready to take hold of his, when he waved it away in irritation, he'd regained his balance, he didn't need help.

She looked at someone who was limping, in a rush.

The detective superintendent who was always in his office at City Police, who couldn't stand to be anywhere else; anywhere else he was just an overweight, balding older man, but in that building he had a name that meant something.

Råby. Or City Police.

Young and hunted. Or older and hunter.

Two worlds. Or the same.

*The only place he can bear to be.*

'Eight thousand flats, Hermansson. Ninety-eight per cent rental.'

He stopped and wiped his forehead with the sleeve of his jacket.

'Twelve thousand inhabitants. Thirty-two per cent leave school as soon as they can without the grades to go on to higher education. Twenty-seven per cent unemployment. Fifteen per cent early retirement.'

Breathing heavily between each clipped word.

'If she's still alive.'

Eight thousand flats. As many storage rooms in the attics and cellars.

'Sorry?'

Ewert Grens looked about, surrounded by high-rise blocks with no colour.

'If she's alive, Hermansson.'

---

When he got closer, he saw that what had partially burnt down was a nursery school, and behind the bicycle shed lay a blackened, sooty moped. Grens had already identified at least two piles of equally sooty tyres and a fence that lay half in ashes. Fragments of pleasure and security. Of wood and metal and rubber. Of community.

'Ewert—'

Ewert Grens waved at Hermansson, she was to stop there by the building, the first one with seven storeys. His phone was ringing and he opened it with clumsy fingers.

Wilson.

'Ewert, we had an agreement.'

'Yes.'

'You're breaking it.'

The road block. He'd got out of the car and in the beam from a small light attached to the barrel of a loaded MP5 Heckler & Koch had shown his ID.

They'd reported it.

'Ewert, we agreed that no one would go in before we were absolutely certain that they were, really were, in Råby.'

*You were there, Erik. You and me, we were there, back then.*

'We had an agreement not to warn those who need to be warned.'

*You stood beside me, Erik. You know where he's heading.*

'They're here. They don't have anywhere else.'

'Ewert—'

'And I don't have much time. I need information. Two hours and thirty-two minutes left.'

———

Tens of thousands of square windows with red and green frames.

Ewert Grens stood on the asphalt path that cut straight through between the buildings with identical windows and knew that they were waiting in one of them, maybe they were taking a cautious peep outside right now, watching the two civilian-clad police officers.

He was aware of the unequivocal order that prevented police officers from going into Råby alone, without back-up. That right now he was exposing not only himself but also Hermansson to extreme danger.

Two hours and twenty-four minutes.

He had no choice. They were here. And those who knew where they were, were too.

'Hermansson.'

He pointed at something, perhaps her feet.

'You stay here.'

Mariana Hermansson looked at him, at the buildings behind him, at the square further back with empty benches and over-turned bicycle shelters, and further away, a deserted platform between two metro lines, and if she stretched up, a glimpse of the motorway exit.

'No.'

'To carry on where we're heading is my responsibility alone.'

He had seen her annoyed, even angry before, her eyes like those he remembered in another face long ago that had been the same age, and worn the same uniform, and disappeared, no longer existed.

'What exactly are you saying?'

He had liked it. He still did.

Someone demanding.

'You know, I grew up in a place like this. You know that. Rosengård, Malmö, what happened there, Jesus, Ewert, Stockholm, you're years behind.'

She stood in front of him with no intention of staying there, and for a moment they were both back in the corridors of City Police and the picture from four years ago of twenty silent, chemically wired children sitting on the floor, each with a brown bag on their lap, who hadn't said a word until Hermansson had hunkered down beside one of them and whispered something in Romanian. For a long time, he was ashamed that he'd heard and had forgotten that she'd told him more than once about growing up somewhere that was so different from anything he himself had experienced, he was still ashamed that he couldn't manage his own life, and even less care about others.

'I don't care, Hermansson. You're staying here.'

She gripped the hand that was pointing at her, or maybe it was her shoes it was pointing at, forced it down, to one side.

'Look around.'

He didn't. High-rises. Asphalt. He had already seen it all. High-rises. Asphalt.

'I can read this better than you can, Ewert. And I'm more protected here than you will ever be.'

She had grabbed his hand, forced it away.

Someone who demanded something.

Ewert Grens smiled, perhaps, he wasn't sure.

She had been sitting in her office when he went to look for her in the middle of the night. People who do that don't need to mix with other people who talk too much and tell you that you're playing your music too loud, they don't need to celebrate Christmas Eve or New Year's Eve or even birthdays which come round with such regularity, because he or she is doing something important and that means that he or she can carry on being alone. She had stood up and he hadn't needed to explain, she had changed out of her uniform into her own clothes, known how high-rises like these, asphalt like this, worked.

His smile, the one that was almost proud.

───────────

A seven-storey building like all the others, rows of even darker windows, balconies with alternate orange and blue doors. Grens tilted his head back, three floors up, somewhere in the middle. The only window with lights on.

They had stopped by the edge of the huge car park that separated the building called Råby Allé 67 from the others. About half of the clearly marked spaces were empty, the other half was a long row of older, well-used cars.

With two exceptions.

The detective superintendent sighed.

Every bloody investigation. So unbelievably predictable. So unbelievably fucking wearisome that they always lived up to the preconceptions, as if they intentionally reinforced the stereotype until they became it. I am a gangster. I put on my gangster costume so you'll know that I'm a gangster because then I look how you think I should look. Even the same bloody car models. This one, the black shiny one that was parked nearest, Audi R8, the sort that people used to escape the police, four-wheel drive, powerful engine. And the one parked beside it, a silver Mercedes CLK 500, the sort that successful criminal role models bought with cash and then drove around in while everyone else admired it and longed for it.

'Sven?'

Ewert Grens had gone over to the gleaming, silver car. With one hand leaning heavily on the bonnet, he looked up into the lightening dark, in his other hand a mobile phone.

'Yes?'

'Are you still sitting in the car?'

'Yes.'

'Go to the Driver and Vehicle Licensing Agency.'

He could picture his colleague waiting in the car, a slim, middle-aged man who now undid the safety belt and leaned over towards the passenger seat in order to reach the computer on the dashboard.

He imagined he could even hear him pressing the three buttons.

'OK?'

'Look up BGY 397 and . . . hang on a moment . . . GZP 784.'

More tapping.

He wondered whether the slim body was still leaning over, or whether it had moved over and was sitting up straight in the passenger seat.

'Mercedes, silver, 2013 model. Current owner, Gabriel Milton. And . . .'

'Yes?'

'. . . Audi, black, 2013 model. Current owner, Gabriel Milton. Previous owner, Leon Jensen.'

Hand still heavy on the shiny bonnet.

He was standing on the other side of the car park, facing the block of flats.

'You don't get it, do you?'

Hermansson nodded at the two cars.

'That this is what it's all about?'

Grens shook his head, rapped the metal with his hand.

'No. I don't get it. You rob a bank. You don't want to be suspected. You don't want the police to see. And . . . then . . . *then* you go out and buy something like this, something shiny for eight hundred thousand. No. I don't fucking get it.'

'Because the benefits of looking rich, Ewert, successful, far outweigh the risk.'

She stood between the two cars that cost as much as she earned in five years.

'Three things – be seen, heard and acknowledged. You need it. I need it. We all need it. It's human. Otherwise we don't function. At all. But here . . . just running around robbing banks and getting loads of money you can't show to anyone . . . that's of no interest. But what *is* interesting, however, is showing that you're successful. And to do that, you need shiny trophies like this. And you show them off and don't give a damn about a detective superintendent with a flat on Sveavägen who doesn't get it. Seen, heard, and acknowledged, Ewert. That's all.'

He rapped the metal of the bonnet once again and started to walk across the car park towards the seven-storey building and a window in the middle where there was still light. Flats that had been just as grey nineteen years ago, he had spent a lot of time in several of them, slowly, gradually herding motivated gang members, one by one, into the witness protection programme and afterwards been so pleased with himself – after all, he had defined what was to be seen as a one-off incident, something that should be observed, but that was part of a passing phase.

He hadn't fully understood the extent of it, the impact. That it would grow, and was still growing.

Ewert Grens nodded to Mariana Hermansson, beside him in front of the dark building and the window that broke the darkness with its light, and they went in different directions along the asphalt that led on to a strip of grass round the back; they met again but still didn't say anything, they didn't need to, another window with the light on up there, the same flat, on the second floor, somewhere in the middle.

The lift in the stairwell wasn't working and Grens panted loudly as he tried to keep up with Hermansson, climbing the stairs that were too shallow, out onto the balcony, the warm dawn air on his cheeks and brow.

He stopped.

The door was waiting, about fifteen steps away.

Name *Gabriel Milton* Personal ID number *931017-0015*

In a search of the police authorities' database just before they left Kronoberg, Ewert Grens had got thirty-two hits when he opened the Criminal Intelligence Database, *observed at Hötorget twenty minutes after an armed robbery of Securitas cash-in-transit delivery at Kungsgatan*, then looked through the Suspect Identification and Recognition Database and got a total of eighteen hits, *questioned in connection with suspected illegal possession of firearms*, and finally eight hits in the police criminal records, *major theft, §4 Chapter 8, assaulting a police officer, §1 Chapter 17, aggravated assault, §5 Chapter 3*. Via three computer screens he had met the teenager who had recently been behind that door.

'We can't go in, Ewert.'

Ear to the door, silence.

'Ewert, right now, no one is suspected of a crime.'

He pressed the doorbell that didn't work, then kicked the orange surface and took a step back.

'And that is why we don't have a search warrant. Are you listening, Ewert? We *cannot* go in.'

'She's lying in a boot. I don't need any damn papers, I need information.'

He kicked the door again, a bit higher up this time.

'If we go in it . . . it would be trespassing.'

He pointed at the name on the letter box – SANTOS, written in spiky letters on a scrap of paper.

'The lad called Gabriel Milton is not paying any rent. He doesn't have a contract. He doesn't have tenure. Someone called Santos does. We're not the ones trespassing, Hermansson. He is.'

Grens had his black gloves in the outer pockets of his jacket, he pulled them out and put them on. Mariana Hermansson saw him do it, opened a holster strapped to her chest and pulled out a gun, pulled the slide back with her thumb and index finger until she was certain that the bullet was ready in the chamber.

'That's not necessary. They're not here.'

He pressed down the door handle. Locked. He balled his hand, moved slightly to the left and hit the oblong window between the door and concrete wall, put his hand through past the jagged edges and turned the lock.

There was only one light on and Ewert Grens walked into a hall, empty but for something leaning up against the wall that was shiny and had rows of identical small white pearls round the edge. He lifted it up, weighed it, a shoehorn.

'They won't be coming back here. But we're looking for information, anything that might show where or how members who are free might help members on the run. If she's alive, Hermansson, we have to know.'

Grens walked towards the kitchen, but signalled to her that she should stay where she was by the partially broken entrance.

A table, some chairs. That was all.

He opened the fridge, lots of empty bottles, some half full, two unopened. Coke and beer. He turned them upside down and emptied the contents in the sink and then left them there, opened the larder and the only thing to be found there was a packet of wine gums. He emptied that as well, no red or green left. He pulled out drawers of cutlery and plastic bags, opened a cupboard above the cooker and emptied a bag of sugar, flicked through a pile of serviettes, lifted the lid on the coffee machine, ran his fingers through a packet of pasta and unscrewed the bulbs in the ceiling lights.

Nothing.

Ewert Grens sighed, loitered by the sink and the bottles – they weren't even old enough to carry the content of those bottles out of the off licence. It was so easy to forget, how young these people who had lived as adults so long actually were.

He carried on into the bedroom, lifted up the pillows and the covers. A big knife slipped in under the mattress, handle like a knuckleduster with sharp points, a long blade that was partially serrated. He reached in under the bed and found a white tube in a ball of dust, *Hydrocortisone-Urea*, sniffed it, smelt of nothing. He got up and went back towards the door but then stopped halfway, poked the red rug on the lino floor with the tip of his shoe. It was thick, soft and didn't belong. He guessed it probably cost more than everything else in the flat put together. He smiled, the lonely pearl-studded shoehorn in the hallway and the thick, soft hundred-thousand kronor rug in here, they were from the same burglary from a large house that wasn't in Råby.

The sitting room.

Empty beer cans, some rogue peanuts and full ashtrays on a sticky glass table. Pizza boxes stacked in a half-metre tower. A corner sofa with a blue fabric cover that was big enough for three sleeping bodies. He lifted up one cushion at a time, pulled off the dirty-smelling covers and turned them inside out, in all five square pieces of brown hash fell out, he guessed about thirty grams each.

Down there, spread out along the bottom of the sofa, gold- and silvered-coloured coins. Grens picked them up, rubbed them with his fingertips, let them rest in his palm. KRONOR – fencer's currency. EURO – drug dealer's currency. And BAHT – for the Thai villages where every small group went to practise their shooting.

Every time the same world came out of trouser pockets like these.

He was heading back towards the hall when he went closer to the flat-screen TV, eighty inches on the sitting room wall, long high loudspeakers on either side.

'Sven?'

He again struggled to take his phone out of one of his jacket pockets, of which there seemed to be so many that trapped his searching hands.

'Yes?'

'Are you still there?'

'Yes.'

'This time I want you to look in CRS.'

Sven Sundkvist stretched over towards the passenger seat again, the computer on the dashboard and the crime reporting system.

'Ewert?'

'A TV. Model number 47LG4000-ZA. Serial number 906WRGX40359.'

Ewert Grens was panting in the way he did on the few occasions he walked up the stairs. Sven guessed he was bending down, squatting in the small gap between the plastic casing and the wall, trying to read the small numbers on the back of the TV screen.

'Reported stolen. Break-in at SIBA's warehouse in Kungens Kurva at the beginning of June. One of a total of one hundred and four items that were reported stolen in the same incident.'

Grens examined both loudspeakers, a Blu-ray player, two computers. Different model numbers and different serial numbers, but the same answer.

He hung up and pushed over the pile of DVD cases that were leaning up against a chair leg. Violence, pornography, pornography, violence, violence, violence. And, he picked it up, he'd read correctly, a cartoon, eight instalments of Aladdin at the bottom of the pile.

So big, and yet so small.

———

He breathed in the humid, late-summer air from an evaporating, but still all-enveloping dark.

A hallway, a kitchen, a bedroom, a sitting room.

They had lacked knowledge when they opened the door and they knew not a bean more when they closed it. Ewert Grens stuck his hand in through the broken windowpane, as before. He reached over to the lock, turned it. Her eyes on his neck, he could feel them, she hadn't changed.

'He *had* no tenure. So, he was trespassing.'

She looked at him, didn't answer.

'And according to police orders, we have a duty as police officers to intervene in the event of any ongoing crime.'

Maybe he smiled.

'In other words, we were forced to do it. Or are you going to stand here and hinder a police order, Hermansson?'

They started to walk back the same way, but not as fast, and when they got to the big car park, Grens pulled a heavy key ring from one of his trouser pockets, rifled through long and short and narrow and wide keys without finding anything sufficiently sharp. Hand down in his pocket again and he swapped the keys for a spare gun magazine, gave a satisfied nod when his fingertips tried the hard edges and then there was a scratching noise as a straight line appeared first on the left side of the silver car and then the right side of the black car, the colour missing, the kind of sound that gives you a sense of power for a moment.

'The trade-in value, Hermansson.'

He looked at his silent colleague.

'It falls after a while, you know.'

They carried on through the high-rise blocks that wouldn't wake up for a few hours yet, but Ewert Grens remained in the flat that those who had the information they needed would not return to.

A knife with a knuckleduster. Some lumps of hash. A rug worth a hundred thousand. An animated Aladdin film. A pile of Thai money.

Perhaps he knew a bit more. He sighed. He knew nothing.

That could be the summary of every gang member he had ever met and would meet.

'Erik?'

The light phone pressed hard to his ear, Erik clearing his throat, he could hear it.

'Yes?'

Half an hour ago, Ewert Grens had hung up while his boss was still speaking.

'Where are you?'

And no one likes to be left hanging in an electronic void.

'County Communications Centre, Ewert. Somewhere that's *outside* Råby.'

He waited again. Wilson's voice had been irritated, but less irritated than it could have been. Ewert Grens might think and say a lot about his new boss, the sort of thing that shouldn't be thought or said about anyone, but he had to give it to him, he was professional, bigger than wounded pride.

'Eighteen years ago, Erik. And this is the continuation. Can you even begin to understand it?'

Someone standing in a vast room, the size of a football pitch, surrounded by computers and screens and staff, the only one who could possibly imagine how it felt, what it was that could hook you, drive you on, give you no rest.

'Ewert . . . what is it you want?'

His voice already different, the irritation over a conversation that had been cut dead had now become the resolve to succeed in a common goal.

'Julia Bozsik. The prison warden.'

Grens was standing in darkness that would shortly be dispelled by a dawn that was already starting some way off, another world.

'Yes?'

'Leon Jensen. Alexander Eriksson. Marko Bendik. Reza Noori. Uros Koren.'

'What about them?'

She was lying in a car boot. And they had put her there. It wasn't just one hunt. It was two.

'The dog units, Erik. And the helicopters. And the patrols on land and sea. They have to continue looking, the getaway car is out there somewhere!'

He looked around. The high-rises, the concrete. And eight thousand flats.

'And send as many here. You know as well as I do, Erik, the others are here!'

'You've already got everyone.'

'I want more people here!'

'You've emptied the entire county.'

'Then ring Uppsala! Ring Eskilstuna, Nyköping! Empty all those bloody counties too!'

'Ewert . . .'

'And then, when you've done that, I want you to wake and send the whole riot squad! Stop every car on the road to and from Råby, identify each person in every seat, turn every metal heap inside out!'

'Ewert . . .'

'They'll find more guns, sawn-off shotguns, axes, knives, truncheons, nunchucks, baseball bats than any of them have ever seen before. They should seize them and put it all in a big bloody pile without recording anything. We haven't got time for that. *She* hasn't got time for that!'

Ewert Grens pointed at Hermansson's left wrist, the watch there, and she held it up.

'And when you've done that, send all the transport police! They'll search every flat, every storage room in the attic and the cellar!'

Her watch, small numbers that were hard to read.

But he was certain.

One hour and twenty-seven minutes left.

———

It had started to rain.

Small, light drops that became fat, heavy when they hit the windscreen, a hollow sound that pounded against your head.

'It smelt vaguely of marzipan.'

'I'm sorry?'

'In the flat. It smelt like the taste of marzipan.'

'Really?'

'They've had dynamite there. Very recently.'

———

Sven Sundkvist had continued to drive through the dawn towards Stockholm and Mariana Hermansson had looked for the light halo that always hovered in the sky above the capital, more and more obvious the closer you came.

Marzipan. Dynamite.

Ewert hadn't said any more and they hadn't asked, it wasn't necessary. Someone who carves up a prison warden and escapes from one of Sweden's maximum security prisons and then, holding an automatic, frees other gang members from two other prisons has decided on something, and explosives, more violence more force, was part of all that.

'Ewert?'

They had left the E4 and Essingeleden when the call came.

Hermansson detached the microphone from the radio set and passed it to the back seat.

'Yes?'

'Where are you?'

'Drottningholmsvägen. Approaching Fridhemsplan. Just . . . turned into Hantverkargatan.'

Erik Wilson again. The voice, tension.

'I want you to come here.'

'And I asked you—'

'Now, Ewert.'

This time it was Wilson who hung up and Ewert Grens who was left holding a detached microphone and echoing silence.

They turned into Bergsgatan, still full of parked cars that would soon accompany their owners elsewhere. Sven Sundkvist slowed down and looked for a space that didn't exist.

'Carry on.'

Ewert Grens had a hand round each headrest, pulled his heavy body as far forwards as the two in the front were pulled back and nodded towards a small park with old trees that was squeezed in between the town hall and the eastern entrance to the police headquarters.

'Go up onto the pavement. And then across the grass.'

Sven Sundkvist turned around and looked at his boss.

'It's urgent, Sven. And it's a shortcut.'

Deep tyre tracks on the damp ground, pass card in the slot by the door, into the stone corridor to security and the glass doors, pass card again, next slot.

'Wait.'

Grens took three steps back and pointed at the security phone.

'Call Lars Ågestam.'

The security guard did not point out that it wasn't his job, and that the public prosecutor was in a completely different building on a different switchboard. He knew who was standing in front of him and therefore scrolled methodically through the computer register before dialling a number and passing over the handpiece.

'Ågestam?'

From the very first day they had worked together ten years ago, they had disliked each other. Perhaps loathed, maybe even despised each other. The older, frustrated detective superintendent was everything the younger, formal prosecutor was not.

'Yes?'

'I want a warrant for a house search and to intercept calls.'

They had avoided each other as much as possible and each time they ended up working together on an investigation, as detective superintendents and public prosecutors sometimes do, the contempt had intensified, so that neither of them could be bothered to pretend any more.

'Reasons?'

Until some years ago, when Grens had ordered a sharpshooter to aim at an incarcerated criminal, only to realise that he'd allowed a person who someone else wanted dead to be shot on false grounds, and had turned to the only man he had sworn he would always hate. Late one night he'd opened the door to his flat, the door that he'd never let anyone else through, for Ågestam and asked for his help.

'Absconding. Helping others to escape. Are you writing this down? *Ana Tomas*, Råby Allé 34.'

Sitting together at Ewert Grens's kitchen table, they had come up with grounds to arrest a national police commissioner, a chief superintendent and a secretary of state, and Grens had on a couple of occasions even called the young prosecutor by his first name. But then they'd both felt uncomfortable about the closeness that neither of them wanted and had in some way, without anything being mentioned, agreed that they would never get that close again.

'Crime classification?'

Ewert Grens pulled out a handwritten note from his back trouser pocket, unfolded it and put on his glasses.

'There isn't one yet. Are you writing this down, Ågestam? *Amanda Hansen*, Västra Ringen 102. *Sonja Milton*, Albyvägen 42.'

'Reasonable suspicion?'

Finger on a row of names, documentation from SAGC and PSIU, known addresses where Leon Jensen and Gabriel Milton had been observed.

'Nothing yet. *Deniz Johnson*, Råby Allé 102. *Wanda Svensson*, Råby Allé 114, *Sofia Eriksson*, Råby Backe 1B.'

'Ewert?'

'Yes?'

'To put it politely, you've never made my work any easier. But this . . .'

'I need it.'

'And *I* need a *reason* to justify a warrant. Without that we will not intercept calls nor carry out house searches.'

A hand slammed the glass wall behind the security guard as the red colour from his face spilt down his neck.

'Get up from that damned desk of yours and go over to the window! Look out! What you see there, Ågestam . . . *reality*. I work out there. There's no alternative this time. In Råby, the way things are now, normal surveillance of the addresses won't work.'

A corridor, two flights of stairs, another corridor.

They entered the heart of the police headquarters, the County Communications Centre, a room full of three screens at every desk and walls covered in considerably larger screens – a room that was alive. Every emergency call in Stockholm county came through here, the position of every police car was registered and followed, the security cameras at Zinkensdamm metro station or Sergels Torg or one of the exits from Nynäsvägen, places that existed here the minute anyone wanted to visit them.

Grens, Sundkvist and Hermansson made their way past occupied work stations towards the round table in one of the corners, to Erik Wilson and the chief of staff and then to P1 and P3k and P7. They were doing what Grens probably should also do but never would, drinking coffee and looking at papers and bemoaning the lack of resources in a seemingly never-ending staff meeting, the only purpose of which was to say that it had taken place.

More coffee cups than usual. Empty, half full.

They had been sitting there for twelve hours – evening had turned to night had turned to dawn – but they didn't look tired, that's how it worked, things happened and would perhaps happen, someone else's trauma or anteroom to insanity, it was never anything anyone said, but was the driving force to what became a policeman's prerogative.

'He'll just continue.'

Grens had sat down on the empty chair to the right of his boss.

'And escape from every prison.'

Erik Wilson looked at him. In the way colleagues do when you talk about something that others don't understand.

'He'll carry on . . . in the way he started.'

They had stood beside each other, white doctors' coats over their uniforms. And watched a life being born.

'You said it was urgent.'

Wilson nodded at the wall with ten screens, each one a metre square – deserted motorways with watchful streetlamps, silent buildings that would sleep on for a while yet, others that captured the odd drunk on his way home, cameras that were all installed high up.

'I want you to look at the bottom left.'

An almost black screen.

Faint light somewhere in the background, a narrow asphalted road in the foreground, a couple of low houses if he peered long enough into the dark.

'We got a call from one of the helicopters fourteen minutes ago. And have since downloaded the picture they wanted us to look at.'

Grens moved closer, he didn't want anything between him and the screen.

'Ten hours in the air. They've concentrated their search on the area north of the tolls, the stretch from Aspsås prison all the way to Haga. But it was when they got here that they put in a call.'

The shape of three cars grew out of the dark next to the last single-storey house at the end of a cul-de-sac.

'Söderby. Twenty-three miles north-west of the city centre. They searched the nearby park with a heat camera, the warehouses are linked by the dense undergrowth. Then suddenly it registered faint heat.'

It was still raining heavily, big drops on the camera lens.

'*There*, to be precise. The lighter car.'

He zoomed in again, a big white car became even bigger.

'The boot. Something giving off heat. Something that isn't moving.'

Ewert Grens found it hard to stand still.

A couple of hours earlier. STORBODA. 19.23. CAMERA 14. Three men had got out of a car and started to run. Then the driver had stopped, slammed his hand on the boot, shouted something.

Grens moved in even closer to the wall of screens.

'Can you call the helicopter?'

Three computer screens and a microphone in front of the operator at the desk beside him.

'Yes.'

'I want it from another angle. I want to see the car at an angle from the front.'

'But the heat is registered in the boot.'

'*At an angle from the front.*'

Ewert Grens, Sven Sundkvist, Mariana Hermansson and Erik Wilson followed every movement of the helicopter as the camera moved perspective and the car became clearer in the bright light.

A bit further down. Slightly more to the left.

Until it fell on the bonnet of the car. And the small round metal symbol that Grens had expected to see.

'Mercedes.'

He turned to the operator again.

'I want you to link up to the position map.'

The square screen to the right of the white car on a deserted street become a road system with hundreds of small shining lights, half moving restlessly in different directions, half standing still – the exact position of all patrol cars.

Grens was standing so close that he could touch them, he searched for light spots closest to where the illuminated car was.

There.

Two small lights that indicated two patrol cars, a road block, the intersection E18 and route 267.

'They're too far away.'

His finger on the flat glass to the left, it left a mark on the sensitive electrics.

'She's lying in there and *they're too far away.*'

There.

Another one.

Ewert Grens measured in the air – not even a kilometre. Unit 2319. A motorbike some way down Rotebroleden.

He grabbed the operator's microphone and turned it towards him.

'Two-three-one-nine.'

All that blasted crackling.

'Two-three-one-nine!'

More crackling. And a faint voice.

'Two-three-one-nine. Over.'

'I want you to reroute. One kilometre east. The end of Söderbyvägen. *Now!*'

---

The room that was so full of life suddenly fell silent and work-stations switched to screen-save as hundreds of eyes focused on a wall where the metre-high TV screens were linked up to become part of one enormous image.

A motorbike moving at great speed towards the centre, powerful searchlights concentrating on a stationary white car.

Ewert Grens had a firm grip on the microphone.

'*The boot.* She's been in there for . . . *hurry up* . . . if she's still breathing . . . *force it open now!*'

The helicopter moved closer. The raindrops were even bigger.

Wide reflective strips round wrists, stomach, shins, that scattered the dark when the motorbike driver stopped, opened one of the panniers and took out two long objects.

A spanner. A screwdriver.

With the microphone, Grens pointed at what was happening only three metres from him, and yet, several kilometres away.

'Give him more light!'

The helicopter sank lower, even closer.

A new searchlight was switched on and the white helmet drowned in the bright light as the screwdriver was forced into the lock on the boot and the end knocked hard with the spanner, once, twice, the third time he hit his hand, then again, the fourth time the screwdriver was forced in sufficiently far, the spanner gripped it and turned the point round a full turn; if there had been any sound they would have heard the lock mechanism breaking.

The motorbike officer turned to the camera briefly, as if he was looking at them so he didn't need to feel alone.

Suddenly the picture vanished, dissolved, gone.

The helicopter had tried to get even closer and the ten large screens slid out of focus. The beam of light doggedly focused on the boot while the helicopter pilot angled the camera, turned, zoomed out, turned, turned again.

And slowly the picture cleared.

It was hard to comprehend what it was they could see.

Something dark, quite large, in the middle of the boot. Something that wasn't moving. *Someone* who wasn't moving.

A body resting on its left side. The face turned away. A woman's long hair. Silver tape stuck to her neck.

The police officer looked into the open boot.

And turned around for the second time, towards the camera, he still didn't want to be alone.

HE SEES THE face, the colour of the skin, almost grey. But the sound, it vanishes.

The persistent sound from the helicopter, not many metres above his head, is no longer there.

Of course he sees it. It's there, big and powerful, the wind beating his cheeks, it comes in even closer, but he can't hear it.

He's moving in a world without sound.

He pulls off the tape that hides her lips, puts two fingers into her mouth, pulls something that feels like material out of her throat, grabs hold of her jacket and shirt and trousers, pulls her towards him.

———————

He sits down on the edge of the boot and puts his hand to her face while he waits for the ambulance, his fingertips lightly on her soft skin.

Now he can see her eyes. Now he can hear again. Now he knows.

THE CAR THAT stood parked in the middle of the grass had cut deep tracks in the small, fragile park with no name that linked the eastern entrance of the Kronoberg police headquarters with the city hall. Detective Inspector Sven Sundkvist opened the driver's door and got in.

He was ashamed.

He was, after all, the sort who would be – a hard-won, cultivated lawn, just to gain fifteen seconds.

Hermansson beside him in the passenger seat, he turned the key, started the engine and waited for the man who was never ashamed to get in too.

'I'm driving.'

Ewert Grens stayed standing where he was until Sven had moved.

'From now on, until the end of this bloody investigation, you'll sit in the back.'

Blue light on the roof and rain drumming on the windows and metal as they turned from Drottningholmsvägen towards Tranebergsbron. Grens drove fast, but still put his hand out for the mobile phone that was lying in front of him on the dashboard.

'Where are you?'

'Where I always am.'

Nils Krantz from Forensics who had been around in Kronoberg as long as Ewert Grens.

'I want you to leave your microscope and come to a car boot in Söderby.'

'A car boot?'

'Yes.'

Quick movements in a laboratory that was at once large yet cramped, sinewy hands packing a forensic scientist's tools into a black bag on his way to a dark blue van in the Kronoberg garage.

'Who?'

'A woman.'

'In what state?'

Grens held the wheel tight with his free hand.

'In what state, Ewert?'

'Dead.'

The crown of Tranebergsbron, a metro train on one side of the car and the oncoming traffic on the other, and way below, the choppy water of the Mälaren.

'Dead?'

'Yes.'

'Who certified the death?'

'No one as yet. But someone at the hospital will. Soon.'

Nils Krantz paused, coughed.

'I'll go. To the body.'

'We're on our way to what is presumably a murder scene. Jump in your bloody bus and stop wittering.'

'The body is also a presumed murder scene. That's where we're going, Ewert. *First and foremost.* The car boot will wait for us.'

Ewert Grens slowed down as the car approached the first set of traffic lights at one end of the bridge, a sharp U-turn, then he made another call, this time to the vast room with the big screens, CCC, and ordered a patrol car to wait at the main entrance to the Karolinska hospital.

'Hermansson.'

He turned towards her, then back to keep his eyes on the bridge and the rain and the road.

'You'll be picked up when we get to the hospital. Go out to Söderby and the car. Make sure that it's cordoned off and guarded by uniformed police, that everything else outside is covered until this lousy weather has passed, and that if anything, anything at all, Hermansson, blows away in the wind, that a picture has been taken of it beforehand. I want to know exactly *how* it was lying, *where* it was lying.'

Sven Sundkvist hadn't sat in the back seat for years. It was Ewert's place. The one he normally chose and where he'd stayed ever since the day that the only person he'd ever cared for died, had for ever left her room in a care home for those who couldn't take part in daily life. Now Ewert was sitting in front of him. In the driver's seat. His broad neck, driving fast and erratically, Sven had thought it was lack of practice for the first kilometre, but now realised it was something else.

Something that had just happened.

When a helicopter sank lower, closer. When a motorbike police officer used a spanner to hit a screwdriver.

When they stood side by side in front of the huge image on the screens and saw a young woman's face.

Ewert had known even then. She was dead. And he'd changed, as he always did when death came calling and someone had stolen another person's life. It usually started with his breathing, heavier, deeper, then his movements, agitated, brusque. His eyes sharper, his neck flushed, the vein on his temple swollen. All adding up to an anger that needed room.

Sven Sundkvist looked at the stocky, furrowed neck in front of him, forced himself not to blink until everything became fuzzy.

An anger that left room for nothing else.

He wondered if that had always been the case. Or whether it had started when someone took the life that had been theirs, his and Anni's, the rest of their life *together*. If that was in fact what the all-invasive anger was all about. Retribution. But not for the victim, as was the case for Sven, Mariana and the other detectives. But for Ewert, maybe that was it, it was the pursuit of his own retribution, the moment when the van he had driven for so long ran over a head, Anni's head. That he was still pursuing it, trying to catch up, to undo what had been done.

Ewert Grens's driving force and Sven had learnt to recognise it.

But this time the anger was different, his movements, his voice, he was driven in a way that Sven had never seen and he didn't know how to deal with it.

The rage that resembled sorrow.

———————

The patrol car was waiting outside the main entrance to the Karolinska hospital, engine running, and two uniformed police officers in front. Hermansson nodded to her boss and to Sven and got out of one car and into the other and disappeared while Grens rolled slowly towards A & E to wait outside the closed gates.

Both vehicles arrived at roughly the same time.

The ambulance from the right, no siren, but the blue light flashing and reflecting in the row of windows. The black or dark blue forensics van from the left, Nils Krantz's tired face behind the wheel.

The gates slid open and the three vehicles drove in and parked next to each other by the loading dock. Grens and Sundkvist stayed in the car, a few minutes were enough to witness a screaming child being admitted further up, blue in the face, about five years old; closer at hand, a drunk young man was already being taken down the corridor, conscious, but with blood pouring from his head and nose.

The A & E ambulance entrance in any major city is a strange place.

Some people who will live on with fear. Some who will not remember. And those who no longer exist.

Sven was watching the ambulance that was nearest, the driver got out of the front seat and hurried to the back, opened the doors, everything looked as it should, someone in a green and yellow uniform sitting beside someone lying under a blanket on a gurney.

It didn't look like it should at all.

Sven could see the face above the green and yellow. He shouldn't be able to do that. The arm should be in the way. It should be moving up and down, should be squeezing the ball-sized BVM resuscitator that covered a mouth and a nose, twice for every two breaths outside her body and then to her chest, taking the other hand and both pressing a point just under her breastbone, thirty compressions to the arrested heart.

'Status?'

The first doctor had come out from the hospital building via the narrow doors to the A & E and was running towards the ramp.

'Young woman, identity not yet known.'

The yellow and green uniform left its place in the ambulance and rolled out the gurney it had been watching.

'Found in a locked car boot. The police ordered transport to Karolinska hospital.'

The yellow and green uniform gave his report as he steered the gurney to the ramp on his own. Sven Sundkvist remained still.

*It didn't look like it should at all.*

There should have been two of them. There should have been someone else walking beside the gurney, who carried on with the ventilation and heart massage while the doctor checked the papers that spewed out of the ECG machine that should be situated above the unmoving woman's head.

'No attempts at resuscitation. Either at the scene or in the ambulance.'

He knew. Ewert knew as well. They had stood side by side and seen her face on a ten-metre wide screen. But that wasn't the way he was made. This fucking fear of death. Or not death, so much as not being alive. And as long as he didn't think about it, refused to see it, then it didn't exist either.

The blue uniform.

She was lying in the foetus position.

The yellow and green uniform continued to roll the gurney in front of him towards the trauma room and the next doctors. Grens hurried behind it, Sven a few steps behind him, watching his boss's face, the tired eyes, the tight lips.

'She's dead.'

The gurney didn't stop. But it did perhaps slow down. The young doctor didn't look at him when she spoke.

'And who are you?'

'Grens, City Police. I want to have a closer look at the body.'

She didn't answer, carried on into the trauma room, as did Grens. The gurney was pushed into the middle of the room and the blue uniform was lifted over onto a bed.

'I'm going to have to ask you to leave.'

'She's dead.'

'Leave.'

'Her body is a murder scene. We need to work with it.'

The doctor looked at him now for the first time.

'*She has not been declared dead yet.*'

The tired eyes, the tense face. That Sven didn't recognise.

'That's just a formality. She's been dead some time.'

———

Ewert Grens had walked away from the bed and the doctor with the sharp voice and emptied the grumbling vending machine of almond slices and sandwiches and then sank down into a sofa in a corner of the A & E waiting room.

'He attacked her, threatened her.'

He wasn't talking to Sven who was sitting close by, he hadn't even noticed, nor was he talking to any of the coughing, snuffling, sick, weak, limping, sore bodies that filled all the chairs in the waiting room, probably not even to himself.

'He stabbed her, kidnapped her, killed her.'

It was just something that had to get out. In the same way that the kind of anger that gnaws and prods you inside has to come out. He thought about pieces from his past: her lying under a tiny, white cross in a huge, impersonal graveyard and about him lying on the floor of a mortuary, shot, and him lying stabbed to death in a shower room in prison, and that it didn't matter whether it was someone he'd loved, or his best friend, or someone he'd never met alive, they all belonged together in a very obvious way that the girl lying on the bed in the trauma room did not.

And only he could see that, feel that.

———

A cup of black coffee. And a sandwich with dry cheese and something red, red pepper maybe.

Grens was restless, wandered impatiently up and down the hospital corridor, fiddled with his mobile phone, dialled the number for the switchboard at the police headquarters in Kronoberg, asked to be transferred to Ågestam, the public prosecutor.

'You again?'

'Have you done what I said? Got up from your bloody desk and gone over to the window and had a look at reality?'

'You'll get a warrant for intercepting phone calls. But not for a house search. Not without reasonable suspicion and a crime classification.'

'Ågestam—'

'And you can shout as much as you like.'

Ewert Grens didn't shout. He whispered.

'She's dead.'

*You.*

'He killed her.'

'He?'

'Yes.'

*It's you.*

'You know who?'

'Yes.'

'How?'

*It just carries on through you.*

'Grens, how do you know?'

'I just know.'

Mobile phone in his hand, if he lowered it, held it closer to the floor, the prosecutor's voice was almost bearable.

'Grens, can you hear me? You wanted a search warrant and didn't get one because I don't have anything to go on. And you know that won't stand up in court. I need evidence. You *know* that too. So I don't understand . . . what is it that you actually want?'

*It just carries on through you.*

*And I'm the only one who can see that, feel that.*

'I want you to prepare. For locking him up.'

The rumble of the coffee machine blended with the regular beeps from the A & E rooms and he raised the phone to his ear again, the prosecutor's voice was clearer.

'Grens, these criminal networks, you know how it works, when you send them to me to send them to court, we can't touch them. *We can't reach them, Grens, not all the way, the gap is too wide.* Old members of the jury, and even older members of the jury who have never walked through a high-rise estate and have never met a gang member, are expected to sit opposite them and try to understand how a criminal network operates; how a core of only a handful of members with high criminal status surround themselves with a large number of younger children whenever they commit crimes, the kind who buzz around and are prepared to do anything, whatever it takes to belong.

That this *really* exists, here in Sweden, *really truly*. Every time I've brought proceedings, I've not succeeded in convincing the court fully of the power, size, how things will look outside our windows very soon if we don't get them to understand.'

Ewert Grens glanced over at the trauma room, the closed door.

'Proof, Grens. Give me proof and I'll bring your murderer down. *Him.* Whoever that is.'

The young woman lying in there, who was there to be used, thrown away.

'I want all four. Blood, DNA, fibres, fingerprints. And then, Grens, the exact time of death. When I've got that, I'll lock him up, and this time for life.'

———

As if it was his fault.

With the last almond slice in his hand, he leant back in the A & E sofa.

*Every intervention by a police officer has consequences.*

*It wasn't his job to evaluate them, weigh them up, try to understand how long these consequences might last.*

He had learnt that. That's how it was.

It didn't help.

He swallowed some dry crumbs, looked around the silent waiting room, closed his eyes.

As if it was his fault.

SHE LAY ON her back with her blue-uniform arms alongside her blue-uniform body.

Her face was pallid. Her eyes frozen.

Her mouth, when he got closer, looked almost as if she was smiling.

Ewert had been at her bedside with a couple of long strides and was standing as he often did, close. Sven stopped just inside the trauma room door, looked at her from there, as *he* often did. If he was afraid of death, Ewert despised it. If he avoided dead bodies, Ewert always tried to get nearer, leaned forwards, prodded what was lifeless. But sometimes, if only for a brief moment, it was clear that his contempt was also fear, perhaps even the same fear that Sven himself struggled with. He had seen it more frequently in the past year, that Ewert seemed to go *too* close, prodded *too* hard, maybe it was even stronger than it was for Sven – for isn't it that contempt is fear wrapped up tight, tight?

'What's her name?'

Nils Krantz was standing on the other side of the bed. The forensic scientist first photographed the whole of her immobile body, then close-ups around her left thigh, then finally her mouth and teeth.

'She's dead.'

'I need to get to know her. What's her name?'

He took out a packet of sterile cotton buds from his black bag, dipped them one at a time in a glass bowl of distilled water and used them to take some blood samples from the torn material at the back of her left thigh, and the blood that had dried on her cheek and in clumps in her hair.

'She *was called* Julia.'

Each cotton bud in a separate protective plastic sleeve with a paper back that was then taped closed with the wiry forensic scientist's name and place of find written on the front.

'Nils?'

Krantz photographed her mouth. Two rubber-gloved fingers against the upper teeth.

'One of her front teeth is loose.'

'Nils, I—'

'Like someone has hit her.'

The rubber gloves opened her still flexible jaws even wider, a new cotton bud to the loose tooth.

'Nils, I want him. The youth who murdered her. I want him in the car with her. I want . . .'

Nils popped the cotton bud in the protective paper bag, meticulously wrote on it, sealed it and then continued with several more cotton buds, tooth by tooth along her upper jaw.

'*Nils* . . . it's like this. I can prove that together they forced a female prison warden through the main gate of Aspsås prison and were then involved in two armed break-outs. I can already get them done for aggravated assault and kidnapping. But him . . . I'm going to do him for murder! And while he's inside, we're going to smash the whole network, break it down piece by piece from the core out, send every member and hangaround and prospect to rehabilitation homes and secure training units and prisons with special young offender units and . . . Nils, *now listen bloody carefully*, we are not going to be able to do that until we can prove that it was *him* who forced her into the back of the car and then into the boot, that it was *his* actions that killed her.'

'Him?'

'Nils . . . *are you listening*? Blood. DNA. Fibres. Fingerprints. *All four.*'

'Ewert, *him*?'

'Yes.'

'There were five of them in the car.'

'*Him.*'

———

The detective superintendent stayed standing where he was, looking into a face that wasn't yet twenty-five, eyes that didn't meet his, lips that didn't ask why he was staring.

'Someone has hit her. I'm sure of it now, Ewert.'

Grens nodded at the forensic scientist who was the same age as him and holding a cotton bud in her mouth, but he didn't hear him.

Not even twenty-five.

And this horrible unease, it wasn't anger and it didn't help to punch the walls.

'Nils, I need *all four*!'

She lay there. And for them she wasn't real.

Leon Jensen and Gabriel Milton had played their own games at an unbelievable speed as children. Impulsive, immediate kicks, *I* have discovered something, *I* want to do it, *I* want to do it *right now*.

*My* gain. *My* satisfaction.

And they were still doing it. Playing. Other games. So the girl lying there who couldn't see him and couldn't speak to him, she wasn't for real either. She was an immediate gain, satisfaction.

Cops and robbers. Only the game had changed names. Cops and *murderers*.

'Several blows. See here. Above the mouth.'

Nils Krantz pulled a cotton bud out from the space between her front teeth and held it up. Grens looked at it and shrugged. A stick. And a bit of cotton wool.

'I don't see anything.'

'Nor do I. But the NLFS will.'

He held the cotton bud up to Ewert's face.

'You want all four. Well, you might have your first here.'

Ewert Grens grabbed his spectacle case from the outside pocket of his jacket.

'I still don't see anything.'

'DNA. From the perpetrator. This ... I guess a scraping from the skin on a finger or maybe the back of a hand.'

---

She is called Julia.

The A & E at the Karolinska hospital slowly got smaller in the rear-view mirror, hands hard on the wheel.

She *was* called Julia.

---

A murderer.

*You.*

---

He had thought he would visit her later on today, in his new jacket, she would probably have liked it. But the agitation that he couldn't explain to Sven and that didn't seem to diminish no matter how long he held onto the wheel or the gearstick or whatever else that wouldn't break when a grown man gripped it as hard as he could, he couldn't bear it. And it was so close. They'd even passed it on the way back. He stopped a couple of hundred metres down the road and parked beyond the entrance that was called Gate 1, then started to walk along the wide asphalted path between the square pieces of grass and big trees and ageing gravestones that roared at whoever passed. When grief had been an unending ocean, it had taken him eighteen months to dare to venture from the entrance all the way in to this part of Norra cemetery which was called Block 19B, for the first time, to a stretch of turned-over soil on Plot 603.

*You can't regulate your grief, Ewert. What you are frightened of has already happened, Ewert.*

Since that first visit, he had continued to walk here several times a week and every time lost himself in the strange calm.

He didn't manage that now.

The guilt that he had carried all his life and that he had decided to bury with Anni, it was there again, looking at him.

He avoided it, stretched over a low, newly built stone wall and took down a metal watering can from an equally newly built but already rickety wooden stand, filled it and then watered the purple bush until every leaf was drowning.

The guilt was still there.

But it wasn't her. Not any more.

It was him.

An eighteen-year-old who breathed criminality and tore people to pieces, classified as one of the most dangerous in Sweden, despite the fact that he was still really only a child, would never manage to get out as he had spent so long making his way in.

Grens looked at the grave, the grass, the beautiful, white wooden cross.

It didn't help.

As if it was his fault.

———

Sven Sundkvist was still in the car, the radio on some commercial station playing music that Ewert Grens couldn't stand, and without asking, he leaned forwards and turned it off and Sven didn't ask why. Every time they headed north and then when they came back, they passed the graveyard. The detective superintendent ordered a short stop, disappeared into the forest of gravestones and always managed to turn off what sounded like music, no matter what it was, before he'd got back into the car with a damp right sleeve and dirt on his shoes.

They drove along Solna kyrkväg, past the Karolinska hospital, and out onto the E4, south towards Essingeleden. Neither of them said anything, both still beside the bed in A & E, looking at a young woman who neither saw nor spoke. Not until Grens sped past the exit at Stora Essingen and then Hornsberg.

'We should've turned off there.'

'No.'

'Have you forgotten—'

'We're carrying on.'

'Carrying on?'

Sven Sundkvist looked at his boss.

'Where?'

'South.'

'Where, Ewert?'

'Back. Back to Råby.'

————

The police station at Råby was a low, colourless building on the periphery of a suburb he had once known so well and now didn't know at all. As far from the exit from the E4 as from the entrance to the metro and it was possible to see both from every identical high-rise. Grens got out of the car in the desolate car park behind the station, walked through the morning for the second time; it was warmer, the rain had stopped and a hesitant sun shone on the wet asphalt.

He looked around – the windows in eight thousand flats looked back.

They're here. *He* is here.

Ewert Grens made for the staff entrance, a small, brown door between two tired rowan trees, and he sighed. Aspsås prison. Österåker prison. Storboda prison. And a young woman who was no longer there.

But despite everything, they'd done the right thing.

The staff who'd let someone go because he was threatening life with a knife, who'd turned the barrel of a gun on the security camera and who'd raised the alarm without putting up any form of defence. It was either that or a bloodbath and Grens didn't particularly care for bloodbaths. He was grateful that those who screamed for prison staff to be more armed had not yet been heard. On a day like this, it would have meant just that: a bloodbath. The more closed and escape-proof a prison was, the more violence was needed to get out; walls guarded with automatic firearms only meant that with every break-out, the absconders would have even more automatic firearms.

One flight of stairs up, a short corridor, past two narrow offices and a small, red kitchen.

He still knew his way.

The coffee machine was new, he noticed, a cup of blackness, he tasted it and approved and pressed for another, even though Sven shook his head, another one, just as black. The door to the office and Section Against Gang Crime was closed, but unlocked. He opened it and they went into a room with more eyes than anywhere else.

The shortest wall, the one closest to the corridor, *Target List Alcatraz*, long rows of black and white photos above carefully worded notes, blue ballpoint, ID number, address, gang status. The most dangerous, all one hundred and fifty of them. Grens and Sundkvist went further into the room, the same eyes once more, but now arranged in groups over two longer walls; the ones staring from the right were defined as established, so multi-criminal that they had left the piles of blue files on the desk; the ones staring from the left had got even further in their criminal development and now could only go further up. Ewert Grens stretched his arm out in an irritated swipe. God, he hated this. A stupid ranking list that became counter-productive the moment it was set: when the authorities defined someone as so dangerous that he moved higher up the wall, that person had succeeded, and would soon know and therefore continued to be even more aggressive in order to get even higher up, be more successful.

He went closer. They all looked the same.

The same staring eyes.

Including the nine faces that had recently been moved over to the left-hand wall, obvious holes from the red and yellow drawing pins in the wall, and two alternative names: *Råby Warriors / Ghetto Soldiers.* He stopped at the top, the leader of this group, eyes that seemed to hate the most and that followed him wherever he went in the room.

————

José Pereira had a plastic cup in his hand. The new coffee machine was quieter than the last one, he hadn't thought about it before, just part of the stillness of dawn.

September, late summer.

A bit lighter. Almost morning.

Only twelve hours had passed, it felt a lot longer. He had, as always, been late and run the last stretch from the bus stop, almost fifteen minutes into the first half when he opened the gate near the edge of the woods at Tallkrogen playing fields, and then stayed there in order not to disturb others, watched the green and white team on the gravel between the trees. The two girls running around out there with headbands over their long hair. Two girls born fourteen minutes apart. From a distance it was so clear that they were quite tall now, almost young women, and sometimes he wondered how much longer he would be allowed to come here, stand watching and then drive the growing, slightly sweaty pair in the back seat home. Or would he be met in the same way that he'd behaved towards his parents, with such embarrassment that they finally chose to stay at home? He had never aged hand in hand with his own children before, and every step they took together was a first. He'd leaned against one of the trees and gradually started to relax as he always did when his everyday surrounded by violent youths was swapped for an everyday with twenty-two younger

322

children running around with a black and white ball, and right then and there that was all there was: the ball, the joy, the disappointment, all the things that are contained between the painted white lines.

That was where he was when his phone rang.

Half an hour into the match, and the number was the opposite of everything there.

Erik Wilson, the relatively new head of City Police Homicide, who explained that two, probably three members of the criminal network that had previously been called Råby Warriors and was now called Ghetto Soldiers, had first started a disturbance in a maximum security prison, and then escaped.

Plastic cup in his hand, half full. He left the coffee machine and his pigeonhole, and walked towards a door that was open, despite the fact that he was quite certain he'd just closed it, the Section Against Gang Crime, an office with walls full of faces.

He had asked Wilson to send two cars, one to take him back to Råby immediately, and the other to drive home two sweaty girls with oversized white socks an hour later. He'd headed back to Råby police station to put together official and unofficial information about the five wanted, violent youths, and had several times turned around to look at the patrol car's empty back seat and the faces that peopled it, faces he had caught as minors and handed over to the Social Services, arrested as fifteen-year-olds and handed over to the public prosecution authority, and as the car approached the high-rise blocks, he recalled all the visits to the kitchens of despairing, single mothers and it was strange to think that he'd just been standing in a reality that should be every young person's reality, and yet sometimes stood in such sharp relief to another that no one had ever chosen.

José Pereira crushed the brown cup and dropped it in one of the bins outside the janitor's office, walked past the kitchen and into the Section Against Gang Crime, through the half-open door that he was now absolutely convinced he had left closed.

———

A beige jacket. Only a few metres in front of him. It didn't turn round. But the big-framed body and bald head and the manner of leaning with one hand up on the wall, shifting the weight over to the right leg, was all too familiar.

'Grens?'

Ewert Grens had heard steps that weren't his own or Sven's, now the voice. They were not on their own any longer and he turned around.

'Morning.'

Grens looked at the policeman who was pretty well middle-aged, but still had thick, dark hair, was still slim, and had friendly eyes, even when he was agitated.

They hadn't aged at the same rate.

'So you're here again, Grens, eh?'

The detective superintendent from City Police shrugged.

'Yes. And I need your—'

'You were here earlier this morning.'

José Pereira nodded demonstratively at his other guest, a younger man, closer to the door.

'You were *both* here this morning. You were clocked. And because you didn't even consider following the directive, you managed to undo a whole night's work within twenty minutes and put *our* strategy in danger.'

Ewert Grens turned back to the wall and the group of nine staring faces.

'I don't know what you're talking about, Pereira.'

'That your bloody unnecessary foray this morning is exactly the sort of thing that we've learnt we don't need.'

The silent, beige jacket.

'Smashing windows and breaking into flats. Warning them. And putting the hostage's life at risk.'

José Pereira stared at the back he had worked with for some years so long ago, until Grens shrugged again.

'I still have no idea what you're talking about. I'm here to work on a murder investigation. Because the murderer is here as well.'

*A young woman in a prison warden uniform.*

Pereira closed his eyes briefly; it sometimes made things more bearable.

He had his mobile phone in his hand, wanted so badly to call the twins who had got into another patrol car later, to hear the voices glowing on the way home in the way voices often do when a match ends three–two, he wanted to keep hold of it a bit longer, the real life, kiss the mouthpiece, hang up.

*A young woman in a prison warden uniform walking beside him down a cold prison underground passage, on their way to D1 Left.*

Only a few seconds, it was so good, simply not to open his eyes.

*She's there, walking, advising a serving policeman not to go into the unit where she herself works alone, because she knows that it would be extremely dangerous.*

She'd had reason to be frightened.

'She said so.'

He stood shoulder to shoulder with the older policeman who had just shrugged then continued to stare at a wall of faces.

'She said that she was frightened, Ewert.'

They'd stood in front of this wall before, in the early nineties, different faces but the same staring eyes, most of them dead now as they always died young, a few others with new lives. José Pereira had spent his first years after graduating working with what was later called the Fittja Commission; Ewert Grens was mid-career in the police and had been tasked with developing and implementing the first – and what later proved to be a very poor – witness protection programme for gang members, their only way out, and during those years they had both, each from their own perspective, discovered a world with no laws.

'His dad.'

Grens was still looking at the group of faces that had just been moved over to the left-hand wall, between *X-Team* and *Red & White Crew*, below *Hell's Angels MC* and *Bandidos*, mostly at the one whose eyes continued to follow him.

Pereira nodded.

'I remember him.'

If they were alike.

If someone who saw them when they were the same age would only see the similarities that he saw.

'We've moved them up.'

'I can see that.'

'Four members were already outside. Five more got out yesterday evening.'

'You know what I think about your lists.'

'Disturbance. Hostage-taking. Escape. Break-out. Murder.'

'They're already here. Outside your window.'

'They'll be at the top soon.'

'They've got nothing else. They don't want to go anywhere.'

'There's always a turning point, Grens. When a ridiculous club of little boys with a ridiculous name becomes something else. When a logo, a top, a tattoo becomes a symbol that doesn't mean anything if it's not given substance.'

José Pereira stood beside the detective superintendent who was looking at a boy's face that was supposed to look dangerous.

'You've got . . .'

Pereira put his hand out to the beige jacket, just below the collar.

'. . . I think it's . . . Ewert, you've got a piece of plastic there.'

He picked off the piece that clung to the back of the collar.

'Thank you.'

José Pereira rolled the plastic between his index finger and thumb, aimed for the waste-paper basket.

'Some little boys who called themselves Råby Warriors for a long time, who we first heard about . . . it must be nine years ago, now. A gang from the southern suburbs that you, if anyone, should know, Grens, the kind that we've got so many of out here that we've lost count.'

A little piece more, there on the shoulder, plastic that stuck to his fingertips when he pulled it off and handed it to the detective superintendent.

'I realised that they'd made their decision sometime at the start of summer. The turning point, the logo that had to be fulfilled. And every time, those we have so many of become something bigger . . . it happens fast. *Ghetto Soldiers*. A name that already existed. A prison organisation established in Aspsås by some of the older inmates, a criminal network inside, power and protection for as long as you're there. I was getting clear indications that they'd decided on the name, that they would adopt it.'

He poked around on his desk that was full of files, opened one of them.

```
X-ray department admission note: young
man, seventeen years old, shot in each
knee.
```

He put four badly lit photographs down on the middle of the desk, all taken by a forensic technician, slightly too shiny, but very clear.

From different angles, a left knee that had been shot.

```
X-ray report: multiple fractures to the
patella, distal femur, proximal tibia,
proximal fibula.
```

'New name, new structure, new rules.'

José Pereira stretched over, the file that was on the floor, he slowly flicked through it, and somewhere in the middle, the plastic sleeve, GHETTO SOLDIERS and ASSOCIATED, three more pictures.

'The first one, the one with the knees, is called Javad Kittu. This one was called Daniel Wall.'

```
Lying between a bunk and heavy fixed
table.
```

'A cell that isn't far from the ones that Jensen and Bendik and Eriksson escaped from.'

```
A lead, probably from the television,
wrapped around his neck.
```

'Multiple shots to both knees. A TV lead wrapped hard around someone's neck. At exactly the same time. Because the two hangarounds didn't scream *police cunts* in answer to every question when they were interviewed in connection with a preliminary investigation that became a long sentence.'

The forensic technician's photographs were still in his hand when he got up from the desk.

'I know that you've got your reasons. And I've got mine. *But we have to catch them fast, Grens*. We're working with the intelligence units in communities with high-rise blocks, the kind of places we pass by, and *these guys, Grens*, right now they're role models for gangs in Stockholm and Gothenburg and Malmö and Uppsala and Västerås and Eskilstuna and Örebro and Gävle and Sundsvall and . . . wherever the fuck you want.'

The middle-aged policeman who devoted all his working hours to various stages of the eyes they were looking into right now, started to systematically pull out the drawing pins that were holding them up one by one, moving one face at a time to the left, to the other side of the ones called *X-Team*.

'I'm moving them again. They've only got two stages left.'

Tiny holes in the white wall as he pinned the young men, or pictures of the young men, in a position that meant even more dangerous.

'They got long sentences, were held in high security prisons, took a hostage, escaped, committed murder. Their logo has been validated now. And every hour that they continue to run around out there, they'll reinforce it, in the way that every little kid we know who dreams about being part of it will one day reinforce their own.'

They both took a step back; it was easier to see the wall then.

'Role models, Grens. They've succeeded.'

THEY WERE HALFWAY across the simple car park when Grens stopped and looked at Sundkvist.

'We're not leaving here, Sven. Not yet. I want you to go back to the flat.'

He nodded at the high-rise.

'The one with SANTOS on the door. And the windowpane that's perhaps a bit damaged.'

*The faint smell of marzipan.*

'A bomb squad and dog will be there in ten minutes.'

*The smell of the taste of marzipan.*

'I want you to be there. And to report back to me.'

'Did you listen at all to what Pereira was saying just a minute ago?'

'Sven?'

'Yes.'

'Just go.'

The detective superintendent looked at his closest colleague, the only one who put up with him, because he had *chosen* to put up with him. Then he turned around and crossed the car park with his stiff leg.

'Ewert?'

'See you at the car in forty-five minutes. I'm going to talk to someone I should have spoken to a long time ago.'

———

He made his way over to one of the proud, guarded high-rise blocks that seemed perpetually to take note, to remember who went where and when.

He wondered if she still lived there.

If the building remembered the last time.

---

A fire engine drove down one of the asphalted paths at full speed. Grens stopped and waited until it had also stopped and he could pass, turned slowly and looked all the way around without seeing any smoke or fire, he knew that it was normally something like a bin, a cellar storeroom.

Råby Allé 64.

A main entrance that looked like all the others and he went into the stairwell and over to the lift.

Strong smell of urine. Four broken floor buttons. Hard to read the graffiti on the walls.

He hesitated. It didn't feel reliable. It wasn't something he did very often, walk up the stairs by choice, he was breathing heavily when he got to the third floor and five identical brown doors. DORDEVIC. MUHAZABI. HANSSON. PITKÄNEN. STENBERG. Two steps closer to the sixth, squeezed in between a fire hose and a fuse box that had been broken open many times.

TOMAS.

The same door. Another time.

It sounded like the doorbell worked.

He waited. Eighteen years ago. He rang it again.

Her eye through the peephole. He heard her, she didn't try to sneak to the door. Then she opened it. And they stood there looking at each other.

'Do you remember me?'

He had stood there just like that. He'd got more hair and been a lot thinner, maybe in his forties.

'Yes. I remember you.'

She looked well. All her teeth. Good skin. No visible ticks. Four years at Hinseberg prison often left more of a mark.

'Will you let me in?'

He had taken her boyfriend from her.

And then stood at her door with a search warrant. A kilo of heroin in a pasta jar in the larder.

Always the girlfriend with no criminal record.

Ana didn't reply.

She could see it was the same face, but from nearly twenty years ago. It was as if someone had put a rubber face over the one she remembered, a temporary face with new lines and furrows and even a different colour. She wanted to reach out and touch it tentatively with her fingertips. She wanted to feel if it was real.

'Will you let me in?'

He moved in a way that showed pain in one leg that made it difficult to balance his weight. She'd heard what he'd said, but remembered how, all those years ago, she'd tried to pull the door shut and how he had grabbed hold of her, forced her to the floor in her own kitchen. And maybe she remembered only a few weeks ago, four young men ringing on the doorbell, just as he had now, and put a foot out to block her door, then they'd come in and left a plastic bag on the hat shelf.

She gave a slight nod and opened the door a little.

'You know.'

He was standing in her hallway but didn't have the answer. How can you start a conversation that's been half a life in the waiting?

'Don't you? Where he is?'

The evening before she had seen her son smiling on a passport photo in one of the many news flashes on TV.

'No.'

'You know where he'd choose to hide.'

'I don't know anything about him any more.'

'Is there anyone else?'

'You know there isn't anyone else. No brothers. No sisters. No grandparents.'

Every intervention will have consequences.

'And no father.'

Every consequence will then give rise to more consequences.

*And no father.*

It had just been a job. To collect. To protect. To hide. To leave. Just a job.

'What *I* know is that he abducted a female prison warden considerably younger than yourself at knifepoint. *I* know that he for various reasons is also suspected of taking her life. *I* know that out there . . .'

Grens indicated behind her with his arm, over there, pointing at one of the windows perhaps.

'. . . there's a lot of policemen ready to arrest him, fully equipped and armed. And *I* know that if you don't cooperate, more people will die. *He* will die.'

She looked at him as she had done since she opened the door, but she didn't say a word.

'Protecting a suspect is a criminal offence.'

'Then arrest me.'

She didn't let him go. Her eyes followed him.

'Again.'

He lowered his arm, the one he'd used to point.

'I'm here to help you.'

'You're here to do your job.'

Her voice, it was scornful.

'You can't help me. You can't help anyone here.'

---

The lift smelt like before.

He avoided it, slow steps down, the blue main door and a lungful of air.

One more.

Something tasted of petrol. Maybe oil. Or metal. He looked to where he'd met the fire engine earlier.

Petrol, oil, metal.

A car.

They hadn't found any more rubbish bins today.

On the wide pathway to Råby police station, he greeted a fireman who was turning off the water and unscrewing a pump from a hydrant, then carried on walking and the taste of petrol and metal got stronger, he guessed it was one of the cars near the police station.

The first thing he saw was Sven.

On a bench by the red-brick wall of the station, phone in hand.

Then he saw the fire engine, the one that was much bigger close up, with four firemen buzzing around it carrying the things that firemen carry. It looked like they'd put out the fire.

Then finally he saw the car. Half of it covered in soot, half of it without colour, and four tyres that had melted into nothing.

He went closer, hand in what was left of the white foam that lay soft and sticky on the bonnet and all the way back to the boot.

*Their* car.

They looked at each other and then at what had until very recently been a new vehicle worth four hundred thousand kronor.

'The last two cassettes were in there, Sven. At the back of the glove compartment. Did you know?'

A vehicle that would never be roadworthy again.

Grens dried the white foam on his trousers, shrugged.

'Are you done?'

Sven Sundkvist nodded.

'I'm done.'

'Well, then we'd better start walking.'

'We don't need to. I've ordered a new one for us.'

'We don't have time, Sven.'

Ewert Grens went over to Råby police station and one of the

police cars in front of the main entrance, a young policeman in the first seat with an equally young passenger.

The detective superintendent rapped on the window.

'We need your car.'

The young driver had wound down the window halfway. Now he smiled.

'Well, I'm afraid we do too.'

'Ours has been set on fire.'

The smile still on his face.

'There you go. But, you see, we're not here to file your report.'

Grens lightly slapped the metal of the driver's door.

'Get out. I'm requisitioning this vehicle from now.'

The two young officers stayed where they were.

'Well . . . you see, we actually work here. So I, and the police command, would be very grateful if you left us now, if you don't mind, it would make things a lot easier for us.'

The man who had rapped on their door and then demanded to take their car was rummaging for something in his trouser pocket and then held it up to the car window. A black leather cover. An ID card and a metal badge, a shield that they recognised in yellow, blue and red and a symbol showing three crowns above the word POLICE.

'Ewert Grens, gold command. The . . . *police command* that you mentioned.'

The two young men studied the ID card and the police badge that seemed to be real and an officer they'd heard about but never seen before.

'We're . . . stationed at Västerort.'

'I see.'

'So we need the car to get back.'

Grens looked at them without answering until they both simultaneously opened their doors and got out. He got in behind the wheel and Sven sank down beside him. He started the car and had driven about ten metres when he stopped, wound down the window and shouted to the two young officers who were standing abandoned on the asphalt.

'By the way, boys . . .'

He stuck his head out so that they would hear him better.

'. . . you do know that police in uniform can take the metro for free?'

———————

They were about halfway into town and had passed Kungens Kurva and Skärholmen, in the middle lane by Segeltorp and Bredäng, by the time Sven started to feel confident enough that Ewert Grens was in control of the new car that he dared talk to him without the risk of distracting him.

'The smell of marzipan that you were talking about.'

The detective superintendent slowed down so that he could concentrate better on listening, and it became obvious that he was not used to this car's clutch and how far to release it in relation to the accelerator.

'The dog searched the hall, toilet, bedroom, sitting room. Nothing. But the kitchen. When it came in there, it went straight over to the kitchen table and lay down underneath it, sniffed around several times, looked up at the dog handler until he lifted it up.'

Grens slowed down even more, and the car lurched forward before settling at a steady speed.

'An English springer spaniel, it moved around unrestrained on the table top and immediately picked out an obvious stain in about the middle, lay down with his snout close by, eyes looking at the handler again.'

The traffic was getting busier and they had to brake more often and Sven tried not to look anywhere other than straight ahead, they only had a few kilometres to go.

'You were right, Ewert.'

The Söderled tunnel and not too many bends left that required manoeuvres involving both the clutch and the accelerator.

'They *do* have access to explosives.'

He didn't notice, but he lowered his voice.

'And people who have access to explosives blow things up. Where? What? *Who* are they going to blow up, Ewert?'

---

Eighteen years.

He had rung the doorbell, as he had back then. He had waited until she opened, as he had back then.

*Do you remember me?*

*Yes. I remember you.*

His questions about a boy who had escaped from prison and then murdered a young woman.

She hadn't answered them because she couldn't.

*You know, don't you? Where he is?*

She'd had a son. She didn't any more.

*There isn't anyone else. No brothers. No sisters. No grandparents. And no father.*

And she hadn't cried, or held her breath to feel the pain when your heart is about to explode.

*If you don't cooperate, more people will die. He will die.*

She opened the door and went out onto the stairs, past the lift, carried on down, she moved fast, she knew that there wasn't much time.

---

He was tired, had probably never felt so empty, forty-eight separate call-outs in one week, two genuine and forty-six intentional: mopeds, cars, cellar storerooms, tyres, containers, climbing frames, fences, bins, bushes, house gables, trees. This one had developed into big flames and black smoke – someone had poured petrol over the car – and the big stones and empty bottles had started to rain on them as usual, but only once they had started to put out the fire and from further away than normal, but the message had been clear enough, *a police car for fuck's sake*, he hadn't been hit more than once on the leg, but the hate felt stronger than usual, the pubescent voices sharper, *it's a police car for fuck's sake, let it burn.*

Thom had just pulled in the hose and pump and opened the door to the front of the large truck when he felt a hand on his shoulder. Someone had come too close. He'd heard footsteps but hadn't registered them and spun round with his arm raised, not more spit and stones, nearly lashed out, his body shaking, when he came face to face with a stranger.

A woman. Thirty, thirty-five years old.

And she pulled back when she saw his hand.

'Oh . . . sorry.'

He lowered his arm, tried to hide it, get rid of it.

'I'm sorry, I thought . . .'

'Don't worry. I understand. It was me who . . . have you got a moment? Have you got time?'

Dark hair, beautiful eyes that weren't alive but that had been alive and wanted to live again.

'Time? For what?'

He had been about to hit someone who wasn't even threatening him.

It wasn't her.

It was not long ago. He had seen one of them who set fire to the car, a young boy who had darted forwards to the rolled-out, water-filled hose and stabbed at it with something that resembled a sword with a curved blade. That was when something even deeper in Thom had burst. He'd ordered the guys holding the hose to turn round and direct the water jet at the child with the sword, they had hit him on the chest and he'd collapsed, screaming *kill* as they normally did, but even louder, *we're going to kill you next time.*

It wasn't her.

'I saw you here this morning.'

The woman with the dark hair and eyes that had once been alive raised her voice to be sure that she was heard.

'Quarter past six, a moped leaned up against a bench on Råby Torg. Engulfed by flames before you got there.'

Maybe she took a step closer.

'Twenty past eight, the blue container by the playground. It was already burnt by the time you came.'

Another step.

'And now. I saw what happened. The third time today. Isn't it?'

Thom listened but felt unnerved, she had watched him, counted.

'I've seen this, them, you, so many times.'

He still didn't say anything, she didn't seem to be sick, he'd met mentally unstable people all his life and she wasn't one of them, but the feeling that someone was watching him, he didn't like it.

'My name's Ana. And I live there.'

She turned and pointed to one of the blocks that looked just like all the others, a couple of floors up, it was difficult to see where she was pointing.

'That's enough. Just leave.'

'I'm sorry?'

'Like I said. That's enough.'

He walked around to the other side of the fire engine, checked the hose and the pump one more time, sorted out what had already been sorted out and hoped that she would have gone by the time he went back round.

She hadn't.

'I . . . I'm a social worker here in Botkyrka, I've been working in the family unit for years, with addictions, so plenty of alcoholics and drug addicts. And a whole lot of young people, even

. . . children. And they . . . please listen, just for while . . . an addict doesn't go *anywhere* unless she wants to. So to get anywhere you have to meet her at exactly the right time. When she's been drinking or shot up her veins long enough, is weak and down and *reachable*, only then will she really listen.'

Thom looked at the woman who was blabbing on about something.

The police car that had just been on fire and the stones and bottles against their body armour and the teenage rants about hate and that he was going to die. And now her. She still didn't look like she was sick, he'd learnt to spot it in their eyes, but still, uncomfortable.

'I'm sure you're a reasonable person. But I have no idea what you're talking about. And I don't *want* to understand either. Please will you just let me do my job?'

He mounted the step up to the front passenger seat, his place, Officer In Charge Front Passenger Seat.

'What I'm talking about? What you are . . . now.'

She followed after him, two quick steps.

'Not an alcoholic, not a drug addict, that's not what I meant. But right now you're just so . . . despairing and weary. You're *reachable*.'

As if she saw straight through him.

He didn't like it.

'You said you live here?'

'Yes, that's my window.'

'Then go back home. And use your time to control your fucking kids instead.'

'I don't have any children. Not any more.'

She just stood there, so he couldn't close the door.

'I want you to come there, third floor, TOMAS on the door. Now, or this evening, or tomorrow morning. I just want to talk to you for a while, soon.'

'Talk?'

'Yes. And maybe get your help.'

She hadn't raised her voice. She wasn't uptight. She seemed to be calm, and that's what was so frightening.

'Just go away.'

'Your help to . . .'

She turned towards what had just been on fire, and what had been on fire yesterday and would be set alight again tomorrow.

'. . . to . . . stop all this. For ever.'

He opened a blue and white door, got out of the car that belonged to Västerort Police, looked in through the window at the glove compartment that didn't contain the two cassettes that for so long he hadn't been able to part with.

Now they had been burnt to cinders, a voice on a piece of plastic had melted in the flames.

Grens and Sundkvist bounded up to Solna coroner's office in three short steps and already caught a glimpse of the body through the window. A young woman in a uniform on her back on a table and Grens imagined for a moment another young woman in another uniform, he had just been to visit her, the white cross in the grass in a corner of the kilometre-square graveyard, carefully watered the purple bush that had a name he'd heard and promptly forgotten. He wondered whether she too had lain on her back on a table, he had been so far away for so long and hadn't even tried to find out – if someone who was going to meet her for the first time, met her like this.

Nils Krantz, the forensic scientist, was standing on one side of the body, and Ludvig Errfors, the forensic pathologist, on the other. Grens went closer, whereas Sven stayed in the doorway.

'So *you're* here as well? Shouldn't you be done and back in your lab with your microscopes, busy analysing? I told you that we didn't have much time.'

Krantz cut away the tape around the woman's wrists with a scalpel, her arms in front when the tape loosened, crossed over her chest and stomach, as if she was protecting her heart.

'I was the one who wanted to see how she was lying *before* the tape and clothes were removed.'

The forensic pathologist had recognised the detective super-intendent's frustration and wanted to avoid adding to it. Grens heard him but his eyes didn't leave Krantz's hands cutting another layer of thick tape and then pushing it down into the paper bag.

'You want four stages of technical evidence that can link them, *him*, as you said, to the car and body. I've already got the first, DNA, from the scrapings from between her teeth and sent that over to the NLFS for analysis.'

'When?'

The National Laboratory of Forensic Science. Grens's body was shaking. The NLFS means Linköping and competition with other analyses.

'I've used our own transport. And I've asked them to prioritise us. And I'm guessing . . . you'll have an answer by this evening, at the latest.'

'Nils, *for Christ's sake*, I said that you had to be fast!'

Krantz opened the bag and held it out.

'And this is the start of the second piece of evidence, finger-prints. Why the rush?'

Ewert Grens didn't look at the brown paper bag or the grey tape.

'Because they've murdered once already, because they're on the run, because they've crossed the line and will murder again, because—'

'That doesn't make this case any different from any others.'

Grens was shaking even more, an arm pointing without knowing where, and a head with blazing red cheeks up close.

'Because they're role models. You know as well as I do that five thousand youths are on their way in and following every single step. And if they succeed? If they carry on succeeding? Nils, it's conta-gious, it'll spread.'

'That still doesn't make it different from anything else. So I repeat . . . why the *damn* rush?'

*A young woman.*

'You just don't understand.'

*A provisional delivery room.*

'Why, Ewert?'

*His job. His decision.*

'Because every intervention a policeman makes has consequences.'

Nils Krantz put the brown paper bag down on the table close to the dead woman's feet.

'I don't understand . . .'

'That's what I just said. That there's no way you can understand.'

It was hard to tell, but it seemed like the forensic scientist was moving even slower when he brushed the woman's hands with carbon dust and pressed her fingers on the form for fingerprints, ten small squares and two large for the palms. And then, without even looking at Grens, carried on, even more slowly, cutting up her clothes and putting them piece by piece in new paper bags and photographing the naked body from every angle.

'See you at Kronoberg.'

The black bag in his hand when he left the autopsy room.

'Remember, we haven't got much time, Nils!'

'You'll have an answer by this evening, at the latest.'

Ludvig Errfors had a pen in his hand, which he pointed at the young woman's face when he took the position where Krantz had just been standing.

'Blunt trauma.'

The forensic pathologist didn't like anger and had no desire to confront the kind emanating from Ewert Grens right now, the kind that was incomprehensible and couldn't be handled because not even the person who was angry knew why.

'Here. The area around the nose, and here, the upper part of the mouth.'

The pen pointing at the upper jaw.

'A fist. And if you remember, the scrapings of skin between her front teeth.'

Grens remembered.

The first blow to her face, enough to make her compliant.

'But if you follow the pen when I draw lightly on her skin . . . apart from the mark on her forehead, which we know comes from the glass at central security, I can identify . . . here . . . three further blows. The first knocked out her jawbone. Full force blunt trauma. And then two more. *After* her jawbone has already been knocked out.'

One punch would have been enough. Another punch had made her as cooperative as he wanted.

But he'd hit her twice more. And those punches were about something else. About respect. Not from her, he already had that, but from the others. He punched her twice for the sake of the others sitting beside him in the car, who needed to see and understand that he still deserved *their* respect.

To harm another person to make yourself good enough.

The kind of assault he witnessed in pretty much all gang-related violence. Grens didn't understand it, and he would never understand it, as to understand it would somehow be to accept it.

He said nothing, it wasn't for anyone else's sake, he just turned away from the table and the woman lying on it, and punched the wall. The forensic pathologist glanced at the detective superintendent's knuckles, dots of blood, then drew new circles on the body in front of them, now on one of her thighs. Grens watched, but didn't listen. He had read in the transcripts of interviews with staff from Aspsås prison that Alexander Eriksson had sliced the face of one warden with a coffee jug, seen pictures of Leon Jensen stabbing Julia Bozsik in the back of the thigh with a piece of metal, and now evidence that he had later punched her in the back of the car, once to make her comply, and then three times more to earn the others' respect.

Violence against someone who in that moment was weaker, not because they had to, but because they could.

Errfors drew on the cold skin and Grens realised that his life revolved around the consequences of violence, the underlying assumption of almost every day in a homicide section. But also how this violence stood out from the lone madman who stabs someone in the chest forty-eight times in a particular pattern, or the frightened, jealous man who kicks against a cunt that no one else wants. The introspective violence for personal satisfaction and the functional violence to get someone to do something that the perpetrator wants. But this was like bleaching teeth so that the mouth was attractive to whoever it was smiling at; it was superficial, injury to achieve favour.

Ewert Grens remained standing under the bright light after Errfors had finished, and didn't move until Sven came closer and put a hand on his shoulder.

His fingers ached. The white bandage, discoloured by dried blood.

He wasn't going to punch any more walls. Not now.

———

Mariana Hermansson was on her way up the steps to Solna coroner's office when Ewert Grens and Sven Sundkvist came down. She noticed her boss's hand was wrapped in a bandage that was white in some places, red in others, and then looked at Sven – they both knew that this was having a deep effect on him and that he was reacting with a different sort of anger than before. She walked the short distance to the car with them, it was important that they listened.

'I widened the cordon around the scene of the crime.'

She couldn't help looking at the bandaged knuckles.

'And as rain is forecast, it's now been covered and transported to the forensics' space in the garage.'

She'd seen him hit walls and furniture and cars before.

'The twenty-two road blocks throughout the county have now been cut to ten, as you ordered, Ewert, and will be reduced further in the next few hours, to four, all concentrated around Råby.'

But never so hard and never with his fist.

'One on the E4 southbound by the bridge at Fittjaviken. One on Glömstavägen by Masmo. One on the E4 northbound by Salem. And one on Hågelbyleden just after Tumba.'

Ewert Grens opened the car door. The white and red fabric was thick and he found it difficult to get hold of the handle.

She couldn't help herself any longer.

'Your hand?'

'It's fine, Hermansson. Four road blocks. Every road in to Råby.'

'Your hand, it—'

'Get into the passenger seat, so I can drive.'

He already had his bandaged hand on the gearstick. She stood by the door, staring at it.

'Västerort Police?'

'Can you please close the door?'

'Why?'

'Let's just say that I requisitioned it.'

'And *our* car?'

'Something about the paint.'

He reversed out of the tight parking space and drove between the parked vehicles to the exit.

'The paint?'

'I didn't think much of the new black colour.'

Mariana Hermansson gave up and turned to the back seat and Sven.

'What's he talking about?'

'It was torched.'

She didn't ask any more. She could ask later, as she often did when she and Sven shared a pot of tea in the Homicide kitchen.

'We've still got two helicopters in operation – one on standby at Bromma airport, and one that's circulating between the four road blocks.'

Grens's movements were still clumsy when he crossed the bridge over Essingeleden, into Gävlegatan and Sankt Eriksgatan. He listened carefully to her without showing it, was struck by her competence, so uncomfortably demanding. He had only once told her that she was good. And would never do it again. It was as if he needed her, the fact that she demanded something from him, and if he was to say it again . . . it would be something bigger, become something else.

'Since eight p.m. yesterday evening, when one news flash followed the next on every channel, the CCC has received around two hundred and eighty-three tips from the public, of which sixty-seven are about the getaway car's possible route. Two are of particular interest.'

A crumpled envelope from a jacket pocket, notes on the back.

'The first, a sighting around nineteen fifty-five hours on Mälarvägen between the roundabout and the petrol station on the Upplands Väsby exit. A driver, I think it was a tanker, has given a time and a registration number. He said that he signalled several times to a young man who jumped out of the driver's seat and without paying the blindest bit of attention to the vehicle behind, went round to the boot, opened it and leant in for a few seconds and "did something with his hands", before getting back into the front seat and driving off.'

*She was alive.*

'The second was a few minutes later on Mälarvägen by Edssjön, when a cyclist on her way home says that she was almost knocked over by a car driving south at high speed. Her description fits the getaway car and she said more than once that she thought there were "several" of them in the car. A few more minutes on the same road and you reach . . . Söderby. The scene of the crime.'

*She was alive when they left her there to slowly disappear.*

Mariana Hermansson had more to report, but stopped. She had looked several times at his bloody bandage since Solna and the way he was now driving through red lights and bumper-to-bumper queues, it was impetuous, as if someone was giving chase who Ewert Grens couldn't frighten off with his bark.

'Ewert?'

'What?'

'What is it?'

'What?'

'I don't know . . . something's up.'

For a moment, he left the cars zigzagging in front of the bonnet and looked at her.

'Something's *up?*'

'Yes, with you.'

Every intervention has a consequence that in turn has a new consequence.

He had just done his job. And if he was to stand there again, he would do the same again.

'Hermansson?'

'Yes?'

'In that case . . . butt out.'

———

'You carry on up. Werner is waiting for you. I'll be there shortly.'

He walked towards what was a garage within a garage, a big, ugly metal box built across four parking spaces. He knocked, but didn't wait for an answer, pushed the door to one side and went in. Nils Krantz was on his knees beside a white Mercedes, which only a few hours earlier had filled ten screens on the wall of the

County Communications Centre, a locked boot and a motor-bike police officer who looked into the camera on the helicopter in order not to feel alone.

'Here.'

The torch shone an infra-red light on the forensic scientist's hand, he then directed it at the fabric on the back seat of the car, but wasn't satisfied and swapped it for an ultraviolet light.

'Can you see? The bloodstains have sunk in.'

It wasn't often that Ewert Grens could in fact see what Krantz was pointing out and talking about. But this time he could. When the light shone on the flecks, they became darker and stood out.

'She received the first blow here. And the second. And the third. And the fourth. And then she was taped up, in the same place.'

Grens balled himself up so he could see more, two grown men kneeling on a back seat was one too many.

'The big stains come from her left thigh which was bleeding heavily. But the splashes slightly further up on the seat could be her blood contaminated with *another* person's blood.'

'The man who punched her.'

'We've got DNA on the way to the NLFS. Brown paper bags with pieces of packing tape for the fingerprint section. This blood, Ewert, might be your third piece of technical evidence.'

'*Him.*'

———

Floor eight.

It wasn't often that he was there, a few times a year, but it always looked and smelt the same, the only corridor with the same persistent smell of sweaty jackets as Homicide. Ewert Grens hurried past the closed doors, slowing by the first inter-ception room, passing it, passing the next one, carrying on towards the one that was farthest away and slightly smaller than the others, for those who didn't belong there, random visitors who wanted to follow incoming and outgoing conversations without getting in the way.

*'Have you fixed it?'*

Sven and Hermansson were sitting by a rectangular table and Gunnar Werner was standing, hunched over, in front of a shelf full of leads and monitors. They each held out a hand and said hello. Grens had known the slightly hunchbacked sergeant in the interception unit for as long as he could remember.

*'I've fixed it. And I told the bitch to clean the flat.'*

Werner got a chair from the stack by the door and put it down in front of Grens who waved it away, with his stiff leg it was sometimes easier to stay standing.

'It might take some time.'

'I'll stand all the same.'

'And I want you to listen carefully.'

Gunnar Werner held up a piece of paper and changed the image on two of the screens.

'We got the tapping warrant you requested six, nearly seven hours ago. We've got four lines. And chose to prioritise tapping the four known hangarounds and prospects – or whatever they like to call themselves – who according to information from the SAGC have most frequently been in the vicinity of Jensen and Milton. They're all minors and domiciled with a guardian. So far . . . thirteen telephone calls and twenty-seven text messages.'

'And?'

*'She did it. And then I told the other whore, no more booze in the flat.'*

'I've gone through all the transcripts. Nothing about the absconders. Nothing about the break-out. Nothing at all about anything that might have something to do with them. Everyone's had their orders. Nothing is said and nothing you might use will be said on the phone.'

Grens couldn't stand still.

'Then you'll have to tap *more* lines. And intercept *more*.'

'I don't have more.'

'Well, get them then.'

'However, Ewert . . . on the security police's orders, we've been intercepting six *other* numbers, so-called unit phones, for the past eight weeks.'

The tall detective sergeant pressed a key on the keyboard that controlled one of the screens.

'*Tomorrow. A grey Mazda.*'

'Mobile phones that we've known about for a long time, smuggled in and hidden by inmates in a total of four units in three different prisons.'

'*A grey Mazda?*'

'I can't tell you why we're actually doing it, which aggravated crime the warrant applies to. Nor can I tell you how we found out about any of the phones. The tapping is in connection with *another* investigation, *another* crime, and what I have been granted special dispensation to play for you is what we call surplus information.'

'*Yes.*'

'*Where?*'

'A conversation from three weeks ago. We are certain that one of the parties, the one with the higher voice, is Gabriel Milton and that the place he is calling from is, within a hundred-metre margin, one of the addresses in Råby Allé. We are equally certain that the other person speaking, the one with the rougher voice, is Leon Jensen, and that the place where he is calling from is almost certainly one of the units in Aspsås prison.'

*'Front seat. And left front wheel. And maybe the sun visor.'*

'A drug delivery. Two phone calls and a crime that has nothing to do with our warrant. Surplus information. Nothing we can or are allowed to use.'

That timeline again. This time without images, just voices on an electronic line on a computer screen.

Gunnar Werner moved the cursor and opened a new document.

'But what I really wanted you . . . *all* . . . to listen to was this. Recorded from the same telephone. But considerably more recent.'

*'Brother?'*

Grens looked at Werner and pulled over the chair indicated. He understood now. And he wanted to listen carefully.

'To be more precise – recorded yesterday evening at nineteen fifty-two hours.'

'Nineteen fifty-two hours?'

'Yes.'

The detective sergeant handed a pair of rather big headphones to each of them and then pulled the door to.

No one else was to listen to this.

'Twenty-five minutes *after* the last break-out. *After* your last trace.'

He stretched over and adjusted Grens's earphones, which were askew. In order to hear the background noises as well, it was important that they covered the entire ear.

'A conversation that stands out from the rest. Someone phones, the call is answered, but the conversation is not between two phones. The voices that are talking are all in the same place and they are only talking to each other, not to the person who has been called.'

'Sorry, I don't understand.'

'I'm guessing, judging by the sounds, that they are in a car. We've identified the position as being very close to the motorway exit in Upplands Väsby. The person has called a voicemail, a top-up card, holder unknown. The person calling hasn't phoned to talk to anyone, he's just called and then lets the voicemail record an ongoing conversation.'

He adjusted Ewert Grens's headphones again, they were still crooked.

'I want you to listen from here.'

The detective sergeant from the tapping unit leaned his long body over Grens's shoulder and arm and pressed the key immediately below the screen with his index finger, which appeared to be shaking.

*Clear sounds from inside a moving car.*
*Then another sound.*
*Once.*
*Once again.*
*Something banging against metal, and yet a muffled, almost imperceptible sound.*

'We've just listened to the phone calls from yesterday evening and last night. And I don't have the transcripts yet. But that sound, Ewert . . . you can't hear it in any other recording.'

Ewert Grens turned to the screen, looking for the timeline.

19.54.22.

She was still alive then.

*The sound again.*
*And again.*
'*Brother, stop!*'

A voice they haven't heard before.

Not as clear as Jensen's hoarse voice and Milton's high voice. Could be from the passenger seat, maybe from the back seat, someone sitting further away who was not holding the telephone.

*And again.*
'*Brother, stop. The screw bitch, she's . . . I can't stand that fucking kicking . . .*'

Ewert Grens looked at Sven, at Hermansson, at Werner. They were all thinking the same thing. The sound of someone lying in the boot and kicking was obvious. So they must have heard her. That's to say, she could also hear them. Tied up with a tape over her mouth and in the dark. It wasn't possible to imagine her fear, or rather, terror.

'*Brother, stop. The screw bitch, she's . . .*'
'*Wait.*'

A new voice.

Lips and mouth close to the telephone microphone, the voice that now spoke was the person holding it.

Leon Jensen.

'*Brother, fuck, should we . . .*'
'*Shut the fuck up and stay there. I'll fix it.*'

Grens sank deeper into the elongated worm that was a sound file.

*The sound of a car door opening.*
*The sound of wind, of traffic, of a car hooting, twice.*

Hermansson moved closer and unfolded a map.
'Upplands Väsby. The roundabout by the motorway exit.'

*The sound of quick footsteps.*
*The sound of a lock opening, maybe a car boot.*

'The horn, Ewert, that's the guy in the tanker, the driver who called in.'

*'I'll fix this. She won't kick any more.'*

The hoarse voice holding the telephone, that had phoned no one in particular and who they recognised from earlier phone calls.

*A sharp sound.*
*'Take it easy, brother, for fuck's sake!'*
*A choked, gurgling noise.*
*'Leon, Jesus, take it fucking easy, we—'*
*A dull sound.*
*Then footsteps, then a car door shutting, then an engine starting.*
*'Let's go.'*
*'What about her?'*
*'She'll be quiet now.'*

Ewert Grens looked at the black line that said no more.
And then turned to Werner.
It seemed as though his long, almost transparent hands were still shaking.
'Anything more?'
'No.'

'No more phone calls? Before? After?'

'Just that. Just the one phone call yesterday from that phone. And without talking to anyone except a voicemail.'

Grens ran his finger along the black worm on the screen.

It didn't move.

'Are you still intercepting?'

'Yes.'

'And if you get any more . . . *surplus information* of the sort you can't talk about?'

'You know that I can't say anything then, either.'

Ewert Grens took off the headphones and handed them back to Werner, but then suddenly changed his mind and put them on again, askew.

'I want to hear it again.'

'Which part?'

'You know which part.'

Gunnar Werner moved the cursor back along the timeline.

*A sharp sound.*
*A choked, gurgling noise.*
*A dull sound.*

Grens looked at his colleague and peer who had been involved in just as many investigations about people who had taken the right to change another person's life.

'Do you hear what I hear?'

Werner nodded.

'Yes.'

'Will you ever understand it?'

'No.'

Ewert Grens got up from the uncomfortable chair and moved towards the door, only to stop again immediately.

'I want a copy of this.'

'You've already got one.'

Gunnar Werner pointed to the CD that Sven had in his hand. Grens nodded his thanks and carried on, more convinced than ever that there were things that he would never really be a part of.

A black line on a computer screen that moved the viewer forwards or backwards in time.

A round, plastic disc that could at any time replicate the voices and sounds that forced someone to stop breathing.

Ewert grens went from one arm of the Kronoberg building that housed various police bodies to another. With heavy, limping footsteps he moved between the walls as fast as his feet would carry him.

And a short phone call punctuated by frequent, noisy panting.

'Ågestam?'

'Yes.'

'It is *him*.'

'You said that the last time you called.'

'And it's still him.'

'So, a DNA analysis . . . you've got one?'

'Not yet.'

'Fingerprints?'

'Soon.'

'Blood? Fibres?'

'In a few hours.'

'Grens, I need *all* four. And when you've got all that – an accurate time of death.'

'You'll get it. And more.'

'More?'

The limping slowed. Ewert Grens was playing with a plastic disc in his jacket pocket, sounds that would not be stilled.

'More.'

The forensics lab was empty. His brown beret was lying on one of the benches, and his black bag stood open on one of the tables, the one that was always there like an extension of his heart at any crime scene. Grens had worked with Nils Krantz for thirty years and as with Werner, a colleague whom he had known for so long, but never met outside work, not even for a cup of coffee at the café on the corner of Bergsgatan, had never talked with him about his family, football, the weather, how high taxes were, the sort of things people talked about together. None of them had learnt to do it.

He sat down close to the brown bags with *autopsy* written by hand on every one. Bodies in particles. Investigations that were to be subjected to microscopes and carbon dust in order to be more than just guesses and suspicion. Surrounding the bags, a pile of used gelatine lifters, tweezers, a magnifying glass, brushes, labels, pins, light leads, toothpicks, plastic containers, rubber gloves – the detective superintendent stood up, impatient, opened one door at a time, the one to the storeroom, to the darkroom, to the fibre room for the perpetrator's clothes, and finally to the fibre room for the victim's clothes.

Nils Krantz was standing there. In the confined space that wasn't much bigger than a cell.

'Fibres.'

The forensic scientist turned with hunched shoulders as he put some black tights and a pair of white pants into a bag each.

'I need your analysis of their clothes, the fourth one, *are you listening Krantz*, I need fibres.'

Her dark blue uniform jacket and light blue uniform shirt were hanging to dry in a humming drying cabinet, cut up arms dancing excitedly against the glass door.

*Frightened.* Grens looked at the empty clothes and pictured José Pereira in front of a wall of faces and his description of walking a short distance with the young woman who had worn them through one of the underground passages in Aspsås prison. *She was frightened.*

'You'll get my analysis when I'm finished.'

She had been lying in the back seat and then in the boot. She had been so close to the man who took her life, her clothes had also been in contact with his. Krantz smoothed out her uniform trousers on the table, cut them into strips for reference samples and put the strips into two baskets – textiles that would later be compared with the prison clothes found in the first escape vehicle.

'Well then, get finished. Give me an answer!'

'You and I don't really do the same thing. Answer, Ewert? You're looking for *your* truth. Whereas I . . . I'm looking for *the* truth. When I'm done here, eighty-five per cent of my work still remains. Compiling reports and records, *the truth*.'

There was a smell of disinfectant. Every trace of the previous victim's clothes had to be purged before the next victim's clothes were allowed in to come into contact with the same scissors and drying cabinet.

'You question someone. And the truth is something that someone chooses to tell you, their interpretation of the truth then becomes your interpretation of their interpretation. But when I write, Ewert, I have to be able to stand up in court with whatever I write! *The truth*. I don't interpret and I don't guess. In a few hours, I will have everything you want. DNA, finger-prints, blood, and this, fibres. But right now, let the ones who have to analyse, analyse. *Then* you will get the truth.'

The sleeves of the cut-up shirt moved more as the heat grad-ually drove out the moisture, as though they were banging against the glass, wanting to get out.

'When?'

'When I'm finished!'

Krantz, who had spent his days with a black bag on his knees on some floor looking for something that no one else saw, was a calm and methodical man who had chosen to be just that, one piece of the puzzle at a time. But he was agitated when he left the room that had now become too small.

'He won't confess, Nils.'

Ewert Grens had chosen to live as the opposite, in constant movement, restlessness, impulses that often conflicted, and he chased after his colleague, who was about to disappear.

'He won't answer any of the questions, none. We have to link him to it with evidence, piece by piece. I want to know that it's him!'

'This evening.'

They were back in the lab with the overflowing tables.

'Nils . . . I want something before this evening!'

When a calm and methodical man who lives for one piece of the puzzle at a time finally breaks, it is often an uncontrolled eruption of anger that flies in every direction. A face that was now flaming red turned, arms slicing the air, sweeping two microscopes onto the floor.

'Don't you ever shout at me again!'

The forensic scientist had seen the microscopes falling but didn't even bother to check the equipment he otherwise protected with his life. He took a step forwards and stopped, his face only centimetres from the person who was hounding him. They had worked together for so long. They were made of the same stuff. They had lived through what would be over in a couple of years now, when someone else would sit in their offices and never ask who had sat there before. All this time and they had never stood so close, they could feel each other's breath, they needed to keep their distance.

'Four hours ago I was in a trauma room in the Karolinska hospital.'

Nils Krantz wasn't shouting. Not yet. He would shortly. He thought at first that he had, but then heard that that wasn't the case, he just wasn't used to it, to raising his voice.

'Three hours ago I was in the autopsy room at Solna coroner's office.'

It was louder, no doubt about it, but not loud enough, his cheeks were burning, it should have been louder.

'Two hours ago I was in a car covered in blood.'

Now he was shouting, he could feel it, his chest opened up, the anger pressed its way up and out.

'And only minutes ago I was in a fibre room so I could tape and dry clothes! I'm going as fast as I can! Is there anything else you can get worked up about that you won't be able to change?'

Ewert Grens looked at someone standing close, shouting. He'd never seen Nils Krantz like this before.

And it was just as tangible when he now lowered his voice.

'I repeat . . . why the damn rush, Ewert? Do you even know yourself?'

Grens had an uneasy feeling in his chest. It was all those words that came so hard and fast. He had no idea what he'd done and after a while he backed away from the face that was doing exactly what he normally did.

'I . . .'

Nils Krantz bent down and picked up the microscopes – they appeared to be whole. The voice behind him, Grens's voice, was quiet.

'. . . I'm not really sure why, but . . . I'm sorry.'

He put them down on the long table, in the same place that they always stood.

'It's just . . . it's as if . . .'

'What?'

'As if it's my fault.'

SVEN SUNDKVIST HAD been sitting waiting in the car outside Kungsholmsgatan for twenty minutes when Ewert Grens waved at one of the security guards, who opened the rotating glass door from where he was sitting in the office, came out and up the steps and then got into the passenger seat.

'That took a while.'

'Krantz.'

'Krantz, what?'

'He seemed to be a bit stressed, you know, off balance.'

Polhemsgatan, Fleminggatan, and Sven was just about to turn right into Sankt Eriksgatan when Grens knocked on the window.

'Left. And then stop outside Thelins.'

Late afternoon in Stockholm, on a main traffic artery. Sven sighed and double-parked.

'I forgot my money. Can you come in and pay for me?'

The sweet, yeasty smell of buns and peppercakes as they walked in and up to the counter, displaying cakes and laden open sandwiches behind the glass.

'I want ten more.'

Ewert Grens turned the plate with almond slices and the young girl behind the counter smiled as though she recognised him.

'More?'

'Yes.'

'And the ones from yesterday?'

'They're still in the box. Have to have enough for everyone, you know, on a day like today.'

Now he smiled too. And gave no further explanation, even though it was obvious that Sven wondered what he meant.

An investigation that was putting him under more pressure and stress than any other he'd encountered.

Almond slices and a smile that was almost disconcerting.

Sven Sundkvist put three hundred-kronor notes down on the counter and waited for the change and a boss he would never understand.

————

Fifteen minutes later he parked yet again outside Solna coroner's office. And stopped yet again on the threshold of the autopsy room, whereas Ewert Grens marched forwards to the table and the body that was lying there.

'Stick by me.'

Ewert had never demanded an explanation, never tried to marginalise or undermine, he had understood and often of his own accord sent Sven off to do an interview or phone someone, anything that was away from the death he was trying to avoid.

'This is important. This time you have to follow.'

'Important?'

'Important for me.'

Sven Sundkvist stepped further into the room that had a naked body on a table in the middle. No explanation. But no more questions either. It was as if Ewert didn't want to see this death either.

Ludvig Errfors had heard his footsteps and pulled a green sheet over the young woman who was lying so still.

'You can take it off.'

The forensic pathologist waited until he had eye contact with Grens and then nodded towards Sven.

'But . . .'

'Today he's going to look.'

Sven couldn't remember the last time he'd seen a body so close; he had long since forgotten how it felt when someone who was no longer alive looked at him. Ewert wasn't forcing him to do it to be horrible, the boss he had come to know wasn't like that. There was a reason, he just didn't know what it was, that was all.

He chose her face. Her eyes. For a long time he just looked at them, but after a while couldn't bear any more demanding looks and therefore chose instead the cut on the white skin of her shaved head, by the ear, focused on the open wound that disappeared round her neck. Just that.

'Why?'

Sven Sundkvist was talking to Ewert Grens but didn't take his eyes off the cut – nowhere else, just there.

'Why, Ewert?'

If it's his DNA, fingerprints, blood, fibres. If the time of death corresponds.

'Because I said.'

If it's him. If it's my fault.

'It's important. For me.'

*'Brother?'*

Grens had been carrying a brown briefcase. He opened it and produced a CD player from one of the side pockets.

'This was recorded last night. In the car where we found her body this morning.'

He placed it between the two naked feet, touched them with the back of his hands.

'I want to know *exactly* when she died.'

The forensic pathologist listened to the young voices from the lower end of the table, his face visibly moved.

'I can't fix an exact time.'

*Clear sounds from inside a moving car.*

*Then another sound.*

'Errfors?'

'Yes?'

'The *exact* time.'

*Something banging against metal, and yet a muffled, almost imperceptible sound.*

Errfors looked at the large detective superintendent, then the shiny machine close to the bare skin, then at the clock on the wall that pointed to small lines and not numbers.

'It's now . . . eleven thirty, you agree?'

*The sound again. And again.*

'Brother, stop!'

One of his hands on her cheek, lifting her eyelid with his thumb and index finger.

A thin syringe in the other.

The pupil was so empty, even when he plunged the injection in and emptied the contents of the plastic tube.

'Atropine, tropicamide, acetylcholine . . . when we die, the eyes sometime continue to live, to open and close, and . . . *there*, did you see that? Now we know that she died sometime between five-thirty yesterday morning and six-thirty this morning.'

Ewert Grens leaned closer to an eye that could no longer see, but had almost winked at him.

05.30 yesterday.

'A twenty-five hour interval.'

You were still at Aspsås prison then.

'Not good enough. I want a more exact time.'

*The sound of a car door opening.*

Ludvig Errfors reached up to one of the metal shelves that caught the light on the white wall, lifted down a small bag and opened it.

A hammer.

He hit her right arm with it, high up and quite hard.

'Nothing.'

He looked at Grens and Sundkvist.

'You agree?'

'With what?'

'You saw nothing.'

'No.'

He hit again, twice, in the middle of her upper arm.

'The bicep muscle. If there had been a reaction – a fast-wave movement that stops and freezes in two bumps – it would be less than thirteen hours. But it didn't. So we know that it must be *more* than thirteen hours ago.'

'Right.'

'So we can reduce the interval. Now we know that she died yesterday between five-thirty in the morning and ten thirty in the evening.'

Grens grabbed the metal hammer, felt it, it was riffled and cold.

'Not good enough.'

*The sound of quick footsteps.*

'This side.'

The white coat moved around the body and the dark patches on the torso had spiky edges that seemed to reach out towards each other.

'She was lying on her left side in the car boot and when the blood stops pumping . . . livor mortis, fully spread, and that reduces our interval as well. Now we know that she died yesterday sometime between eleven thirty in the morning and ten thirty at night.'

11.30.

You were still somewhere in the prison corridors then.

'Not good enough.'

*The sound of a lock opening, maybe a car boot.*

Her left arm was hanging partially extended from her naked body, she had been bound, tape around her wrists, and when Ludvig Errfors applied full pressure and pressed it to the table, there was a loud, snapping sound.

'Maximum rigor mortis. Muscle fibres that have contracted and stiffened reduces the interval by a further four hours. She died yesterday sometime between three thirty and ten thirty p.m.'

15.30.

You were sitting locked in your cell then. You'd had your tools made and delivered then. You had started to cut through the metal bars then.

'Still not good enough.'

*A sharp sound.*

*'Take it easy, brother, for fuck's sake!'*

A square plastic box on a trolley with small wheels that squeaked when a white coat sleeve pulled it closer, two blue cables from the middle of it got slowly shorter as the forensic pathologist first slid them over and then under one of her eyes.

'The iris sphincter responds to electricity, fifty hertz, fifty volts . . . *there*, you see, the whole eyelid contracts.'

The grey face, the black lips. Sven Sundkvist couldn't take any more.

This time she really had winked at him.

'That closes the interval by another four hours. She died between seven thirty and ten thirty yesterday evening.'

19.30.

The final image. STORBODA, CAMERA 1. The car moved off down the drive, suddenly stopped.

You leant out then.

You held the automatic in your hand then and shot at the camera and high gate.

'Not good enough.'

*A choked, gurgling noise.*

*'Leon, Jesus, take it fucking easy, we . . .'*

'Then I'll have to ask you to turn around.'

Sven Sundkvist was already looking the other way. Ewert Grens looked at the bare feet, the white legs, the blotchy body.

'Turn around, Ewert. For her sake.'

They concentrated on the light-coloured wall, on the metal containers and metal instruments lined up on metal shelves.

'I'm measuring the body temperature in her rectum. How far it has sunk will of course depend on how warm it was in the car and now how warm it is in this room. Some people prefer computers. I still use Henssge's equation and . . . yes, we can lose another hour. Time of death . . . sometime between seven thirty and nine thirty p.m.'

It was you. It was me.

'Still not exact enough.'

Sven suddenly turned round again, the woman lying there, he looked at her again.

'Ewert?'

'It's important. For me.'

*A dull sound.*

*Then footsteps, then a car door shutting, then an engine starting.*

Another square plastic box, this one looked more like a microwave oven.

'After this, I can't do any more.'

Ludvig Errfors got the box and put it on the table right up to her skin and then immediately syringed the eye that has so recently winked.

He withdrew the needle until the barrel was full.

'Vitreous fluid.'

And then emptied it into a test tube that was positioned in the middle of the plastic box.

'The longer she's been dead, the more potassium there is.'

A small window in the middle of the box, chemical symbols, electronic lines, numbers and commas.

'Around zero point nineteen millimoles per litre an hour.'

'I see.'

'So I can reduce the time interval a little more.'

'Well?'

'Sometime between seven thirty and eight p.m.'

Ewert Grens looked at the lines and numbers that were the amount of potassium in a dead person's eye.

'Are you absolutely certain about that?'

'I'm not absolutely certain of anything. But I would witness to it in court.'

*'Let's go.'*

*'What about her?'*

*'She'll be quiet now.'*

The voices at her feet had finished speaking and the detective superintendent looked for the button at one end of the machine that would stop the CD and cut off the loud rushing noise.

'The time when he stops talking is exactly nineteen fifty-four twenty-two.'

Ludvig Errfors waited while Grens's hands stowed away the plastic disc in his briefcase again.

He was obviously deeply affected.

'We do autopsies on around thirteen hundred people a year. Full autopsies. Seven specialists and a staff doctor – and I'm convinced that none of us have ever listened to a murder *while it was happening*.'

An accurate time of death.

Grens suddenly started to move, eyes that knew no peace, Sven and Errfors recalled the bloody knuckles and looked at each other in relief when he disappeared towards the exit.

'What is it you're not telling us, Ewert?'

Sven had followed him into an office and stared at the person who had collapsed onto one of Errfors' chairs.

'I've already said. You don't need to know.'

'Last night you smashed a window when you broke into a flat, unarmed, inhabited by several young men who are classified as highly dangerous. You forced your way into the trauma room and declared a woman dead. You've annoyed Pereira. You're harassing Krantz and Errfors.'

The detective superintendent looked up and Sven nodded.

'Yes, they've all spoken to me.'

Ewert Grens stared at his colleague in indignation and then swapped the chair for a coffee machine that didn't have coffee but could provide hot chocolate. He tasted it and poured it into the paper bin.

'And now . . . you're moved by a dead person. I've never seen it affect you before. Except . . . yes . . . well.'

'You said it.'

'I want to know.'

Grens pursed his lips, as if to make it absolutely clear that he had no intention of answering.

'Ewert, I know . . . I can feel . . . something's not right.'

'You can *feel* it? In the same way that Hermansson thinks that *something's up*?'

That indignant expression again when he turned towards a young woman who no longer existed. Ludvig Errfors was still standing by her head, perhaps he had realised that it was best that the conversation was only between Grens and Sundkvist, perhaps he just didn't want to leave her alone. He had removed all the instruments that had together measured the time of her demise and the immobile body somehow looked smaller, as if she had started to die for the second time.

'We know that she had a sock in her mouth and her mouth was taped.'

The forensic pathologist put a gentle hand on her cheek.

'What we just listened to . . . they stopped the car, and someone pulled off the tape.'

*A sharp sound.*

'Pushed the sock further in.'

*A choked, gurgling noise.*

'And then closed the boot again.'

*A dull sound.*

'It was at that moment she choked. Six minutes later she was medically dead.'

HE HAD NOT thought about visiting her again that day, or that week. But when the car turned out of the car park at Solna coroner's office, it was as if it steered itself towards Solna kyrkväg and Norra cemetery and then chose to stop in front of Gate 1.

'Do you want to come?'

Ewert Grens was on his way to her grave. To Anni. And he had asked someone else to come.

Sven didn't answer at first. Ewert had never even considered the question before. This was his private place, a part of Ewert Grens that no one would ever get close to.

An extraordinary question.

The uncomfortable silence while his boss stood there with the door open, waiting for an answer.

'No.'

He wouldn't go.

'Thank you, Ewert, but no.'

Grens walked through the grounds with silent graves. For a short while something akin to peace in his heart. The place he had so long feared and not dared to visit was now a peace that he found nowhere else.

He watered again, straightened and pushed down the white cross until it stood firm.

Every Tuesday for twenty-seven years he'd gone to the same nursing home, and continued to go there even though someone else was living in her room. He had stood close to what had once been her window and thought about her sitting there, looking out, looking for something. Until that morning when he had walked around on the grass and on the terrace and a

373

medical student called Susann, who had once warned him against *hoping for too much*, had come out and talked to him about something he was unaware of, that he had timetabled his grief, that he lived *for* the grief and not *with* it and he had to remember that what he was afraid of had already happened.

It felt good to stand by her grave and cross.

With her, on this day.

A bit more water, to be on the safe side.

––––––––––

Sven Sundkvist was sitting on the end of the bonnet when Ewert came through the gate from the cemetery, which was always open. His face resting in the September sun, he had his eyes closed, a scrap of summer left on his warm cheeks.

'A little longer, Ewert.'

The detective superintendent seemed to be calmer, his bulky body less in conflict with everything around him.

'Jump in. You can sunbathe more another day.'

Without being aware of it, Sven listened to the voice in the way he always did, comparing it with other Ewert voices. This one was friendly. He didn't just look calmer, he *was* calmer.

'I've just spoken to one of the guys from the bomb squad.'

'And?'

'The flat that you thought smelled like marzipan, the stain in the middle of the kitchen table.'

'Sven?'

'They've analysed it. Nitroglycerine. The active component in dynamite.'

They were still standing outside the car, hadn't got in.

'The dog noticed something on the same table, two centimetres away, something that looked like white cake crumbs. ANFO. Bulk industrial explosives. Extremely powerful, normally used for blasting tunnels.'

Hands on the warm metal body of the car.

'And on another visit, just now, they found some pieces of white and green plastic casing in the doorway to the sitting room. Detonator wires.'

In one single movement, one single breath, Ewert Grens lost the peace he had taken back with him.

'Dynamite. ANFO. Detonators.'

'Yes.'

'You know what that means.'

'I think so.'

'They've built a bomb, Sven.'

THEY HAD JUST reversed out of the parking space in front of Gate 1 and started to drive down Solna kyrkväg towards Solnavägen and Vasastan when Grens pulled into the side and stopped.

Eight thousand council flats in identical blocks.

'We won't manage it in time.'

They would have to open every door, window, cellar.

'Sven, *we won't manage in time.*'

He switched off the engine; it made it easier to speak.

'The six addresses that we've got a warrant to bug. Places where Jensen and Milton have been observed. Just bugging isn't enough. *We have to go in.*'

'But we can't. We've got a warrant to intercept, but not to search. None of them are suspected of a crime.'

'Six break-ins, Sven, at the same time in six flats. Using the same tactic.'

'That's illegal.'

'Stun grenade and tear gas and Sig Sauer 226 and Heckler and Koch MP5A2.'

'It would be a breach of duty.'

'Every person in every flat on the floor. Every room and every wardrobe and every drawer, no matter how small it is, ransacked.'

'Ewert . . .'

'A dead young woman, Sven. A bomb. And you're sitting there talking about Prosecution Authority forms?'

He opened the wardrobe. Mirror on the inside of the door. The beige jacket, he liked it a lot.

He put out the plate of almond slices and bag of pastries, went down the corridor to the coffee machine and pressed first for a cup of hot water and then three coffees, one black, one with double sugar and one with whitish-yellow powder that was supposed to resemble milk. Carried on to the kitchen, a teabag and a tray for carrying the four full cups.

'*Extra* sugar.'

He put the first warm cup down with great care by one of Hermansson's notebooks.

'And this one . . . something like milk.'

He smiled vaguely at Sven, who moved his mobile phone to make room.

'Tea. Yellow and red packaging. I've never managed to learn the different kinds.'

Lars Ågestam accepted a cup of the tea that was kept in square boxes in kitchens in soulless workplaces and tasted of absolutely nothing. Grens made sure that each of them had got the right cup while he himself held the one with black coffee.

'Help yourselves.'

He turned down the edges of the white paper bag and held out the plate. Sven and Mariana looked at each other, they were thinking the same thing: only once before had Ewert Grens ever got coffee for anyone other than himself.

'Almond slice. And pastries in the bag.'

Danish pastries with yellow custard in the middle. Almond slices with pink icing.

He took one of each when the others hesitated, and met their eyes, one at time.

Satisfied. That's how he looked.

'Because it's a perfect day for almond slices. Go on, take one. Before they're all gone.'

He broke off another half, chewed, drank up what was left in the plastic cup and then got up and went over to his desk.

Grens had a yellow mat on his desk.

At least, that's what it looked like when he lifted it up and held it towards them. But if they leaned closer they could see that it was yellow Post-it notes side by side, on top of each other, each one with something written on it.

'Every time I come in here it looks like this.'

He put down the underlay and pulled off one of the notes.

'Vincent Carlsson, Swedish Television.'

He crumpled it up and dropped it in the waste-paper basket.

'Johanna Linder, Swedish Radio.'

He crumpled that one too, then ripped it to pieces to be sure, and let the pieces float down towards the first one.

'Viveka Lind, Tidningarnas Telegrambyrå. Jovan Mravac, *Expressen*. Sune Johannesson, *Kristianstadsbladet*. Riita Strömberg, *Göteborgs-Posten*. Lisa Erixon, *Sydsvenska Dagbladet*.'

One at a time, scrunched up, into the waste-paper basket on top of the others.

'No doubt they're all good people, from all right newspapers. But none of them will talk to me or you. I don't want anything public yet. I have no intention of helping to bolster a murderer's criminal status.'

Half of them left. His palm against the mat when he swept them all at once to the floor.

'I'm not going to answer a single question. And you're not going to either. You won't hear *gang war* and *murder hunt*. The only thing you're going to do is to make sure that any press conferences arranged by the people who are paid to do that, are as far away as possible and about as little as possible. They have . . . to see themselves on TV . . . they thrive on the attention and are not going to get any air from me.'

Ewert Grens bent down to the floor and gathered up the yellow Post-it notes that hadn't landed where they should, and then went back over to the sofa and the plastic cups standing beside a paper bag and a greasy cake plate. Sven, Hermansson and Ågestam had all drunk nearly half of their cups and eaten an almond slice as well as a pastry.

Thus far it had been a very good first case meeting.

'We know that they've committed murder. That they have a bomb at their disposal. And that they are expanding fast and about to succeed.'

And in exactly thirty seconds everything would be even better.

'We have no choice.'

They would go in where they could, close in on the fugitives and then disappear.

'From now on, we have to use coercive measures.'

———

Wanda wandered aimlessly through the rooms she so seldom visited, her own flat in the middle of Råby. It felt good to be here and her body relaxed, music in the kitchen and the hall and she danced a few steps. Gabriel didn't like listening to voices singing, it made his head spin, and here she could choose whoever she liked and turn the volume up loud. It was the middle of the day and she had just woken up, she was so tired. As she swayed and twisted to the refrain she held a hand on her stomach that had not yet started to swell, but still felt so big. It must have been later that everything happened at once. The crash of a window being broken in the kitchen and the black thing that wobbled, then rolled fast across the sitting room floor and the terrible bang and the light that was all white so she couldn't see and then the next bang from the sitting room with more bright white light and the door in the hallway was broken in two and everything moving around her and she couldn't see properly, could only make out shadows that came closer and pushed her to the floor and held her neck down firmly and pulled her hands behind her back and clicked hard metal round her wrists. She guessed four or five or six from the front door and one or two from the kitchen and maybe one or two from the balcony, and if all the movement around her was people and if the black things on their heads were helmets and the thing in front of their faces was a visor, if that was the case, then there were about ten of them up close and even though blood was running from her eardrums she heard them shouting and the one on top of her was so heavy and pushed even harder when she tried to get up.

––––––––––

Lars Ågestam took another small bite of the pastry that seemed to swell in his mouth and get even bigger whenever he tried to swallow. He couldn't do it. He sat still and looked straight ahead while he pushed it back between the cake plate and the cup of tea.

'Coercive measures?'

The public prosecutor wouldn't lift up the brown plastic cup once more.

'Later, Ågestam.'

Lars Ågestam had thought of asking again, but chose to nod instead, pretended to carry on chewing and then smiled when he pointed to Grens.

'You've got a new jacket. And bought us cakes.'

Ewert Grens didn't smile back. He tried, he did every time, but it didn't work and he was still not entirely sure why. Perhaps because the young prosecutor who had risen to chief district prosecutor within only a few years represented every-thing he wasn't, he worked as hard, spent just as much time in the corridors of the police headquarters, but for different reasons – Grens worked because he liked working more than not working, Ågestam did it because he liked promotion. Perhaps it was because one had been educated by life, the other by university, so they viewed the way forward very differently. Perhaps it was because one of them was younger and still had all the big decisions ahead of him, and one of them was older and could only make the decision once more.

Grens moved the plate of cakes and two of the cups and then went to get his computer, which he positioned in the middle of the coffee table so that everyone could see. The image that had assaulted CAMERA 7, Österåker prison wall, top corner.

He had looked straight into the camera, posed, his face uncovered.

His posture, his features, it could have been the same person, they were even the same age.

'Leon Jensen. He looks the same, moves the same. As his father.'

The cursor on his face, he froze the picture, zoomed in.

'Daniel Jensen. That is what his father was called before he disappeared. The first person in our witness protection programme.'

Ewert Grens's hand knocked the screen as he pointed, the finger that outlined the face had tried to push it down from the wall.

'He gave us his friends. His girlfriend. And we gave him a new identity and a stay in a hostel in Småland where he had no contact with his past. It worked for six months. Drugs. If you're craving drugs and don't have any money, you have to turn to crime. He went to prison again, under his new name, a destructive but intelligent young man who changed into a bumbling small-time dealer, in and out all the time.'

The quality of the security camera picture wasn't particularly good and when Grens took them even closer by zooming in a bit more, Leon Jensen's face turned into big dots that didn't stick together and his eyes became two empty holes.

'Since last night, I've tried to go back, *remember*, but all I can pull out is as blurred as this damn picture. Only one day is clear. The third and last time that I visited him. A red house in the woods, just outside Nässjö. I'd gone there to tell him that his girlfriend had been pregnant. And that she'd given birth to his son the day before. It was later that evening that he told me to go to hell, fell off the wagon again and left both the red house and the witness protection programme.'

———

Deniz was standing in the bathroom when she heard the lift stop on the sixth floor and the doors open without anyone getting in or coming out. She adjusted the mirror and then brushed her newly washed hair and smiled at the naked woman who was over forty and now dared to look at herself without seeing and magnifying the things that no one else saw but that it was so easy to imagine that was all they saw. She had learnt to identify the sounds in the building that housed forty-eight flats and in the past few minutes had heard several different kinds of feet. Midday on a Sunday, there weren't usually that many people around so high up, even on a weekday morning – she guessed there were four or five pairs that stopped when they got to this floor. She towelled her hair one more time, a quick glance in the mirror, long enough to be proud of herself – all the energy that young women wasted on trying to outrun self-loathing – and the acceptance that comes with middle-age. A ring on the front doorbell. Someone had pressed it, two short signals. She didn't open. She never did. But she could hear voices and then one of them opened the letter box and shouted in, and when she left the bathroom to see what it was all about, she heard the noise of a ten-centimetre piece of steel in the lock and another sound that was a crowbar breaking open the door, mixed with the screams of her five-year-old daughter who came running out of the sitting room, but most of all, the noise of her own thoughts about Eddie, who was still out there, somewhere.

———

'Does she know?'

'I'm sorry?'

'That you took her boyfriend from her? She was pregnant and she wasn't told. He just disappeared. Does she know now?'

'Does she know what?'

'What happened? Where he went?'

'No.'

Mariana Hermansson didn't take her eyes off Ewert Grens, it was important that he should feel it, even though she had learnt long ago that that face meant the same as no answer. And she wasn't going to ask any more either. About why a pregnant woman hadn't been told. Not yet. He probably couldn't even answer the question himself.

Grens emptied the plastic cup that had already been empty for some time, the final few drops hiding at the bottom. He put a hand on the coffee table, drew it across the surface, as with the Post-it notes a while ago, only now it was pastry crumbs and he swept them over the edge of the table onto the floor.

The picture on the computer screen that was zoomed in on a face that was dots and holes now turned into a film sequence that was almost six years old, from a security camera that was far from any prison wall.

A jeweller's shop. One of the wide avenues in Skärholmen shopping centre. The camera was positioned high up behind the counter.

They all leaned in again.

The picture was black and white. It wasn't as jumpy as security camera films often are, and the focus was good. Jewellery in glass cases. A shop assistant straightening a pearl necklace on one of the shelves by the window. Then someone comes in through the door. Light-coloured shoes. Dark tracksuit bottoms. A grey top with the hood over his head. Another person behind him. And another. Until there are about twenty of them. A couple of them in puberty, the others yet to reach it.

'There's no sound. But several witnesses describe the same silence in real life. They say nothing, just walk in and position themselves.'

Twenty-one hoodies all in a row, a big U along the walls. And at the edge of the picture, a further ten outside the shop. One of them has a paving stone in his right hand, raises it, throws it at the window. The shop assistant, a middle-aged woman, runs out of the shop and then disappears out of the picture at the moment when the line of twenty-one turns around and smashes all the display cases with hammers and stones and gloved hands, then takes out folded plastic bags from the front pocket of their hoodies and empty the shelves of wedding rings, engagement rings, necklaces, watches, christening gifts, earrings, bracelets, silver plates.

Until Ewert Grens pressed pause and froze the picture.

'Leon Jensen was twelve years old. And had already learnt how to exploit his friends for his own means.'

Grens pressed the tip of his index finger against the screen, against the one who had thrown the paving stone and then taken a few steps into the shop and stood there, directing every movement without speaking once.

The sequence carried on.

Twenty-one bulging plastic bags, as they calmly walk out of the empty shop and through the shopping centre's wide main avenue, held triumphantly high above their heads.

'That very same morning, he'd run away from a special training centre in Örkelljunga, five hundred kilometres away. And in order to get home, to get here, and rob this jeweller's shop in the afternoon, he'd stolen a total of four cars, all Mercedes. Each to their own. But the head of the centre had a Mercedes. And Leon Jensen was shown by the others who were there how to steal it. He *learnt* Mercedes. School for crime, twelve years old, that would be sixth grade, wouldn't it?'

The security camera from the jeweller's shop continues to roll from its position above the counter.

Large pieces and tiny pieces of glass all over the floor.

'And from then on ... abuse, robbery, arson, blackmail, minor drug offences, assaults on officers, aggravated blackmail, serious drug crimes, abduction, armed robbery, aggravated assault, attempted murder.'

The first curious onlookers in the left-hand corner of the picture, they look in and one of them points.

Then suddenly one of the hoodies comes back.

*Him.*

'He was only missing one thing, and he notched that up last night.'

The onlookers move slowly back while the twelve-year-old boy opens the door to the shop, goes in, walks over to the window, and picks up the square paving stone.

'Murder.'

He holds it in his right hand, goes further into the shop, approaches the camera, turns to face it, looks straight into it briefly, then throws the stone and the picture goes dark.

'And her?'

Mariana Hermansson tried to pin Ewert Grens down with her eyes, looking for the answer she didn't get before.

She was like her boss. The sort who never gave up.

'The dad – she still doesn't *know*? Why he disappeared? Where?'

'Her son who became so good at throwing stones was taken from her immediately at birth. A social worker and senior social worker were waiting in the cell by the bed and an ambulance was on standby outside the window. As far as she was concerned

he had a mother in prison and a father who had disappeared.
That was all she knew.'

'She doesn't *know*?'

'How many times do I have to say it?'

'*Why* doesn't she know?'

'Because it wasn't part of my job.'

'And now?'

'It's still not part of my job.'

––––––––

Ana was sitting in the kitchen that she loved so much, by the
kitchen table she'd had since she moved from home, since
before Hinseberg prison. She drank the lukewarm coffee, always
nearly half milk. She hadn't crept past the empty hat shelf for a
few hours, hadn't even bothered to look out when more fire
engines came, she was tired, almost peaceful. She filled the cup
up when the doorbell rang and someone shouted *police, open
up*. She finished her coffee, still wrapped in peace, put down her
cup and went out into the hall towards the voice that was still
shouting. She stopped on the doormat, she knew who it was,
knew why. It was good that they'd come, they always did and
she couldn't stand waiting any longer. She stood just by the
letter box, *police, open up*, and felt the eyes looking at her feet.

'It's not me you're after.'

'Open up. Or we'll break down the door.'

'It's nothing to do with me––'

'Open up!'

'––I'm on my own here.'

'You know how it works. We'll break your door down.'

'It's open.'

She went back into the kitchen, half a cup more, then lay
down on her stomach with her hands behind her back and
waited. She had lain like this before, a long time ago, the big
policeman had pressed her hard against the same kitchen floor.

There were more of them this time, eight, and they pressed her arms closer, heavy bodies on hers, she looked out into the hallway, at the hat shelf, it was still empty.

————

No more almond slices. Only half a pastry left in the bag. Ewert Grens held it out to his guests who all shook their head, so he took it himself.

Hermansson changed the image on the screen, twelve-year-olds robbing a jeweller's shop in Skärholmen now became a white car leaving Storboda prison and an eighteen-year-old laughing as he leaned out and fired wild shots with the gun in his hand.

'Nineteen thirty-three. Almost seventeen hours. The last picture we have.'

The map was still spread out, crooked, between the two windows.

She loosened the tape in two corners, tugged it gently, then pressed the tape again, considerably straighter.

'We've got more now.'

With a red pen, she started to draw on the green and blue that was the northern part of Stockholm municipality.

'Storboda prison. The last break-out. I'm fairly sure that in order to get south, they drove here – through Rosersberg – and here – Norrsundsvägen that crosses Stockholmsvägen – and here, through Upplands Väsby.'

She looked at them. And didn't need to explain. They had all heard a road tanker hooting at someone in a car who got out of the driver's seat and opened the boot.

'Then . . . Mälarvägen, past Edssjön – the cyclist who was almost knocked over – and on down to here, Söderby, where we found the car this morning.'

A new map on top of the other, she taped it up and they were both straight now.

'We know that three stolen cars were reported in the Söderby area this morning. One of them was a Mercedes Benz, registration number EBN 927. We've checked all the speed cameras within a ten mile radius from where the car was found. *And we have one hit.*'

The red felt pen carried on more or less directly south, getting closer to Stockholm.

'Twenty twenty-seven hours. Location, Bergslagsvägen by Åkeshov. The stolen car. And through the window . . . well, you can see for yourself.'

She held up a very enlarged picture, handed it to Grens who studied it then put it down on the table between Sven and Ågestam.

Two faces in the front seats. Leon Jensen to the left. Alexander Eriksson to the right. Behind them, another three, not as clear, but for someone who had studied the full face and profile photographs of Marko Bendik, Reza Noori and Uros Koren through the morning, they were in fact clear.

'My guess is that they got here via the Lunda industrial estate and Bergslagsvägen past Vällingby and Råcksta. But I actually *know* which route they took after that.'

She drew a line from the speed camera at Åkeshov to Brommaplan, south-west past Drottningholm and onto Ekerövägen.

'They passed by here – the very tip of Ekerö. Some woods. There is a sharp bend in the road down to the water and it meets another road precisely *here.*'

She drew on the map with her felt pen. A cross. Something that had four legs. And perhaps a gun.

'A hunter in his sixties, at around nine o'clock yesterday evening. Out with his dog to see if he could find a deer that he'd shot. His description is reliable and detailed. The dog had picked up the trace of the deer at the Jungfrusundsvägen–Bryggavägen crossroads when a car approached at high speed. He'd raised his gun in anger, followed it in the night vision scope, he could have fired, he said that several times, young men trying to run over his dog. He aimed, could see them clearly. Then this morning on the news – the same faces, he was certain of it.'

She pointed at the green and blue and sometimes yellow map. At the tip that was stretching out into the water.

'I've just come back from there, met the man . . . here. Then carried on in the direction that the car was heading until the road stopped. Carried on along the water's edge. Didn't need to go very far. It was parked . . . here.'

It was less than a kilometre from the abandoned car to the other side of the bay. To the mainland. To the high-rise blocks in the southern suburb called Hallunda.

And from there, a twenty-minute walk in the dark on asphalt.

To Råby.

He gathered up the plastic cups and cake crumbs and moved one of the chairs, hadn't noticed that anyone was hovering in the doorway.

'I wanted to talk to you.'

Grens turned round to face the voice that shouldn't still be there.

'Did you, now.'

Hermansson. And she looked at him with an expression that wanted an answer.

'Coffee?'

'We just had coffee.'

'Another one then. The café on Bergsgatan?'

He sometimes went there in the morning and had a cup of black coffee and a wholemeal roll with cheese, the round table in the corner by the window. He liked to leave the office and sofa and walk across the street to read the newspaper, watch the people going in and out, sometimes had a chat with the girl who worked there who had such a loud laugh, and then he'd go back to the office, knowing that he didn't need to see any more people today.

This time he sat down, but not alone. An odd feeling. *His* table. And Hermansson pulled out one of the three vacant chairs, beside him.

'Wouldn't it be better if you sat there?'

He pointed at the empty chair opposite. She nodded, got up and sat down there.

'You're right, then we've got eye contact.'

'And you're further away.'

Never too close. Even on the short walk over here, through the police headquarters and over the street, she was there, walking *too* close, and he'd wanted to take a step to the side.

She smiled.

'And it's easier for me to put my hand on yours, like this. Like you do when you're talking in confidence.'

As if she'd hit him.

He was so terrified of looking like an old man getting too close to a young woman, of human warmth becoming invasive and too much.

She knew that. And let her hand rest on his until he realised that it was there and he pulled back and looked out of the window at nothing in particular.

'Did you manage to triangulate which mast the intercepted call from Leon Jensen's mobile came from?'

'I'm sorry?'

'The murder. When he . . . the conversation we listened to. His mobile phone was connected to some transmitter or another. I want to know exactly where he was when he phoned. Which mast . . .'

'Ewert?'

'Yes?'

'I heard what you said. But we're not here to talk about telephone masts.'

Intimacy. Integrity.

He can't see the difference. He has no idea.

Just like them.

'I know that Sven has tried to talk to you. And that you wouldn't answer. The cakes, Ewert. That was nice. But that doesn't somehow fit with . . . whatever it is that is anger, and yet, somehow not. You're haranguing us. Yourself.'

He was still looking out through the window. An older woman stopped to talk to an old man while their dogs sniffed each other.

'I'm worried, Ewert. And I want to know.'

He often saw them out here, a brief chat, the dogs sniffed each other, then off they went in opposite directions.

'Anni?'

'What?'

He left the window.

'This isn't about her.'

'Your grief, moving on, you have to—'

'This is not about her.'

'Ewert, you have to—'

'*This is not about her.*'

He had stood up, so she grabbed his hand and pulled him back down again.

'Don't you understand? You're just like them.'

'The telephone masts, Hermansson.'

'Intimacy. Integrity.'

'I want to know which mast his phone was connected to, where he was.'

'They can't see the difference. Despite all the words. Someone who says *love*. Someone who calls you *brother*. I don't think they know what love means. But I do think that they feel something. That it feels good when they pat each other on the shoulder and say *well done, brother, you knocked that bastard down, well aimed, one love, brother.* When you don't really know "Oh, is *that* what love is?" "OK, that's what it feels like."'

She wasn't sure whether he was listening. Or whether he'd closed off a long time ago like he normally did when she tried to talk to him about the only thing they never talked about.

'Do *you* know, Ewert? What love is?'

If he was listening, he was certainly careful not to show it.

'Ewert? Will you ever love another woman?'

'That's none of your bloody business.'

At least he was listening.

'Will you ever—'

'This is not *about* Anni.'

He got up again. This time she didn't stop him.

'It's about Leon Jensen.'

He didn't wait for her when he crossed Bergsgatan and went into the police headquarters.

---

Lars Ågestam leaned against one of the lift walls for support. In the mirror, a sweaty neck, tense jaws. *From now on we have to use coercive measures.* He was shaking. Forty-five minutes ago, he had left Ewert Grens's office full of cake, following an update on an investigation that was going nowhere. He had walked from Kronoberg and Kungsholmen to the bridge that was like an arm reaching over to Norrmalm, into the offices at Kungsbron 21, up to the sixth floor and had just gone into one of the public prosecution authority cloakrooms when his phone started to ring in his jacket pocket. *Coercive measures?* He had put on again what he had just taken off and run down the steps that were not made for running. *Later, Ågestam.* He had run without stopping all the way back to Kronoberg, in his suit and shiny shoes, past dogs on long leads and young secondary school pupils on their way to the 7-Eleven to compensate for the lunch they'd skipped, not stopping or breathing until he got into the lift that he now stepped out of.

Kronoberg remand jail. Sixth floor. The women's unit.

He hurried over to the glass cubicle, knocked hard on the window hiding a young security guard.

'Name?'

'Let me in. Unit 6A.'

'Name *and* purpose?'

'Chief District Prosecutor Lars Ågestam. Let's just say releasing the innocent.'

He walked towards the unit door that remained locked, no matter how many times he tried it.

'Open up.'

'Why?'

'Six charges who were locked up no more than an hour ago. They're to be released.'

'Why?'

'Because I say so.'

'We actually need written release papers up here.'

The prosecutor's jaws were as tense as they had been in the lift.

'And where I come from written arrest warrants are needed. Open up!'

'I'm sorry.'

Lars Ågestam didn't try the locked door any more. He ran back to the opening in the glass, slid a finger through, lifted the cover until he could get his whole hand through, grabbed the pile of paper lying in the middle of the desk, duty rosters, and pulled it towards him, turned over the top sheet, wrote something on it with the pen that he always had in his shirt pocket and then threw it back in.

The young remand guard studied the handwritten instruction and then Ågestam and then the writing again.

'What does it say?'

'There, it says *Chief District Prosecutor*. And there, it says *Lars Ågestam*, and at the top it says, *Release them, dammit!*'

————

The young remand guard was much taller and considerably heavier than he'd looked when he was sitting in the glass cubicle. Lars Ågestam followed the broad back through Kronoberg remand's women's unit, past cell doors that hid the seven square metres behind a barred window with a view to nothing.

*Sonja Milton. Sofia Eriksson. Deniz Johnson. Ana Tomas. Amanda Hansen. Wanda Svensson.*

He had tried to get through to the detective superintendent

for a long time now, put up with him, his disdain, he had tried and tried and then stopped trying, and had been deeply touched one night when he was the first person ever to be invited into Ewert Grens's home – he had thought that they'd finally had a dialogue, but realised now that they would never speak the same language.

The first door. The remand guard bent forward for a quick look through the small square hatch, then keys and the sound of a lock turning twice and someone standing up inside.

When the guard stepped out of the way, the prosecutor met a woman who had just been lying down, her hair was tangled – especially round her neck, even though she hadn't slept – and her eyes tired. He guessed she was around thirty-five, she was small, possibly looked even smaller in the grey, baggy Prison Service clothes.

He held out his hand.

'My name is Lars Ågestam. I'm the chief district prosecutor. And I sincerely apologise for the manner in which you've been treated.'

She didn't answer, didn't take his hand, didn't even look at him.

He understood her. He would have done the same.

———

Hermansson had looked at him with an expression that demanded an answer and he had hurried to meet Sven and the car and she had followed, and they sat in silence as they always did, all the way to Råby and the police station on the edge of the estate of high-rise flats that were hiding a murderer.

Ewert Grens looked over at her, sitting beside Sven, waiting, at a round meeting table in the Section Against Gang Crime. A red Adidas bag between them, which was the reason why they'd come here and why he would soon sit down. But first he had to try to understand seven new faces with staring eyes.

The same wall. The most dangerous ones. And the label with two names, Råby Warriors/Ghetto Soldiers, in the same place and under the nine faces that had been there before – four who were free to come and go, and five who he was sure were also somewhere outside the window. The other seven were completely new. They obviously belonged, even though the pictures were different – taken at a distance, cameras with zoom lenses, surveillance pictures of him walking over Råby Torg, and him sitting behind a flat window.

'They'll do whatever it takes to be part of that group of staring faces one day. We can't really put them under surveillance. Can't track them. But I . . . the way things are now, Ewert, you need all the knowledge you can get.'

José Pereira looked at the seven young faces beside those who were not much older. It was for them that he'd left two girls and the first half of a football match the evening before. Ahead of a night at the police station, to put together ten years' surveillance work around kids of the same age who lived a life that was miles apart.

'Eleven. And he's twelve.'

As dawn had turned to daylight, he couldn't bear it any longer, and had gone home to an empty flat and another reality, so that he could carry on. Laura and Maria had left visible traces of a late breakfast and he put the muesli and cereal back on the bottom shelf in the larder, wiped the plastic tablecloth clean of cream cheese and marmalade, washed up what was standing by the sink and then lay down on the sofa in the sitting room, fell asleep and slept for a couple of hours in a world with no thoughts or anger or a young woman who was scared and now dead.

'None of them are older than fourteen. One of the things that make organisations like this work.'

Ewert Grens looked at the surveillance pictures of children.

And then at the face beside them, that had been hounding

him since last night. He remembered a paving stone and a twelve-year-old boy who had raised it and thrown it and then watched over the others while they emptied a jeweller's shop.

*You. Just recently. And them. Very soon.*

'The ones we can't arrest. But who could be a link.'

José Pereira moved closer to the photographs that he'd taken himself of the eleven- and twelve-year-olds on their way to or in the company of experienced criminals who were only a few years older, but had profited for a long time from the kids' yearning to belong.

'They may well have the knowledge that we don't have. They're always there – close to *them*.'

Pereira took down one of the pictures, the boy walking over Råby Torg, and handed it to Grens.

'I had him in for questioning a couple of weeks ago. The third time. He came with his mum, sat with a rucksack on his lap, and we talked about two shots that had been fired at close range at two knees. He sat on the chair that Hermansson is sitting on now and knew everything and nothing.'

Ewert Grens held up shiny photographic paper that would stick to an open palm. A child. Skinny, still no signs of puberty, a thick, gold chain, shiny slicked-back hair.

*You. Very soon.*

'I don't like this wall.'

'I know.'

'They're dying to get there. And they're always in the know. A strange game, Pereira. We can confirm that they're expanding.'

The red Adidas bag in the middle of the table.

In a wide circle around it lay two bulletproof vests, three balaclavas, a bayonet, a stiletto, two sets of nunchucks.

'Six synchronised raids. Eight riot police at each flat. And this was what they found.'

Sven Sundkvist pulled one of the bulletproof vests over and held it up so they could all see – someone had sewn a badge on the chest on the left-hand side, two words, GHETTO SOLDIERS.

'Brand new. We've compared them with ones that we've previously seized, and . . . completely different quality.'

He put it on, it fitted, almost exactly the right size.

'The best body armour you can get. Reinforced metal that even protects against bullets from high-velocity weapons.'

He opened the red sports bag, the zip got caught.

'Bulletproof vests, balaclavas, guns, as always. But this was under a bed in the flat rented by Gabriel Milton's presumed girlfriend.'

He dug down to the bottom of the bag with both hands.

'And this is interesting.'

A bundle of papers in one hand. He moved the balaclavas and bayonet down onto the floor and put out the eleven sheets of A4 paper side by side on the table.

A letter. Handwritten. Spiky letters that someone had struggled to keep as even as possible.

'This . . .'

There was a knock at the door.

'Yes?'

'I just wanted to say that we're in position.'

Sven recognised the face that popped in through the door. The bomb technician who had identified traces of dynamite in the Santos flat.

He had been about to close the door again when Grens shouted. 'When?'

'I'm sorry?'

'What you found, if someone has put it together, if it's anywhere in the area . . . when will it explode?'

The bomb technician was quite tall and more than a bit overweight, considerably younger than Ewert, but similar in shape.

He opened the door fully now.

'When someone *wants* it to.'

He walked over to the table and from a smaller side pocket by his knee pulled out an aluminium pipe as long as his index finger, a thin white plastic lead and an equally thin green plastic lead out of only one end.

'A detonator. Completely harmless. Right now.'

The large body was unexpectedly supple when he bent down to the socket near the base of the wall and pulled out first the plugs to the four computers on the desks, and then the six land-lines. Finally, he got out his own mobile phone and turned it off.

'Now you turn off yours as well. And all radio equipment.'

He waited until four more mobile phones had been turned off, then out of the pocket by his other knee he pulled one of his bomb gloves and from another pocket, even further down, a pair of nippers. The detonator was in his hand when he cut off the white and green leads. And then again, a bit shorter. And again, making sure to get as close as possible.

'From now on, however, it's deadly and can be activated at any moment.'

He put it down in the bomb glove with great care, and then wrapped it in a rubbery material.

'DS Grens?'

'Yes?'

'Could you turn on your mobile phone again now?'

Ewert Grens muttered with irritation about buttons that were too small, while the equally large bomb technician turned his mobile on without any problem and put it down on the table next to the bomb glove.

'You've got my number?'

'Yes.'

'Call it.'

Dialling was easier. The first signal went out. They all looked at the glove, at each other. The next signal, they could hear it clearly, and simultaneously, the other sound, the dull explosion as the glove jumped to the floor.

'One call to a mobile phone. Enough current to trigger a det-onator if the fuse is cut short enough.'

The smell of an explosion, sharp and penetrating.

'They've got dynamite, explosives, detonators. They've got a telephone positioned nearby. One call to that whenever they want . . . when they *choose* to do it, to trigger the detonator that will explode the rest.'

The big man turned and shrugged. Even his movements were similar to Ewert Grens.

'And they will do it in a small space. No bigger than this room. This type of explosive does more damage if the space is limited.'

Grens, Hermansson, Sundkvist and Pereira all sat in silence as the bomb technician picked up the remains of two trimmed plastic leads and a test-exploded glove and left the room.

The current from a telephone call in a world where mobile phones were ringing constantly.

At any moment. Anywhere.

When they *chose* to do it.

'The letter.'

Sven gathered up the eleven pages of A4 that he'd just laid out on the table when the bomb technician knocked on the door, and gave them a few sheets each.

'Found in the bedroom of Gabriel Milton's girlfriend. But she's not the recipient.'

*One love best brutha!*

They read.

Like a child had written it.

But they didn't smile. They knew. That this was for real.

*Miss u so fucking much.*

Ewert Grens gave up first and

*Brutha seriously ARMED and very TIGHT unit!!! 200%*
*love respect pride bruthahood duty belonging honor.*

threw his sheets down on the table.

'One of all the bloody pompous letters written the minute he feels lonely by some jacked up little gangster who hasn't learnt to spell. Brother this. Brother that.'

José Pereira was not going to throw down his sheets.

'They've murdered someone.'

'Same bloody crap. *Love. Brother. Respect.* Same bloody dreams that someone will love them if they're mean enough.'

'They might sound like kids. But their violence is grown-up. I've seen so many letters like this, he's young and angry and sitting in a room in a youth detention centre or a prison cell with only his grandiose thoughts to keep him company. But there's an undertone here, Ewert, and you can see it too. The person writing it has already started to fill out the empty phrases.'

This time no one knocked at the door. Instead it was flung open. And someone ran into the room.

Lars Ågestam's face looked as weathered as Ewert Grens's.

'Grens!'

The detective superintendent heard him. But did not move.

'Turn round when I'm talking to you!'

Back to the door, he stayed sitting where he was.

'When you were *not* granted search warrants, how the hell did you go ahead with six?'

The agitated besuited legs, arms in the air, fringe to one side and glasses that jumped up and down when he shouted.

'I'll say it again, Grens! You ask for search warrants! You don't get them! But you carry out six all the same!'

Ewert Grens turned round for the first time and looked at the prosecutor who was standing so close to his chair.

'Ågestam?'

'*And carry out six!*'

'Did no one teach you to knock?'

The staring faces on the wall. The staring faces around the table.

Lars Ågestam's neck was even redder and his voice even louder when he held six pieces of paper up in the air, then slapped them in front of him.

'Sonja Milton! Sofia Eriksson! Deniz Johnson! Ana Tomas! Amanda Hansen! Wanda Svensson!'

He threw them down on top of the eleven-page letter.

'A police officer with a senior position carries out several illegal raids! With the help of the police force! Forty-eight riot police commit a crime on the orders of a superintendent!'

'Are you done?'

'I've opened a preliminary investigation into unlawful intrusion, unlawful interference, unlawful exercise of authority! You'll get done for this!'

'Look . . . this morning I stood beside an autopsy table with a very young woman on it who had been stabbed in the back of her thigh, punched badly in the face, tied and bound and dumped in a boot and left to choke to death—'

'You are not the law, Grens!'

'—and out there, a long way away from your desk, a murderer is still running around free. I don't give a damn what papers you write your initials on. There are no laws in Råby right now. Certainly not our laws, as they mean nothing here. So we have to find new ways, Ågestam, ones you won't find in your law books, we have to do what *they* do.'

'Six law-abiding citizens who are not suspected of anything at all, other than being in the same family! Grens . . . you would *never* have used the same aggression if the owners of those flats had been called something else and lived somewhere else!'

Ewert Grens had been sitting down. Now he got up.

His face was red, the veins on his temples standing out, his stiff leg pushing against the floor.

'You little bastard . . .'

The large detective superintendent took hold of the public prosecutor's collar, pulled him up close.

'What the hell are you insinuating?'

'That you're giving yourself licence to treat people differently.'

Hands even firmer on the collar, a sharp shake.

'You bastard . . . I don't give a monkey's . . . it's people like you, who are so far removed from reality and so fucking frightened of doing or thinking the wrong thing, or having the wrong opinion, of appearing to be prejudiced, when in fact you're just that! It's people like you who are so caught up with your fear of being an outsider that you can't see it when other people are! It's people like you who think that if they just don't say the truth for long enough then it's not the truth! And one thing you can be damn sure of – I would do exactly the same in rich Djursholm and rich Öster-malm and even in the public prosecution offices if needs be!'

Ewert Grens let go and pushed the jacket and public prose-cutor away from him.

The room remained remarkably quiet while Lars Ågestam straightened out his shirt, tie and jacket collar. It was the first time he had been to the police station in Råby that was involved in so many of his preliminary investigations now. In recent years he'd used reports filed by José Pereira and the SAGC more and more frequently and had often thought of coming to meet them, but certainly not in this way.

He looked around, nodded to Pereira and Sundkvist and Hermansson, then headed to the door.

'I've already opened the preliminary investigation against you.'

He walked out and the door had swung closed when he sud-denly wrenched it open again.

'And one thing you can be damn sure about, Grens – I know exactly what day it is!'

They listened to the footsteps fade down the corridor. And looked at each other. It was as if all the energy in the room had followed the prosecutor out and all the loud words and naked rage lay around them on the floor and table.

José Pereira gathered up the bulletproof vests and weapons and balaclavas – the result of six flat searches – but left the eleven-page letter where it was.

'They've murdered someone and they won't stop there.'

He had twice started to decipher the handwriting, but hadn't managed to finish it yet.

'Wanted, successful, they're flourishing now, they're building.'

So now he continued, one page at a time.

'They have no other option. Just more, further afield.'

---

There was a tiny lawn just outside the main entrance to Råby police station.

It wasn't particularly green and nobody used it.

But this afternoon it greeted six uniformed policemen and six dogs, eager to start work.

'Sven?'

'Yes?'

'Every flat, every storeroom.'

Sven Sundkvist nodded towards the police station and the window on the second floor where a prosecutor had just held forth about his breaches of duty and violations.

'Are you absolutely sure?'

'They have access to a bomb, *a bomb*, Sven, just one mobile phone call away. Yes. I'm still totally uninterested in his bits of white paper.'

They were so impatient and yet sat so still. Six dogs. Sven identified at least four different breeds. The one that was a bit smaller, about half a metre high and brown and white with long ears, English springer spaniel, the sort that Jonas had asked for every Christmas and birthday for years, only to be disappointed by skis and computer games. One that was bigger, fluffier somehow, a Belgian shepherd. Further back, two Alsatians, two Labradors. Different kinds of nose, some fast, some slightly slower, trained to see what no one else could see.

'I'm guessing about ten minutes per flat, on average. Eight thousand flats makes it eighty thousand minutes, divided by six dogs.'

Sven Sundkvist took a small notebook and pencil out of his jacket pocket. There weren't many who could do that any more. Pencil, lined paper.

'Two hundred and twenty-two hours. That's nine days, Ewert. If they work round the clock.'

Ewert Grens had recognised the bomb technician who'd just demonstrated how a telephone signal could cause a catastrophe. Now he looked at the dogs that would prevent that. A couple of them, the two smallest, had started to bark loudly and impatiently at their leader who would soon give orders.

*You're here. You've built a bomb. You've put it somewhere.*

The dog handlers and dogs set off, and Sven followed them, to start searching the first blocks to the east, the ones that constituted Råby Backe.

*And you're going to use it.*

———

He watched their backs until they disappeared, then went round to the car park at the back of Råby police station, and Hermansson who was waiting by the car, the door open and pointing at the emblem.

Västerort Police.

'Perhaps time to deliver this back?'

Grens opened the other door, to the driver's seat.

'Not yet.'

And looked at her briefly before getting in.

'If they torch another one, better that this one burns. Rather than one of the City Police cars.'

He didn't drive particularly fast, but they still managed to get to Skärholmen before either of them said anything.

'You're scared, Ewert.'

He slowed down a touch more.

'After that grilling. In the café. I put my hand on yours. I know that you don't like it. Because you don't know the difference between intimacy and integrity. Because you're like them. And that . . . scares you.'

'No.'

'Scared of getting too close.'

'No. Because what I'm scared of has already happened.'

'Ewert?'

'What?'

'That's just words.'

'That's what people say to me. *And that's the way it is, Hermansson.* What I'm scared of has already happened.'

'Just words. If you don't understand them.'

'Look . . .'

'Scared. Still. No matter how often you repeat other people's truths.'

He didn't look at her. He focused on the car in front, only looked at that.

'I'd like you to stop now, please.'

'And I want to talk about you. About your feelings. About your life.'

'Listen . . . my life is my business.'

'Your life, Ewert, your fucking life is anyone's business who happens to get in the way. Your life, you bastard, has affected those of us who've had to work with you for years!'

Ewert Grens stopped. In the middle of the E4. In the middle of the middle lane.

A few seconds, then the first angry horns behind them and beside them.

The exit to Fruängen and Bredäng was near enough, he

could have chosen to turn off there. He stayed where he was. His hands gripping the steering wheel.

'Hermansson? Go to hell.'

Mariana Hermansson didn't really know why. After all, she was the one who had started pushing his buttons. But it was as if years of anger, tiptoeing around him, his inability to give anything back, more often not cooperating at all, as if everything came to a head at once.

'Don't talk to me like that!'

She looked at him when she gave him a slap around the face, and when she undid her seatbelt. But looked away when she got out of the car and started to walk down the middle of the motorway.

Grens drove slowly behind her and she carried on walking between the cars that were passing so close.

He wound down the window.

'Get in.'

He shouted a bit louder to be heard above the vehicles passing at a hundred and forty kilometres in a ninety-kilometre zone.

'Hermansson, get in!'

She turned round, just once.

'Go to hell.'

And then carried on walking.

―――――

The empty platform came closer.

She tried to see out of the metro-train window that had become a scratched film in the strong sunlight. Råby. Penultimate stop on the red line, the station between Hallunda and Norsborg, she stood up when the doors opened and got out at a station where no one got in.

She was wearing a pair of yellow trousers and an orange top.

They had shouted outside her door and forced her to the floor and she was still in her dressing gown and slippers in the back of the police car when they drove away. The yellow trousers and the orange top, some kind of misplaced kindness, one of the men in helmets and overalls who had locked her arms in handcuffs had opened her wardrobe to take out two pieces of clothing that she no longer wore and certainly would never wear together.

Ana stopped on the platform, waited while Deniz ran her fingers through her hair, which had been wet when they were taken in, and now was uncombed and sticking out every which way, then straightened her dress that was too long, which some police officer in a helmet and overall had chosen from *her* wardrobe.

In the car, they had continued to stare at her and repeated *where* and she had looked straight ahead and continued to say *it's not me you're after*, and the sharp edge of the handcuffs had bitten her wrists *where is he* and her shoulders had ached because her arms were being pressed so hard against her back *this has nothing to do with me* and when they got to the garage at Kronoberg they had led her from the car to the lift, up to the fifth floor and then released her hands and pointed at a cell with a green door. The woman in a police uniform had followed her in and sat down on the only chair in the cell and there were more questions, longer questions *where is Leon Jensen right now, where is Gabriel Milton right now, are you aware that you are now guilty of protecting a criminal* but the answers were just as silent. The uniform had left the cell after a while and she had sat on her own on the end of the bunk in complete silence and looked at the locked door until the one and a half hours now were as long as the four years in Hinseberg prison, all that time ago.

Deniz had tidied her wild hair and dress that was too long and they walked together to the end of the platform and out into Råby, without saying anything, it wasn't necessary, they had recently just sat on either side of a mute cell wall. They had been taken from their homes with force and raised voices and it felt as if in order to return they had to walk through it all again with heads held high – Råby Torg and police cars and uniforms that *get the fuck away from me* were searching two young men and at the same time holding a group *don't touch me you pig bastard* of even younger men at a suitable distance. The asphalt pathways and a bus OPERATIONS CENTRE parked in the area that was otherwise used as a small football pitch. Several more police uniforms as they got closer to Råbyvägen, that was formed like a wide circle, its protecting arms embracing the high-rise blocks, someone hooted and someone else *get out of the car for fuck's sake* screamed in the queue of cars up by the road block, a metal barrier stopped all traffic going in and out and they were searched and guarded by police with automatic weapons. And as they got closer to Råbygången, even more police uniforms accompanied by dogs, tails wagging, ears pricked, eyes watching the handler's hands, moving from one stairway to the next, doing what they were trained to do and longed to do. Ana and Deniz had been in no rush, now they stopped, gave each other a hug, and then continued their separate ways towards their own front doors, Deniz towards Råby Allé 102 and Ana even further up to Råby Allé 34.

She opened the door and was in the stairwell when she caught the smell of smoke.

She turned around, and now she saw it, from a building four blocks down, she started to run, tried to guess how many times the fire engine she passed had been back and forth today.

She recognised his back.

He was holding a microphone in his hand, the lead disappeared into the neck of his heavy overalls, some kind of communications radio and she waited until he was done.

'Hello again.'

He hadn't heard her coming, turned around and saw the woman he'd hoped not to see again.

'You?'

'A moped at quarter past six. A container at twenty past eight. And a police car just before ten. That was the morning. How many times have you been here since then?'

'I asked you to let me be.'

'I've been in town for a few hours, but if I was to guess . . . seven more, a total of ten times? If it's been a normal day for you, that is. And this, well, this looks like . . . yet another rubbish bin.'

He turned his back to her again, the one she knew so well, hurried over to a colleague and a hose that had to be attached to the pump.

She followed him.

'I need your help.'

She looked at the back that didn't answer.

'Put it this way . . .'

She went up to it, prodded it, tugged at his black and yellow and brown overalls just where EMERGENCY SERVICES SÖDERTÖRN met LEADING FIREFIGHTER.

'Why do you bother putting them out?'

He turned around.

It was hard to tell whether the tension in his face was the sort that stemmed from anger.

'Because it's my job.'

'So your job is to protect Råby even when the people who live here want it to burn?'

He was listening, she was sure of it.

'You stand there and put out burning mopeds and fences and rubbish bins ten times a day. And still you don't understand? That what's happening will carry on happening until someone makes sure it won't happen any more.'

His voice wasn't aggressive, not even annoyed.

It was tired.

'Let me ask you again. Please, just leave me be.'

The smell of grey and black smoke faded the closer she got to number 34.

When she went into the lift and up to the third floor, it disappeared completely.

She stood in front of the door to a flat that had been hers since she left home so long ago, and yet it was as if a part of the security it had taken so long to build up had been taken away at the same time that she was. Gingerly, she put her hand on the door handle, turned it, opened, went into what was no longer hers and sat down on the kitchen floor in the same place where she'd been forced down a few hours earlier.

The man who put out fires. She needed him.

If no one was to get hurt.

———

His cheek was still burning. She had slapped him hard.

She had called him an old bastard, hit him, got out of the car and started to walk down the middle lane of the E4. He had rolled along behind her and after a while put on the flashing blue light. He didn't understand. It was *she* who had pushed *him*. He'd never really worked her out, she made him uncertain now and then, didn't see him in the same way that others did, laughed at him sometimes and made him feel embarrassed. Ewert Grens remembered a time five years ago, when they had arrested an American man with a death sentence over him, how in the middle of such an intense case she'd forced him out to a dance hall in the middle of Stockholm and that time slapped a drunk man who had asked how old Grens was and how much he'd paid for his foreign tart, then asked the band to play 'Everybody's Somebody's Fool' by Siwan, asked him up, helped him to enjoy dancing together with someone for the first time in twenty-five years.

The daughter they never had.

'I hear that Ågestam had some pretty strong opinions about your raids, Ewert.'

Erik Wilson had stopped by Grens and the coffee machine in the Homicide corridor at the police headquarters.

'Yes. He obviously didn't have any forms that ticked the boxes for violent eighteen-year-olds who are classified as dangerous and who, within the space of a few hours, first escaped from a maximum security prison then forty minutes later from another lower security prison, and then forty minutes later from yet another low security prison, who have committed murder and built at least one bomb, who are still on the run and frightened and aggressive and will become even more frightened and aggressive as time goes by. And when those forms don't exist, the desk sometimes becomes smaller than reality.'

Violent eighteen-year-olds classified as dangerous. They weren't talking about him. And yet they were.

'Right now I've got fifty-seven messages from journalists whose questions I'm trying to avoid and I'm on my way to a meeting with the national police commissioner and then with the minister of justice to answer more questions that I'm trying to avoid, as I don't have any answers. Do what the hell you like, Ewert. You've got my full support. I want you to carry on looking for them, no matter what – *and to find them*. Meanwhile, I'll fill out all the forms for Ågestam.'

Half a cup of machine coffee.

He had loathed the kind of police work that Erik Wilson was responsible for previously. Criminal informers who committed crimes in order to solve other crimes. Lies and truth in the same corridor. But right now, his outlook, flexibility, made him far easier to work with than his predecessor.

'So what have you got?'

Grens shrugged.

'What have I got? Photographs of a white Mercedes. A red Adidas bag with a letter from a kid who wants to be dangerous and is just like all the other bloody letters written by kids who want to sound mean. A bayonet. Two sets of nunchucks. A pile of balaclavas. And body armour that could withstand a scud missile.'

Half a cup more.

'That's what I've got.'

Erik Wilson was drinking tea. The green kind.

'How much longer, Ewert?'

'I don't know.'

'It's nearly twenty-two hours now.'

'He's there.'

'And his mum?'

They looked at each other.

Someone they had long since forgotten. And who could no longer be forgotten.

'One of the ones Ågestam didn't give a warrant for, one of the ones he believes we committed a crime against.'

A baby had lain on her stomach and two police officers had stood on guard in front of the locked cell door. One who had already served half his working life and was in his forties, and one who was still fresh, no more than twenty.

'Nothing?'

'Nothing.'

They were older now. And they both wanted to say more. That it was all a part of the greater whole. That everything was always a part of the greater whole.

'So what is it you want, Ewert?'

'We've intervened, controlled, searched and got nowhere. I want to go further. I want a state of emergency.'

'A state of emergency is passed by the government.'

'I want Råby cordoned off. I want a curfew. So that from now, no one can come or go from the place without being seen and checked.'

'A state of emergency, Ewert, is granted when a society's structure or very existence is threatened.'

'Yes.'

'Yes?'

'South of Stockholm. West of Stockholm. Gothenburg. Malmö. The suburbs are burning. The staring faces of young men who write letters like small children. Boy club rules that take whatever there is to take. In the Råby area alone, we reckon there are seventeen gangs! And five thousand youngsters waiting in the wings, who watch and admire ones like the lot who are about to succeed. Role models! No matter how little we give away and how pointless we make the press conferences, they've been in the media spotlight for almost twenty-four hours now. They're the new celebrities! They've escaped and killed someone and planted a bomb that they'll set off when they *want* to set it off! I want a state of emergency for the people who right now are creating their own state of emergency!'

'You won't get it.'

'Then we'll call it something else.'

The green tea bag had done its job and Erik Wilson dropped it into the bin, tasted it, the water was still a bit too hot, but not bad, considering it came from a coffee machine.

He looked at the older man who had been *his* boss, once upon a time.

It had been simpler then, a long time ago.

'Then we'll call it something else.'

———

The sofa, the desk. A room that was the only place he could find peace. The mirror in the wardrobe; he checked to make sure that the jacket still looked good, metal comb through his thin hair until it stayed almost where it should. He wondered whether she would have liked what she saw, he possibly wasn't identical to the man she'd met in the lecture theatre for police cadets, way back then, as tall but possibly broader and with a face that had aged in the way faces do. He lay down on the corduroy sofa. On this day, a few years ago, he'd done what he always did on Tuesdays, gone to the care home where she no longer lived and the window where she no longer sat and been told that he was no longer welcome. The following Tuesday he'd got into the car and driven towards the care home, but then stopped on Lindingö Bridge, *I don't want to see you here any more*, he'd turned around and driven aimlessly through a city that had forgotten the lonely, then suddenly stopped at the edge of Solna in front of the building that had once been the police college, long ago, and the place where they'd met. He had started to walk through what had then been trees and bushes and was called Nothing Woods, and was now blocks of flats and cement, and after a while had ducked into a renovated building and found a café in the same place that they used to drink a cup of smooth black. New staff, shiny interior, but it had felt good and he had since gone there every Tuesday at the same time, a thirty-year date with a care home and someone who'd already stopped living had gradually been replaced by somewhere she had been alive and well and a date with someone he now knew was dead. He grieved, would always grieve, for her sake, no longer for his own.

Footsteps out in the corridor.

Maybe he'd fallen asleep. It certainly wasn't as light outside the window.

Footsteps that passed by his door. That stopped. That turned. That opened the door.

Hermansson.

Her brow was sweaty along the hairline.

'You and I are going to have a conversation later.'

She had looked in, said something, and was already closing the door again.

'Hermansson—'

She shook her head.

'Did you carry on?'

'A *long* conversation.'

'In the middle lane?'

She didn't answer, he hadn't expected her to.

Ewert Grens stretched his limbs that creaked loudly. A circuit of the office in silence to loosen up. He stopped in front of the map between the two windows with the red line in felt pen that had meant freedom for the youths driving the car and death for the young woman who was lying in the boot kicking against the metal. If he went closer, carried the line that stopped at the water on across the water, about twenty minutes' gentle walk to Råby, it didn't look particularly big from above, white squares around a yellow stripe that was the asphalt on a motorway and a black line that was the metro tracks.

'Sven?'

He had called someone who was at that moment walking around in one of the white squares, in a passage down in the cellar, behind a bomb technician and his dog.

'Yes?'

'So far?'

'Nothing.'

'It's not good enough.'

'Six hundred and five hours. We've managed to go through one hundred and eighty doors. We need assistance.'

'Tomorrow.'

'Seven thousand, eight hundred and twenty flats left, Ewert.'

'You'll get six more dogs at half past six tomorrow morning. Two from Malmö police. And four from Customs and Excise.'

'And locksmiths, Ewert. Two, maybe even three. For inhabitants who refuse to open the door.'

'They can be there in an hour.'

He drew another line on the map on the wall, a fierce, mint-green colour – if the motorway was one side of a frame, and the metro lines another, then only two short sides were needed to link them together, a long chain of road blocks, patrols, dog handlers, uniformed policemen and civilian policemen who from now would surround Råby and become a net that it was impossible to break through.

There was a knock on the door. Again. *You and I are going to have a conversation later.* So soon?

'Come in.'

Lars Ågestam.

'You?'

'Were you expecting someone else?'

'Say what you want and get out.'

He was carrying something in his hand. And his voice was considerably quieter than it had been a few hours ago.

'You're working late today.'

'What do you want, Ågestam?'

'Thought that maybe you wouldn't. Not today, I mean.'

Grens shifted his weight uneasily.

'Right?'

'Is everything OK, Ewert?'

'Do you want something or not? You've said enough today and I'm tired.'

'You can still be a total idiot sometimes, Grens. And you made a mistake. But that's not why I'm here.'

Ewert Grens snorted at the person who was still in his office, but he didn't shout and he didn't chase him out.

'Earlier on today . . . you gave us coffee.'

'Yes . . .'

'And cakes.'

'There's none left, Ågestam.'

It looked like the detective superintendent had combed his thin hair again and not that long ago either, and Lars Ågestam couldn't remember it ever lying like that for several hours in a row. *And one thing you can be damn sure of, Grens – I know exactly what day it is!* He held out the rectangular wooden box that he'd been carrying, put it down on the desk.

'I ordered this from Systembolaget. A good vintage. From 1952. Which is exactly sixty years ago.'

Ewert Grens didn't reply. But he reached over for the box and opened it. A beautiful bottle. And so strange. Such deep discomfort at the idea that someone should know and approach him and be part of his day. And yet it felt almost nice that someone had. He let it stand between the stacks of files and studied the label in great detail in order to avoid looking at Ågestam.

'Some things do get better with the years.'

He lifted the bottle up, still without answering.

Sometimes it was good to have a glass in the evening. Like now, for instance.

Lars Ågestam was holding something else in the other hand, a corkscrew and two cognac glasses.

'You should really have coffee with it. But you normally drink enough of the stuff, so we'll skip it today. Any presents?'

He filled the glasses to just over half.

'Must be thirty years since the last one.'

Raised glasses, the first mouthful.

'But you've already got what you wanted.'

'Armagnac? That's lovely.'

'A murder.'

Another mouthful, a full flavour, good vintages often were.

He smiled a touch.

'Yes, a murder.'

They didn't say anything else for a few minutes while they stood relatively close and drank a few centimetres at a time until they were both holding an empty glass.

'And you'd prefer to sit here on your own for the rest of the evening?'

The detective superintendent nodded and Ågestam took with him an empty glass and an empty wooden box when he left the room. He'd gone as far as the photocopier and kitchen when Ewert Grens caught up with him and held out his hand.

'Um . . . thank you.'

The strange feeling persisted.

Grens went back to the beautiful bottle and felt happy. Not because Ågestam had known. But that he had known and yet not said anything, but had come himself and left after a short time; he'd understood.

Ewert Grens had been twenty-nine the last time he had shared, really shared, this day with anyone else. He remembered with horror his fiftieth birthday, sitting in a garden on a wooden chair between Sven, who had understood, and Bengt and Lena who would never understand and how he'd cringed every time he was forced to smile and say thank you to those who had come to surprise him without saying anything.

It hadn't felt like that at all now. He'd had a glass of something strong and looked at Ågestam and it had tasted good.

Maybe next time. Sixty-one.

Maybe then.

———

'Are you finished?'

*I have an accurate time of death.*

*If I get DNA, blood, fibres, fingerprints.*

'Soon.'

*If I have all four.*

'Nils, I need . . .'

*Then it's not my responsibility.*

'Ewert?'

'Yes?'

*It's not my job to worry about the consequences.*

'You can come down here.'

*Not even when I arrest you, put you in prison, again.*

He had pressed Nils Krantz as far as he could. It was late in the evening and he would soon have answers that it normally took twenty-four hours to get. It was his day and he had got his present. A murder. And now he wanted to open it.

'Light jacket. And now you smell of alcohol . . .'

The forensic scientist was standing by one of the long tables in the laboratory with his black bag only an arm's length away.

'Yes.'

'I've never seen you in anything light-coloured before. And I've certainly never seen you drink a glass of what you smell of right now.'

'That's probably true.'

'Ewert?'

'Nothing.'

'I've known you for over—'

'Absolutely nothing, Nils.'

Two men looking at each other in a room full of bags that say autopsy and white cotton buds with the remains of blood on them. Two men who could have been sitting in an armchair watching TV a long time ago, but who this evening, like every other evening, preferred, no matter the time, to be here, where there was a context, than in an empty flat where there was nothing.

They were now standing on either side of three different documents,

```
In the victim's mouth AB/4409-12/G234
(stains between two teeth on the upper jaw
examined) evidence of secretion/DNA. The
result confirms that the secretion/DNA comes
from Jensen (Grade +4).
```

Grens followed every line with his finger,

```
In the back seat of the escape car AB/2344-
12/G342 (stains on lower part of textile
cover examined) evidence of blood. The
result confirms that the blood comes from
Jensen (Grade +4).
```

Krantz underlined with a pencil the keywords that would later be summarised in a final report.

```
On the victim's trousers AB/4513-12/G018
(stains on lower part of left trouser leg
examined) evidence of fibres. The result
confirms that the fibres come from Jensen
(Grade +4).
```

'Three out of four.'

'Yes, and if you only knew how much I've pushed the NLFS and got them to—'

'And the fourth?'

'Sorry?'

'The fingerprints. I explained that I wanted *all four*.'

The forensic scientist had only a few hours earlier raised his voice and then pushed over two of his microscopes.

It hadn't been worth it. He would never do it again.

'Soon.'

White rubber gloves on when he carefully extracted the piece of tape that he'd ripped from the dead woman's wrists a few hours ago, and put it on the grille in the red metal cabinet.

Fifteen drops of superglue in an aluminium tray on the hot-plate at the bottom of the cabinet.

One hundred and fifty degrees and the white gas looked quite beautiful through the glass door.

'Your jacket? And the alcohol?'

'Absolutely nothing, Nils.'

A dish of warm water and a tin with a vibrant yellow powder which the forensic scientist mixed, stirred, whisked, then poured the yellow liquid into a bottle.

Ten minutes. The whitish gas had become transparent. Krantz's rubber gloves took out the tape, studied it with a magnifying glass and nodded.

Obvious fingerprints.

The yellow liquid over the tape, rinsed off with water, and the prints had become luminous. *The one who first taped her mouth and later pushed a sock down her throat.* The forensic scientist moved closer to the lamp, which made them clearer even for Grens. He compared them with the fingerprints that he'd secured during the autopsy and were now in a line on the transparent foil.

'So we can confirm then that those are hers.'

'Are you sure?'

'Yes.'

'And . . . who else?'

'We'll know in a couple of minutes.'

Side by side down the Forensics corridor, Grens's great lumbering body and Krantz's considerably smaller, a closed door to a room at the end.

'The forensic engineer. That's his chair and he's the expert. But at this time of night . . . and as you're so . . . I'll do it myself this evening.'

A narrow room. The forensic scientist moved the fingerprints that had been luminous only minutes ago from the scanner to a computer and Ewert Grens tried to stand behind him so he could see. He didn't manage, the walls and cabinets kept knocking his back.

'If you turn the screen a little. You know, the light, Nils, maybe it would be better if I sit here.'

He had three already.

And if he could get the fourth.

This anxiety, Grens didn't understand it, it had hounded him since a conversation in the middle of the night.

'One *detail*.'

Now, with the fingerprints on a big white screen, it was getting stronger and becoming decidedly uncomfortable.

'One more.'

Krantz had traced a papillary ridge to the far left that split into two, a *fork*. He needed at least eight to ten details, preferably even more. Unique patterns on a person's fingers that were there before birth, there after death. The next line ran slightly closer to the middle only to suddenly break off, a *gap*, before continuing again.

'And there, the right loop, you see? Curved. One *delta*.'

In Krantz's hands, each new detail became a red dot on the screen, a network that bit by bit became an image that would become a pattern.

'Eleven. That's enough for us to be certain.'

It quite possibly only took a few seconds.

The computer compared the patterns of one hundred and twenty thousand fingerprints with the ones here.

But the anxiety that had been rampant for nearly twenty-four hours now and had deepened to great discomfort, understood nothing about time.

'Hit.'

Ewert Grens looked nervously between the two pictures. Red points that showed an identical pattern. The anxiety, discomfort, in that moment changed to something else.

Something that perhaps resembled relief.

'Completely sure?'

Krantz pointed at the red line that linked what could only be found in *one* individual.

'Eleven details. Yes. I'm completely sure.'

One press of a button away.

931020-0358

One more.

Jensen, Leon.

––––––––

He wasn't tired. The dark and the car and the southbound motorway. Every time the same strange feeling when thoughts were clearly washed away by adrenalin and anticipation, and the energy that should have run out surged again.

He'd had three.

```
On the duct tape around the victim's wrists
AB/10942-12G009 5 identifiable prints, of
which 1 palm. Data search carried out. The
prints definitely originate from Jensen
(Degree + 4).
```

He had all four. And a time of death. He had all five.

He was driving fast, on his way to a woman who had given birth to her child in a prison cell. He'd been standing beside Erik Wilson and she had looked at him afterwards. She was only seventeen and had felt it lying quietly on her stomach for a short while.

The motorway exit past the police station, over there, one of the delayed evening trains that raced into the platform at Råby station, and exchanged people on their way home for people on their way out. A blue and white car with a police emblem on the door, he seldom travelled in one of them, so much easier when he turned onto one of the paths for pedestrians and cyclists and drove right up to the door of Råby Allé 34.

The smell in the lift was just as strong. But this time he chose to hold his breath and go up, even tried to read the spiky scrawls that had replaced the mirror, if they meant anything, it wasn't important to him.

Third floor. And there she was. Feet that didn't shuffle when he rang the doorbell, a hall light glimpsed through the peephole.

'Enough's enough.'

'I've got something I want to show you.'

'You were here this morning asking questions. A few hours later you sent a whole troop of policemen to pin me to the floor.'

'Open up. Let me show you what I've got. Then I'll go, I promise.'

A stairwell is home to many noises. On this floor alone, six flats, he guessed around fifteen people moving around, doing their own thing, only a few metres away.

She turned the lock. He could see one of her wrists through the opening, the red bracelet, irritated skin, the handcuffs had been tight.

'Listen to this.'

He held out a CD player and some earphones.

'I don't understand.'

'Ten seconds. No more.'

She stood in the door opening, reluctantly took the head-phones and put them over her ears.

'Now.'

*A choked, gurgling noise.*

'Can you hear that?'

She didn't answer.

'I'll play it again.'

*'Let's go.'*

*'What about her?'*

*'She'll be quiet now.'*

Ana looked at him. Her face showed nothing.

'You know what you're listening to?'

She didn't answer. She looked past him. He didn't exist.

'Can I come in?'

She opened the door wide, came out on to the landing and then closed it behind her.

'You will never come into my home again.'

'What you just heard—'

'I know what I just heard.'

He waited until she had taken off the earphones and felt that she was ready. Then he held up four pieces of paper.

'And if you could read these, please.'

She didn't sigh. She wouldn't give him that.

She held the white A4 sheets and read about duct tape around the victim's wrists and the back seat of the escape car and the victim's trousers and the victim's mouth and what was called Grade +4 and then she opened the door again, went in without looking at him and closed it.

———

'He'll contact you!'

Ana was still standing in the hallway. The hat shelf was empty, but still sagged in the middle, it was clearly weighed down by a plastic bag with nothing in it.

She stood there without crying or collapsing on the floor.

'And when he does . . . then I want *you* to contact *me*!'

She walked past the bedroom and the desk drawers that had been pulled out and were lying higgledy-piggledy on the floor, the sitting room and the pictures that had been taken down and were leaning in towards the wall, into the kitchen, stepped across the rug that was scrunched up by a woman's face while arms held her down, and over to the kitchen table and the cup of coffee that was almost stone cold now. She took a sip and lit a cigarette without bothering to open the window or turn on the fan.

He was standing out there, ringing her doorbell, shouting something.

She had listened to a recording of someone taking another person's life. She had read the four sheets of paper.

*But she hadn't fallen to the floor and cried.*

He rang the doorbell again, was probably down on his knees, mouth to the letter box.

'Don't you understand? We need your help!'

She could have shouted back. *Enough's enough.* But she didn't. She drank the cold coffee until the cup was empty and lit another cigarette and stared out at the buildings that all looked the same.

Your dad.

You.

The ones who will see you on TV today and tomorrow and long to be like you.

He rang the doorbell again. And again. Then he gave up, she heard him go into the lift, going down, away.

She waited for a while to be sure. Still silent out on the landing.

The stairs down to the next floor and the rubbish chute.

She opened it, put her hand up, felt around in the cement tube, four bits of tape, she loosened them, one at a time.

It didn't feel like anything any more.

She held the plastic bag in her hand, swung it gently back and forth, then let go, a thud when it hit the bin at the bottom.

Her steps were light when she turned back.

Cold coffee and a cigarette, she looked at the closed front door, whispered.

*Enough's enough.*

———

'About to call it a day?'

He'd known that Werner would still be there.

'Not yet.'

A building full of old men who didn't want to go home.

'Did you want something?'

He hadn't expected her to give him an address or to run and get her son from somewhere – he'd just wanted to give her a nudge so that she would be ready to do so when she knew. But she had been harder to reach than he'd imagined. Kneeling down and shouting through the letter box had not been part of the plan.

'The telephone, Werner.'

The asphalt path back through the high-rise blocks and the sliproad onto the motorway to the centre of Stockholm.

'What about it?'

He wasn't driving particularly fast and it was nice to talk to somebody in the dark that deepened when it started to rain.

'Has it been used again?'

They had stood on the eighth floor in one of Gunnar Werner's tapping rooms and distinguished a choking sound, a gurgling sound and a dull sound.

'No. Nothing more than what you've already heard.'

The mobile phone of one of the inmates in Aspsås prison that had been hidden somewhere and that Werner couldn't talk about as the tapping warrant applied to another investigation.

'And *if* it were to be used?'

A telephone that they now knew had moved out of the unit inside the prison walls, had been in a car, and was probably still with the young man who had killed someone.

'You know that I can't talk to you about it.'

'The same kind of thing as when we met earlier?'

Grens couldn't hear Werner smiling. But he did.

'Yes, the same kind of thing.'

————

He parked in one of the Homicide spaces and sat in the car for a while, the big garage under the police headquarters, so deserted at night.

He felt a bit chilly, which he didn't often do, somewhere that was cool on the warmest summer's day was nearly cold in early autumn.

He started to walk towards the lift, but then changed his mind halfway and headed for the metal box that was built across four parking spaces, a part the garage reserved for forensics.

Silent. Empty. He turned on the light. The car was still there. A white Mercedes.

Grens tried the door handle, unlocked, the smell of glue hit him when he opened the door. Krantz had taped the walls and floor and seats and then superglue-vapoured cigarette butts, drinks cans, scraps of paper.

He sat down on the protective plastic covering on the worn-out front seat. *You were sitting here when you heard her banging against the metal.* He moved into the back seat. *And you sat on her here, and punched her three times for glory.*

She had still been alive at that point.

He went round to the back of the car, stopped by the closed boot, tapped on it absent-mindedly. A sound that skipped off round the concrete space, bounced off the walls and into his lap.

He opened it.

It wasn't particularly big. If he leaned forwards, curled up and pressed himself in, he had just enough room, his large frame pressing against every bend in the metal.

He stretched up his arm, reached for the door handle and pulled it towards him and a thin crack let in light and the air tasted of oil.

*She was lying here and you killed her.*

He now had enough evidence for a court to convict an eighteen-year-old boy of murder.

He had the whole prosecution. But he still didn't have the prosecuted.

Ewert Grens stretched as well as he could in the restricted boot, it didn't get any bigger.

No tape over his mouth, no sock down his throat.

He could breathe.

And he yawned, relaxed, the protective plastic covering on the floor of the boot rustled a bit when he tried to find a more comfortable position.

# now

## part four

### (thirty-seven hours)

IT'S DARK OUTSIDE. He can see through the window. But it can't be a window, can it, as there's no bars on it. He must be asleep, dreaming that he's lying here and the rattling at the metal door, like metal doors rattle when a key is being turned in the lock by a girl who says good morning until he answers.

*The light's not on.*

Someone screams. He hears it. But a long way off. And a car starts. And an aeroplane flies over.

*Who's turned the light off?*

Leon lay back down, stretched, looked around.

It *was* a window.

There *was* someone who screamed and there *was* a car and there *was* an aeroplane.

And he couldn't hear the key rattling and the voice that demanded a good morning. Because she was dead. As were there three empty rooms and five thin mattresses on a parquet floor.

He had slept naked without a sheet.

He had clothes, Gabriel had left them in the car, but he didn't want to sleep in them.

A black hoodie – and he who only ever wore grey ones. Black trackies, Adidas, narrow at the bottom – they were good.

Beside the mattress, piles of empty frozen-pizza boxes, empty paper bags with sugar at the bottom, empty beer cans with cigarettes butts in them, a mound of peanuts, half a cheese.

Barefoot over the warm floor to stand in the middle of the room, closer to the window.

He listened.

Another car. A bus. Some distant voices maybe.

Råby Allé 124. Sixth floor.

He opened the blinds a touch, looked out over the concrete, buildings, car parks, still his world.

They'd slept all day. The rhythm that had been theirs for so long, living only by night. It was as if his body had already forgotten the five months of wake-up at seven a.m. and lock-up at seven thirty p.m.

Alex was asleep beside him, on his back, a gentle snoring. Reza and Uros over by the door to the hall. Marko in the kitchen, in front of the cooker and fridge. He let them sleep, the less they moved the better.

There was a clock on the wall. Quarter past twelve. Six hours to sunrise. He'd always slept with the light on, longed for the light to protect him and show him *where* as soon as he woke up, now he wanted the opposite, the dark that would hide someone on the run.

He was about to make some phone calls. Two phone calls. The first to no one. And the second that meant everything.

Every time he thought about it, the rush, racing round and round inside, forcing his heart to beat faster, making his cock get hard in the way it had when he stabbed the piece of sharp metal in the screw's thigh and pressed it against her throat.

*New name. New rules.*

There was still a knocking in his head. She'd banged so hard against the walls of the boot, she'd twisted and turned and he'd stopped and taped her arms a couple of times more by the Upplands Väsby roundabout, she'd lain there and looked at him and he'd ripped off the tape over her mouth and pushed the sock in as far as it would go, she'd looked at him and he hadn't looked away.

He angled the blinds a tiny bit more. The darkness of Råby outside.

He was home.

*Riot. Escape.*

It was where it always was, in the pouch on the front of his hoodie.

Mobile phone in his hand. He knew that it was tapped. He knew that they were even recording it.

*Kidnapping. Murder.*

It was like she was still banging on the metal when they'd left the car in a dead end on an industrial estate and he'd stopped in front of the closed boot and shouted that she should shut the fuck up and then hadn't turned round even when she continued to knock and they'd got into another Mercedes and driven off. Several times they'd nearly crashed or run someone over and had laughed with a sense of what felt like release and sang along at full volume to the adverts on the radio and halfway into the city, a fucking police camera had flashed in their faces.

He closed the blinds again. A mouthful of tepid beer from one of Alex's cans, a handful of pick 'n' mix from the bag beside it.

The first number was the telephone's own number. The second one was the one written in black felt pen on the kitchen worktop.

He recognised Gabriel's way of holding a pen. The big movements when he pressed hard and always went over the two loops of an eight one more time. His beloved brother who'd made all the necessary changes on the outside so that one of them would always be able to look after things outside when the other one was inside. The escape, break-outs, getaway, it was as much Gabriel's plan as his, their shared desire to rise higher up the wall. They'd been nine when they started to chip away at the morphine and amphetamine market, and now they were there, together.

He trusted him. The only one who he – who had never trusted anyone – had *chosen* to trust.

He missed him so much.

When they'd turned off with the pigs' flash in their face at Brommaplan, they'd driven through Ekerö and into the darkness that had no form and he'd turned up the music and driven even faster and the hare had hit one of the headlights and the dog that had been so close, they should've run it over, and they screamed enough to drown out the radio when the water was finally there, and the beach and the boats and only a few minutes in a skiff to the other side.

Papers. TV.

Ten digits on the worktop. *I'm going to kill them all.* In a while, when he wanted to, higher up.

They'd run along the shore and the two small boats had had padlocks that were easy to cut off with an angle grinder and the guns at their feet on the bottom of the boats and they had been close to land when the helicopter had swooped down to the water with its searchlights and circled and circled and they had pressed themselves against the wet wooden bottom of the boat until they jumped out by Slagstabadet and he knew exactly where they were.

He clutched the mobile phone and felt the rush inside again, right up into his chest like it sometimes did when he was alone and didn't want to be, even more and even stronger than when he'd held the piece of metal against her throat. He'd known that it was bugged when he dialled the number to his other phone just before he had left the car and before he forced the sock down her throat, had listened to nothing while he spoke. And he was going to do it again. And they would listen again, like before, and they would come here, be here when he made the call to the other number.

Explosion

Leon was breathing heavily and his hands were shaking when he looked into the dark windowpane that was a mirror for his huge pupils; he could feel it, he knew it, it was real.

That whoever got highest up couldn't get any further and didn't need a wall any more.

————

Someone was standing outside the door.

Gabriel was sure of it.

He lay down on her sofa. He'd had his own key since they met, but had hardly ever been there. But there had been two civvy pigs coming through Råby and the kids had warned him and he'd known where to go.

He wasn't suspected of anything and couldn't be arrested.

Nor Big Ali, nor Jon, nor Bruno.

But they were looking for them, for their pointless interviews about something no one had any intention of talking about and they'd split up, each gone their own way from the garage, he had crept under the cars between Råby Allé 67 and Råby Allé 114, a route that only he, who had always been here, knew.

There *was* someone there, outside. He could hear them.

He had locked the door, pulled down the blinds and lain down on her sofa to wait. It was too early to visit Leon. And he had a phone that he wasn't to talk to anyone on. He'd fallen asleep. Slept the evening away.

Someone was trying the door handle.

Gabriel reached down to the floor, Glock 17, it lay so well in his hand and he pulled back the trigger with his index finger, the only gun he'd ever held cocked like this and he liked it, the feeling of more control.

The door opened. He couldn't see who it was. Gun in hand, finger on the trigger, he was ready.

Her.

His body went soft again, he relaxed, let go of the trigger.

'Hi.'

She looked so happy. And she sat down beside him on the sofa, kissed his cheek and forehead and neck, snuggled up closer.

'I was there today, before the pigs came.'

She didn't normally look this happy.

'The antenatal clinic.'

She laughed a lot, to be fair, but not like this.

'A private antenatal clinic.'

She took his hand, put it to her womb.

'Here, you see? He put an ultrasound stick up to get close enough. They don't normally do that here, not so early, only in other countries. But I wanted to. And I had the money.'

He'd once given her a film that he thought was the best. He'd watched it with Leon when they were little, again, again, and again, he knew every movement and was prepared every time the main character got wild in the eyes. It was lying on the white shelf under the TV and he put it on.

'It's called an ectopic pregnancy and it's dangerous. And I wanted to know. And I don't need to worry! Gabriel? He said that I'm five weeks pregnant! Can you believe it?'

*A Clockwork Orange.* He liked the first scene best. With the alcoholic who lies there and the others come walking along the tunnel all dressed in white with black hats and beat the loser with sticks while he keeps rattling on. After the very first time, an old DVD player that they'd hidden at Leon's mum's, they'd run side by side to the metro and Skärholms Centrum and Åhléns and smashed the display window and gone up to the first floor and the hats that were there, they owned the fucking place, they'd been eleven years old and danced like in the film and with hats on and he'd understood what it was all about.

'It's already five millimetres.'

Wanda kissed his cheek again. And bent down to the DVD player, ejected his disc and put in her own.

'There. Gabriel, can you see it?'

The picture was grey and black and white and grainy and blurred and she went over and pointed to it and he looked at her finger that was nothing.

'Five millimetres. Measured from head to bum.'

She held her hand up on the air, two fingers in front of his face, measured a space as big as a gram of methamphetamine in a yellow capsule.

'Like half a nail on my finger. But already . . . a person.'

'Turn it off.'

'The heart, he said it wasn't much bigger than a speck of dirt, but that it had already started to beat. And liver and kidneys, they're not developed, but they're there. And little buds that are arms and legs. And even an appendix. And—'

'Turn it off, I said!'

'—the face, it's starting to form, the jaws and nose and eyes. You, Gabriel. And me.'

Whatever it was that was grey and white and nothing was still on the TV screen and the entire picture moved slowly slowly, like he'd had something to smoke and was feeling good, even though he hadn't at all.

'Your earrings?'

'What about them?'

'Where the fuck are they?'

He was still lying down and she was sitting on the floor beside him, her ears at his level. The earrings. From the jewellers on Kungsgatan, two crosses with a small diamond in the middle.

She had chosen them herself. So she should wear them.

'It was them that I . . . well, sold.'

'What the fuck did you say?'

'The ultrasound. The film, the one you're watching, it cost money. So I sold them. And there's enough for—'

'. . . you fucking . . .'

'—another visit, another film.'

Gabriel didn't call her a whore any more. He didn't hit her either. Once he'd vacuumed her. There was nothing left he could do. But he did pull out her film, throw it towards the kitchen and put his own back in. There was another scene that he liked, when they ring on the door of a big posh house and mr and mrs don't want to let them in but do in the end and they're singing 'Singin' in the Rain' with clown masks on and white clothes and black hats and tape up the man and woman's mouths and use their sticks again, more than once.

─────────

He'd made the first phone call. To the phone that he was holding in his hand, the one that was tapped, he'd called himself and they'd listen, trace it, come here.

Leon ran his fingers over the empty kitchen worktop. Ten digits in black pen. Gabriel's writing and the number to a phone that was wrapped in plastic, protected against water. When he was absolutely certain that they were there.

*I'm going to kill all of them.*

Four snoring, snuffling teenagers on mattresses on the floor. Pigs running around all over the fucking country looking for them, and they were lying on a dirty floor only a few metres away, sleeping. He'd leave them be for a while, go and get something and they'd still be asleep when he got back. That was why he was going there. To get something. That's what he thought, at least. She hadn't been to see him once in Aspsås prison. Or Mariefred prison. Or Eknäs young offenders institution. If he worked it out, he didn't need to work it out, he knew exactly, it was two years and four months since they last saw each other. Even though they lived in the same place between his stints inside. And he hadn't been prepared that time, neither had she, they were suddenly just standing there beside each other on the platform at Råby station and she was wearing a black coat and jeans and she had her hair up in a way that made her look old. It was three minutes until the next train and there was no one else there. He hadn't said anything and she hadn't said anything. They'd stood still breathing so quietly that it couldn't be heard until he'd suddenly said at least *hello*, and he knew that she'd heard but she didn't turn around and he'd been about to say it again when the train rolled in and they'd gone their separate ways.

He opened the door, the stairs were empty. He would go out, but not into the concealing dark, he'd go down into the garage and the way they always went when they didn't want to be seen.

———

He couldn't sleep.

They were lying side by side on her white sofa and he was sweating and shivering and he'd got cramp in his feet and calves like he used to when he was little and the skin that had disappeared had still burned.

Gabriel looked at her. She was asleep and she had no earrings in. He rubbed her soft earlobes with his thumb and index finger. She'd sold them. And bought a grey and black picture.

He had a smoke. He drank two cans of beer. He even got out his gun that was lying in a bag in the hall and took out one bullet at time and put one bullet at a time back in, but it didn't help; what he was feeling just got stronger, weed and alcohol and holding a gun normally made him feel calm but not now, it just got worse all the time.

Her disc. He put it in and started it.

There was no sound.

He hadn't thought about that, last time. The grey and black and grainy, the thing that was moving so slowly, you couldn't hear it.

*He couldn't see anything.*

A heart. Two kidneys. Buds that would become arms and legs.

440

*And if he couldn't see anything, how could it be there? And moving so fucking slowly?*

It wasn't there.

He was there. And Wanda was there. And soon Leon, his beloved brother.

He would be able to touch him for the first time in five months, that was all there was, not her fucking picture that was her fault.

———

That time, the last time, he'd said *hello* and she hadn't even answered.

She could have turned around, looked at him. But she said nothing, pretended not to hear, just got onto the train and turned her back.

He was going to get the package. That was the only reason. She would open the door and he would take it and she could be as silent as she fucking liked.

Leon hurried down the stairs of Råby Allé 124. He should maybe have stayed where he was, but it was night and the others were asleep and would still be asleep when he got back – and he'd be moving around in the dark – and he'd made the first phone call – and they'd be moving very soon anyway.

He'd known it so well, the place called Slagsta Strand, but he'd lain there between Alex and Marko on the wet planks at the bottom of the boat until the helicopter had done its last sweep and disappeared. Råby was two kilometres and a hundred police officers away. They'd sat on the beach that they used to run to as kids when they were at school, when they'd swum at night, washed away whatever was sticking to their skin. He remembered what it was like to be naked and light and that it was always cold and that he always shivered a bit afterwards, but nothing more; he'd been so young and it was so long ago, faded and hard to get hold of and he felt nothing when he thought about it, nothing except that fucking lump you get from feeling nothing.

The grey door, right at the bottom, opposite the lift. He opened it a few centimetres, listened.

They'd split up at Hallunda Centrum and he'd run over the big hill behind the metro line and down the other side and the helicopter again, the searchlight, flying low, he'd had to lie in the ditch in the short stretch between Botkyrka church and the Shell station that they'd robbed four times the summer they were twelve, he'd got up when the helicopter flew towards Södertälje and he'd run alongside the E4 to the concrete pipe that went under the road to the other side and he'd felt a surge in his legs and stomach and chest when he'd seen the windows with no curtains in the distance and caught the smell that only existed there.

He was sure. There was no one else on the other side of the door. He dropped down onto the hard surface and crawled out into the garage that connected the whole area underground.

The helicopter had turned back but the sound was still distant and it was dark and he had started to walk, step by step closer to the buildings that were his childhood and he'd seen blue flashing lights and pigs with bright torches, and then suddenly in the pit of his stomach, far down in his balls, as if he were proud, helicopters and road blocks and motorbikes and cars all because of him. He had sneaked past the first few buildings, loud music from an open window and then another with a man and a woman screaming at each other, next building, and the next building, he'd been so close. *Stop.* Someone had shouted behind him, it had been a man's voice. *Stand still.* A pig voice, he knew exactly what they sounded like. And he'd managed not to run, took several deep breaths, so fucking close, and then turned round.

He crept through the garage, between the cars that were standing there, he knew every dent in the concrete wall, every pipe, pillar, rubbish bin, pile of tyres.

A man's voice had shouted *stop* and he'd turned around. They were waiting a bit further up by one of the entrances to a stairwell, four pigs with torches, and they'd been shouting at someone else. He'd pressed himself in against the wall while they searched through someone's pockets and checked someone else's ID and then moved on. Someone else. He'd run the last stretch to the door and into the garage he was now lying in, and he'd waited for Alex and Reza and Marko and Uros while the kids had blocked the lifts and the stairs to the flat at the top with the mattresses on the floor and beer and pizza in the fridge.

Leon breathed in the smell of the garage, the second time within twenty-four hours, crawled slowly under the cars and faster over empty parking spaces.

A couple of metres away, the grey door called Råby Allé 34.

He knew exactly how it would feel. Strange how our first experiences follow us. He had slept in other beds in recent years, walked up other stairs, but every step here, he wanted to laugh out loud and hit someone, he wanted to be alone and surrounded by the people he knew, every time on these stairs, he could feel it the whole way from top to bottom.

The third floor. He rang the bell.

He heard her, put his hand over the peephole, she wasn't going to stand there looking at him.

'Open up.'

He pressed down the door handle. It was locked.

'Open up, for fuck's sake!'

He was standing in front of a door that someone had unlocked for them for the first time when he was four and a half, and she had come home.

'Open, or I'll kick it in!'

And he was there to collect the package. That was the only reason.

'What do you want?'

'You know what I want.'

'You shouldn't be here. I've explained to you before. And yesterday . . . the girl, the car boot, the pictures . . . *you're never coming in here again.*'

'Open up!'

Ana stood by the closed door and looked through the peephole that was covered by a hand.

She had stood in front of him that time. The day before he turned sixteen.

Her son.

And she'd explained to him that she had opened the door for the last time, whispered something about being frightened even though you love someone, about the strength that doesn't come back no matter how much you try, that with Gabriel he'd been unreachable for so long, and even more so with the others who seemed to make him so much stronger, but that he'd also become unreachable when he was alone and that when a person couldn't get any further she had to give up or go under, and that's what she'd done, given up.

'I want to talk to you!'

'Never again.'

'About my dad.'

She looked through the hole that was black.

He was standing on the other side. Thirty centimetres away.

The black, his hand, she could almost touch it. *About my dad.* He'd never said anything like that before.

She turned the key, pushed down the door handle, opened.

She saw a boy, eighteen years old, tense face and unkempt hair, clothes like they all wore. He saw a woman, thirty-five years old, tense face and long hair that had started to turn grey, a dressing gown that looked like all the other dressing gowns she'd had. Maybe she was smiling slightly, or maybe it was one of the expressions a face makes when it recognises something and for a moment sees something else. Maybe he wanted to touch her, his palm brush her cheek, but he didn't reach out his arm and if you don't stretch out your arm you can't reach and can't touch.

'Where is it?'

'Your dad. You wanted—'

'I wanted you to open. Where is it?'

He was standing in her hallway and she was so small, just like that time on the platform, and he wanted to say *hello* again, talk, about whatever.

'Where *the fuck* is it?'

He smelt of beer. And his clothes smelt of sweat.

'It's not here.'

'*Where*?'

'I threw it away.'

He was standing so close.

He'd instructed Gabriel to give her the plastic bag, she was to look after it even though they could have given it to someone else. And he'd just rung on this door out of all the others, after lying hidden on a mattress for twenty-seven hours.

He didn't care about her.

'You have not.'

And why should he? A thirty-five-year-old cow who didn't want to open the door?

'I know that you haven't thrown it away.'

She should never have thrown it away, it protected him, helped him to survive, he knew that somehow it would always be like this.

Maybe he had wanted to reach out to her, touch her. He didn't do it. He hit her.

'Just like your dad.'

He hit her again.

'*Just* like your dad.'

He walked towards her as she backed away, down the hall he'd run along so many times as a kid, into the kitchen that had been breakfast and lunch and supper and sometimes when it was cold outside, tea that she made herself that tasted of raspberries, and yet didn't at the same time.

He raised his hand to hit her again.

'Out there.'

She pointed to the hall, the door.

'The rubbish chute. At the bottom.'

He lowered his hand that was still shaking, prepared, and walked over to the kitchen table where they had sometimes baked some round, heavy bread together and where he and Gabriel had divvied up packets of morphine in the beginning, and that he'd plunged a knife into four times one evening, the great gashes were still there if he lifted up the plant pot and tablecloth that she always put over them. There was a drawer between the two chairs and he pulled it open, screwdriver on the left, red and long. He took it with him and hurried back out into the hall, her black coat on a hanger under the hat shelf, keys always in the left pocket.

'So you won't be able to lock anyone out.'

He should have gone down the stairs slowly, quietly. He ran. Down to the ground floor, on, stopped at the bottom by the door into the garage. And then turned round. Another door, equally grey, but not as thick.

Screwdriver against the doorframe, by the bolt.

A hard push.

The gap opened, another push, again, again until it was wide enough for him to lift the door, force it open. The stench of rubbish, he didn't breathe, rummaged around among the plastic bags that were leaking and milk cartons that weren't empty, cutting himself twice on broken bottles.

It was lying there. A white plastic bag with strips of heavy tape. In between four large bags that reeked of fish. He leaned over the edge of the container and managed to reach the bottom with his fingers, which slipped on the wet plastic surface before he managed to get hold of it and he stood up with the gun in his hand.

Lahti L-35. Finnish. He aimed into the air, his arm slightly to the side, even when he opened the door and went into the kitchen.

She was sitting there, a cup of coffee as always, and a cigarette.

'Like a child.'

He aimed at her now.

'What did you say?'

'You're standing there . . . posing like a child.'

He didn't let go of the gun when he hit her again on the right cheek.

She fell and he kicked her on the thigh, the hip, her cunt.

'You'll show me some respect, whore!'

She lay there, her neck sore when she gradually lifted her head and looked at him.

'*Just like your dad.*'

———

Wanda was still asleep beside him on the sofa, without her earrings. Gabriel had crept back up beside her and she hadn't noticed, he'd stroked his fingers over her bare lobes and she'd turned towards him in her sleep, her face to his.

Freezing. Sweating. It didn't stop.

He'd seen something moving slowly that was grey and black and five millimetres long and a heart and kidneys and buds instead of arms and legs. And for the first time in ages he'd thought about a fire that had taken a father he couldn't remember and a little brother who he sometimes remembered in the mornings and eighty-five per cent of his skin that he missed every day. He'd sunk into the picture that wasn't of anything and stood in the middle of a fire. He'd waited in front of a door that was locked and his father was standing on the other side and he was seven years old and had pulled at the door to get into the flames that were so high and his dad who was shouting at him that he had to let go and get out and when he hadn't done that, shouted that he'd get a good beating if he didn't leg it – he'd let go and he'd run away from the fire and that fucking fucking picture in front of him that moved so slowly and he couldn't see whatever it was that was five frigging millimetres. He'd thrown the remote control at the TV screen and pressed himself closer to Wanda and that was where he was lying now when he took her arm and shook her and when she didn't wake up, slapped her, but not as hard as normal and shouted *it's your fault* and started to walk away and out, he was going to meet him now, only one brother, only one love.

---

The image was gone. How did that happen?

When he closed the front door and went down the stairs, it stayed in there. With her.

Gabriel stood completely still.

It didn't come. It hadn't followed him.

He carried on. He took out his gun like he usually did, but this time opened it and took out the only bullet, spun the chamber and fired at his temple, a clicking sound.

---

Four cellar storerooms. Five flats.

*Paragraf 1. Famly never asks. Famly gives orders.*

This was the first one and where he'd be for the next few hours.

It had been five months.

And he would be able to hug him again soon.

*Paragraf 2. A soldier always stands ready for the famly.*

Gabriel went up the stairs of Råby Allé 124. The whole building was silent. Ordinary tenants who were sleeping so they could get up early tomorrow morning and live ordinary lives.

It didn't feel like he'd thought it would.

He'd gone up three nights earlier with Jon and Bruno and Big Ali, cardboard boxes from the supermarket full of pizza and beer and sweets, suitcases with bedding and pillows, and then once more with four newly stolen boxes that had been stored in the trailer in the garage that Leon wanted to be kept in one of the wardrobes. He'd filled the fridge and put out the mattresses and he'd felt it in his chest, his brother was going to sleep here and the whole fucking country would know that Ghetto Soldiers had escaped and later, to be able to hug him again, it was already in his body, something laughing inside.

And yet it wasn't like that. He was on his way to something else. The fire once again.

*Paragraf 3. The famly before everthing.*

He stood in front of the door. If he continued. If he took Wanda with him and the thing that couldn't be seen. If he opened and went into a flat full of another kind of love, the kind that he and Leon had written rules for.

*Paragraf 4. Or else punishment.*

———

Gabriel stood in the hall. And when he breathed, he was almost calm.

Most of all in his stomach. And throat. If he was angry or frightened or sad, that was where he felt it. Now there was nothing. Every breath slipped in and down without pressing and pulling and burning inside.

Alex was lying on one of the mattresses over by the wall in the sitting room. Uros and Reza were closer, by the door. And if he stretched over and looked into the kitchen – Marko Bendik, in the space between the cooker and the fridge. They heard him, nodded, but couldn't say anything yet.

The fifth mattress was empty.

A step further in. He could see him now.

Leon was standing by the worktop in the kitchen, his back turned, the white plastic bag beside him – the one that only a few weeks ago had lain on a seat on the metro between Norsberg and Råby, only a few weeks ago, that they had then left on a hat shelf – the gun in three pieces, the slide on one side of the bag, frame on the other, and the actual barrel in one hand and a cleaning rod in the other, slowly in and out.

He turned around. They looked at each other, started to walk towards each other at the same time, arms outstretched. A hug. Long. Warm.

'One love, brother.'

'One love, my only brother.'

That feeling. But it wasn't everything at once. It had always been that. All his yearning and joy and security and trust and someone who was part of him.

He tried to feel it. He *wanted* to feel it.

The first hug had always been everything at once. He held on to Leon and neither of them wanted to let go and Gabriel waited for the feeling that didn't come.

Another feeling instead. He recognised this too. Shame. Stronger than he'd ever felt it before.

They hugged until Leon let go and walked over to the cupboard in the hall, opened it and took out four cardboard boxes, carried them into the sitting room, unpacked four recently stolen portable television sets, mounted the small aerials and put the four remote controls down on the floor in front of him.

'I've been waiting for you, brother.'

He picked up two of the remote controls and held them out.

'You put on SVT and Sky News. I'll put on Text TV and TV4.'

Gabriel tried. But it was hard to meet Leon's eyes.

Shame.

He took both the remote controls, weighed them in his hands.

'Brother . . .'

'Switch them on.'

'We have to talk, brother.'

Leon was standing in a sitting room with no furniture and bare walls. He nodded at Alex, at Marko, at Uros, at Reza, held one of the remote controls over his head, pretended to aim and shoot, switched on the TV set to the far right. Text TV, page 100. The square with the yellow letters that was at the top, *Head of investigation warns the public*, the square with blue letters just underneath, *Biggest police operation since Malexander*. He aimed and fired and switched on the next set, TV4 and a special news-flash, *escape, hostage, break-outs, murder*, every half an hour.

'Brother, turn them on!'

'Talk, brother. We've got to talk.'

'Turn it on! We'll talk later.'

He'd never known that shame could be so invasive, that it could grab you by the throat and never let go. He tried to look into his beloved brother's eyes and pretended to aim as well, pressed the remote control, pointed it at the TV to the far left. News special on SVT. A woman he recognised and then pictures of the prison wall at Aspsås and five passport photos of faces that right now were looking at themselves and then some other pictures of a white car with an open boot.

'The other one.'

'Brother?'

'Later.'

It wasn't much of a pretend aim and pretend shot. He couldn't. His fingers didn't even want to press but did, because he forced them to. Sky News. And sports news, baseball, no matter how many times he tried.

Leon's face, maybe it was disappointment.

'Turn it off.'

Three TV sets on, the fourth silent. They stood, sat and lay in front of the images that switched between reporters talking and close-ups of barbed wire and the black and white slightly grainy ones from various security cameras.

*About them.*

Leon stretched out his arms again, embraced Gabriel, pressed hard.

'See that? It's us!'

'Now, brother. We *have* to talk.'

'In a while. I've got a phone call to make first. This one.'

He held up his mobile phone.

'They'll be listening this time. Then we'll shift. And ring the other one. Those fucking TVs, you know, they'll just keep coming!'

He pointed the remote control at the pictures of himself and Gabriel looked at them and then looked away.

'I want out.'

Gabriel wasn't quite sure if he'd said it out loud or not, maybe it had just been in his head.

'Did you hear me, my only brother? I want out.'

———

When Leon turned down the volume on all three televisions, one set at a time, it was totally silent.

'You understand, brother? I . . .'

They were all looking at Gabriel.

'. . . I . . . fuck, Wanda . . .I'm going to be . . . a dad.'

———

The first blow hit him on the right shoulder and the top of his arm.

'So I . . . I *want* out.'

The next one, more on the chest, almost his heart.

'Her belly, inside . . . about this size . . . like a little person.'

He held his index finger and thumb up in front of him a few millimetres apart, like Wanda had done.

The third punch was to his jaw and cheek.

'You can never leave.'

'Love you, brother.'

'Gabriel, *Gabriel*, you're a part of the plan, you can't just fucking leave . . .'

The remote control in Leon's hand, it was shaking.

'. . . *no one* can leave. You know that! It was *you* and *me* that wrote that.'

'I've made up my mind, brother. You know . . . love, I feel . . . her fucking belly, like you and me, like you and your mum before, you know . . . love, brother.'

———

His cigarettes and a lighter were in the pouch of his hoodie.

Leon opened the packet and lit a cigarette. Just one drag. He left the smoking, glowing cigarette on one of the silent TV sets, picked up a remote control instead and looked at Gabriel, standing like a statue, who met his eyes and let his arms hang loose at the side of his torso, he gripped the oblong piece of plastic in his hand when he punched him with full force on the left temple and then waited while Gabriel fell to the floor.

He lay there.

Arms pressed even closer to his body, still obviously passive, and Leon looked him in the eyes when he aimed the first kick to his thigh.

'No one leaves.'

The next kick higher up, his ribs.

'*No one.*'

———

Gabriel lay on the floor, without moving, when Leon sat on his chest, one leg on either side of a body that knew, was waiting.

The smoking cigarette on the TV, Leon turned, took hold of it and looked at Gabriel's silent face when he pressed it for the first time against the fifteen per cent of skin that had never been damaged, on the forehead.

'Your *dad* was burned alive.'

The second time, on his left cheek.

'My *dad* disappeared.'

Left cheek, once more, but this time lower down, the glowing end stuck a bit when he pushed hard.

'Alex's *dad* kicked the shit out of him and Reza's *dad* drank himself to death and Uros's *dad* sits on a bench on Råby Torg and shouts cock at anyone who passes and Marko's *dad* . . .'

He turned to Marko who was standing by the window in front of the closed blinds and pointed a finger to his head, fired.

'. . . blew his brains out.'

Leon pressed the cigarette into the healthy skin again, on the right cheek now, twice.

'And you . . . you say that you're going to be . . . *a dad*?'

Gunnar Werner closed the door to the eighth floor and the Section for Electronic Communications Interception and went over to the lift. It had been one of those evenings; he had stayed a bit longer, then a bit longer still – a late-night sandwich in a real home, in front of the telly, the news and half an hour of Frank Sinatra with his eyes closed in the sitting room armchair had become more and more distant – as if he had been waiting for something without knowing what.

Now he knew.

And he had to be quick.

His mobile phone ready in his hand as he approached the basement. In the space of a few minutes he'd made twelve calls and each time after a few rings had been transferred to Detective Superintendent Ewert Grens's voicemail. After some minutes he'd worked out the possible position of the phone – it was, within a sixty-metre margin – somewhere in the car park under the Kronoberg headquarters.

He stepped out of the lift and into a concrete space.

Many more vehicles than were there during the day. The air was different, less pollution and less oil. And another sound, he could hear the humming monotone of the air vents in the silence.

He dialled again. No answer. He called again and started to walk behind the rows of cars listening out for what he should be able to hear. He carried on ringing until he came to the main door, turned to the right, round the next corner.

It wasn't until he approached the closed-off area that belonged to Forensics that he heard it.

Faint at first, then clearer. In there? He opened the unlocked door and went in.

Only one car. A white Mercedes. He'd never seen it before, never stood so close, and yet it was as if he'd sat in it, driven it through the Stockholm suburbs. He knew the sound of it accelerating and braking suddenly, when someone lying down banged on the metal, even how it sounded when someone stopped breathing in the large boot.

The ringing was louder and he went closer, it was coming from *inside* the car, somewhere near the front seat.

He opened the door on the passenger side. There it was. The dashboard with a small shelf in the middle, between the speedometer and the clock.

A mobile phone. But no detective superintendent.

There was a strong smell of glue. Thin plastic like a membrane covering each seat and red and white flags to mark blood stains. He stood with the door open and realised that what had seemed urgent was probably too late, he closed it again and started to walk towards the exit when he thought he heard someone breathing.

He turned around, *there*, a black shoe.

He approached the pale skin between dark socks and dark trouser legs that was sticking out from the boot.

Ewert Grens. And he was asleep. On his side, legs pulled up, head turned, his body touching every metal wall.

'Ewert?'

No response.

But the large man was breathing steadily between soft snores. Gunnar Werner put a hand on one of the crushed trouser legs, tugged at it gently.

'Ewert?'

'Yes?'

His face was creased, his eyes squinting as he looked for the voice that had spoken.

'Ewert, you were asleep.'

'No.'

'You were sleeping in Nils Krantz's murder scene.'

'I was working.'

Gunnar Werner smiled as he put his hand down into the boot.

'Good, Ewert, good. That you're so meticulous.'

Grens saw the same-aged hand and took hold of it, Werner pulled and a large, aching body unfolded. His leg that hurt when he couldn't lie with it straight. His neck that hurt most of the time. He sat on the edge of the boot and stretched his arms over his head.

'You obviously wanted something.'

Ewert Grens was smiling vaguely now too.

'Important enough to interrupt an examination of the crime scene.'

The much taller and thinner detective sergeant who was an expert at intercepting and listening to phone calls held out a small digital recorder.

'I didn't go home this evening. I sat watching a long thin line on a computer screen. And sometimes, you know, we get surplus information.'

Grens was on his feet and Werner closed the boot, put the recorder on top and checked his watch.

'Twelve minutes ago. And twenty-eight minutes ago. At zero zero twenty and zero zero thirty-six.'

They listened in the cavernous garage that had walls and a floor that carried the sound, made it grow. A faint peep from a button being pressed on a phone immediately became something sharp that penetrated into the recently rested brain.

'Someone dialling a number.'

'I can hear that.'

Ten digits, ten peeps like small daggers. And then another, a peep that was longer knives with shorter intervals.

'Engaged tone.'

'I can hear that as well.'

Gunnar Werner would shortly go back to the Section for Electronic Communications Interception. The fact that he'd spoken to Grens about something he wasn't supposed to only hours ago was bad enough, but standing here talking again in a place where anyone might pass was risking more than it was worth.

'Leon Jensen's phone. Both calls. And he's ringing himself.'

'Him . . .?'

'Himself. Engaged. The phone he shared with Mihailovic, that he took with him from Unit D1 Left. The one he used in the car during a murder and that we already have a tapping warrant for in connection with something else.'

He stopped the recorder, put it in his jacket pocket and started to walk slowly away.

'Two calls from the same place.'

He waited for Grens who hurried after him, his heels clacking loudly.

'And I'm almost certain I know where from. From which building, and even from which floor.'

It smelt of burnt flesh.

An unpleasant smell that invaded your nose and overpowered every other taste in your mouth.

He'd phoned twice, they'd listened to the engaged tone and were on their way, they would sit down there, together. The first call would bring them there. The next call, the number that Gabriel had written on the worktop in the kitchen, just one signal to a mobile phone wrapped in a plastic bag in a cistern behind a toilet.

Leon stood in the hall of the empty flat that they'd slept in for twenty-four hours and had to leave immediately. Thirty minutes max, maybe twenty, no more. Four to choose between, all connected to the underground garage and with a view of Råby police station.

Five white circles.

Gabriel was still lying on the floor in front of images on TV screens with no sound.

Five white circles with small black specks in the middle, like corns of ash on snow. Two circles on each cheek and one on the forehead. In a few hours, seeping blood blisters, in a few days, infected wounds, in a few weeks pink craters in the skin, in a few months tender scars.

Leon stepped over the silent TVs and went out to the kitchen worktop. *You will never leave us*. He pulled the plastic bag that only recently had been lying at the bottom of a rubbish container towards him. *You will never leave me*. He lifted up the bolt and barrel, fitted it to the slide and frame, pushed in the full magazine, eight bullets. *You're my brother, my only brother, we're on the top fucking wall, you and me, you and me, Gabriel!* One piece left, a decimetre long, black, round piece of metal, he picked it up and screwed it onto the muzzle.

'You can burn the rest. I won't be back.'

The long, black thing on the muzzle of the gun was a silencer, it was easy to see when he held it up, pulled back the safety lever with his thumb and aimed at the burnt circle on his forehead.

'Do what the fuck you like. I've made up my mind. I'm out.'

Leon aimed, finger on the trigger.

And then turned around, fired one shot at a time, a hole as big as a five-kronor coin in each screen.

'Well, fifty thousand then, *Daddy*.'

'You're not getting any fucking money from me.'

'That's what it costs.'

'It was fucking well you and me that built this up!'

'Fifty thousand. And then you can leave. I don't need you.'

---

Ewert Grens walked with Gunnar Werner through the Kronoberg garage to a car with the Västerort Police emblem on the door.

Twenty-eight hours of silence from someone on the run. Then suddenly . . . a sign of life.

Werner had picked up a telephone signal.

Twelve seconds the first time and eighteen seconds the second time.

You rang yourself. Twice. You risked being discovered. As if you wanted to be discovered.

'Address?'

'Råby Allé 124.'

'Floor?'

'Six.'

That rush – closing in on a murderer, someone who has declared that another person's life is less valuable than their own and has taken it with them – it came from deep down inside and carried him through nights of hell.

Grens looked at the telephone that had been lying on a plastic surface on a passenger seat.

Sixteen missed calls.

Werner.

He nodded, thanked a police sergeant who had done more than he needed and was now on his way back to other voices that would become sound files in a court case.

'Where are you?'

Ewert Grens had got in, turned the ignition key and made a call.

'Råby, the big office. And I've finished putting together the information about the minors. Even when I don't include the ones who don't really have enough connection, there's still twenty-seven left. I've got addresses, observation logs, reports . . .'

'Not necessary.'

'. . . a list of . . .'

'Pereira, it's not necessary.'

José Pereira's voice was tired, but not because it was night or sleepy, but due to lack of sleep.

'I'm listening.'

'He's there, Pereira. Close to you.'

'Where?'

'Less than four hundred metres away.'

*Ewert Grens had seen him being born.*

'I want you to wake the duty special firearms command team.'

*José Pereira had seen him grow up.*

'I want them to do a raid.'

*They'd known ever since where he was heading, where it would end.*

'In fifteen minutes.'

————

Leon turned off the mobile and put it in the pouch of his black hoodie. A bugged telephone can be traced. That was what he'd wanted and he knew that it didn't matter who he called, what he talked about or for how long. He didn't want it any more. They had about five, he guessed, max ten minutes left. Alex, Uros, Reza and Marko were on their way out into the hall and he'd hung back by the TVs on the sitting room floor that had just shown a face from the front, profile from the left, profile from the right, by the crossed out digits in black felt tip on the kitchen worktop that was the number of a mobile phone in a plastic bag in a toilet that he would ring when *they* were there. And by someone who had been the only person he'd ever trusted and who now had five circular marks on his face.

'If I was you, I'd get my ass out of here, fast.'

He held open the front door, turned around.

'And don't forget . . . fifty thousand.'

He closed it. Opened it again straight away. Gabriel was still lying on the floor and they looked at each other. Not for very long, neither of them had much time, but enough for it to hurt.

————

Ewert Grens had perhaps driven faster out of the city than ever before as he headed south on the E4.

*He'd seen him being born. He was going to see him arrested.*

Someone who was wanted had turned on the phone, phoned himself, waited a while, then turned it off.

*Is that what you want, to be found?*

The road block they'd been stopped at the night before, Grens wound down the window to the same helmet and bullet-proof vest, a lowered gun with a sharp beam of light.

'We met yesterday.'

'We did.'

'And this time?'

'This time I reckon I'll let gold command through.'

The helmet and vest smiled briefly, then grinned when he saw that the person he was smiling at was smiling back.

The motorway exit and the main road and then the asphalt walkways to the door of Råby Allé 124. Ewert Grens parked between the deserted playground and two park benches, walked over to three police vans and two police cars and another two from the dog patrol.

'Sixth floor?'

'Six flats. Hit them all at the same time.'

Two policemen on either side of the main door, dark helmets, visors down, new uniform and automatic weapons in their hands.

'When?'

'Four minutes ago.'

The detective superintendent carried on over to the stairs when one of the dogs, an Alsatian, jumped up, front paws on his shoulders, growled in his face, snapped at a beige jacket sleeve to show that he'd come too close. Grens pushed his hand against the animal's chest, a hard thrust, and it lost its balance, four paws on the ground and he looked at it, shouted *sit* in a loud voice until it did. He nodded to the dog handler who had a dog that did its job, and carried on up the stairs, running as far as he could up the six flights of steep stairs.

A lift that was standing still. Five flats that were temporarily sealed off. And the sixth that was open, or rather, didn't have a door.

He went closer.

The door had been removed and leaning against the wall by the entrance, splintered wood where the hinges had been – a piston and the pressure of compressed air.

He paused briefly in the hall. The smell, faint but recognisable, of burnt flesh. And it was stronger in the sitting room, by the four TV sets in the middle of the floor, each screen with a hole in it and if he got down on his hands and knees and felt them with his finger, bullet holes. Mattresses, pillows, he counted five beds. Empty beer cans and half-eaten cakes. The parquet floor was covered in splinters of glass from two windows, a rope outside each that was moving gently in the wind, forced entry from two sides at the same time.

'I've spoken to the neighbours on this floor.'

José Pereira picked up a box and shook it, which according to the picture on the side had had a TV in it.

'Three of the flats were abandoned in full haste. They saw what was happening and got frightened and vanished so they wouldn't need to talk. So that leaves two. The neighbours on . . . *this* side, a family with three children who've seen nothing, they were all asleep when we forced entry. And . . . *here*, two sisters, I'm guessing Polish, who described being woken up by loud voices and then what they called a dull bang, three, maybe four times.'

They turned and looked at the four TV sets that didn't work any more.

'They crept out to have a look through the peephole, two at different heights, so they could both look at the same time. And they both agree. Five young men, all in hoodies and tracksuit bottoms, left the flat first and then some minutes later, a sixth one left.'

Ewert Grens kicked one of the cardboard boxes lightly and it slid across the parquet floor. TV sets?

'When?'

'They reckon about ten minutes before we got here.'

'And they're reliable?'

'Yes.'

So near. And yet so far.

'Then they'll be in the next flat already.'

THE COFFEE IN Råby police station was much worse than in the corridors of Kronoberg. Bitter, almost sour, and ridiculously weak. It wasn't often that Grens said no to a plastic cup of warmth, but having really tried with the first and poured out the second, he just shook his head when Pereira went to get a third.

They stood in front of the wall. The one he scorned and the one that the kids out there aspired to and that always seemed to be in the middle of the office, no matter where he was in the Section Against Gang Crime.

Nine young faces and seven even younger faces, far too close.

As they had become more violent, José Pereira had moved them from the desk to the other wall and then further up and then to the main wall, and further up. Two steps left. Two groups above them. Bandidos and Hell's Angels. Until Grens took the pictures one at a time and put them on the top.

'If you insist on having your damn rankings. These ones . . . they're the most dangerous. Not the fat arses on motorbike. These guys are younger, have more hate, they've invited themselves in and taken their place in the only way they know how.'

He had just been standing in a flat with no door, left-overs and shards of glass and mattresses on the floor next to four TV screens with bullet holes in them.

'We've looked up and checked out all the sources close to the group, the ones you described as stable, reliable, well-informed. And nothing. No one has seen or heard anything, none of them know.'

You didn't disappear ten minutes before a raid by chance, did you?

'And the bomb dogs, yesterday evening, last night, nothing. Fourteen hours and five hundred and four flats. Seven thousand four hundred and ninety-six left.'

You let us listen to you committing murder – the only phone call during your escape, to a voicemail – as if you wanted us to hear. And then you're not there when we got here – next phone call, and this time to yourself – as if you wanted us to know and strike.

You had the initiative. You lent it to us for fifteen minutes. And then you took it back again.

'It's them, Pereira, it's *him* who decides!'

I'm surrounded by houses and flats and you've got access to several of them, ways to get there that only someone who is born here would know, the sort of ways that ten or a hundred or even a thousand police officers would never find without the local knowledge they will never have.

'And we . . . we can only wait!'

---

Fourth floor, Råby Allé 146. Leon checked the time on his mobile phone. It had taken them less than three minutes.

This one was bigger, one more room, with five new mattresses and pillows and blankets on the floor and a fridge full of beer, Coke, pizza, even some packets of crisps and sweets, and Gabriel had written the phone number down in felt pen on the worktop in this kitchen too, the number he would ring shortly.

Leon lifted the blind, looked out into the same dark Råby that would sleep for half a night yet.

She had jeered at him, *just like your dad*, and he had hit her once on the chest and kicked her twice in the thigh and hip.

He had hugged him, *my only brother, I want out*, and he'd pressed the cigarette into his forehead and his cheeks and he'd just lain there, passive.

He didn't need her. He didn't need him. He would never see them again, or talk to them, or even think about them.

Leon opened the blind a crack more. He could see the police station now. And the window on the first floor where the light was on.

They had broken down the door and run into an empty flat. And they'd gone back to the room that he'd expected them to go back to. Down there. There in the building about a hundred metres away. They were in there, he could see them moving about, the dark shadows back and forth across the window, and his hands were shaking and his cock was hard; they were sitting there.

———

Ewert Grens moved closer to the wall and the circle of new pictures round the nine faces that called themselves Ghetto Soldiers, the blurred ones that José Pereira had taken from a distance and the brightly coloured ones that he'd cut out of school yearbooks.

'Here.'

Pereira had picked up a folder from the top of one of the piles on the desk and was holding it out.

'All the information about the ones under fifteen. Twenty-one of them. Personal details, family situation, behavioural patterns, status in the gang, observation reports.'

Grens opened it, children sitting on various benches, smiling, next to other children.

'Known names for the last six months as least. The ones who look after guns and sell drugs and move stolen goods around.'

Ewert Grens nodded at Sven and Hermansson who came into the office while he was looking through the documents about the cut-out children's lives, a personal ID number by every face, he worked out that the oldest was fourteen and the youngest was eleven.

'We'll pay them all a visit. One at a time. Some of them must know.'

He tossed the folder back to Pereira who had to stretch over to catch it.

'Which one, Pereira?'

Grens waved his hand at the wall, by the faces that were valuable until the day they could be sentenced.

'Which one shall we visit first?'

Pereira looked at the restless detective superintendent, then at the wall, pointed at one of the faces, with slicked-back hair and a thick gold chain, posing eyes.

'Him. Eddie Johnson.'

Ewert Grens looked at a child.

'He's the one who was sitting on that chair only a few weeks ago and who'll be sitting there, at the top of the wall, in a few years' time.'

————

The low building. The big office with the light on. They were there. And no one had blown up a police station before.

Uros was lying on the mattress next to him, breaking off small bits of frozen pizza that he couldn't be bothered to heat – it was a year since he'd smashed the window of one of the lorries that transported bulk industrial explosives to a rail tunnel in Södertälje and driven off with it, seven sacks, one hundred and seventy-five kilos. Alex on the mattress in the kitchen and he was already asleep – six months since he'd made a hole in the roof of a construction site work store, some big house in Tyresö, sixty-two sticks of dynamite and a couple of thousand detonators. The mobile phone from when they robbed the shop on Kungsgatan in the middle of the morning and the rucksacks that Bruno went in and took from the outlet shop on Skärholmen.

The light was on in the office.

They were sitting and walking around down there, a couple of steps away from what one of the kids had taken in and hidden in the cistern behind the toilet.

One single phone call.

One signal of radio waves that reached the detonator and cut-off wires – a bomb that would be a blast wave that would rebound when it hit the external walls and would press and blow to bits any bodies that were in the way.

No one had blown up a police station.

————

It wasn't particularly cold outside.

It was still some time until morning and the dark was full drizzle, Grens had started to button up his jacket but then he stopped and undid it, puffed his astonishment into the almost warm September night.

'Fourteen years old?'

'Yes.'

They were going to visit them one at a time.

'Thirteen?'

'Yes.'

Ewert Grens and Pereira were going to go in one direction, Sven Sundkvist and Hermansson in the other.

'And this one . . . twelve?'

They weren't even out of sight when Grens stopped and turned around.

'Hermansson?'

She heard his voice bounce off the walls and she stopped on her way to another twelve-year-old, a piece of white paper in hand, a photograph of a child, but a description of grown-up crime.

'Can you come here a moment?'

She turned and went back to her boss, who was standing still, and had asked Pereira to wait a bit further up.

'Yes?'

'Did it feel good yesterday?'

'Good?'

'No one has ever slapped me before.'

When she'd placed her hand on his it had felt like she hit him.

When she hit him hard in the face, he hadn't even felt it.

'It was about time.'

Without realising, he rubbed his cheek where she'd hit him, palm against what had been flushed. He hadn't understood. It was she who had started, kept pushing, asking things that were none of her business.

And then walked away down the middle of the E4.

'Maybe.'

He was quiet, cleared his throat, looked down at the ugly asphalt.

'And well . . . you . . . maybe you were a bit right.'

She heard what he said and should have been overjoyed, hugged him, it was more than she could ever have wanted from someone who found it so hard to get out of his own head.

'About, well, that . . . fear.'

He coughed again, searching for the words.

'And that it's about Anni. And about Leon Jensen. But mostly . . . mostly it's about . . .'

His eyes left the asphalt, looked up, but not at her, at the blocks behind her.

'. . . loneliness.'

She didn't dare move, or breathe, anything that might frighten away this timid creature.

'When the only person you've chosen to trust disappears . . . you're well . . . alone.'

He looked at her for the first time.

'And sometimes . . . I don't want to be, any more.'

She dared to say something now.

'Ewert, you . . .'

'So there.'

He was done.

'So there, Hermansson.'

He had said what he wanted to say and didn't need or expect an answer, and had already started to walk towards Pereira who was waiting on a bench outside the school.

'Oh, and by the way . . .'

He'd turned round.

'In the car, yesterday.'

'What?'

'Comes under assaulting a police officer.'

He smiled.

'And obviously I'm considering reporting it.'

They walked through an area where José Pereira could always find his way, no matter how dark, and that Ewert Grens had randomly become part of over the past twenty-four hours, past the block that housed a female tenant on the third floor who would never let Grens into her home again, the parking place where two new cars had long, vivid gashes from something sharp across the paintwork, stairs up to a flat with a broken window by the door and a lonely shoehorn in the hall and a hundred-thousand-kronor rug in the bedroom. They were close to Råby Allé 102 and the document at the top of the blue folder.

'They take all sorts of risks, commit crimes constantly, every new thought and action is the start of another crime.'

Pereira held up the piece of paper, on it a face that lived in the building in front of them with his mother and little sister.

'But never for their own gain. The drug deliveries, gun running, break-ins are not for themselves, but for the family, members who exploit these kids' desire to belong.'

Ewert Grens went in through the entrance and into the lift, took the piece of paper that Pereira was holding out.

And he sighed.

I'm sixty years old. I'm on my way to see a twelve-year-old. I'm walking through a suburb with buildings I only visit in connection with crime. I don't belong here. I'm out of place. I shouldn't be doing this.

A bell that was louder than normal. And then silence. After a while, quick steps across the floor and the door was pulled open.

A six-year-old girl. Maybe five. Even four. Grens couldn't tell the difference.

'Is your mum at home?'

The long hair was tousled from sleep and she looked only at Pereira.

'You're a pig.'

'Yes. I'm a pig. Is your mum in?'

'You've been here before.'

'Yes, I have. Is she there?'

She tugged at her long hair, stared at him, and when she was done, she stared at Grens, until she turned suddenly and disappeared down the hall.

They waited.

'Mummy?'

And they heard her voice blend immediately with another, older one.

'Yes?'

'The pig and an old man are here.'

She had also been asleep, her eyes tired, a dressing gown around her barely conscious body.

'Yes?'

'Deniz?'

'What do you want?' Her voice was brittle. 'Eight of you . . .'

She had just washed her hair, brushed it in front of the mirror in the bathroom.

'. . . broke open the door.'

They'd rung on the doorbell, shouted through the letter box.

'That was yesterday.'

The loud screams of a five-year-old daughter who'd come running from the sitting room and her worries about Eddie, who was out there, somewhere.

'Tonight I want to be left in peace.'

José Pereira looked at one of six women who were not suspected of any crime, but had been forced to their own floors and driven to the remand jail and locked up.

'I heard about that. Some policemen make the wrong decisions.'

He turned towards Grens who refused to meet his eye, looked at him for a little too long.

'And I apologise for it. That you were treated like that.'

He waited for an answer that didn't come.

'Eddie isn't here.'

'Then maybe you can help us.'

She couldn't bear to answer, just stood there and held on to the door handle.

'How about it? Will you let us in?'

---

He had memorised the black felt-tip number from the kitchen worktop and dialled one digit at a time.

The feeling of holding the whole fucking world in his hand, a push of a button away.

Then the lights in the room had been switched off. He'd had one number left. A few minutes later Pereira had come out the front entrance followed by three others, a big guy with a limp, a smaller one and then someone who looked like a woman.

They'd left the office. But he stayed by the crack in the blind with the mobile phone in his hand. They'd be back soon enough.

---

She hadn't answered. Just left the door open and gone in. They closed it, walked down the unfamiliar hall with big furniture and pictures on the wall, frame to frame.

'As you're still here.'

A coffee pot in one hand and three cups in the other. Ewert Grens pulled out one of the kitchen chairs and sat down by the table.

'Thank you.'

She filled them to the brim and then asked her curious daughter to go to her room.

Grens tasted the warm liquid that was so much better than what he'd tried to drink earlier in Pereira's office, then he nodded to her.

'Ewert Grens, the old man. And I'd like to ask you some questions.'

It looked like he was smiling. So she smiled back.

'OK.'

He finished the coffee and this time took the coffee pot and filled the cup himself.

'I'm sure you understand why we're here.'

She didn't answer. It hadn't been a question.

'We want to know whether your son has been in contact – *and really, any kind of contact* – with the wanted men?'

'You know he has.'

Grens looked at one of all the women who had given birth and loved and probably still loved, but lacked the strength to counter the other love that called them, the one out there, that saw and heard and acknowledged and led them astray.

'I mean now. Within the past twenty-four hours?'

She took her first sip of coffee. It was still night, a long time until morning. But she wouldn't get any more sleep.

'I don't know.'

José Pereira held up a piece of white paper with a young face on it beside a list of documented crimes, put it down on the table between them, as if to justify their visit. The first time, he wondered if she remembered, he had been sitting in one of the cars watching someone who was nine and hung around with members of a gang who then called themselves Råby Warriors, he'd taken him into the car, driven him home to a mother and little sister, and realised that something that would never end had just begun.

'You don't know?'

Two weeks later he'd driven him home again and in the months that followed, she herself had called the police authorities and social services several times and asked for help to take him into care, relocate him, put him somewhere, anywhere but here, she'd explained that he was slipping away, and that no matter how hard she tried to hold on, it was happening more and more often, longer. Slowly her efforts had ebbed away, and now they only met when her son was arrested for a crime or called in for questioning which required the presence of a parent.

'I don't know. And I don't want to know.'

Her eyes, as if they'd given up, the knowledge deep down that her son who was twelve today would be eighteen tomorrow.

'Has he been home over the past couple of days?'

'He's my son.'

'Have you heard him talking on the phone over the past couple of days?'

'I love my son.'

'Has he had any visitors?'

'I miss my son.'

They weren't going to get any answers. As she had no answers to give.

'I . . . everything. I've tried everything, I've . . .'

She shook her head, but didn't cry, she had already done that.

'I'd like to have a little look round his room. Do you have any objections?'

She shrugged.

'Over there. On the other side of the hall.'

Ewert Grens really only knew one child, Sven's son, Jonas, and they sometimes chatted when he visited the terraced house and the boy would stay in the kitchen for a while between football matches and hockey matches. No one else. When Bengt was alive, he'd known two other children, but that was then, and they'd be big now.

So he didn't have much to go by. But it seemed like a fairly ordinary boy's room.

A bed, a desk. A mirror, posters. A tin of hair wax on the shelf, he opened it and sniffed, remembered the picture of a boy with greased-back hair, an open collar and shiny chain. He lifted up the mattress, leafed through magazines and turned on the computer, some games he didn't understand. He went down on his knees, a sports bag under the bed, he pulled it out and opened it and one of the pockets smelt distinctly of acetone, not long since some form of central nervous system stimulant had been in there.

He sat down on the edge of the bed, stretched out his legs, unfolded Pereira's unofficial documentation. Serious drugs crimes. Arson. Serious firearms offences. If he'd been of age when he was arrested for just one of the crimes, he would have been sentenced to anything from fourteen years to life.

In a few years. You're him. And it's *you* we'll be looking for when *you* have succeeded. And no matter what I do, no matter how much your mother in the kitchen does, it won't make any difference, you've already been discovered, you will never be anything, the only thing you'll do is serve time.

He leaned back and lay down on the bed, head on a pillow with a picture of Bambi, it was soft, like the sofa in Homicide.

---

Leon stood by the angled blinds, mobile phone in hand, a number on a kitchen worktop already saved. He would stand there until the lights in the office were switched on again, until they sat down on the sofa and the chairs and looked at the wall.

The very first time.

They'd been selling Gabriel's morphine for nearly a year and expanded into amphetamines. Pereira had arrested him and he'd sat in the big office with the desk and the policemen and the files, and he'd been so proud, *arrested, for real*, until he'd seen the wall and all the names and faces that he admired and *they hadn't been there*. He'd sat in front of it, waiting, he'd been nothing, then the social worker came and Pereira was given permission to ask his questions. His mum. The social worker had been his mum and they'd gone home together afterwards and he hadn't been on the fucking wall and he'd stabbed a short knife in the table four times.

Five arrests later and they were there. Right at the bottom of the second wall.

*Is that me, in the picture? And that one, that photo, is that Gabriel?*

He'd really liked the pictures that looked like all the others and every time he came back and was waiting to be questioned, he would look up at the wall, and every so often they'd been moved higher up and someone who had got to the top couldn't get any further, and someone who eight years later was at the top when the wall disappeared, would stay there.

---

Ewert Grens rolled over onto his right side, left arm pressed against a small shelf as he slid over the edge of a boy's bed and onto the floor. It was considerably harder getting up from a piece of furniture designed for a body that was one metre five and weighed forty-five kilos, than it had been lying down.

There was a book under the bedside table. A jotter, European geography. He looked through the texts that were illegible, not one single word was spelt correctly, not one sentence that had a function, the same hand that sold drugs with authority, hid weapons and threatened people to death – a high achiever in crime. Hand on the shelf as he stood up, he went back out into the hall, thanked the woman who'd made up the bed with colourful Bambi and Mickey Mouse bedlinen and fought against a force she could neither see nor understand. He carried on out through the door that still bore witness to forced entry and out into a neighbourhood that was still asleep, on his way back to the police station and new faces for the next visit.

————

Grens stood for a while on the steps in the warm air before going in. All these windows that seemed to be watching each other.

*You're here.*

He wanted to wave, to shout out loud, anything that was more than nothing.

*And maybe it's you that's watching me right now.*

Twenty-four hours. He was no closer.

————

José Pereira was standing in front of the wall in the Section Against Gang Crime when Grens came in, folder in his hand, studying cutting after cutting.

'And now . . . who?'

'I don't know yet.'

One of the pictures from a school yearbook, one of the ones sitting in the middle of a row arranged by height in a photograph that strived for symmetry, another face with only a few signs of puberty.

'Perhaps him. Just as involved in criminal activities, just as young. The same prognosis.'

Ewert Grens looked at yet another twelve-year-old – as if it was the same face and the same body, over and over again.

'Råby Backe 23. A mother and a younger brother. Give me five minutes, Grens. You start to walk, I'll catch up with you.'

There were three large windows in the room. Ewert Grens looked out through the one in the middle, he still had the urge to wave and shout out for a sign, just one.

*You're there. I know it.*

You phoned yourself. Twice and a bloody engaged tone. You gave yourself away. You *wanted* to give yourself away! You wanted us to come here and to strike and to fail.

And I can't grasp why.

He looked at Pereira who held up a hand showing all five fingers, I'll be there soon, and he started to make his way out into the warm air again, slow steps while he waited for company and this time the light wind carried a smell, he was sure, something he knew but couldn't put his finger on.

───────

Now.

He pulled the blinds up the whole way.

The lights were on again in the room on the first floor of the police station, glaring ceiling lights, and someone was moving around in there.

They were there.

They'd escaped, broken out and been brought together, they'd climbed to the top and now were going to do what no one else had done.

Leon gripped the mobile phone hard in his hand, index finger on the green ring button. He pressed it. And the signal made its way to a telephone hidden in a toilet only a few hundred metres away.

*Now.*

───────

The smell.

It came with the wind. It was inside. It was in his head and chest, chasing around and wanting out, it smelt stronger, more.

Ewert Grens stopped.

You're here. You wanted us to come here. You *knew* that we were listening to you when you murdered her and you *knew* when you called yourself a while ago, and you *know* now, and you're using us.

The smell.

It's in my head, inside. I can smell it again now.

*The one that's like marzipan.*

---

He ran. He wasn't particularly far away.

He ran towards the police station and Pereira who was inside. And he thought about a motorbike officer who had run towards a car and hammered a screwdriver with a spanner and opened a car boot, and afterwards told that he did it all wrapped in a peculiar silence.

The one that Grens was running in now.

Not even the sound of his own footsteps.

He had got halfway when he saw the first windows being blown out, shattering, falling to the ground.

And still no sound, as if there was no explosion at all.

SHE LOOKED AT the cloth in the middle of the table, arranged to cover the four holes from four stabs of a knife. He'd been nine years old and forced the sharp edges into the soft wood.

It was lying on the edge of the white cloth, her tooth.

Ana had played with it for a while, pulled at it, it was loose, one of her upper front teeth. His fist had hit her cheek, mouth and jaw. She left it on the kitchen table when she went over to the sink, a glass of cold water, one more, then out into the hall the pain stabbing with every step, her hip, her thigh, he had kicked her twice, the third time between the legs.

He'd never hit her before. It had always been there on the few occasions that they'd run into each other in recent years, the hate, the aggression, but Gabriel had always been beside him and she'd never been frightened, he had never exploded in the same way when Gabriel was there to balance, to neutralise.

She stopped. Her hand on the brown wallpaper.

She had decided so long ago. She just hadn't understood it then. She had waited for them in a room in the social services office and gradually become a part of the sickness. The long queues of young boys — children — who instead of coming closer, only got more distant. They had just started out on their journey and would never change direction. They had sat on the chair in front of her desk and she had sat on the chair next to them in front of the police desks and the only thing the two authorities could agree on was that it was too late.

Hand against the wall, the pain eased a bit and she hobbled over to the window, opened it, breathed in the darkness that was still warm.

A disease. Outside her body. That was what it felt like at first. Until the afternoon when José Pereira had phoned and asked her to come down to the police station to be present at yet another interview with yet another minor, which turned out to be an interview with a minor who this time was her own son.

The gentle breeze on her cheeks, Råby dawn, she needed air, the kind of air that was to be found on the other side of these concrete walls.

The symptoms of the disease had also worked their way into her body. Gang formation, criminality, alienation. Leon. Her son. And she had screamed and cried and watched and embraced, but the ones who gave the diagnosis, who had the authority and power, hadn't recognised the disease, understood how it developed, it was still happening outside *their* bodies and what cannot be seen does not exist and symptoms that are not stopped and continue to spread, slowly become death.

Another controlled intake of the warm dark.

She had decided then. And again when the policeman who had once forced her onto the kitchen floor had stood at her door and asked her to listen to a murder. And again only a couple of hours ago with the first punch.

She almost laughed.

How many times can a woman make a decision?

She knew that what had slowly died had to be buried in order to make way for what would grow and renew; she had decided that that was the case and now she had to get the fireman to decide the same.

She leaned out of the window. Over there, the empty square and the empty shopping centre, the snorting metro.

And the other noise. That sounded like a big bang.

The strange thing was, she was certain that it was somehow also connected to Leon and the disease that they had driven past on the E4 without seeing.

Gabriel lay down on her white sofa and looked at them. He was bleeding a bit, the material took on another colour.

He had almost never been to her place. Now it was his only home.

He'd known before they even rang the bell and told her that she had to go out, he'd known they would come. She had to go out and go anywhere but here. Wanda had cried for a while, protested, but without raising his voice, he couldn't do it, his ribs like knives, he'd held her by the shoulders and walked beside her to the door and the stairs, and then gone in again without locking the door, without even closing it.

He was lying there now while they went through her flat and aimlessly picked up her things that meant nothing to any of them but was just a demonstration of power. They'd sat down at the sitting room table, Jon, Big Ali, Bruno. He could have challenged them. Maybe even hurt them, even killed. But he hadn't challenged – they weren't doing anything wrong, just as Leon hadn't done anything wrong. The kicks, the punches, not even the five round burn marks on the only part of his skin that was untouched, Leon had just done what he had to do.

And that fucking awful moment when he was lying on his back on the floor and Leon opened the door again and they'd looked at each and known that it was the last time.

Gabriel undid his trousers and pulled them off, nodded at Big Ali, Jon, Bruno. Their eyes that weren't laughing and weren't crying. He was grateful that they'd taken knock-off Rohypnol, eight milligrams each no doubt; it was his fault, not theirs, they had to look at him without feeling. He lay down, it would be easier for them to get to it then, and Jon pressed the round sanding disc against his right thigh and the month-old tattoo that was still raised, and Big Ali put the plug in, *you've got fifty thousand in fines*, he bled heavily when the sanding machine reached maximum speed, but he said nothing and they stopped after a while, sat down by the table while his thigh bled all over the rest of her white sofa, *you won't get fucking fifty thousand, it was fucking me who started all this*, they had to wait for half an hour, four milligrams more of Rohypnol and the beginnings of a scab that they sanded again, *fifty thousand in fines and you've got three hours*, and between each round, a bit more colour bled away, he moved after a while so that a big pool wouldn't develop, and that was when he heard the explosion and felt a flutter of pride; he knew exactly what it was.

THE WOMAN HE had never met before closed the door and he had stood for a while outside. There was nothing more to say.

Ewert Grens gripped the steering wheel with both hands as he drove away, he would drive until this was over, one hand to the wheel when his mobile phone rang.

'Ewert?'

Gunnar Werner from floor eight. He'd stopped.

'Yes?'

'Zero four forty-two.'

'Yes?'

'You were right. He called. Again. *Exactly* then.'

That smell. Inside his head. The smell of marzipan when he ran through the soundless dark without footsteps and without shattering glass blasting out and falling to the ground.

They were hunting for someone who was also on the hunt, who knew that they were listening and wanted them to be there just then.

04.42.

He'd rung. And a building had exploded.

'Where from?'

'I don't know yet.'

'Werner, I . . .'

'I need four masts to determine the exact position. I've only got two. The others . . . one of the servers isn't responding, but to hazard a guess, another ten minutes to get an update, perhaps quarter of an hour.'

She had closed the door and he had stood outside. Silent. Empty. He, if anyone, should know, there were no words.

A white cross on a patch of grass that was called Plot 603.

They had embraced him and talked and comforted and asked and phoned and been in the way.

There were no fucking words.

Martha Pereira had asked him to leave in a friendly manner and closed the door. It was the third time that he'd had to tell a spouse that the life partner she was waiting for wouldn't be coming home. The first time – a couple of years after Anni – still just a constable, he'd accompanied a superintendent to explain that a woman's husband had been shot by a wanted criminal. Ewert Grens had stood beside the detective superintendent who had been very emotional, and the woman who had lost everything, and felt nothing. Until she collapsed and they both had to carry her to the kitchen table, where they then had taken it in turns to make sure she was conscious. He had felt it then. But not what he was allowed to feel. He felt the tension. It was the first time he reported a death and he didn't feel grief, nor fear. And after a while, the other feeling, shame, of not feeling the right thing, of being unable to feel anything at all for someone else. He had avoided it after that. Every time he'd asked someone else to do what he should, often Sven, one of the few people who knew how to talk to others. He had waited until he had no choice, his only real friend, Bengt Nordwall, had been shot to death in one of Stockholm's morgues by a trafficked prostitute and he had gone to the home of a woman he knew well, explained that they would never see the man they both held dear again. She'd hit him in the face, screamed at him, *what am I supposed to say to the children, Ewert*, and then held him tight and he had stood quietly without knowing what to do with his hands until she had stopped crying – he had left and realised that it was still possible to suppress death, his best friend and he still felt nothing, he had told his wife and comforted her and seen Bengt's loved one react, whereas he had only registered it; he had stood to one side and stayed there.

This time he had been forced to do it again.

*Pereira has a wife, Ewert.*

*Someone has to go and tell her, Ewert.*

*You, Ewert.*

And he'd had no idea where Pereira lived in town. They hadn't known each other like that. A turn-of-the-century building on Södermalm, *she won't be home*, and he'd knocked on the door, *she won't be home*, and had already been on his way out again when she answered the door.

This time, it was the hardest thing he'd ever done.

He'd seen the children, the two girls, twins, he was sure of it, he'd hoped that they wouldn't be there, if only for their sake, if only for their mum's sake, maybe even for his own, he'd felt their fear and their grief and then the terrible anger in his own breast, for them, for himself, *he no longer exists.*

---

She had closed the door. A single parent with two children. The person she had chosen to share her life with would never open the door again, sneak up behind her, kiss her neck, whisper her name, ask who was going to pick up the two girls from football. Grens held both his hands firmly on the wheel. That's the way it is. No one sneaks up behind you, no one whispers your name, no one kisses your neck. And you don't react in the way others expect you to react because you've never understood how you're supposed to react. So you let the image of what's no longer there block out the images that press in on you because you don't understand that what you're frightened of has already happened.

'Ewert?'

Gunnar Werner and the mobile phone and just one hand.

'Yes?'

'Zero four forty-two. We're there. We know where from. And how.'

'Werner?'

'A call from one mobile phone to another. The exact position of Leon Jensen's phone – Råby Allé 146, fourth floor. The exact position of the receiving phone . . .'

'Yes?'

'. . . Råby police station. In a corridor right outside the Section Against Gang Crime.'

Ewert Grens checked the dashboard clock: 05.37. Nearly an hour, like last time, he was long since gone.

'You were right, Ewert. He called. And detonated a bomb.'

---

Even when he had ordered twelve members of the special firearms command and four civilian intelligence officers to raid the flat on the fourth floor of Råby Allé 146, he'd realised that they would be hiding somewhere else. An hour and thirteen minutes was an eternity in an anthill with passageways to eight thousand flats and as many cellar storerooms.

Five mattresses and five pillows. Beer cans and cake wrappers.

Grens looked out through the open window, Råby police station down there, you could see it so clearly from here, the three big windows on the first floor that were gone, one of the fire brigade's small red command vehicles parked in front of them, alongside Nils Krantz's dark blue forensics van, the curious and distressed onlookers on the paths trying to get closer, and at the front, the pens and cameras that he always avoided.

You were standing here. When I turned round and looked for you, when I went in, when I went out, you could see me all the time. You knew and you were in control. And now you know that we know that you knew. And you don't have control any longer.

Ewert Grens adjusted the communications radio that was hanging from his breast pocket.

The voices, hectic, but he could follow them.

They had managed to move somewhere else, but this time he

had three dog patrols at his disposition, which had already picked up several trails and disappeared in different directions.

'He lost it down by the door to the cellar!'

Something scraping, laboured breathing. Grens turned up the voices in his breast pocket.

'But he picked it up again, I'd guess about twenty-five metres away!'

The fugitives had separated for the first time and were no longer running in a pack. They would never leave Råby. And splitting up here, in such a limited space, increased the chances of the dogs keeping track of at least some of them.

Grens left the window and walked towards the abandoned front door.

He had got closer.

---

The crowd was bigger than it had seemed from above. Several rows, tightly packed, and the crush that always develops when lots of bodies wait together, moving forwards, a wave of energy. Ewert Grens systematically elbowed his way through, climbed over the police cordon at precisely the spot where he'd turned and run back a few hours ago when he'd realised what was about to happen.

Three big holes where there had recently been windows, the Section Against Gang Crime where he had spent so much time over the past day or two. Large and small shards of glass on the ground, he walked over several, an unpleasant jarring sound as they were ground against the asphalt. He had got as far as the red command vehicle when he *Detective Superintendent Grens* heard the first voices that he'd never understood the point of and *just a minute, Detective Superintendent Grens* had therefore never paid any attention to. They wanted something and he was supposed to give it. He wasn't interested in such one-sidedness. So he did what he always did, didn't bother to turn round. Until one of them jumped over the cordon and ran after him, put his hand on his shoulder.

'We need a statement, Grens.'

Ewert Grens stopped in his tracks.

Quite a tall man, at least ten years younger than himself, thrusting a horrible little recorder to his mouth. Grens counted a further twelve reporters, at least, behind him, and as many photographers, and he could see four TV cameras.

'Take your hand off me.'

'Just one—'

'And then walk carefully backwards and stand behind that blue and white plastic cordon again.'

The tall man did as he was told, started to walk backwards, waving his recorder in the air.

'We need facts! A statement! Answers, Grens!'

Every step they took, every new scrap of information, there wasn't a newspaper, radio or TV channel that wasn't constantly writing or talking about *serious organised crime* and *the Stockholm suburbs* and for twenty-nine hours he had crumpled up the yellow Post-it notes with names and telephone numbers that were still being left on his desk by hands that couldn't find the bin.

And there were no fewer after the police station had been bombed.

'Hey, you.'

The tall man who had just clambered over the cordon held out his recorder and leaned forwards.

'Yes?'

'You want answers?'

'Yes, please.'

Ewert Grens turned and swept his arm towards the building that was missing three windows.

'So do I.'

He carried on towards the main door. That's how it was, if you decided not to hear when someone behind you was shouting at your back, you didn't.

A strange feeling, to open the door, now, afterwards. To walk into what had so recently been alive and was now dead. On his way up the stairs, he met a fireman on his way down. They greeted each other, had never met before, but right now were connected by someone who was no longer alive.

A well-built man, as tall as the reporter who'd waved his recorder around out there, LEADING FIREFIGHTER on his helmet, jacket, trousers.

'Ewert Grens, City Police.'

'Thom Håkansson, Södertörn Fire Brigade.'

The fireman carried on, but Grens caught his hand and made him stop.

'In there . . . the extent?'

He waited until the detective superintendent let their hands slip.

'No more than you see yourself. Explosives with low-detonation velocity that extends the blast wave. I've turned off the electricity and water. You can carry out all the investigations you need.'

All the way up the stairs, corridor to the right towards the SAGC, just as it had been an hour and a half ago, apart from the long, gaping crack down the ceiling.

He had run, José Pereira had still been alive then.

The toilet had been on the other side of the wall from the office. Big chunks of porcelain thrown all over the floor and there, crouching down in the middle of a pile of shattered plasterboard and ripped wooden beams, Nils Krantz.

'It was in here.'

Grens went closer.

'Most probably hidden in the toilet cistern, made of the same components that we identified in the kitchen in the flat. I've secured traces of ANFO and dynamite.'

He went further into the room and an internal wall that was no longer there, the faces no longer staring.

'Bulk industrial explosives. A person's body in the same room is exposed to extreme pressure for a long time, so Pereira was pressed together, everything inside him squeezed until he burst, he exploded from the inside.'

A spot on the floor. All that was left.

José Pereira had been sitting there, thrown against and then supported by one of the walls that remained standing, which then pushed back and reinforced the blast wave. And Grens, who had never avoided dead bodies at a crime scene – in fact, he often got closer, touched, forced himself to show that he felt nothing – had looked away, walked away, alarmed.

That bloody spot.

He stood completely still, looked at it, felt himself starting to shake, faint at first, then violently.

Sven. And Hermansson.

He could have lost them.

'A piece of a battery.'

Krantz pointed to a centimetre-long piece of metal lying about two metres into the room, and then another.

'A piece of a printed circuit board.'

There were a few more similar pieces, the forensic scientist picked them up with his latex gloves, one at a time.

'A couple of hours ago, Grens, they were all part of the same mobile phone.'

The one he'd called. One, maybe two rings. Enough current to activate the detonator.

*It was here. While we were in the room next door.*

Grens needed air, three windows to choose between, gaping holes. He leaned out and avoided listening to the people right at the front, shouting his name, and instead focused on what was behind, the other Råby that was waking up.

'A new trail, I'm sure of it.'

Electronic beeps followed by voices in his breast pocket, he turned them up, held the radio in his hand so he could hear it better.

'I can see them!'

The loud barking, the tense voices.

'Two of them! I'm sure!'

And the dog handler's footsteps got harder, slapping on the asphalt.

'They've got guns . . . don't let the dog loose!'

---

It smelt of smoke.

Gabriel was certain of it, but not in here and he raised himself up from her sofa, looked around the sitting room.

He was stuck. The red on Wanda's white fabric had dried and got darker, almost brown, and was sticking to his thigh. He was freezing, the pain that earlier had come from inside now blended with what came from outside, his swollen thigh, the sanding disc against his skin and muscle and sinews. He didn't know how long he'd been lying there, a few hours, maybe two. They'd sat at the coffee table in front of him and he'd heard the muffled bang and looked at his thigh that was oozing blood and tattoo ink, it was him who'd made the bomb and sorted out how to get it there – it was like running away, backwards, looking at what he was leaving behind.

The smoke really was there, it was obvious now.

Gabriel peeled the material away, went into the kitchen and then the bedroom, it was strongest out in the hall by the front door; he opened it.

The stairwell was full of smoke.

Jon and Bruno and Big Ali were standing at a distance, he could make them out through the grey mist. They were holding the entrance door open, and the draught was blowing the smoke inwards, towards the flat. He heard the fire alarm going off, *fifty thousand, Daddy* and it was only now that he saw what was burning, *within the hour, Daddy*, a pram, the fabric was almost gone, and they shouted to him before they closed the door and left.

———

Ana stood on her toes, she hadn't been able to see much more than the building's shiny roof and narrow chimney, she was short, and somehow – when sharp elbows shoved – she always seemed to end up further away. She leaned cautiously back so that she wouldn't bump into anyone who was standing close by, and if, at the same time, she leaned slightly to the left the powerful and regular pulsing almost disappeared. It started in her mouth and the hole where her front tooth had been, carried on down into her chest and culminated round her hip and pelvis. She had only ever experienced such all-consuming pain once before – a bed in a cell in a prison, he had pressed against her so hard from inside and then closed his eyes when he lay on her stomach, until now, almost the same pain.

She had been standing by the open kitchen window in the flat, watching the dawn, when she heard the dull explosion and realised that it was connected with Leon and the disease. She had run down the hall and down the stairs and out the back towards the noise that had already disappeared. It was still quite dark but she had already from a distance seen the smoke pouring out through the three windows with the light from the police station office shining above it, and what was grey and swirling became so clear, almost beautiful. She'd been one of the first to get there and there had been plenty of space, she'd stood quietly and looked at the room that she'd visited so many times and she could hear his voice, surprised by his big nine-year-old movements, he had been so proud, she'd sat beside him just as she always sat beside them and no matter how much she'd reached out to him, it hadn't been far enough.

She had stopped some distance away from the windows that were no longer there and watched the smoke diminish, more people had come and it started to be crowded and then the cameras had come and there was more of a crush, and one of them, she couldn't remember who, one of them had a recorder and a pen, had whispered that he'd heard from reliable sources that a policeman had died in there. She'd looked at him and he didn't have a clue who she was and that she'd given birth to a son eighteen years ago and she'd just nodded vaguely and realised that it was true, a policeman had died, and she cried tears that were no longer there and screamed a scream that could no longer be heard, and the crowd had grown without understanding that a disease like this, when no one sees it and treats it, it will continue to spread.

She had recognised the fireman as soon as he'd climbed out of the car, which was considerably smaller than the truck he normally used and it had LEADING FIREFIGHTER written on it. A couple of the police officers who were on guard had made sure that the mass of bodies dispersed somewhat and then removed the blue and white cordon when the red car drove up to the front door and parked by the broken glass that lay all over the asphalt.

She would wait for him. She had decided.

She would wait until he came out again and this time she would not stop talking until he had understood.

———

*To harm people.*

Thom had stopped halfway down the stairs out of Råby police station to talk to a large detective superintendent from City Police, who had a limp.

*More than buildings.*

He had carried on down towards the crowd and the red car, opened the door to the driver's seat and sat down with his chest heavy on the wheel.

And hadn't got any further.

He had the key in his hand that was shaking so much that he immediately dropped it on the floor in the space between the accelerator and the clutch. He had gripped the wheel with hands that slowly slipped down, off. A person he had come to like had been sitting in there. On the floor. Leaning against one of the external walls, in his lap the organs that had been squeezed out of his inside.

Thom leaned forwards. If he held his left hand hard around his right wrist, if he could just keep his fingers still, he would be able to reach out and pick up the oblong piece of metal and put it into the ignition and start the car and leave this place.

It was quite simple, he couldn't take any more.

And maybe that was why he heard both the quiet spoken call from the communication radio on the dashboard, as well as the regular beeping from the pager in his front pocket, despite the fact that they were simultaneous. Perhaps that was why he'd let the key stay where it was between the pedals and opened the boot and taken out the powder extinguisher and started to run towards the entrance a couple of minutes away. Perhaps a very ordinary call to a burning pram would for a short while force him to think about something other than someone who was not breathing.

––––––––

Ana had leaned a little more to the left and a little more back and just there, just as she was about to fall onto the curious and upset onlookers beside her, it was as if the pain didn't reach her. The tall fireman had disappeared into the building twenty minutes ago and she kept an eye on the entrance and his red car. The police station wasn't burning any more, it was quite a while since she'd seen the smoke become transparent in the bright lights, he was done and could come out any moment.

The office that was missing three windows.

Leon, who she hadn't managed to reach out to, no matter how much effort she made.

The social worker who had seen other Leons with other mothers who also did their utmost, but still didn't manage. She often thought about them, where they were heading, which prison they would go to, which prison wardens they would harm, kill, how they would look at their mothers as they raised their arms to hit them for the first time, what the policeman who worked in the police station they would blow up was called. But most often she thought about the boy who had also been nine the first time, but now was twelve, the one who was called Eddie and who over the years was the one who was most like Leon. His mother had sat beside him and made a plea, in the way that Ana had pleaded for them to take over, do whatever to get him away from what she didn't have the power to reach. Afterwards they'd sat in the Social Services office and had a coffee. After every new interview with Eddie, who was too young to be prosecuted, they had continued to drink coffee. Ana really liked her company; they had both seen what those outside did not want to see, the disease and its symptoms, and from her conversations with Deniz she had come to understand that even if someone has long since given up hope that she will ever manage to reach the one she loves, she can perhaps make sure that others do.

She had jumped when the detective inspector, who had once forced her to the floor, had worked his way through the crowd, climbed across the cordon and gone into the building, the anxiety that came in the wake of his lumbering frame never seemed to diminish. A few minutes later, the tall man she had been waiting for came out through the door, hurried towards to the red car and had then sat for a long time behind the wheel without going anywhere. She had started to push her way towards him, with a lighter heart, when he had suddenly sprung up, taken a fire extinguisher out of the boot and began to run.

She had run after him.

She hadn't taken her eyes off him, run, *run*, Råby Allé 114, he had disappeared in through the door.

Ana was standing outside now.

She closed her eyes, gathered what was inside and let it sink to her stomach, let it lie there, feel it, let it slowly up through her chest again, up through her throat, until it rested between her temples and forehead and she once again trusted her ability to speak and move with control.

'Hello.'

He was standing in front of a blackened metal frame between the doors to the two flats on the ground floor. There was the pungent smell of burnt fabric, but there wasn't much smoke now. She went closer – this time they had set light to a pram.

'I want to talk to you.'

He hadn't heard her come in and spun around, studied the woman who had tried to engage him several times before.

'You . . . again?'

'I . . .'

He put down the fire extinguisher beside the burned metal frame and waved his hand at her.

'Go.'

'I won't go. Not this time.'

He shook his head.

'Then I'll go.'

A last look at the extinguished pram material before he picked up the fire extinguisher that hadn't been used and walked towards the door.

She ran in front of him, stood in his way.

'I need your help.'

'Please can you get out of the way.'

'You can help me.'

'*Move!*'

She kept her eyes on him all the time; he wasn't going to look away. As she started to take off her clothes.

Item by item in a pile on the stone floor.

The fireman shook his head in pity and turned away so he didn't have to see the pale body that was cold, bastard Råby that was suffocating him with its frustration.

'Look at me.'

She moved, round him, *wasn't going to let him look away.*

She had decided.

'I'll stand here until you look at me.'

Thom closed his eyes, swallowed. Then he turned round to face her again.

'Thank you.'

He had already caught a glimpse of her face, the blue cheek and swollen chin and upper jaw, the gap there, a missing front tooth. She took hold of his hand with care, and pointed at her right breast, her voice still slightly too loud.

'I want you to look at this.'

He had never seen a discoloured, swollen woman's breast before.

Underneath it, he could rest his eyes there, a hand's width of pale, cold skin.

And then her hip and the red mark that was gradually changing colour, her thigh, both of them, someone had aimed at her pelvis.

'Don't you understand?'

*Leon beside her on a chair at the police station, nine years old, she had stretched herself without reaching him.*

'I need your help . . .'

*Eddie beside her on a chair at the police station, nine years old, Deniz had stretched herself without reaching him.*

'. . . with this, with what's . . . happening . . . to get it to . . . stop. For ever. Without hurting anyone.'

She pointed at the pram behind him, then at the police station, maybe also at the buildings out there, or maybe it was the sky.

'I don't understand.'

His hand, she hadn't let go of it.

'What . . . is it you want me to do?'

---

The burning pram, the grey smoke. And Jon and Bruno and Big Ali who had seen him and left.

Gabriel lay down on the white sofa. He wasn't bleeding any more. He had emptied Wanda's bathroom cabinet of painkillers and whatever it was that was pulsing slowed down, the enormous hole on his right thigh stung more than stabbed.

A sooty black metal frame with metal wheels outside the flat door.

He knew what that meant. He'd done things like that himself. Alex who had been arrested for various reasons on suspicion of assaulting one of the greengrocers who had a stall on the square, who hadn't paid his monthly dues and a woman had seen it and reported him and decided to stand witness. She had three children. And Gabriel and Leon had set alight the same number of prams and rolled them into the lift and up to outside her door. She'd understood and the same evening withdrawn her witness statement and Alex had been released without charge and escaped a year and a half in prison.

He tried to feel something. Leon had won. Pay or we'll hurt your family. It didn't feel like he'd expected it to feel. It didn't feel of anything.

It was easier to get up from the sofa this time, all his weight on his left leg when he went into the kitchen and pulled out and turned round the top drawer in the cupboard beside the sink and pulled off one of the rolls of banknotes that were taped to the back. The flat door again, the metal frame was standing there and he kicked it, quick glance through the glass at the large crowd outside the police station. He would have liked to be able to go there and stand amongst the onlookers and see the consequences of the explosion he himself had planned and created. As they had nothing on him. As he wasn't formally a suspect, just as Jon, Big Ali and Bruno weren't formally suspects. The police search out there was for the five fugitives who had killed a prison warden first, and now a policeman. He should be able to go out there, move around freely, but knew that someone who is not suspected of anything, and therefore cannot be arrested, might well have information and so could be pulled in for questioning and information and he wanted to avoid that, sit there in that building, look at the floor and refuse to answer the questions. So he hurried past the glass door two floors down and chose – when he cautiously opened the metal door into the underground garage and spotted a couple of police cars on guard by the entrance – to crawl along the filthy concrete between the rows of parked cars to the rusty Chevrolet that had stood in the same place for a few years. And that no one touched. Their postbox. He had detached the roll of tape from under the bumper and attached the banknotes in their place near the back left-hand wheel, one hundred five-hundred notes.

Leon had won. And he didn't feel anything.

———

Ewert Grens was still holding the communications radio in his hand, careful to catch every word. 'I can see them again!' He rushed out of the half-blasted office that had once constituted the heart of Section Against Gang Crime, crossed a floor covered in bits of porcelain and plaster and wood and the sort of metal that was used in mobile phones. 'Still two of them! On their way in the door!' Out of the building, past shouting mouths and four hundred and fifty metres to a vandalised entrance in a graffitied wall, Råby Backe 17, he got there at the same time as fourteen members of the Special Firearms Command.

———

Gabriel lay absolutely still behind the lorry that was parked two spaces away. A couple of minutes, here they came, Jon and Big Ali, creeping as he himself had just done. They knew exactly where to feel with their hands under the rusty Chevrolet that had stood in the same space for several years. One hundred five-hundred notes just by the back left-hand wheel. He waited until they'd disappeared, then crept back towards the stairs and ran past the stripped pram and into the flat.

———

Both in hoodies and tracksuit bottoms lying side by side on their stomachs, arms out at an angle, hands behind their necks. The three dogs waited eagerly, barking and wagging their tails, hoping that one of them would move.

The SFC took over from the dog handlers, a firm grip on their arms and legs when they ran with them, screaming and swearing, towards the floor of the waiting van, they had both been bitten on the lower leg and were still bleeding when the vehicle left the place.

Ewert Grens sat down on one of the park benches that had once been green and now were a tapestry of sprayed colours.

They had caught two of them.

The biggest police hunt since Malexander and they had caught two of the five and the only thing he felt was this damn fury.

Alexander Eriksson. Reza Noori. They meant nothing.

He was still out there.

The one who had murdered and who was a continuation, as every intervention had a continuation.

———

She was sitting on the bloodied sofa when he came back, holding a mobile phone in her hand, and looked at him in a way he didn't like.

'Leon called.'

Gabriel was all ears, moved closer.

'He said that you have to pay.'

'I *have* paid.'

'He said that you have to pay seventy-five thousand more.'

'*I have just . . .*'

'He'll cut out the baby. That's what he said. *If Gabriel doesn't pay seventy-five thousand more, I'll cut that fucking foetus out of your belly.*'

Gabriel looked at Wanda but felt a knife. Deep in his body. And it was cutting something out of him, throwing it away. His first thought was to hit her as he always had when he felt like this, raised his hand and held it high but then let it fall and grabbed her mobile phone to dial the most recent incoming number. No reply. He sank down into the sofa that was brown with coagulated blood, towards the coffee table and his own mobile phone, the number that could only be found there.

'Brother?'

The breathing, he recognised it.

'You're calling me? On this phone?'

'I tried the one you'd called from. You didn't answer.'

'You put—'

'Enough, brother.'

Threats, violence. More threats. He knew how it worked.

'You're not my brother. Are you?'

'Leon, enough. I've paid my fifty thousand. And I don't give a toss about you burning the rest of my face. *But don't touch her.*'

He had done it himself, used violence against anyone who doubted, after all, he was one of the ones who'd made the rules, and he didn't feel any hate, Leon was his brother, after all.

'No one leaves us. And you, Gabriel . . . *Daddy* . . . you don't leave me. I want seventy-five thousand more.'

―――――――

Sven Sundkvist ran towards Råby Backe 17, the heavy bomb suit snagging with every step, making them shorter. Halfway there he pulled off the visor and hood and helmet, air around his neck and face, and there, down there on the bench, Ewert.

Nineteen hours and six hundred and eighty-four flats. Seven thousand, three hundred and sixteen left.

Six bomb dogs had become twelve when reinforcements from Malmö and Customs and Excise joined the search which had become even more urgent following the explosion in the Section Against Gang Crime office, where a person he had recently got to know had had his internal organs squeezed out. A colleague. A father. Of children the same age as his own son. If it had exploded twenty minutes earlier, half an hour later. He had been sitting there, the bomb was only a few metres away, ready to be detonated at any moment. If it had been him. If it had been Anita that Ewert had gone to see. If it had been Jonas who no longer had someone to call Dad.

There had been a bomb and someone had detonated it when they wanted it to be detonated. There might be more.

He was running a bit faster now, the vandalised entrance in the graffitied façade, they had arrested someone, this damn madness was perhaps nearing its end. Ewert sat on the park bench, his bulky frame sagging, hands on his knees.

'It was me that started this.'

He didn't look at Sven, not even when he sat down beside him.

'I came as fast as I—'

'Two down.'

'—heard that—'

'Two down and it makes no difference at all.'

The detective superintendent's hands were rubbing the fabric of his trousers hard against his knees, got hold of it, pulled at it.

'He's still out there.'

'Ewert?'

'*He's still out there.*'

Ewert Grens whispered, he didn't often do that and Sven didn't like it.

'Ewert, you . . .'

The detective superintendent got up and started to walk, he didn't limp and his neck wasn't stiff, Sven had never seen him move like that.

'It was me who started all this. And it's me who's going to finish it.'

———

The flat he hadn't visited for eighteen years and that he had now been to twice in less than twenty-four hours. This was the third time. Ewert Grens rang the doorbell. She didn't open.

'You and I have to talk.'

He continued to ring the bell, he could hear her inside the door.

'I explained to you yesterday evening. You—'

'We were talking about your son who had murdered someone.'

'—will never come into my home again.'

'He's murdered someone else now.'

———

Grens saw it immediately. She'd only opened the door a crack, but had obvious injuries on her face, perhaps also on her torso, the way she was holding her body and weight.

'Are you in a relationship at the moment?'

He studied her again, she was leaning to the right to ease the pain, and one of the blows had been hard, to her neck on the left-hand side.

'Well, are you?'

Ana wanted to whisper *what kind of a fucking question is that?* But she didn't. She knew why he was asking.

'No.'

He lowered his gaze demonstratively to a pair of men's boots in the hall. A type he recognised. A fireman's boots. He thought he'd heard someone moving in the sitting room already.

'Have you got a visitor?'

'Yes.'

He indicated her hip and face.

'Was it him who . . .?'

'No.'

'Are you sure?'

'It wasn't him.'

Ewert Grens had his gun in a worn, brown leather holster across his shoulder. He undid it, the black gun in his hand when he cocked it and forced his way past her and made for the sitting room, gun aimed and at the ready. The fireman who had left his shoes in the hall and was now sitting in an armchair, looked very like the one he had just met on the stairs on his way into the destroyed police station and who'd had LEADING FIREFIGHTER written on his helmet, jacket, trousers. The detective superintendent nodded at him, lowered his gun and put it back in the holster before returning to the obvious injuries to her body.

'If it wasn't . . . the fireman in there, and it wasn't a boyfriend . . . then *he's* been here.'

She shook her head slowly at the floor.

'You're standing there asking me to report him?'

'I—'

'You're standing there . . . *making demands?* And who . . . who are you to make demands? Where were you when the only big shop we had, the haberdashery shop, moved to Älvsjö two weeks ago, to avoid being constantly burgled here? Where were you when the last restaurant closed after the seventh break-in this year – I think they'd driven a car into the window? Where *the hell* were you when the ticket collector on the metro was murdered and Stockholm Public Transport refused to let their staff work here for a long time, when the post office closed down, when the ATMs were dismantled, when . . .'

She swallowed, tried to catch his eyes which were focused on the swelling on her left cheek.

'Your colleagues don't even bother to come here to investigate any more because *it's too dangerous*. We're encouraged not to go out after ten in the evening because *it's too dangerous*. The rights and obligations that are so important for all the other citizens in this country, that are talked about so much – how they should be upheld and maintained – they don't apply here.'

When he chose to concentrate on the other swelling instead, the one that merged her chin with the greater part of her right cheek, he could see that it had grown a bit.

'I—'

'They don't apply here!'

'I know that—'

'They don't apply here because everyone, society, has long since abandoned us, moved away, bit by bit! And you . . . you stand here making *demands*?'

'Your injuries, I know that he . . .'

She shook her head slowly again, laughed. Not very loud, not very merrily.

'The first time, yesterday. You asked if I remembered you. I said that I did.'

She opened a bit more, took a small step towards him.

'I said that I did because I remember every word, every nuance of your face. When you stood here all that time ago, outside my door with a search warrant. When you produced a pasta jar with a kilo of heroin in it. When I asked you about my man and you shook your head, just as I'm doing now. When I gave birth alone. And when you some years later said *when you need my help, call me* and never got in touch again.'

The light was falling on her face, making it clearer, and he concentrated on her mouth, one of her upper teeth was missing.

'Do you know how that feels?'

'No.'

'Don't you understand how—'

'No. I've never had children. No matter how hard I try, I can't understand how it feels. The only thing I know is that every intervention has consequences. It's . . . still happening.'

She could fear her son, even hate him, Grens had met her before, so many like her, mothers who feared and hated, but who had carried and given birth and therefore were always a part of something they no longer understood.

'It will stop.'

He had no idea what she was talking about.

'I see.'

Ana put her hand to her tender cheek and mouth.

'What's happening can't be allowed to carry on happening. And only the one who started it can stop it.'

'I'm sorry?'

'Only that.'

A park bench. He had just been sitting on a park bench and said exactly that.

Another voice. *His* voice.

'What . . . are you talking about?'

Her eyes, harder than before and her lips tighter, tense.

'I'm talking about just that. That only the one who started all this can stop it.'

———

Gabriel lay on the sofa's layer of blood. Wanda beside him, so close.

He wanted to touch her in the way that she often touched him, his hand on her cheek. He couldn't. He had seen others doing it, Leon's mother's hand on his cheek when they were little and sitting beside her at the kitchen table. Wanda's hand that he so often accepted. But he couldn't. He'd never done it. It felt false.

It was easier to hit.

*Leon called. That's what he said. If Gabriel doesn't pay seventy-five thousand more, I'll cut that fucking foetus out of your belly.*

The knife through his body.

He went into the kitchen, another drawer this time, cutlery and white serviettes and small tealights that Wanda liked to put on the table, he pulled it out and took a roll of banknotes from the back and hurried down into the garage to the Chevrolet and the same hiding place by the back left-hand wheel, back over the floor and in through the metal door to the cellar, and it was there, in the dark, that Jon aimed the first blow with a heavy iron pipe against the back of his thigh. He fell forwards onto the stairs and Big Ali and Bruno were waiting on either side and kicked his body and when he then curled up and protected his head, they kicked his arms and hands until he let go, the last kicks to his chin and cheek as they whispered *a hundred thousand more in an hour or we'll cut the fucking baby out* in his ear.

————

Her face, swollen and blue, and the pain that she'd tried to hide in the doorway.

Leon Jensen had been there. He was moving around, despite all the road blocks, dogs, helicopters, in a world of meandering asphalt walkways and besieged flats and broken-in cellar store-rooms and loyal hangarounds that were an impregnable advantage to those who were born here, which anyone who was just visiting without an informal map in hand would therefore never be able to keep up with.

Grens zigzagged through the crowd that had thinned out a bit. The grey smoke floating almost transparent in the air, glass splinters crunching uncleared. From the outside, Råby police station looked intact, except for the three windows, despite the fact that a body had recently been squeezed to death in there.

He stopped by the lantern with a candle in it that someone had lit and put down in front of the entrance beside a bunch of red roses.

'Ewert?'

A car had passed through the cordon and was approaching at great speed, yellow, some Japanese make that he recognised from the Kronoberg garage and the face inside the wound-down window was familiar.

'Yes?'

Gunnar Werner.

Despite having worked together all these years, Grens had never seen him outside the police headquarters.

'So the detective superintendent is still awake?'

The policeman from floor eight had only a few hours earlier discovered an outstretched leg, followed shortly by a whole sleeping body in the boot of a murder scene.

'I wasn't asleep. I was resting my eyes.'

When he got out, Werner was holding a laptop which he opened and put down on the car roof.

'I want you to listen to this.'

*'Brother?'*

'Gabriel Milton.'

*'You're calling me? On this phone?'*

'And Leon Jensen. Fifty-seven minutes ago.'

*'Enough, brother.'*

*'You are not my brother.'*

'A phone call from Råby Allé 114, ground floor. Tenant, Wanda Svensson. Phone call made to Råby Allé 172. Fifth floor. Tenant, Linn Holmgren.'

*'Leon, enough. I've paid my fifty thousand. I don't give a toss about you burning the rest of my face. But don't touch her.'*

'He wants out.'

Leon Jensen's best friend since he was nine. One of the gang's two leaders.

'Werner, he wants out!'

Ewert Grens hit the car roof with his hand.

'He's being threatened. His girlfriend is being threatened. And he's going to be fined and threatened and fined for eternity. If we get hold of him . . . from now on, you see, he's the way to Jensen!'

———

He lay on the cellar floor. He could feel it most on his left side, more than one of his ribs were broken and the pain turned his body inside out with every breath, forcing his muscles to cramp when he pulled himself up one step at a time. His face was swollen, two fingers on his right hand broken, his back ached and his thigh, where they had sanded off a tattoo, was burning like before.

Gabriel didn't meet Wanda's eyes when he opened the door, went over to the sofa, lay down. They couldn't stay here much longer. The conversation with Leon was equal to the pigs suddenly having a reason to question someone who wasn't suspected of a crime.

He started when she turned on the light in the sitting room, which always happens when eyes meet light after concussion. She sat down and put her hand on his cheek, in the way that he couldn't.

'This is never going to end, Gabriel.'

He didn't answer.

'Your face, Gabriel, five cigarette burns! Your thigh, they've sanded the skin off! They've beaten you up and you've paid and they were going to cut the baby out if you didn't pay again. So you paid again and they beat you up again and now he wants you to pay. Again! And Leon, is it still true, Gabriel, is he still your fucking brother?'

'He's doing what he has to do.'

'It's never going to end!'

'It was Leon and me who wrote the rules.'

'Don't you get it, Gabriel . . . *it's never going to end!*'

He closed his eyes to block out the light and the nausea.

'I want you to call.'

She took his hand and he looked at her, the fragile face and body that couldn't take any more.

'Ask for help, Gabriel.'

That was it. He knew it.

There wasn't any other way.

He got up and started to retch immediately, coloured the floor and rug. He tried again, reaching out for the mobile phone and dialled a number he had long since learnt by heart.

'*Police.*'

It's never going to end.

'Well . . .'

He would pay.

'*Yes?*'

As long as he had the money, they would make him pay.

'Um . . . that investigation.'

'*Yes, so?*'

'The ones who . . . escaped. Råby. The guy who's leading it . . . he's the one I want to talk to.'

And when the money ran out.

That was when they would kill them. First the girlfriend. Then the traitor.

He was one of the ones who'd written the rules.

'*I'm sorry. But I can't transfer you directly to him. What was it about?*'

'A tip-off.'

'*A tip-off?*'

'I know . . . where they are.'

It was as if she was considering for a moment. Whether she

should let another weirdo through. Whether she risked missing someone who really knew.

'*OK. I'll put you through. A detective superintendent from Homicide. He's called Ewert Grens.*'

———

A deserted flat.

He'd known that it was pointless, wasn't even disappointed, the third time after more than an hour. The door had been removed, the rope outside the broken window. The same approach but against another kind of flat. The other two had had mattresses and pillows on the floor and had otherwise been empty. This one was furnished, lived in, a young woman's home, someone whom the gang had forced out and then given some kind of compensation under the false pretence that it was a mutual agreement, paid a few thousand a week in rent.

His mobile was ringing and Ewert Grens answered.

'Yes?'

'*Switchboard. I'm transferring a call.*'

'Who?'

'*I don't know. Someone who claims to have a tip-off.*'

A faint humming.

'Yes?'

Nothing.

'Hello?'

Someone hung up.

Grens closed the phone again and looked around.

He had ordered another raid at the same time that he knew would be equally futile, with no result apart from another earful from Ågestam and another report to the internal committee on breaches of duty. On the flat where Gabriel Milton had been when he called the only phone he wasn't supposed to ring.

Nothing there either.

Except for a heavily blood-stained sofa and fresh vomit on the sitting room floor.

So now the only link to the one they were looking for had also disappeared.

---

Sven Sundkvist had stayed on the bench outside Råby Backe 17 and watched Ewert Grens who had neither seen nor heard him, even though he was sitting so close.

Fear came creeping. That feeling that had accompanied him since the first meeting in the middle of the night in Ewert's office.

When Anni, Ewert's wife, had died a couple of years ago as a result of an operation after half a life in a care home, he had sat on the floor in the Kronoberg archives with a twenty-seven-year-old investigation in his lap, and was unreachable. When Bengt Nordwall, his oldest and closest friend, was shot to death in a morgue, in the course of pursuing an investigation he had chosen to destroy some evidence for the sake of his friend, at the risk of his own career.

Both times he had responded with shock, but not grief and he had never been frightening.

Now he was frightening.

Sven saw someone who was being eaten up from the inside, an animal – a strange picture, but the only one he got – a wounded animal that neither limped nor lay down despite the fact that it couldn't move, as though the pain was smothered and drowned out by large amounts of adrenalin, until it was no longer there. The kind of animal that races around in the forest until the adrenalin runs out and it falls down, lifeless.

Seven thousand two hundred and eighty more flats. They would have to wait.

Sven Sundkvist had already pulled off the green helmet, hood, visor, and now he took off the armour designed to protect against blast waves and splinters, the knee protectors and gloves, and finally crept out of the warm overalls and carried the equipment he'd borrowed from one of the bomb experts over to the car parked at the back of the damaged police station, drove the distance to the city and his own workplace, hurried to the CCC and the large room and the round table with a perpetual, live staff meeting.

'I need your help.'

Sven turned to the man with both his elbows on the table, reminding him of another table a few years earlier, Jacksonville, Florida. They had sat opposite each other at a lunch restaurant with a computer on the white tablecloth and tried to comprehend that the picture they were both looking at was the exact moment when someone had been shot to death. Now Erik Wilson was the head of Homicide and so both Grens's and Sundkvist's boss, and this was perhaps the first proper conversation they had had with each other since then.

'You do?'

'It's about Ewert.'

'OK.'

'I'm worried.'

Erik Wilson excused himself from the meeting, asked Sven to come with him to the enormous wall of screens, out of earshot.

'You're worried?'

'I'm frightened. Everything is going to pot. Since this all started . . . Råby, I don't know why, but it's really affecting him.'

A room with bars on the window and a woman on a bed and a young policeman in his twenties beside an older man in his forties.

'Erik . . . is there something I should know?'

He had stood in the closed cell and looked at a colleague who was restless, wasn't in a good place, and when the birth was over, who'd gone forward to the young woman who had had the baby on her stomach for a short while, the great lump of an older colleague who never touched anyone, had put his hand to the child's cheek, cupped it round the soft skull.

'No.'

Erik Wilson had been twenty-two, newly employed and on one of his first postings other than doing the beat on the streets of Stockholm. He hadn't yet understood that the detective sergeant would go on to become a detective superintendent and would spend his days and nights in an office filled with the songs of Siw Malmkvist, that what had happened in front of them would be the only time that the now detective superintendent who approached dead bodies with as much intimacy as disdain, would be confronted with the opposite: life, a birth.

'I don't think so, Sven.'

He looked down at his papers, straightened a pen that was lying crooked on the desk between them, started to walk back to the still ongoing meeting.

'That there's anything you should know, that is.'

———

Gabriel lay with his cheek against a cold and hard stone floor, under the rubbish chute, on the sixth floor between three flats.

He had been throwing up violently since he got up from her sofa and had taken the last roll of banknotes from the drawers in the kitchen and crouched down with Wanda when they left the flat and moved towards the lift that took them as high as they could go. He had known that the pigs were listening to the calls on Leon's phone and would now be looking for him too, someone who was weak and might want to talk, but with the concussion and vomiting he hadn't been able to move any further away.

He'd rung the police switchboard, but when he'd been transferred and a pig had answered, he'd hung up.

He had decided to pay for a third time. But every attempt to get up had ended in more retching and she had had to go and do what he should have done. He had been ashamed and explained where and how; she had taken the lift down and gone into the garage and put the third roll of five-hundred kronor notes by the back left-hand wheel of a rusty Chevrolet. When she had started to crawl back between the cars, they'd been standing there. Jon and Bruno. They hadn't said much, *one hundred and twenty-five thousand more in the next hour*, just that. She'd pointed to the car and the five-hundred kronor notes, run up the stairs and sat down beside him on the floor. He'd almost managed to stand up and hold her when she whispered, *Gabriel, it's never going to end.*

A TELEVISION SET of the old-fashioned type, big, heavy, a piece of furniture that requires space and therefore dominates the room. He'd sat down in a comfortable armchair, been drawn into the frozen image on the screen of a young face that he'd got to know several years ago, while he listened to the detective superintendent, whom he met earlier by the entrance to the police station, stand in her doorway and ask questions that she didn't answer. She had closed the front door and gone into the kitchen and poured two cups of coffee, made them a cheese sandwich each, then come back into the sitting room and the other armchair and pressed play on one of the remote controls; a recorded news programme that for the first twelve minutes switched between pictures from the security cameras in three prisons and a photograph of some young men from the police archives.

'Brother, stop. The screw bitch, she's . . .'

They sat beside each other, not close, they didn't know each other, and listened to a recording from a getaway car, agitated young voices.

White letters over two black lines. Text at the bottom of a TV picture.

It was even clearer then.

'. . . I can't stand that fucking kicking . . .'

Thom looked at her, the swollen face, already a faint yellow in some places, adjusting the flowery cushion behind her back in the armchair.

Her body that ached when she poured them more coffee.

What . . . is it that you want me to do?

She'd sat in front of him naked and beaten up and talked to him until he'd understood what it was she wanted, and that it was absolute madness, and then later that she wasn't after all, mad that is. He had helped her put her clothes back on and together they'd left the metal frame which no longer had the fabric of a pram in the stairwell that smelt of smoke and walked towards the flat that was her home and sat down in her armchairs and he had continued to listen and understand.

*'I'll fix this. She won't kick any more.'*

It was a long time since he had decided never to allow himself to be provoked, never give his anger to anyone who spat or threatened, while someone else's saliva ran down his throat onto his chest. But then he had cracked when the gold chain and hair that was shiny and slicked back had first cut up yet another hose and then pointed his index finger at Thom's head and pretended to cock a gun and fire and whispered *I'm going to kill you.* And he'd continued to break a bit more when the friendly and decent policeman he liked so much had looked at him with empty eyes in a bombed building. *Right now, you're just so . . . despairing and weary. You're reachable.* She had seen straight through him and he had tried to avoid it, avoid her – there were fires here twelve times a day and he put them out twelve times a day. A forest fire that's what it was, isolated incidents at first, but when the wind is in the right direction it grows, spreads, in an instant. He talked regularly to colleagues from other towns and cities with other Råbys that were also burning and had to be put out if they weren't to get out of control.

On the TV screen, again, *that* picture.

A motorcycle police officer moving round and the helicopter searchlight comes closer, gets stronger; she had been attractive.

Ana stopped the recording and stood in front of the frozen image of an eighteen-year-old who had talked on the sound recording and who in all likelihood had taken the lives of two people in the past few days.

'They've abandoned us. Those of us who live here, really live here. Can you hear it . . . shhhhh . . . can you hear them whispering? *Let the bastards shoot each other – we'll go in and get the bodies afterwards.*'

She went over to the glass TV screen, pressed her hand against it, the face that no longer existed.

'I undressed and showed you the consequences of a balled fist and a pointed shoe so that you would see me, listen to me. I can't undress for the whole of Stockholm or Sweden. Do you understand? We're going to do exactly what I did. Only bigger. We're going to show them the damage, force them to see.'

When the hand left the glass, a damp print remained, the frozen image slightly blurred.

'There has to be a deafening explosion, so that they will hear – a bombed police station still isn't enough. This is our everyday reality, a lawless country ruled by a mere few, and no one out there must fail to understand that.'

She looked at Thom and they put on their outdoor clothes and left Råby Allé 34 for Råby Allé 12, went in the door, she was in front now, down some steps and she pressed the call button for the lift, waited, opened the lift door, wedged it there.

Some more stairs down into the cellar.

With her fingers she picked out the thin, blue-painted screw that was difficult to see, just above the lift-door handle, which hid a square hole.

She took out a ten-centimetre long piece of metal and pushed it into the square and turned it round until the lift door opened.

She lowered herself into the lift shaft and jumped the metre or so down to the bottom.

She waved at Thom to follow, turned on her torch and lifted two black blankets.

Two full twenty-five kilo sacks of ANFO, the cheapest and least shock-sensitive of all explosives. A box of three hundred and fifty detonators, like small pipes with green and white wires at one end. A packet of dynamite sticks, he counted eleven.

'And in the others?'

'Only one twenty-five kilo sack. But the same amount of detonators and sticks of dynamite.'

'Are you sure about that?'

'Råby Allé 25. Råby Allé 34. Råby Allé 57. Råby Allé 76. Råby Allé 102. Five more lift shafts.'

He stood there, the torch beam moving back and forth, he followed it as it fell on the explosives, detonators, dynamite.

'How . . . did you know this was here?'

'You don't need to know that.'

'How *long* have you known this was here?'

Drugs when they were small. Stolen goods, weapons when they were twelve. This, explosives, she tried to remember, nine, maybe ten months.

'That's not something you need to know either.'

She was on her way up from the bottom of the shaft, turned and looked at the fireman she had been speaking to all day and would continue to speak to once they got back to her flat. She wanted him to climb up and follow her, someone could come by at any time.

He stayed standing where he was.

'OK, not how. Nor how long. We won't bother about that. But if you don't tell me *how many*, I'll walk away, now.'

'How many?'

'How many others have you told about this?'

'No one.'

'If you knew about this before the explosion took Pereira's life, if you—'

'If I talk about it, I'm . . . dead. That's the way it works. *You*, of all people, should know that.'

He knew that.

A light foot on one of the twenty-five kilo sacks.

'Bulk industrial explosive. Just like that used in the police station. Does more damage to anything that's living than explosives with a high detonation velocity.'

'I'm sorry?'

He bent down, opened the sack and filled his hand with small, round, colourless balls.

'This explosive, in the sack, ANFO, has low—'

'What are you trying to say?'

'I'm trying to say that Pereira was killed by a slow blast wave. The kind that doesn't break through load-bearing concrete walls, so it bounces back against human bodies again and again.'

He turned off the torch, a long one-metre step up and out of the lift shaft.

'And I guess I'm also trying to say . . . it will work.'

Ana locked the door with the square piece of metal and waited quietly for him to finish.

'What you want to do, it will work. If you put together the detonators, sticks of dynamite and sacks of explosives. If you cut the green and white wires. With all this, to destroy the flats . . . all we need are the garage doors to be well closed and someone to make a quick phone call.'

He had propped himself up on the stone floor.

Dizzy, about to be sick again, but he wasn't, he could stay sitting up.

Wanda's hand holding his arm, but he pushed it away, he could manage alone and her face was so tired, her eyes black, her lips dry.

Domestic sounds from inside the three nearest flats. Music from the one to the left, maybe Greek, a TV from the one in the middle, and someone hammering in the one to the right. Gabriel supported himself with one hand against the wall and one against the rubbish chute as he tried to get up, but was forced to sit down again. The dizziness had intensified, his legs turned to jelly. He tried again, she held his hand and he didn't push her away, she was stronger than he'd imagined and he managed to stand up for several seconds this time.

'I want you to call.'

The Greek music and the TV and the damn hammering and her voice.

'Gabriel, you know it's never going to end. You have to call again!'

Threats. Fifty thousand. Violence. Threats. Seventy-five thousand. Violence. A hundred thousand. And threats.

*One hundred and twenty-five thousand in an hour.*

'Gabriel, you have to ask for help!'

She gave him the mobile phone.

'Thirty-five minutes left.'

He held it, fingered it.

The Greek music had disappeared, the TV programme had changed, the hammering was replaced by first a drill and then a vacuum cleaner.

'Thirty-five minutes left.'

He dialled the number. Two rings.

*'Police.'*

He hung up, looked at her, and she looked at him.

He dialled again.

Two rings.

*'Police.'*

'Um . . . the guys who escaped . . .'

*'Yes?'*

'. . . the man who's in charge of the investigation, I want to talk to him.'

*'I can't just transfer . . .'*

'And he wants to talk to me.'

*'He does?'*

'If he wants to know where those guys are . . . then he wants to talk to me.'

One ring. And one more. The voice, the same as the last time. A man, an older man.

*'Grens.'*

'. . .'

*'Hello?'*

'You . . . you're leading the investigation?'

*'Who's asking?'*

A deep breath.

*'Hello?'*

More, deeper.

*'I can hear that you're still there. Who is it that's asking?'*

That carried on.

*'If you want to talk to me, talk now.'*

A throat being cleared.

'I . . .'

*'Yes?'*

'You have to . . .'

Gabriel clutched the handset, looked at Wanda, her face, her stomach.

'. . . help me.'

———

Ewert Grens drove the red Volvo towards the garage door that whined as it rolled up. The instructions were to pass the police car that was on guard and then carry on into the underground garage and swing to the left after the first three rows of parked cars. He counted the grey metal doors, the seventh, an old Chevrolet, he was to park in the space behind it. He turned off the engine and put his gun on the seat close to his left thigh.

He didn't realise until he looked around. He had been here before. Eighteen and a half years ago. Another gang leader who had asked for help, after he'd tried every way he could to get out, he'd phoned, arranged a meeting.

Leon Jensen's dad.

'Grens?'

He opened the door to the passenger seat. Tall, Ewert Grens guessed about one metre eighty-five, short hair, black hoodie and black trackies. He looked like all the others. If it hadn't been for the dried blood all over the clothes. The wounds on his face. Eyes with different-sized pupils and a right leg in spasms. And the way he bent over when he looked into the car, broken ribs.

'You're the pig who's . . . working on this?'

Grens recognised him. Despite all the injuries. He'd seen him several times in the past twenty-four hours, high up on a wall.

The other leader. Gabriel Milton.

'Sit yourself down. You're not wanted. You haven't formally committed any crimes.'

He'd done time in prison and served sentences for other crimes. According to all available sources he was a serious criminal and one of the two brains behind one of the country's most criminally active gangs. But for the moment, innocent until they could prove otherwise.

'Even though I know that you know where Leon Jensen is. And even though I know that you've got something to do with the explosion that killed one of my colleagues.'

An uncomfortable silence, they sat side by side in the front seats and looked into the gloom of the garage, each waiting for the other.

'I . . . need help.'

He turned a fraction, groaned, he was in pain.

'Your help, I mean. Yours. The pigs.'

A strong smell of sick on his breath in a closed car.

'I have to get away. *We* have to get away.'

'I see.'

'Don't you understand, you bastard? *We have to get away. And we need help.*'

'Why?'

'I can't answer that.'

Ewert Grens glanced over at him, he was sitting there talking to a policeman in the way that he'd always spoken to the police – he didn't know any other way.

'If you want my help, you'll answer my questions.'

His breath, like vomit. Grens wound down the window on the driver's side.

A car drove into the garage, he followed it in the rear-view mirror until it disappeared down to the next level.

'*Why?*'

'Someone's threatening us.'

Ewert Grens looked at his face properly for the first time. Five round marks, burns from a cigarette. He remembered the earlier documentation about Gabriel Milton, the description and pictures of burn scar tissue all over his body, *except* on his face. And he remembered the smell of burnt flesh.

'Who?'

'I can't answer that.'

Grens raised his voice.

'This is not a fucking interview. This is a conversation. About how you're going to survive today. *Who* is threatening you?'

He lowered it.

'There are only two ways out. Either you die. Or you hand over your brothers and are given witness protection.'

'That's just bullshit. To get me to grass up.'

'You can call it whatever you like. I call it an exchange. I want to know where Leon Jensen is. And then where Marko Bendik is. And then where Uros Koren is. I've been doing exchanges with gangs in Råby since before you were born. You'll be dead by twenty. Or you'll inform on your brothers under a witness protection programme. *There is no other fucking way out.*'

The smell of vomit. Or the smell of a dusty garage. He didn't know which was worse, but decided to wind down the window a bit further.

'I won't inform on my only brother.'

'To be part of our witness protection programme, you *have* to inform on him.'

'I won't hand him over.'

'Then you can leave.'

Ewert Grens looked straight ahead, out into the grim garage.

Even when the eighteen-year-old in the seat beside him opened the door and got out, walked towards the grey door, bent double.

———

He stopped. Dizzy. A pain in his side and his chest, a rib digging even deeper in. He stood in the dark when the pig bastard started his car and drove off, waited as the door rolled open and the car disappeared. Then he went to another exit, Råby Allé 34, took the lift up four floors.

Gabriel stood in front of her door for a long time, the name plate, TOMAS, it had always been there.

He rang the bell. Maybe she wasn't home. She was, he heard her turning the lock, lifting the security chain.

'Can I come in?'

Ana opened the door, but only a couple of centimetres. She saw a boy she'd known since he was nine and her instinct was to close the door and hate everything he now represented. But she also saw something else, eyes that didn't look away or through her, then the bad injuries, and she knew who.

'Can I?'

It was hard to see if there was anyone behind him through the narrow crack. But she was sure there was no one else there.

The stairs were empty.

And he had asked for permission. That was a long time since.

'It's just me.'

He seemed different. Not so aggressive. Almost reminded her of the boy she had met and let in so many years ago.

'Come in.'

Gabriel walked down the hall he knew so well, past Leon's room that was no longer Leon's room – repainted, it had been green and now it was white, a TV set where the large desk had been – past her bedroom and the big bed that they'd jumped on and hidden stolen goods under, into the kitchen and the table he had sat at almost every day. He lifted the table cloth, four marks from four plunges of a knife.

'I don't know anyone else.'

There were two full cups of coffee on the table and he'd seen a pair of big boots in the hall.

'Is there someone here?'

She picked up the two cups and poured out the contents.

'No.'

He stayed sitting and looked around the kitchen and she saw

a little boy who was big and had chosen the same chair as back then.

'Leon . . . you and him . . . like me and him.'

He curled up, he was in pain.

'I don't know . . . love . . . I don't really know, do you understand? Leon is love, like her fucking belly . . . and Wanda . . . I'm going to be . . . a dad, do you understand?'

Five round burn marks on his face, the skin he had always been so proud of.

She understood. One love, brother.

And she put her hand on his cheek, bristly, unshaven, fingers around the burns from a cigarette.

He didn't move.

'He's my only . . . brother. Do you understand?'

'No. Because it's *you* that is *his* only brother.'

He was crying, great tears down the torn cheeks.

'Brothers! Do you understand? And now . . . he's . . . not there.'

Ana sat in front of a person who was heading somewhere, in the way that she was heading somewhere, it was perhaps not visible, but you could feel it.

'It's not him that's not there. It's you that's not there any more.'

Her hand still on his cheek, it was getting wet, sticking slightly.

'But you, you . . .'

'I love him. But I don't have a son. Not any more.'

He should have got hold of it, forced it away. But he didn't.

'And you don't have a brother. Any more.'

And he cried as he had sometimes done back then and she held him as only she had ever been allowed to hold him. She looked at him, then at the empty place beside him, the other boy who used to sit there.

––––––

Gabriel walked slowly down to the cellar and out into the garage and back to Råby Allé 114, keeping his eyes closed as much as he could to keep out the light, bending forwards to ease the stabbing pain around his ribs.

He sat down on the lift floor.

He had paid and the debt had grown. If he continued to pay, it would keep growing, if he didn't pay, they would die, both of them.

*You can't leave me.*

The sixth floor, he got up onto his knees and crawled out. No Greek music, no hammering. Wanda was sitting by the wall under the rubbish chute and stretched out her arms when he got there, held him.

'The pigs?'

'No.'

She moved apart slightly, her cheeks flushed.

'It's an hour and five minutes now!'

'I . . .'

'And you haven't paid, you know, *you know what they'll do*!'

He didn't answer.

'Gabriel? An hour and six minutes!'

'I won't inform on them.'

'You'll die! I'll die!'

'Never, not my brothers.'

'Then I'll go there myself.'

She had just reached the lift when he got up, took a couple of shaky steps, regained his balance and hurried after her.

The first time outside since the escape, fresh air and slightly damp, it was going to rain. The sharp sunlight sliced his brain in pieces and he screwed up his eyes, pulled the hood over his head. A wide circle round the area to avoid being seen, round the back of the police station and the small car park and he saw it immediately, the red Volvo, he was still there. Gabriel sat down behind it, took the mobile from Wanda's hand, phoned the City Police switchboard, and asked to be put through to Ewert Grens.

---

He'd never gone into the police station via the staff entrance before, up the stairs, the limping pig bastard moved as slowly as he did.

He'd sat there, in the Section Against Gang Crime, several times before.

Opposite Pereira, conversation, conversation and information, questioning.

But it had never looked like this. The walls were gone and the paper faces were strewn in small bits across the piles of porcelain and wood and plaster and without thinking, he looked for his own.

*They had been at the top.*

Every breath still cut him up inside. But he couldn't feel it. Because he was smiling.

*They had done exactly what they had decided to do.*

'I want those two out.'

Gabriel spat at a middle-aged man and a younger woman who were sitting on chairs in the blasted room, dressed in civvies, but still obviously police.

'Sven Sundkvist. Mariana Hermansson. They work with me.'

'And I'll only talk to *you*.'

Ewert Grens nodded to Sven and Hermansson, they were to leave the room, then sat down on one of the two chairs and pointed at the other one.

'Sit down.'

The eighteen-year-old boy stayed standing.

'No recorders.'

With exaggerated, clear movements, Grens turned off the recorder and took out a pen and paper.

'And no notes.'

The detective superintendent paused, then dropped both to the floor, the pen bounced and rolled away, while the paper floated, hesitating, then fell into place between their feet.

'We will, sooner or later, link you to the escape. *Protecting a criminal.* To the car. *Vehicle theft.* To the gun that was used to threaten. *Serious firearms offences.* And with your record . . . I'm guessing four years.'

'I can do my time.'

'That's not good enough. If you want our help – we want yours.'

'I will never inform on my brothers.'

Two chairs facing each other in the remains of an office. Grens got up and walked on whatever it was crunching beneath his feet, stopped in front of one of the piles of unsorted rubbish and moved the pieces of porcelain from a toilet that lay on top. The broken plaster boards gave off a cloud of dust when he pushed them to one side, then some way down he found what he was looking for, a piece of metal from somewhere. He cleaned it on his trouser leg, then on the sleeve of his jacket, a thick layer of white dust divided into a cloud in the air and a loud stripe on the material.

He held it up.

'Look in this.'

The boy who was in so much pain did as he was told.

'And?'

'What do you see?

'What do I . . . see?'

'Yes.'

'Like a . . . mirror. I see . . . me.'

'You can see your face. Five craters. *He burnt you.*'

Gabriel searched in the piece of metal. He hadn't known what it looked like.

'Yes.'

532

'And?'

'I'll do my time. But I won't inform on my brother.'

The piece of metal in the air, it landed on the pile again, clattering before it got wedged between two legs of a chair.

'Take a look at this.'

The laptop had been in Grens's bag.

'I was sent this by three colleagues only a couple of hours ago.'

Pictures from a security camera in a petrol station outside Nyköping, a young man assaulting a woman and then pointing a gun at the head of a man who rushes in.

'Not even a week ago.'

'I'll do my time. But I won't inform on my brother.'

Pictures from a security camera on a pedestrian street in Jönköping, a young man running out of a bar and smashing a shop front.

'You can show me whatever you like.'

A third security camera, pictures from Copenhagen police, a young man on Hovedbanegården, robbing an amphetamine dealer in the early morning.

'I won't inform on him.'

'Aggravated assault. Serious threat. Gross theft. Armed robbery. All in less than twenty-four hours. If I were to guess, eight, maybe ten years in prison.'

'What is it you don't understand, pig bastard? *I won't inform on my brother.*'

Ewert Grens was close to screaming. But not here, not now. They were both fighting for the upper hand. Instead, he left the chair without a word, out into the corridor with footsteps that whipped the walls, and into the staffroom, over to the table where Sven and Hermansson had been banished and were sitting with a cup of coffee each.

'Sven?'

The vexed detective superintendent was red in the face.

'Your baton.'

Sven Sundkvist had heard what his boss said but stayed sitting where he was.

'Now, Sven!'

His jacket was hanging over the chair beside him. Sven took the twenty-centimetre-long black baton of sprung steel out of the inner pocket and handed it to Ewert, who pressed the button at the bottom, waited for the sound and the feeling when it extended to three times the length. First he hit the concrete wall above the cooker, then the back of a chair – which split in two places.

'Thank you.'

Grens handed it back without attempting to close it, then back through the corridor and into the gang room to someone who was half lying on the chair.

He had explained that by the end of the investigation they would be able to link him to the escape, four years. He had let him see a ruined face. He had shown clear pictures of a frustrated teenager's rampage through Sweden, eight years.

Ewert Grens had played all his cards. Except one.

'You came here because you needed my help.'

The laptop again, no pictures this time, just sound against a black background.

'A telephone conversation. Only a few hours ago.'

*'No one leaves us.'*

'He's threatening you.'

Ewert Grens leaned in to the eyes that looked away.

*'And you, Gabriel . . .'*

'He's threatening your girlfriend. What she's carrying.'

*'. . . Daddy . . . you can't leave me.'*

He reacted.

The boy who was sitting in the place he hated most, but who didn't have a choice, who had come here and asked for help, Grens was sure, he'd reacted.

And he moved the cursor, played one single word again.

'. . . *Daddy* . . .'

He paused, moved the cursor, one more time.

'. . . *Daddy* . . .'

'Do you want to hear that again?'

He could see it clearly now, a slight shift in the face that was so hard.

'He's threatening your child.'

Grens moved the laptop down onto the floor.

'A child . . .'

The eyes, it always started there.

'. . . you won't meet it until it's finished school.'

Lips taut, jaws tense.

'*You* choose. You join a witness protection programme. You tell me where Leon Jensen is. And I . . . I might not press for two new preliminary investigations, *protecting a criminal, vehicle theft, serious firearms crime* and *aggravated assault, unlawful threats, gross theft, armed robbery*, to be opened and completed, as no one else seems to know about them. And . . . I guarantee that your pregnant girlfriend will be given full protection from now on.'

His face, he wasn't even trying to conceal it any more.

'You choose.'

And he left the chair and went over to the internal wall that wasn't there any more and the toilet that had been on the other side. It had been just there, the bomb.

'Where was he standing?'

'Who?'

'Bastard Pereira pig. When he died.'

Ewert Grens knew what he was after, a final shred of power in the only way he knew how, but his heart was beating so and his cheeks were flushed.

'He was standing exactly there.'

'And then? Where was the pig lying?'

Grens's anger was on its way out; he couldn't hold back what he so needed to hold back.

'He wasn't lying. He was sitting. Leaned back against the external wall, that one there.'

The eighteen-year-old who still hadn't said the only thing that Grens wanted to hear was going to cling to any sense of worth he still had for just a little bit longer.

'See . . . did you see him?'

Not yet. This raging fury. *Not yet.*

'Yes. I saw him.'

'With his intestines in his lap? That's what I heard. And how . . . did it feel?'

It was so long since he'd hit a person.

The regimental commander when he was nineteen, one single blow, he'd fallen to the ground in the middle of the barrack square on P10 and he deserved it. A pathetic stoned bastard who'd stolen his bike one night from a bar by Kungsträdgården that had been called something in the seventies that he'd forgotten. And the long-haired guy who owned the newsagent and had made fun of Anni, he hadn't hit him, but pushed him hard against the wall.

But when the rage pressed until you no longer had a choice, the grinning face with five craters from a cigarette had repeated *bastard Pereira pig* and *intestines in his lap* one time too many and Grens had stood up, raised his arm to hit someone who right then lowered his head.

———

It was over.

Gabriel Milton had lowered his head. He hadn't been able to take any more.

And Grens had stood there with his balled fist in the air and it was still a long, long time since he'd hit a person.

———

'Do you know how it works?'

'Wanda?'

'You can't ever come back.'

'Wanda, for fuck's sake!'

'We'll look after her. You won't see each other again for several years.'

WHAT HAD EARLIER been warm and damp was now gentle rain, the first drops tentatively wetting the roof of the red car as it moved from one police station to another. Grens got into the driver's seat and Sven and Hermansson got into the back from either side, and the boy in the hoodie and tracksuit bottoms covered in dried blood stood there and waited his turn.

'Here.'

Grens nodded to him as he stood with his hand on one of the back doors, looking in at the full back seat.

'In the front. You can sit here. You've not been arrested for anything.'

He'd been on his way to the place where he always sat, hand-cuffed between two police officers.

Ewert Grens made sure that the cars were in place with their engines running, gave the all-clear sign to the one driving in front and checked in the rear-view mirror that the one following behind kept the right distance.

The rain got heavier, the sound of the drops falling harder on the roof blended in with Gabriel Milton's irregular breathing. Grens asked Sven to take his mobile phone from his jacket pocket, to dial the last called number and then hand it to him.

'What have you got? Where?'

Erik Wilson.

'I don't know yet, but find two available safe houses.'

The first secure, protected place. He only needed it for a couple of days.

'One in Rosvik – somewhere between Piteå and Luleå. And one in Korsberga, Småland – the road from Vetlanda to Växjö.'

'Too far away.'

'There isn't anything else.'

The windscreen wipers were working harder, it was going to start pouring.

'Then I'll sort it out myself.'

He looked over at the boy whose cheeks were getting paler and paler.

'But I need some help with clothes. Male, one eighty-five tall, normal build. Anything that isn't a hoodie and trackies.'

He hung up and turned to the passenger seat.

'A brown corduroy sofa.'

Gabriel didn't look at him, didn't answer, didn't even register that someone was talking to him.

'It's comfortable to lie on. If you need to.'

———

The City Police Homicide corridor.

Sven just in front, Hermansson just behind, and Grens beside him. Gabriel Milton was moving even slower and his breathing was even more laboured, as if he had started to relax during the journey, now that his girlfriend had protection and he himself had made a decision and was on his way, somewhere.

The detective superintendent stopped by the coffee machine, selected the button without sugar and milk, pressed and filled a plastic cup.

'Would you like one?'

The young face didn't answer.

'Anything to eat? An almond slice? A roll?'

Now it turned away.

The door to Ewert Grens's office was open, on the desk in a pile between the telephone and the alarm clock – a pair of blue uniform trousers, a white T-shirt, black socks, white pants, white trainers.

'I want you to take off what you're wearing right now. And if you've got anything in the pockets, mobile phone, money, put it in that plastic bag there.'

Ewert Grens had explained what Gabriel already knew.

*You cannot make any phone calls. You cannot take anything with you. You leave your past behind here.*

But the clothes, he went over to them, lifted them up, dropped them again.

'Those?'

'Yes.'

'Not a chance, fucking pig.'

'Just for today. From the police stores. You'll get new clothes, bought in town, tomorrow.'

He went through the pile that was so off the mark, turned towards Grens.

'How the fuck would you feel in my trackies? In here? It's the same fucking thing.'

He looked at the pile of clothes again, then pulled off his hoodie, his T-shirt.

'Do you want me to wait outside?'

Mariana Hermansson had stopped by the door.

'I'd rather get undressed in front of you than those two.'

The gaping wound on his right thigh, bruising over his whole body.

Grens tried to see how his stomach and chest were looking, the ribs, but couldn't tell.

*You have nothing left that can be traced back. And then we'll empty you of information, over several hours or days, as long as it takes.*

He had changed into new clothes. He was no longer the same person.

Sven and Hermansson pulled out a chair each while Grens rolled out his desk chair and pointed at the sofa until Gabriel sat down.

The last drops of coffee, plastic cup on the table.

'Are you sure you don't want any?'

Gabriel shook his head with small movements and the detective superintendent went out only to return almost immediately with two new cups and a cheese roll. He kept one coffee for himself and put the other and the cheese roll in front of his guest.

'If you change your mind.'

Grens drank another half cup, Sven closed his eyes, Hermansson sorted out some white papers on her knees and Gabriel after a while fell back against the brown sofa, it eased a bit then, the stabbing in his side.

'You can relax now. You can't get much safer than here. The building is full of police.'

Ewert Grens held up his key ring, jangled it, then held up a square piece of plastic.

'I need to use my keys twice and my staff card three times to get in here. And then just as many times to get out.'

The young man in the blue police-uniform trousers and a white T-shirt had not heard what he said. His face was creased with pain and he sank back and down into the sofa with his head on the armrest, where Grens had had *his* head all these years. He let out a load groan, sweat on his forehead and temples, a couple of minutes, then his breathing was more normal again.

Ewert Grens lifted up the recorder that had been sitting on the floor, put it in the middle of the desk and pressed the button that switched on a small red light for recording.

IT WAS SO silent. Someone should be singing. This office, without music, without her voice, it lacked time.

Ewert Grens leaned forwards, a beige jacket elbow on the only free surface on the desk.

He didn't have anything against time. It wasn't that. Getting older didn't frighten him at all. It was more that he had no relationship to it. He had never fully grasped how to divide it up into small bits and give them different names and then decide that they meant different amounts.

That's not the way it worked. Not for him.

A second in a car when the back wheel hits a woman's head was still longer than the thirty-two years that had passed since then. Fifteen minutes by a plot of ground and a white cross would always be as long as the lifetime it had taken to get the courage to go there.

The other jacket elbow equally heavy beside the one already on the desk, hands under his chin as he looked at nothing in particular.

That's just how it was.

The moment that had been a person's birth and first breath, the only life he had seen begin, was now, even eighteen years later, so much more than the sum of all the deaths he had already forgotten.

———

'I want you to give us Leon Jensen. I want you to give us Marko Bendik. I want you to give us Uros Koren.'

He had put in an order for lunch, coffee, dinner, coffee, sandwiches, coffee, for four.

'I want you to tell us all the crimes that you yourself have committed and not been prosecuted for.'

He had asked Sven to ring home to Anita and explain that they wouldn't be watching TV together this evening.

'I want you to tell us about all the crimes that all the other members, hangarounds and prospects have committed and not been prosecuted for.'

He had contacted the medical staff at Sankt Görans hospital and a youth hostel about two hundred kilometres away.

'I want the names of every single minor you have ever worked with. I want to know what the structure of Ghetto Soldiers looks like. I want to map out your criminal network in detail.'

For a long time, he had looked at a very young man who was sitting on his sofa in his place and who in so many ways had lived as long as he had.

'In short, I want to know everything that you think I *shouldn't* know.'

———

There were times when he'd had to sit here like this for three days to gain all possible information. Sometimes two. It could also be over in a matter of minutes.

The meaning of seconds, hours, years evaporated as it always did when hands were fumbling for the key that would open the door out.

———

'Where is Leon Jensen?'

Ewert Grens was still sitting there, his jacket elbows on the desk. Sven Sundkvist had twice got up to open the window and then when the buses on Hantverkargatan had got too noisy, closed it again. Mariana Hermansson offered cigarettes and coffee. Gabriel

Milton leaned forwards ever so slightly, not much but enough to be noticeable, breathing carefully.

'Wanda?'

'She's fine.'

'What's she doing now?'

'Now?'

'Yes.'

'She's sitting well protected between two police officers in a room in Råby police station.'

'And me?'

'I've explained that.'

'I want to hear it again.'

'We'll transport you to where we've agreed you will go.'

'Good.'

'Well, then?'

'You said *map out your criminal network in detail*?'

'I said I wanted to know where Leon Jensen was.'

'If you're going to map out our criminal network in detail, you'll need a pen.'

Three hours and twelve minutes.

———

He didn't like his new clothes. His way of sitting, moving, a body that screamed in discomfort, wrong, overdressed.

He drank his first cup of coffee.

He poked with a plastic knife at the lunch slop that was meatballs and gravy.

'Wanda.'

'Yes?'

'Now?'

'She's sitting in the same room. Between two police officers.'

'Good.'

'That's what you asked for.'

544

'I said good.'

'More coffee?'

'You *want to know what the structure of Ghetto Soldiers looks like?*'

'I want to know where Leon Jensen is.'

'The structure? Are you writing this down?'

Five hours and thirty-eight minutes.

————

He asked if he could lie down. Grens nodded. Hermansson got one of the cushions that were lying on the floor behind the sofa. He breathed easier for a while, his face relaxed.

'*The name of every single minor?*'

'Leon Jensen.'

'You said *the name of every single minor you have ever worked with.*'

'I said Leon Jensen and that I want to know where he is.'

'Do you want them or don't you?'

Eight hours and four minutes.

————

Coffee. Coffee. Dinner. Ewert Grens guessed cod, maybe coalfish, some sort of fish that tasted of nothing.

Coffee. Coffee. Sandwiches. Meatballs again with beetroot on dry, dark rye bread. And some white bread with cheese.

He seemed to be asleep.

An eighteen-year-old's face, nearly relaxed.

Hermansson adjusted the cushion, he didn't move.

She looked at him, then glanced over at Grens.

Then looked at the boy's face again.

If you don't know what love means. But you feel something.

How can you know?

'You said *I want you to tell us all the crimes you've ever committed and not been prosecuted for.* Is that what you said?'

He wasn't asleep.

Maybe he'd got a fright when Hermansson's face came so close.

'You said *I want you to tell us all the crimes that all the members, hangarounds, prospects have ever committed and never been prosecuted for.* Is that what you said after?'

'What I said was that I want to know where Leon Jensen is.'

'And I want you to go toss yourself off. Are you writing this down or not? *All the crimes?* You'll need a lot of paper then.'

Fourteen hours and four minutes.

———

He had his eyes shut again. Hermansson was still sitting beside him on the sofa, close to his face.

He was in pain. It didn't help to lie down any more.

She moved nearer.

He had known love. *Well shot, brother.* Then something had changed. His girlfriend had got pregnant.

She straightened the pillow again.

Someone who had never been close, who couldn't understand, if it happens, if he realises, starts to love himself, then that other feeling, it will change as well, from inside.

'*I want you to give us Marko Bendik? I want you to give us Uros Koren?*'

'What I want is for you to give us Leon Jensen.'

'Marko Bendik. Uros Koren.'

Eighteen hours and sixteen minutes.

———

Ewert Grens hadn't ordered breakfast, had forgotten that others ate in the morning. He had emptied his top drawer of ten-kronor coins and with them then emptied the vending machine. Rolls wrapped in plastic, cinnamon buns, apples, yoghurt, almond slices, two chocolate biscuit things. The boy who was lying down had pointed at the chocolate, eaten both and then lain down again.

The young person who was breathing more and more heavily and who was to be exploited – of information – had several times been about to fall asleep and Sven and Hermansson had taken turns to prod him.

He could sleep later. When they were finished.

––––––––

They were so close.

He was lying there because he'd decided. And they knew that, all of them, him too.

'Not my brother.'

Sometimes he tried to shout, but gave up when the pain was too much. He still sneered, of course he did, challenged them, but it all got lost in the weakness.

'I've given you the others. But you won't get my brother.'

When he had cried for the first time, Grens had leant out of the open window, contacted the Special Firearms Command, and whispered that they should get ready and wait for orders.

––––––––

'More coffee?'

'No.'

'Lunch?'

'No.'

'I've got cigarettes here if—'

'Five.'

He cried again, darker this time, from deep inside.

'We prepared five flats.'

Grens didn't move, nor did Sven or Hermansson move, what had just started could stop any moment.

'Råby Allé 124. Råby Allé 146. Råby Allé 172. Råbygången 68. Råby Backe 4.'

He was crying in pain, and because he was no one.

'And four cellar storerooms. Råby Allé 16. Råby Allé 143. Råby Backe 192. Råbygången 146.'

But most of all, he was crying because of the excruciating loneliness.

'You've already raided three of them. And he'll never go back once he's left. Work it out for yourself.'


Twenty-three hours and forty-seven minutes.

'HE NEEDS TO go to hospital. A broken rib has punctured his lung.'

Sven had heard what he said. But didn't leave his chair. He looked at the eighteen-year-old who was lying there and then at his boss.

'A lung? How long have you known that?'

Ewert Grens was already on his way out of the room.

'Ewert, *how long* have you known that?'

'As long as he's known where Pereira was when he died.'

The Homicide corridor echoed when he turned around.

'And I care about it as much as he cares about how Pereira is.'

Twenty-four hours and four people between closed walls. *He'll never go back once he's left.* Grens followed the stumbling body between Sven and Hermansson through the dust and dark. *Work it out for yourself.* Unsteady steps as he disappeared.

A member who'd defected and informed on his brothers.

And who had just been given a new identity and would soon be registered at Sankt Görans A & E under that name, stay on the surgical ward and be taken care of for a couple of days under that name, be transported in a civilian car to the Hargebaden youth hostel just outside Askersund under that name, without drugs or family or friends, would get a contact person, pocket money and food under that name.

Never ever to return.

He would live the rest of his life, perhaps even survive his brothers, under that name.

A PIECE OF plastic, temporarily covering the blown-out window, was in the way. He tore it down, wanted to see better, be able to lean out.

'Ninety seconds.'

He moved the communications radio closer to his mouth.

'Seventy-five seconds.'

Ewert Grens was standing in Råby police station and rested his gaze on the almost cloudless blue sky, then after a while looked for a window high up and far away, and another one much lower and closer, then the doors that were in between and hid the dark cellar passages. He had ordered a total of fifty-five officers from Special Firearms Command – MP5 reinforcement weapons, shock grenades, stun guns – to carry out simultaneous raids on a flat in Råby Backe 4 – seventh floor and SUVOROV on the door – and a flat in Råbygången 68 – first floor and DAHL on the door – as well as storeroom 86 accessed from Råby Allé 143, storeroom 342 accessed from Råby Backe 192, storeroom 798 accessed from Råby Allé 16, storeroom 976 accessed from Råbygången 146.

'Sixty seconds.'

The units ordered to strike against the flats were to do it from two places: the front door and the windows. The units ordered to strike against the storerooms were to do it from three places: the two entrances from the cellar corridors and a third group would wait outside the narrow cellar windows.

'Thirty seconds.'

He had arrested his father, then his mother.

'Fifteen seconds.'

Was this the consequence?

If those arrests had become this arrest?

'Ten seconds.'

And then what?

If he was to arrest again now?

'Five seconds.'

It wasn't his job to weigh up, assess.

'Four seconds, three seconds, two seconds, one second.'

It wasn't his job to try to understand how long such a conse-quence might last.

'Arrest him.'

# now
## part five
### (ninety-two hours)

IT WAS EVEN darker outside the window. He had slept well and long in the brown corduroy sofa.

He'd used the same cushion and it smelt a bit different, someone else had slept on the same sofa and under the same blanket, which also smelt a bit different. Not bad, just different, and he wasn't used to anyone else.

An eighteen-year-old boy with a punctured lung, and not long ago.

Ewert Grens stretched and sat up on the edge of the sofa. The beige jacket was all creased, he should have taken it off. Half a cheese sandwich left on the table from breakfast, and still soft when he took a bite. A nearly full cup of cold coffee. He walked slowly through the silence over to the bookshelf with black files and two tired cacti in the place where a cassette player had once stood, beside the tapes that he'd recorded and mixed himself and the photo that he'd taken and framed, the voice and the picture of a woman who no longer sang in this room. Two steps over to the window and the dark over the Kronoberg courtyard and he looked up to the eighth floor in the next building and Gunnar Werner who was walking around listening to new voices in new investigations, then the next section of the building, Kronoberg remand jail, and another eighteen-year-old who had been detained there for about as long as Grens had been asleep.

He went out into the equally silent corridor and down three flights of stairs, through the two doors into the archives, past the metal cabinets full of investigations – he could choose to reopen any of them and find traces of his thirty-seven years as a working police officer in Stockholm.

The room at the back, and the glass booth furthest in, he knocked on the closed hatch and a man with small, round glasses and thick grey hair popped up from behind a computer screen.

'I'm looking for a document that only people like you can authorise.'

Ewert Grens nodded in the direction of the room without windows behind the glass office, the archives innermost room and the special documentation that was stored there on behalf of the Swedish Security Service, Interpol, the CHIS unit, witness protection programme, and the division that he disliked the most, Control Unit: internal investigations. He himself accounted for some of the content in the division's files, reported and investigated on twenty-two occasions, disciplined four times.

'OK.'

'Witness protection. Nineteen ninety-three. Sonny Steen.'

The round spectacles and grey hair pressed some keys on the keyboard, looked at the screen.

'It's here.'

'I'd like to sign it out. A few days, maybe a week.'

The archivist gently shook his head.

'It's one of the documents that are subject to particular secrecy and can only be signed out by the head of investigation or investigation authority at the time.'

'Yes.'

'So . . .'

'It was me. The . . . head of investigation *at the time*.'

More tapping on the keyboard and a couple of seconds over onto the next page without looking up.

'ID, please.'

'You know who I am.'

Grens met the eyes that he'd always disliked and that disliked him back. He smiled briefly, didn't have time, put his police ID down on the glass plate under the hatch.

'I've been signing things out here for thirty-five years. You've been sitting here almost as long. But still insist on all this nonsense.'

'What's secret should be kept secret.'

The grey-haired spectacle user disappeared through the door into the heart of the archives and was very careful to close it behind him, returning a few minutes later.

On top of the police ID on the glass plate.

CONFIDENTIAL in black capitals against a yellow background, across the front of the file.

'A week.'

'Don't you worry.'

'And what is the purpose?'

'I'm terribly sorry. This is one of the documents that are subject to particular secrecy and can only be signed out by the head of investigation or investigation authority at the time.'

Ewert Grens picked up the folder of documents that was several centimetres thick and turned to go.

'But you have to be careful with it!'

The heavy, rather cumbersome detective superintendent stopped abruptly.

It was as if the man sitting behind the glass window, who lived his life amongst secret documents, was signing out something that belonged to him personally, that he would prefer it to stay just where it was under lock and key, so that it remained untouched and in perfect order.

Grens turned around.

'I'm just going to photocopy it. And then distribute it. To the editor's desks at all the national papers. So no need to worry at all.'

Then he carried on walking without listening to the voice that followed him down the gloomy corridor and into the lift up to the seventh floor and Kronoberg remand prison. He got out, approached another glass booth, with two prison wardens sitting comfortably on chairs, and one of them got up when he requested it and then walked ahead of him when he said that he wanted to visit one of the cells in the left-hand remand corridor.

He waited while the blue uniformed arm opened up a rectangular hatch in the middle of the cell door and looked into an enclosed space.

'Visitor.'

His voice jumped in the silence.

'You've got a visitor, Jensen.'

'You know that I don't want any fucking visitors, bastard pig!'

The remand warden noticed that the detective superintendent was moving impatiently behind his back and took a step to the side just as Grens stepped forwards.

'My name is Ewert Grens.'

He was there.

He flashed past the hatch as he moved swiftly to the only place in the five-metre square remand cell where he couldn't be seen. Right beside the hatch, with his shoulders pressed hard against the inside of the door.

'I don't want any visitors. And I'm not going to talk to any more pig bastards.'

'If I want to talk to you, then I will. But that's not why I'm here. I'm not here to chat. I'm here because I want to *show* you something that I know you want to see.'

'Not interested.'

'You will be interested when you see what—'

'If you want to flash your dick around, show it to someone else.'

Half a metre between them. On either side of a green metal door.

And completely without contact.

Ewert Grens started to walk back to the door. The young voice *fucking bastard pig* continued to scream *fucking pig cunt* at him several times until the detective superintendent stopped and screamed back *exactly what your father said when I locked him up* and he didn't wait, he knew that the shouting would stop immediately.

HE LOOKED AT the alarm clock on the desk between the telephone and the lamp; nearly two, he wouldn't have to wait that much longer, he was certain of it.

Grens ran his middle finger over the letters that tried to look important as they shouted CONFIDENTIAL, opened it and read the only line of text on the first page of the document.

`Daniel Jensen`

Then a photograph of him taken on the day he was arrested, a scenes of crime officer's documentation of a staring face, profile left, full face, profile right.

He looked through the first couple of pages, another picture, a red house in open forest. A youth hostel. The place where he was sent under the witness protection programme once he'd been exploited. An eighteen-year-old photograph. Ewert Grens remembered it well, he had taken it himself on the first of three visits.

He closed the folder. An absent father. And it went on and on. He still didn't understand it. He himself had had an absent father, but he hadn't become a bloody criminal as a result.

He left the desk in favour of the corduroy sofa.

He'd had a father. It wasn't something he often thought about. About him. They'd met twice. At least, that was all he remembered. Once when he was four or five, a good day, a sailing boat far out on a sea that was endless, somewhere close to a lighthouse called Tjärven. The second time was harder to recall in detail, even though it was much later. His mother had died, he was forty-one and one evening, alone in her attic, bent over cardboard packing boxes, he'd suddenly stopped his preparations for the valuation of her estate the next day. He'd grabbed the telephone directory, looked up, found, and said his name out loud, then gone to the address listed, Kolbäcksgränd 34 in Bagarmossen. He'd sat in his car outside the 1950s building for two hours before going in and up the stairs to the door on the first floor. He'd rung the bell and said nothing when a man twenty years his senior had opened the door, and without saying anything either, had looked at him then turned around and closed the door. Grens had stayed out on the landing and listened to the footsteps disappear into the flat. Nothing more, nothing less. It meant nothing. He had long since grown up and an absent father was still just an absent father.

Someone knocked on the door, opened it carefully, looked in.

One of the young security guards he recognised and sometimes spoke to briefly as he passed the night entrance on Kungsholmsgatan.

'I knew that you sometimes sleep here.'

Behind him, another face, a uniformed prison warden from Kronoberg remand prison.

'I'm not sleeping, I'm working.'

The guard pointed at his uniformed colleague.

'From the remand jail. They've tried to ring you several times. But your phone's switched off.'

'It always is. At night. I don't want to be disturbed when I'm *working*.'

Ewert Grens got up from the corduroy sofa with great difficulty just as the remand warden came into the room.

'I know that it's a bit late . . . I just wanted to ask you if you'd come with me to the seventh floor, left-hand corridor. To a detainee who's been screaming without stop in his cell for several hours. And every time any of us ask him to calm down he just threatens us, *I'm going to kill them all*. He even managed to set light to a couple of books and a sheet not long ago.'

The detective superintendent pulled his fingers through his thin hair, listened and smiled.

He had been certain that he wouldn't need to wait particularly long.

'He's got one demand. He wants to talk to you.'

Grens looked at the alarm clock. It had taken eight and a half hours.

'He does, does he?'

'Yep.'

'How did he articulate it?'

'Sorry?'

'What did he call me when he explained that he wanted me, in particular, to come? I hardly think he remembers my name.'

He was still smiling, whereas the warden's pale cheeks took on a pink tinge.

'He asked for . . . a meeting. With you.'

'If you want me to come with you, then tell me what he said.'

The pink deepened to a darker shade.

'Exactly?'

'Exactly.'

And the throat that was flushed the same colour was cleared.

'He said, well . . . that he wanted to talk to – and I'm quoting now – *the pig bastard who limps.*'

A thick folder from the archives with confidential papers under his arm and two plastic cups of black coffee from the machine in the corridor. There was a total of six locked doors between Grens's office and the left corridor on the seventh floor: the three first still in the City Police section and opened with Grens's square plastic card, the last three in the Prison Service's section and the warden's identical plastic card was the key.

It was half past two in the morning. But the left remand corridor was brightly lit.

Outside the locked metal door where Grens had waited a few hours earlier, there were now five uniformed wardens armed with thick mattresses in the event that an attacker needed to be forced back against the wall, and behind them, a doctor in a white coat with a syringe in his hand.

'I would like you all to leave before you open up.'

Ewert Grens nodded to the warden who had walked with him through the police headquarters.

'And . . . yes, you, too.'

'We'll stay here.'

'Right now, your uniforms alone will provoke him. I'll deal with this myself.'

'He murdered one of our colleagues!'

'I'm aware of that. And he'll go down for it. For a long time. But if you want to put a stop to the threats and any more fires, you let me go in and you'll disappear along with your colleagues.'

The prison warden unlocked the door and then joined the group of seven people who stood waiting and watching at a distance, from the end of the corridor.

Grens stood on his own outside the door.

Then he opened it. Two steps into the small cell. Careful to close the door behind him.

A strong smell of burning. On the floor, two blackened books. He tried to make out the titles, but couldn't, the text was no longer there. Further away, a half-burnt pillow. Grens looked at the mattress, he'd tried to set fire to that too, obvious signs of soot at the end. Leon Jensen was lounging on the bunk, supporting himself on one arm.

The detective superintendent put one of the plastic cups of black coffee down on the table that was attached to the wall, the other on the window ledge in front of the bars. He drank half of his, then pointed to the one by the window.

'It's good.'

'That?'

'Coffee machine. It doesn't get better.'

The plastic cup stood untouched.

'You wanted to talk to me?'

'I don't talk to pigs.'

He'd been causing a disturbance, making threats.

'You don't know me.'

Now he said nothing.

'But I know you.'

An eighteen-year-old who remained silent as he didn't know how to talk about what he wanted to talk about.

'I've got plenty of time. Nights generally just get in the way.'

But when he finally started to talk after several minutes of silence, he talked about something completely different.

'The walls.'

'Which walls?'

'The pictures. Of us.'

Grens knew precisely what it was like not to talk about the only thing you wanted to talk about.

He was like that himself.

'What about it?'

'Have you seen them?'

'Yes.'

Leon Jensen raised himself up.

'Where were we?'

Now he was sitting up, still on the bunk, with the pillow behind his back and his knees pulled up.

'On the wall that we bombed. Where were we?'

'Is it important?'

'On the one to the left? Or the one to the right?'

'Well, is it?'

'Left or right, you pig bastard!'

Grens emptied the plastic cup.

'Left.'

'Left?'

'Yes.'

He was proud, Ewert Grens was sure of it, something about the expression round his mouth.

'Fuck, the left. High up?'

'Yes.'

'How high?'

'As high as you can get.'

That expression. Tight lips that caught a smile.

Grens pointed at his plastic cup.

'Are you not having any?'

'I don't drink pig slop.'

'OK if I take it then?'

The eighteen-year-old who looked so proud shrugged. Ewert Grens reached over for the brown cup, drank the now cold coffee.

'You have no idea what you're missing.'

Three long gulps.

'You wanted . . . you said, you bastard, that you wanted to show me something.'

A cup of coffee. Some meaningless chat about a wall. Maybe it didn't seem like much. But something like that could sometimes be the kind of warmth that a tired detective superintendent only occasionally felt all the way from his feet to his belly.

'Yes, I did.'

He picked up the folder and opened it.

'A fucking investigation report? I've seen it all before.'

'Not this one.'

Ewert Grens held the first document up in front of the boy on the bunk and he moved back.

'You should read it.'

Even further back.

'Or, maybe, would you like me to read it for you?'

Leon Jensen still didn't answer. Grens moved the document closer to the young face again.

'Maybe it should've been you, you fucking pig.'

Ewert Grens arrested his movement, about halfway between the two of them.

'Maybe it's you I should have blown up. Not Pereira.'

And now retracted it, put it back in the folder.

'Excuse me?'

'Maybe it should have been you who spewed up your own intestines. Maybe it should have—'

Grens stood up, opened the door, walked out and closed it behind him, then turned to the hatch.

'As you like. Your choice.'

He started to walk away, seven blue uniforms and one white coat over there, mattresses and injection at the ready.

'Oi, you, pig.'

He screamed through the hatch, like yesterday.

'Listen to me, you pig bastard!'

And perhaps Grens walked a bit slower.

'Yes. I'm listening.'

'What was he called? You said yesterday . . .'

'Jensen.'

'I fucking well know he was called Jensen!'

'Daniel Jensen.'

He didn't shout any more, and Ewert Grens didn't stop walking.

LATE EVENING AGAIN. That must be why he never went home to bed. Because it simply wasn't worth it. The days and nights passed so quickly that they blended into each other and more often than not, he stood, as he was now, by the window looking out onto Kronoberg courtyard and realised that he didn't know whether it was the darkness of evening or morning.

It *was* evening. He was sure of it this time.

The night's conversation in a remand corridor with an eighteen-year-old who wanted to know and was frightened and called him pig bastard, it was as if it had generated energy. He should be tired. He'd sat at his desk for the rest of the night and through the dawn, then in the morning and afternoon had had preliminary meetings with Wilson in an office further down the same corridor and with Ågestam over at the public prosecution offices and with Krantz, in amongst all his microscopes and brown paper autopsy bags in the forensics lab, then watched Sven and Hermansson question boys who behaved like old jailbirds and either remained silent or whispered *I don't need to answer that question* or just sneered, all these waking hours and still that unfamiliar feeling of not being quite so alone.

He suddenly started to hum. And it took a while before he realised, heard it.

Siwan's version of 'Everybody's Somebody's Fool'.

Music that would never be heard in this office again. He turned towards the bookshelf and the files and the cacti that filled a hole. He didn't feel angry, or disappointed. On a couple of occasions previously he'd caught himself in the act when he'd hummed or taken a few unconscious dance steps and every time had punished himself, without understanding it, by shouting at other people.

He didn't this time.

He just stopped humming, but smiled, sheepishly, instead.

Ewert Grens sat down on his chair and continued to leaf through the documents he had already looked through. The picture from the youth hostel outside Nässjö, one of the very first participants in the new witness protection programme. The man who had been called Daniel Jensen the day before and now looked at the camera as Sonny Steen. They had travelled there together in the same car, a silent eighteen-year-old beside him in the passenger seat, watching the only place he'd ever known shrink in the rear-view mirror. Only once during the four-hour journey had he spoken: an irritating scraping noise from somewhere in the front of the car had resulted in a breakdown just outside Mjölby, and before Grens could do anything, the boy had opened the door and then the bonnet, asked for a spanner, and after a couple of minutes mumbled *the solenoid*, and explained that the car should start again now. Grens held the shiny picture closer, it was a good one, he remembered that he'd taken more, varied the aperture and lens, and this one with the red house at the edge of the forest was so clear and had a definition that made him wonder why he stopped taking photographs.

He needed his glasses to look at it in a bit more detail.

A neutral face. Closed, straight mouth. Eyes that looked straight at the camera. Hair that was long and moved in the gentle breeze.

That wasn't all though.

The irritation, the anger, wasn't visible.

When Grens took the picture, the eighteen-year-old gang leader and drug addict had spent the first two months of his witness protection programme in a red house in a forest under a new name and had had no contact with his past – and only a drug addict's days without drugs could cause the kind of restlessness that any policeman in Stockholm so often met and recognised.

He straightened his glasses and tried to get even further into the frozen past.

The eighteen-year-old in the picture was wearing a black polo-neck sweater. Ewert Grens remembered the irritation that had accompanied major withdrawal symptoms, but also that when he had stood there with his poker face looking into the camera, he had insisted on wearing the sweater despite the summer heat and when Grens had asked him to pull down the neck, he'd screamed no and so had answered his question. He had injected in his neck. He'd had a relapse. He was on his way to losing, unsuccessful witness protection programmes often looked like this; relapses every few years at ever shorter intervals until drugs, crime, prison once again become daily life and the only hope for a gang leader and drug addict to jump ship and start again was already lost.

Ewert Grens paced backwards and forwards between the bookshelf, the sofa and the window, as he often did, turning his mind to another eighteen-year-old he'd visited one evening, one night and would visit one night again, at least, who had been sitting in an interview room with Sven and Hermansson all day and carried on with that damned silence lark that Grens had come to hate and would never learn to manage, which was why he'd harassed Krantz and Errfors and Ågestam and Wilson, so that he could conclude the case without a confession and still safely link a young murderer to an equally young prison warden.

The bookshelf and the sofa and the window one more time before he went back to the desk and opened the forensic scientist's final report *the secretion/DNA comes from Jensen (Grade +4)* that started with the results he had been given earlier from the National Laboratory of Forensic Science and the fingerprints unit and that *the prints definitely originate from Jensen (Grade + 4)* were connected to the restlessness and unease that he'd carried in his breast for so long.

He continued, probably didn't hear the careful knocking on the door.

*One photo* of Jensen's left hand, marks across the back of his hand, someone had bitten hard with a force that only comes from fear, teeth marks that matched those of the dead Julia Bozsik.

*One photo* of the T-shirt Jensen was wearing when he was arrested, marked with seventy-four white circles around blood stains, blood from Julia Bozsik and Leon Jensen, and yet another person, Gabriel Milton. Grens vividly recalled a burnt face and beaten-up body.

Another knock on the door and he still didn't hear it.

*Several photos* of stolen goods that had been found under the beds of fourteen minors.

*Several photos* of weapons that had been seized from lockers in public places and lockers in schools.

An irritating noise – as if someone was hammering somewhere.

*One photo* of three tyres in an empty flat, all back left-hand tyres with traces of amphetamines and heroine.

*One photo* of a fragment of undetonated bulk industrial explosive, the same as was found in Råby police station and the toilet next door to the Section Against Gang Crime that was the centre of the explosion, which was also found in small amounts on the floor of a flat in Råby Allé 67, the tenant of which was a certain Eduardo Santos.

Nils Krantz's report carried on and Grens immersed himself in every step of the report that would result in a judgement and long sentence.

It was only when there was a fourth knock, and Grens tried again to ignore the disturbing noise, that he realised that it was at his own door.

He checked the alarm clock beside the phone. 00.30. One and a half hours earlier this time.

And then he looked over at the door that would open on his order.

'Superintendent Grens?'

'Yes?'

The same security guard from the Kungsholmsgatan entrance. The same warden from Kronoberg remand prison.

The same night shift.

'Jensen.'

'What about him?'

'He's shouting and making threats. And wants to talk to *the pig with the limp*.'

'Not the *pig bastard* with the limp?'

'Not this time.'

He hummed quietly to himself. 'Everybody's Somebody's Fool' again. And then louder. When they were on their way out of the lift.

Just like the night before. A group of uniformed wardens outside a cell door, armed with mattresses, and a doctor in a white coat armed with sedatives. And Leon Jensen's voice screaming *I'm going to kill them all*.

This time they seemed to be relieved when they saw the detective superintendent who usually slept in one of the Homicide offices, didn't ask to stay where they were but moved after silent nods down to the end of the remand corridor and then waited there, watching as Grens stepped up to the cell door.

He knocked on it. Opened the hatch.

'You wanted to talk to me again?'

'Maybe.'

'But not . . . blow up?'

He didn't get an answer. He hadn't expected one either. But nor did he get any threats when he opened the door and went in.

The smell of smoke was gone.

Everything seemed to be in order.

The eighteen-year-old was sitting on the edge of the bunk, it was night, but he didn't look tired. A remand cell didn't exactly offer anything other than days that could be slept away. Ewert Grens put down the two cups of coffee, one on the table, one on the window ledge by the bars, then opened the folder, drank half of his cup while the one on the window ledge remained untouched.

'It's good.'

'That stuff?'

'Like yesterday. From the coffee machine, still doesn't get any better.'

Grens drank the rest of his cup and watched Leon's arm reach out for the warm liquid, lift it to his mouth, swallow and then promptly put it down again.

'Are you trying to kill me, you pig bastard?'

Ewert Grens leaned towards the barred window and caught the almost full cup, emptied it, crushed it and smiled.

'Your dad.'

The folder on his lap, the top document, and Leon didn't pull back, not like yesterday. But he didn't look at it either, avoided it, eyes to the side, above, below. Not even on the single line of text, the name he'd already heard.

'Daniel Jensen.'

The next document, a picture, the exterior of Hinseberg prison for women and a grey day, a lot of snow, it looked cold.

'He disappeared. Just before you were born.'

'I know.'

'Then you know—'

'That's what they told me. That he was on his way there when he disappeared. To Hinseberg. To . . . me.'

Ewert Grens had started a sentence that he wouldn't finish. If that was his truth. If that was the truth he wanted.

Next picture.

A barred window in the background. And a slightly blurred newly born baby on a stomach.

'You were born there because your mother was being threatened and your father had been too.'

The eighteen-year-old sitting on the remand bunk stood up abruptly, *was being threatened*, they were talking about something that he knew more about than most people.

'Why?'

'I can't answer that.'

'*Fucking bastard . . .*'

'It's simple – I don't know.'

It was hard to determine whether he believed him or not. But he sat down again after a while and the loud voice died down.

Next picture.

A woman in a blue dress with the baby on her lap.

'Who's that?'

'You.'

'And the other person?'

Grens turned the photograph round so he could see it better, looked closely at the picture that was starting to fade.

'A midwife. You were in care even before you were born.'

They were silent again.

Rain outside the cell window, drops that drummed monotonously on a piece of brown metal.

The kind of downpour that would last a while.

'Did he want to?'

'What?'

'Come. When I was born.'

*That's what they told me.* If that was the truth he wanted. *That he was on his way there when he disappeared.*

'I don't know.'

'What do you think?'

'I don't have children.'

'What the fuck do you think, pig man? If he hadn't overdosed. If he hadn't . . . died. Would he? Would he have come?'

Ewert Grens would often leave at the sound of voices like that. Or raise his own in response.

This time, he didn't.

'I think . . .'

Sometimes a lie was perhaps better. When you still can't talk about everything.

'I think he would have wanted that.'

But a lie often needs to be bigger and grander in order to sound like the truth.

'He nagged and he threatened. A bit like you. He wanted to go. But when we let him, when he was given permission to be there for your birth . . . he was just like all the others, given the chance, he had to take it, if he had the chance to escape and get a hit, then he took it . . . like all drug addicts, first himself, then everyone else.'

The eighteen-year-old boy sat quietly on the bunk, listening. He was possibly a bit calmer too. It was always hard to tell when someone wore their aggression, refused to let it go.

'Craving.'

'I'm sorry?'

'That's what we feel.'

'*We?*'

Ewert Grens smiled. And Leon Jensen almost smiled. A lie begets a lie. As close as he would ever get to his father.

Grens held on hard to the folder, hand over the photo he had thought of showing next, taken just a few years ago, after the most recent judgement and before the sentence that the boy's father was obviously serving right now, the photo that was above the name that the detective superintendent had not yet revealed. The truth. Sometimes it's simply not needed. Ewert Grens kept his hand there when he closed the folder, making sure that neither the text nor the photo could be seen.

'You've never considered, well . . . rethinking?'

It wasn't something Ewert planned to say. So he had no idea why he said it.

'I think . . . that if you *don't* rethink, sooner or later everything will go to the dogs.'

'Rethink?'

'How you want to live.'

'Live?'

'Your life is important!'

Leon Jensen looked at him with scorn for the first time that night.

'For who?'

It was not something he'd planned. So he didn't know why he'd said it. Which was why he didn't really understand what he was thinking himself.

*For me.*

'For you.'

*Your life is important for me.*

'Your life is important for you. For your mum. For—'

'Shut the fuck up!'

There hadn't been much more to say.

Grens had got up, folder in his hand, and both the plastic cups in his jacket pockets, when he pointed to the lamp, which was on.

'Turn it off. Try to get some sleep.'

He'd walked towards the door, opened it and then stood there.

*He's not going to turn it off. He never turns it off.*

And then he turned round again.

'Or else . . . leave it on. I normally do.'

And when he was about halfway down the remand corridor, the voice that always screamed shouted: 'Respect.'

He had heard and the strange warmth spread from his feet all the way to his stomach again.

'Respect, pig bastard.'

HE WAS HUMMING something when he got back to Homicide, felt something in his chest. Maybe he would dare. Without needing to fall headlong into the bottomless pit. He had always been frightened before. Memories were the past and the past was the only place where he'd had the courage to be content.

Maybe he should dare after all.

Ewert Grens hurried back to his office and the silence he'd never really got used to. He'd learnt to tolerate it, sometimes felt almost proud of it, but was tired of doing it. It was as if all his thoughts got bigger in the silence, more visible; he couldn't escape them. He didn't want to hear the clock on the desk, the buses on Hantverkargatan, his own coughing and footsteps. He had already hummed a few times without feeling angry or frightened or disappointed. She wasn't dangerous. Her voice didn't pull him back any more. He felt something and that *respect, pig bastard* and . . . it was so long, not even once in all the years without Anni. He looked at the bookshelf and snorted at it without expecting it to snigger back and then went over to the files and the cacti that were standing there to fill the hole that had appeared when he packed away all the other stuff that had stood there and been a part of his life for thirty years.

He took down first one file, then another. A cactus. And then another. He tentatively ran his hand over the hole on the bookshelf and then bent down over the desk and his telephone list and the number for Einarsson, the head of the property store.

It took a while before he answered.

Maybe he'd been asleep.

'Yes?'

'Einarsson? Grens here.'

'At this time?'

'Yes.'

'It's the middle of the night.'

They hadn't spoken to each other for over a year, since the morning when Grens had taped up three boxes and carried them down there and started to take detours past the storeroom in the basement that was normally where stolen goods were kept in connection with preliminary investigations.

*'I've got some boxes. I want you to look after them.'*

The tired voice at the other end of the line coughed briefly and there was a scraping on the receiver as if the hand that held it almost dropped it.

'Ewert?'

'Yes?'

'I was asleep. I want to carry on sleeping. What do you want?'

It wasn't even two o'clock. And he sounded so tired.

'I want to retrieve my cardboard boxes again, Einarsson, how do I go about it?'

*'Them?'*

'Yes.'

'When?'

*'PI Malmkvist. What the hell is that?'*

*'Preliminary investigation Malmkvist.'*

*'I realise that. But I've never heard about the case.'*

*'Closed investigation.'*

'Now.'

'It's the middle of the night.'

'So?'

'The property store is closed. Unmanned. And I'm at home. And I'm going to go back to bed again very shortly.'

'I'll go down there myself then.'

*'I want you to keep these. In a safe place.'*
*'Ewert, I . . .'*
*'Einarsson was silent, looked at Grens and the boxes for a long time.'*
*'I don't believe it.'*
*'A closed investigation.'*

'Ewert?'
'Yes?'
'Don't do it.'
'Now.'
'The last time you went in there yourself, it took us several days to sort out the place.'

> *'In that case . . . investigations like that are better stored here. If the goods are unique, I mean. Rather than in an unsecured attic or a damp cellar. Sometimes I mark certain investigations clearly with confidential. Because it is, isn't it?'*

'Tonight, Einarsson.'
The tired silence again, then a cough, a throat being cleared.
'Are you sure about this, Ewert?'
'I'm sure about it.'
'Hang on a moment then.'
Ewert Grens heard bare feet on a bedroom floor, then another conversation, presumably on another phone.

A couple of minutes later, the scraping noise again, and Einarsson's tired voice.

'You can go there in quarter of an hour, Ewert. And wait outside. Until you see a young man who works as a caretaker at NPB. He'll find what you want.'

It had taken him five minutes to get from Homicide to the property store. No windows, no lights, no sound. Few places were as deserted as the basement of Sweden's largest police station at night.

His first thought had been to throw it all away.

He couldn't remember why, but he'd then changed his mind and decided to store it here, and he was glad he had.

The boy, because it was a boy, appeared out of the dark on light feet, opened up and then turned to the detective superintendent whom he'd never seen before, but who was working late on something that was urgent.

'It's the Malmkvist investigation. PI Malmkvist.'

'So I gathered.'

'I want to sign it out.'

The young caretaker vaulted effortlessly over the wooden counter and disappeared in amongst the shelves.

'PI Malmkvist – what's that?'

'It will be with the closed cases and archives.'

'Why do you want it then?'

'It's being reopened.'

'And you're heading it?'

'I've been heading the investigation for thirty years.'

It didn't take long, young arms lifted down and carried three cardboard boxes and stacked them on a trolley with small, wide wheels. Ewert Grens looked at them, they were intact, even the hole near the bottom of one of them, a hard kick with his pointed shoes.

'I haven't been here very long . . . but thirty years?'

'Yes.'

'I've never even heard it mentioned.'

Grens slapped his hand on the top box, then picked off the red tape with CONFIDENTIAL and ONLY TO BE OPENED BY AUTHORISED PERSONS.

'Sometimes you don't, I guess.'

'Any conviction?'

'Malmkvist was influential, we know that much. We're going to listen to what she has to say again.'

A firm hold on the trolley handle and he started to walk, heavy boxes that were light.

'Superintendent Grens?'

The young caretaker was still standing behind the counter.

'Yes?'

'I'm a bit curious, but after thirty years – is there anything new?'

'That's what we don't know yet. But between you and me, I guess it will probably be . . . the same version.'

---

He sat on his desk chair. On the edge of the desk. Lay down on the sofa. Stood by the window.

He thought about alcohol. He seldom drank, it didn't interest him, but he understood the feeling, someone who had made the decision never to drink again, who went to AA meetings and then bought that bottle again, put it down on the kitchen table and looked at it and knew exactly how it felt, and how it would soon feel again.

It wasn't fear, more anticipation.

Because it wasn't a grave that he'd opened. Because Anni was somewhere else now. Because this was just Siwan and the music that he and Anni had shared, for the first time he felt quite sure of it, that *this* was not the same as *her*.

He opened the three boxes. He unpacked the tapes and photographs and cassette player and filled the shelf.

And he listened.

And he danced.

With himself, in the lamplight in the middle of the office, as before.

And if it hadn't been the middle of the night, people passing by would have heard the same song over and over again.

*The tears I cry for you could fill an ocean*

The music, the voice, it hadn't been like this for so long.

*Outside* his skin.

And thoughts that were too loud already took up less space.

*But you don't care how many tears I cry*

He sat down at the desk, sweat dripping down his spine and brow, his jacket over the back of the chair when he pulled the telephone over and called the switchboard.

Sometimes you just had to share things.

'The caretakers' office at NPB. I want to talk to a young man there who released some boxes from the property store just a short while ago.'

He turned the music down while he waited, it was difficult to hear when the voice that answered transferred him.

'Yes?'

'You wondered earlier if there was anything new?'

The young caretaker who had looked like a boy sounded surprised that a detective superintendent from Homicide would take the time to call and report back.

'Yes . . . yes, I did.'

'We've now got her to sing again.'

'Who?'

'The key person in the Malmkvist investigation.'

'Right.'

'And just as I thought. Between you and me. The same version. Exactly.'

He hung up. And stood up. Danced a couple of steps into the middle of the floor.

He woke early.

A couple of hours of deep sleep between five and seven and he was rested, the soft sofa and the music, every muscle relaxed, easy in his heart that so often raced.

As if he had bought that bottle. As if he had put it on the table, opened it and drunk. And started to understand. He had always thought that it was good. But he now realised that it was the effect he hankered for; her voice, and the songs he could hum along to whenever he wanted, were something else. Siwan, the music, the memory he had chosen to live for and missed, that was the feeling, the alcohol effect.

He stood up and put in another tape, Siw's version of Patti Page's 'Don't Read the Letter', it was the same music that sounded different. He still loved the melodies and lyrics from another time, but for different reasons, as if this was the first time and they were new and stood for something else.

Before he'd felt happy for a short time – then melancholy.

Now he felt happy – and could continue to feel happy.

Her voice in the room once more when he sat down in front of the pictures on the computer and the eighteen-year-old he'd visited two nights in a row. A ninety-minute escape divided over forty-three cameras and three prisons. The thin timeline on the bottom of the screen moved him forwards and back with the same unmasked figure. He paused for a long time on the picture from the prison wall, leaned back to focus on the unfocused. First the hands that were carrying a serious firearm along the top of the wall, which meant power, having power. Then the face, so proud when it looked into the camera and shouted something.

No yesterday. No tomorrow.

You neither live before nor after, but only have now to lose.

But if I don't move the timeline any more this time. If I stop and zoom in on your eyes instead.

I see something else.

What you're actually frightened of, I, if anyone, can see it, how damn lonely you are.

He turned from the computer to the open folder and the eighteen-year-old photograph that he'd taken himself outside a red house.

He compared them.

The picture of Daniel Jensen, who under the witness protection programme had become Sonny Steen and was standing outside a youth hostel, and the picture of Leon Jensen who would never be anyone else, standing high up on a prison wall.

They were the same age, the same height, the same slim build and tight lips and staring eyes.

They could have been brothers. They were father and son.

You could change the name.

But not the past.

Grens turned around and put in a new tape. He opened a new window on the computer screen, the *population register*, and first wrote in *date of birth 1975* and *Jensen Daniel* without getting any hits, an old name that no longer existed, then he wrote in the same date of birth, but this time with the name *Steen Sonny*.

Hit.

He existed. And he was alive. People who had abused drugs so much and for so long seldom were.

*Current address.*

Ewert Grens read it, looked away, read it again.

Box 38, 175 23 Aspsås.

He got up. He sat down again.

The PO box was in the post office in Aspsås. The address of

every inmate in Aspsås prison. Daniel Jensen, who was Sonny Steen, was living out his sentence in the prison where Leon Jensen had so recently been serving *his* sentence.

The heat in his throat and cheeks, he didn't like that pulsing sensation.

The same prison.

Grens's restless fingers on the keyboard opened another window, logged into the police *criminal records register*.

He had housed him in a beautiful youth hostel outside Nässjö, under a witness protection programme that had lasted for two months, until his first relapse. According to the register, he got his first conviction only six months later. And since then, in and out, twenty-seven convictions, sentences of two months to a year, drugs offences, burglary, a couple of assaults.

He reached for the phone.

'Good morning.'

'How can I help you?'

'Ewert Grens. I'd like you to help me with a name.'

He'd called Lennart Oscarsson, the governor of Aspsås prison.

They had only met on a couple of occasions, the first time long ago when a misjudged decision had led to the release of a convicted paedophile who had killed again, and then more recently a couple of years ago when the governor's orders had forced a CHIS to kill two inmates.

'OK.'

'Sonny Steen.'

'What about him?'

'I want to know which unit he's in.'

'Why?'

Ewert Grens had opened the door to a home in the middle of the night, in a terraced house where time had stood still, he'd put severe pressure on an already stressed man in his own kitchen and Oscarsson had in desperation taken off his uniform and cut it into tiny squares.

'Would you rather I came to your house? Again?'

Lennart Oscarsson didn't answer.

The sound of another keyboard, a few seconds, no longer.

'Block D.'

'Right?'

'Unit D1 Left.'

The same feeling as just a few minutes ago when he'd read and reread a PO box address on the computer screen.

His throat, his temples, pulsating.

'D1 Left.'

'Yes.'

The folder on the desk – the one who was eighteen years old and standing in front of a red house. The frozen image on the computer – the one who was eighteen and standing on the edge of a prison wall.

'It's the same unit. It's the same unit!'

'Same as what?'

It was quite a cool morning, mid-September, and his breath became small clouds when the moisture met the cold air. Ewert Grens walked the short stretch between the police headquarters on Bergsgatan and the public prosecutor's office on Kungsbron, took the lift up seven floors, he saw Ågestam already from a distance and rushed into his office without knocking.

'I want you to do me a favour.'

'You didn't knock.'

'I want you to place Leon Jensen in Aspsås for the remainder of his time on remand, before the hearing.'

'For someone who thinks that knocking is important, you're pretty damn bad at it yourself.'

'In the same cell as before he escaped.'

Lars Ågestam sighed and put his pen down in one of the two desk organisers.

'Leon Jensen is on remand with full restrictions.'

Grens took a step into the room. But he didn't sit down. He couldn't remember ever having done that here.

'You've already got everything you need for a judgement. Blood, DNA, fibres, fingerprints, time of death. You have probable cause. You know that he'll be convicted.'

'And I'm saying no.'

'You couldn't keep him in a more secure place than in that prison, *and that unit*, where the young woman he murdered worked. With her colleagues, Ågestam! They will, believe me, watch over every visit to the toilet, change of underpants, every wink of the eye, twenty-four-seven. And they will wait and hope for a chance to get . . . even more control.'

The public prosecutor wasn't as young any longer, Grens could see obvious wrinkles that he'd never noticed before around his eyes and his hair was starting to recede. Ågestam straightened his glasses and tightened his lips.

'I have never previously even considered moving a murder suspect, a *double* murder suspect, from a remand cell to a cell in a normal unit *before* he's been sentenced.'

One more step. And then, the detective superintendent sat down for the first time in the office he disliked so much. It was hard to decide whether Grens or Ågestam looked more troubled.

'It's very important.'

'Important?'

If you dare to believe.

'For me.'

'I don't understand. Why would it be important?'

Someone who is going to be locked up for the rest of their life for murder.

Someone who is going to be locked up for the rest of their life, because the need for someone who builds machines from bits and pieces doesn't exist on the other side of the wall, where bits and pieces are allowed.

*If you dare to believe.*

'That's all I can say.'

Lars Ågestam looked at the large man who seemed so small on the low chair. He had once called him by his first name, Lars, he had said, and Ågestam had, without understanding why, been filled with horror and hoped that he would never hear it again from Ewert Grens's mouth. Now the detective superintendent had sat down on a chair in his office for the first time, and from the low piece of furniture was forced to look up at the prosecutor behind his desk. This, this was even worse than *Lars* and he would remove that chair after this visit, never risk having to be in this position again.

'Ågestam, he's going to end up there. And the only thing that remains for us to do, for you, is arrange a couple of hearings, and I'll take responsibility for that, we'll go to Aspsås and hold the hearings there.'

The still relatively young public prosecutor and the considerably older policeman.

They would never understand each other. And they didn't really want to either.

'OK, we'll do it. But it's your responsibility, Grens. From now on, you are personally responsible for the consequences.'

A DAY PASSES so quickly.

After his visit to the public prosecutor's office, Ewert Grens had gone back to his office and stayed there. There was no time for any other investigation until the next nightly meeting. He had plundered the vending machine out in the corridor of strawberry yoghurt and dry, plastic sandwiches, while he read his way through to the end of the folder about what had happened in the past – it was dark outside when he stopped at a report at the end of the investigation that was nearly two decades old, two handwritten pages, tightly spaced, about an arrest in a flat on the third floor, Råby Allé 34, TOMAS on the door. His own handwriting in blue ink. He tried to remember why it was not written on a machine, if it had been more urgent than usual, if he hadn't wanted to hand it to anyone else to print and copy, it only took one hand to be involved in a witness protection programme that didn't play ball for lives to be put at risk. He sat down by the open window and read the text of a man who was twenty years younger. One of the few reports that included the name Ana Tomas, as well as Daniel Jensen. A young member of a criminal gang, classified as highly dangerous, who was being threatened and was frightened after losing an internal power struggle, had asked for help from the enemy, the only way out, had turned to the investigating detective sergeant and been exploited, told them about all the members, hangarounds, prospects and finally, about his pregnant girlfriend, who on his orders, was storing a kilo of heroin in a pasta jar; she would subsequently be arrested, held on remand, convicted and sentenced, and then transported to Hinseberg prison for women, and six months later would give birth to a son there.

Leon Jensen.

Now he was being detained in the left-hand corridor, several floors up, accused of murder.

Meanwhile Marko Bendik was in Huddinge remand prison, Uros Koren in Uppsala remand prison, Alexander Eriksson in Nyköping remand prison and Reza Noori in Gävle remand prison, without any means of communication, accused of aggravated assault and kidnapping. A total of five hangarounds had also been sent to various remand prisons in northern Sweden, three prospects to different Paragraph 12 secure training units and eight minors called in for questioning in the presence of their single mothers at the social services offices.

And the girlfriend.

Gabriel Milton's girlfriend.

They had arrested her on a concrete floor at the top of a building after he'd told them that she had acted as a courier for several months, and now she was also being held in the building – in the women's unit in Kronoberg remand prison.

Drugs supplies to Aspsås prison, Österåker prison, Storboda prison, filled plastic bags up her vagina. Serious drugs crimes and four, maybe even five years in Hinseberg.

A generation later. But the same consequences. Even a pregnant girlfriend.

It was past midnight.

Carrying the folder with him, he left the office and took the lift up to the remand jail. And when he stood beside the warden and knocked on the door, when the hatch was pulled to one side, he saw a bedside lamp that was on.

'You?'

'Yes.'

'I haven't asked them to call you.'

'Your last night here – tomorrow night you'll be sleeping in Aspsås again. I still have things I want to discuss with you.'

Plastic cups just like before, one on the window ledge and one in his hand when Grens sat down.

'I've known you all your life. Or that's to say . . . I've known about you all your life.'

He held up the photograph they had looked at together once already, and that now didn't seem to be as frightening.

A newly born baby with wet hair on a wet stomach. A barred window visible in the background.

'The photo, it was me who took it.'

The eighteen-year-old boy reached out his hand. For the first time, he held the photograph, himself.

'I was there. When you were born. I only had a few seconds. That was how long you lay there. Before someone else took over your care.'

'You were there?'

'Yes.'

'And I only lay there for a few seconds?'

'Yes.'

'You didn't say that yesterday.'

'I'm telling you today.'

Leon Jensen held the paper, picked at the photograph until it started to come loose at the edge.

'But we also met another time. When you stayed with me. For two weeks.'

Leon didn't say anything. Maybe he didn't understand.

Ewert Grens searched for the face far beneath the other one that was now so hard and tense, searched for the two-year-old in between various homes.

'Your mum called me from a phone booth in Hinseberg prison. She was crying. And asked me to look after her son until the next foster family had been sorted out. I still don't understand why, but, well – a policeman – a prisoner is always allowed to call the police.'

Grens pointed at the picture that was now slightly frayed at the edges.

'You didn't like porridge. You refused. But you loved rosehip soup.'

She had phoned the policeman who had arrested and questioned her. And he had mumbled yes and for two weeks had looked after a child. A holiday, he'd said. The only child who had ever been in the flat in Sveavägen. He'd never had a clue about what to do with children, but the boy had eaten and pooed and slept and was still healthy when he was collected by the new foster family one Sunday evening.

He had no doubt said afterwards that she could phone him if she needed help. But had never contacted them himself. Not the mother. Nor the son. He knew that she'd called again several years later and that he hadn't answered, let her report the boy's first conviction and sentence on an answering machine, and could Ewert do anything about it? He had then registered every new conviction and sentence for a while and thought about getting in touch, but hadn't done it; it wasn't a conscious choice, he just never got round to it.

'Pig bastard.'

His voice wasn't hard when he said it. No scorn. And then for the first time he drank more than a sip of the coffee.

'Pig bastard! Rosehip soup?'

Leon Jensen was almost smiling, some more coffee, then a long silence until Grens coughed.

'What I said yesterday. That he was a heroin addict, that he was on high doses, took a gram at a time and was scared of doing cold turkey and of being locked up and that's why he disappeared when he got permission to visit your mum when you were born.'

'Yes?'

'That was a lie.'

'A . . . lie.'

'As I can't tell you the truth. But I'm going to, all the same.'

Leon sat completely still. And over the next couple of minutes, Ewert Grens gave him a summary of an eighteen-year-old investigation involving a gang member who had informed on his brothers and was one of the first to join a Swedish witness protection programme.

'No overdose?'

'No.'

'So how did he die then?'

'He was placed in a youth hostel.'

'How did he die?'

'He got a new identity.'

'Did you not fucking hear what I said, pig bastard? How did he die?'

'No contact. He wasn't allowed any contact. But after a while, the drugs, the other life, he relapsed, started to commit crimes again.'

'What is it you don't understand? *How did he die?*'

'He got caught. Was convicted under his new name. And since then . . . he's been going in and out.'

It was only now. That he understood.

'What the fuck are you saying?'

'I—'

'That . . . he grassed on the others?'

Grens nodded.

'Yes.'

'That he grassed on the others, like Gabriel grassed on me and that he's . . . alive?'

'I don't know anything about Gabriel. But yes, he's alive.'

'That . . .'

Leon Jensen was shaking when he stood up from the bunk and took a step towards his visitor. Grens got up at the same time, they stood opposite each other, close, and the detective superintendent watched the teenager's balled hands closely. Until the young body turned round and punched the concrete wall with full force. And again. Ewert Grens wasn't particularly good at placing a gentle hand on someone else's shoulder, but he did, and Leon turned back, shaking, spitting. Twice he spat at him, the first time on the left shoulder, then the right trouser leg by the knee. Grens stood still and looked at him, even when he took out a handkerchief and wiped the beige shoulder and grey trouser leg.

It was the kind of saliva that was gone the moment it disappeared.

That wasn't always the case with saliva.

But he had nothing more to say, so he turned and closed the door behind him.

'And now, fucking pig bastard?'

The rectangular hatch. Every time. The mouth that didn't know what to say until a back had been turned.

'What the fuck is he called now, fucking pig bastard?'

*He's called Sonny Steen.*

'I don't know what he's called now.'

'And where—'

*In the unit where you were so recently.*

'And I don't know where.'

'Fucking bastard pig, I—'

'That's the way it works. I'm not supposed to know. What he's called. Where he is.'

The lift down. The dark corridor where he felt so safe. The coffee machine greeted him as he passed.

A small strip of light. An office with the door ajar. He stopped, his face suddenly in her doorway.

'Are you still here?'

'Are *you* still here?'

Mariana Hermansson had headphones on, they got caught in her hair when she took them off.

'Today's interviews. And Jensen is saying nothing. Not to me, not to Sven.'

Ewert Grens went further into her office. The piles of paper that previously covered most of her desk had now been divided into several smaller piles on the floor. She had summarised all communication between the fugitives in the form of diagrams, lists and maps, from the evening when Julia Bozsik was suffocated to death in a car boot – all mobile phone traffic and the eight masts the calls were transmitted from.

'We've got enough evidence. But I want a confession.'

'Maybe you'll get your confession, Ewert. When I carry on questioning him tomorrow. At *Aspsås prison*.'

She looked at him. She wanted to know why.

A prison before the prisoner was convicted?

He didn't answer, sat down on the chair in front of her instead and waited.

'How are things, Ewert?'

'What do you mean?'

'You're wandering around here in the middle of the night.'

'I've always done that.'

'You have always done that. But you look . . . you look like you . . . the past few days, Ewert, there's something.'

He didn't need a rectangular hatch. His mouth still had no idea what it was about to say.

'How many murders have I investigated?'

Mariana Hermansson looked at someone who wanted something, it was the middle of the night, and who didn't know how to go about it. And instead of doing what he normally did, had sat down and started talking about something completely different.

'The last time . . . you asked me to count, do you remember?'

He remembered.

'You have investigated two hundred and eighteen murders. Including these two.'

'Two hundred and eighteen.'

'Yes.'

'And I've always been relieved, often proud, when I've sent a murderer to where he belongs. To a cell. Locked up. As I think that murderers should pay. It sounds so simple. But then I am simple.'

'Yes, you are so simple, Ewert.'

'But this time . . . I don't know, I feel . . . something different.'

'What?'

'I don't know.'

'Why?'

'I don't know that either.'

'So, if you want me to help . . .'

'You'll be good enough to leave.'

He pointed to her door.

'We're in *my* office, Ewert. You're sitting on *my* chair.'

He looked at her. And then looked around, stood up and started to leave.

'That's good, Ewert.'

'What?'

He stood in her doorway and threw open his hands.

'*What's* good?'

'You've never felt anything. If it's not been about you. If you're feeling something now, if it's confusion, frustration, whatever, Ewert, if for once it's about someone else, that's good.'

'Good?'

'Yes.'

'How can it be good to solve a murder and not feel . . . relieved? Or proud?'

He shook his head and carried on walking.

'Only you know that.'

She smiled.

'Did you hear that? Only you know that, you old bastard.'

He had been on the way back to his office. He wasn't any more.

He went in the other direction, to the seventh floor again and the left-hand remand corridor and a cell some way down and a final visit. And he thought about a father who was still alive, because a policeman called Grens had helped him out of a world where those who stayed died young.

He was alive, but had been dead to his son.

That was how it always was. Moments, decisions that will affect someone else's life for ever.

Moments that you can't influence yourself, but that are fixed, steer, take over. *What you are scared of, Ewert, has already happened.* He had learnt that, in the end.

But the boy on the edge of the wall holding a heavy weapon and shouting loudly at the security camera? Ewert Grens would always despise anyone who assumed the right to injure a life, but this time, it was the circumstances he despised, the ones that created the person who injured, *what you are scared of, Ewert, has already happened and will happen again.*

He knocked on the cell door and opened the hatch.

Leon Jensen was lying on his back on the small cell's narrow bunk. Grens could see that he was awake, his eyes closed, but his breathing shallow.

'You asked a question earlier.'

'And you can fuck off, pig.'

He turned over, his back to the door.

'You wanted a name.'

'I spat on you.'

'Well, you'll get it. The name.'

'And I'll do more than spit at you next time.'

Ewert Grens opened the folder he'd had with him three times without showing the only pictures that were important.

'This.'

He held up the first one. Someone sitting on a chair in an interview room, who had been arrested on the first day he was criminally responsible, who would be locked up shortly, the three fixed angles, from the right and the left and face on.

'This is your dad.'

Leon Jensen turned slowly back, looked over to the hatch, across the distance, at someone who might be familiar.

'That? Fuck, that's just a kid!'

'He's fifteen in this picture. But in this one . . . he's eighteen. Just like you are now.'

The photograph of the red house outside Nässjö and someone who looked a little more familiar. Leon sat up and leaned forward, only a few metres away.

'Him?'

'Eighteen years younger than he is now. Before the amphetamines and heroine ravaged him.'

Leon came over to the hatch, so close that he could touch the picture in the middle of a white sheet of paper.

'Steen.'

Ewert Grens loosened the corners of the photograph, took it off completely, turned it round and showed the full name, written in pencil, on the back.

'He's now called Sonny Steen. And if I've understood correctly . . . he finances his drug habit by making tattoo machines in Unit D1 Left in Aspsås prison.'

Leon didn't spit, didn't hit. But he was shaking.

'Piss off.'

His hand was shaking furiously when it pointed at him through the hatch.

'Just piss off, pig.'

LENNART OSCARSSON HAD stopped counting.

His whole working life, he'd read through the Transport Services lists and then totted up the number of years that were leaving to continue elsewhere and the number of years that were arriving to be longed away under lock and key. But he who was so fond of routines, who was in fact utterly dependent on them, had barely a week earlier put that particular day's lists to one side, and from that morning on had quite simply decided not to count and hadn't done so since. That was an evening and a night and a dawn since three inmates had escaped from Block D, since they had stabbed someone, taken a hostage and decided that one of his employees had no days left to live. And after that, thinking about *their* time, trying to understand how the inmates felt, was suddenly of no interest. Each and every one of them could from that morning on do their time and he would never allow himself to be part of it.

He stretched, and through the large window in his governor's office at Aspsås prison, tried to follow the steps of a young man across the asphalt square between the prison gate and central security. Handcuffs, body cuff, leg cuffs. Oscarsson had earlier that morning received information from Kronoberg remand prison that Leon Jensen had run amok in his cell the night before, been violent and aggressive, had threatened to kill the staff, broken everything in the cell that could be broken, bed, chair, basin, how he'd banged his head off the concrete wall, and then with a bloody forehead and cheeks been pressed back against that very same wall by the remand wardens armed with mattresses, had been sedated by a doctor armed with a syringe of

597

CPZ, and then when he was unconscious, had been carried to a padded cell with restraints.

The young man was closer now, in front of the central security window and exactly two storeys down from Oscarsson's window. It was obvious from the way he dragged his feet and tossed his head when he tried to avoid getting light in his eyes that the CPZ was still working.

The prison governor stood very still.

His hands gripped the window sill, he pressed his forehead to the glass. He had never previously felt like this about a prisoner.

Fury.

Sharp, messy, insistent, peculiar absolute fury.

He who had been so careful day to day. Never personal. Always professional. Always, always, with every individual inmate, don't see someone bad, see someone who has done something bad.

He couldn't.

He ran to the door and down the stairs and to the reception area and Leon Jensen who was standing in the middle of the concrete floor with his arms out to either side and a prison warden's latex-clad finger looking in every bodily orifice.

'You . . .'

The naked body dropped its arms and turned around. The face almost relaxed, eyes distant.

The drug would do its work for a few hours yet.

'We're not finished here.'

The prison warden with a latex glove in one of Jensen's armpits looked at his boss, and Oscarsson took a step back, nodded, he would wait, the mouth, the anus and the scalp, it never took long.

The fury.

He couldn't shake it off.

Lennart Oscarsson waited between the lockers and the barred window behind a teenager who held his arms out like this and bent over like this, like so many times before. He focused largely on his legs, a huge new tattoo on the right thigh and something smaller on the left thigh that the owner obviously wanted to be rid of, an infected wound and a hard scab that would soon be picked off again.

'You killed one of us.'

She had sat on the sofa in his office, looked at him, a voice that was easy to like, calm and matter-of-fact and more mature than her twenty-one years.

'Yes.'

The relaxed face looked at him, the naked body stretched, Oscarsson was sure of it, he was . . . proud.

'I did.'

'Then . . . then you killed a policeman in Råby, whom I liked a lot.'

'Yeah. First her. Then him.'

The relaxed face looked at the prison governor, *proud*, then at the two prison wardens who were standing so close.

She had been their colleague. It could have been one of them.

It hadn't been her in particular, they knew that, it had been her in her capacity as someone who happened to be there and could be used and then thrown to one side.

And they found it hard to stand still, in uniform and under the supervision of their boss, they couldn't help but throw his new clothes at him a little too hard, hold him a little too roughly, perhaps even push him in front of them in such a way that his head hit the doorframe, that some blood trickled down his teeth and lip when he looked at Oscarsson.

'She was lying down, the screw bitch. On her left side, I think. But the pig man, he was sitting, so I heard, leaned up against the wall.'

Lennart Oscarsson clenched one hand around the bars across the window, the other balled deep in his right trouser pocket. He looked at the two wardens who were shaking for a long time, then at the young, proud face.

And then he lowered his voice.

He knew that when someone doesn't hear even when a mouth shouts out loud, then the only thing to do is whisper.

'You are not going to have it easy here.'

THE DOOR WAS shut, but not locked.

He sat down on a mattress on the stone floor of a cell that had been cleared and cleaned, but still lacked a sink, wardrobe, table, chair, lamp, bed. He could scream. Maybe even threaten them. They were expecting that. The thin mattress was the only thing that resembled furniture and both screws had looked smug when they said that. Cell 2. One of the ones they hadn't managed to repair yet after the riot a few days ago.

Leon didn't scream.

He got up, looked at the metal door and the barred window and the prison yard and the wall.

A fucking cell with a fucking mattress in the fucking corner.

And he felt nothing.

———

Over the past few hours he'd heard the others coming back, one by one. Some from the classroom, most from the workshop. He'd stayed on the mattress and listened to the sounds he knew so well and was part of, someone playing cards, someone having a shower, someone laughing too loud, someone going out to the kitchen to get some food. But he didn't participate. Not yet. Leon opened the door and went out into a corridor with both half-open and closed cell doors. He passed them one after the other and stopped in front of Cell 10, right at the end of the row of even numbers.

He'd heard him. He knew he was there.

———

Leon didn't knock.

The skinny shoulders and dirty, straggly hair, Smackhead was sitting with his back to the door, but turned towards the sound of steps coming into his cell.

The ravaged face that twitched from the eye down the cheek.

He looked scared when he smiled.

'Don't fucking smile at me. You know that.'

Smackhead looked down, away.

'Stop fucking smiling!'

Leon went closer, he could have hit him if he wanted, but he didn't do it.

He tested his voice, first quietly inside, he wanted to be absolutely sure that it would carry, then out loud.

'I want you to make something for me.'

———————

The man who was sitting there and was now called Sonny Steen and who had, a few weeks earlier, built first a tattoo machine from a Braun shaver and then a cutting torch from empty bottles, felt pens and a vacuum cleaner lead, looked at him and shook his head and smiled like he always did.

———————

'A zip gun.'

That fucking smile.

'I want you to make a zip gun for me.'

'No.'

'No?'

The smile, it was still there.

'No.'

———————

He hit him.

He'd thought about it all night and morning, how it would feel.

He didn't feel anything.

———

'*You're going to make me a fucking zip gun.*'

There was blood on Smackhead's forehead, and cheek, and neck. And he smiled. Because he didn't know how not to.

'Who?'

Leon looked at him, didn't reply.

'Who are you going to use it on?'

He still felt nothing when he left the cell and passed the three intervening doors, when he opened the door to Cell 2 and sank down onto the thin mattress that filled the void in one corner.

He couldn't get any further away.

The closed metal door was cool against his back when he leaned against it, he had never stood like this before, not in someone else's cell, and if he was to guess, it was two, maybe two and a half metres to the barred window.

Leon tried to feel something.

Anything.

The thin shoulders in front of him, arms, hand that carefully placed one part at a time on the unmade bed, slow, exaggerated movements. Breathing with deep sighs, that fucking fucking smile, eyes and cheeks caught in irregular spasms.

He tried to hate.

'You, Smackhead . . . *make it.*'

It had taken the fucking junkie barely twenty-four hours to get all the parts. Now he was squatting down with them in his hands, moving them around on the bed, shaking his smiling head.

'Don't think so. Don't think so at all. Two hundred and fifty g. Remember the cutting torch?'

*'You got everything?'*

*Glass bottles. Felt pens. Vacuum cleaner lead. Electrical tape. Nail clippers. Carbon rods.*

*'I've got everything.'*

'If you do, if you remember, then you'll maybe remember that you owe me something?'

*'I want half a kilo.'*
*'You want to be part of this? Or what?'*
*'Yes.'*
*'Then you'll get two hundred and fifty.'*

'And . . . if you remember the cutting torch, and you remember your small debt, then maybe you'll also remember things didn't happen quite the way we'd agreed. You escaped – and I stayed here.'

*The one who was waving, then banging frantically on his window. The lips forming the words 'I'm supposed to be coming with you.' Leon who looked at the face that always smiled, hated it, turned around.*

Leon pressed harder against the metal door that was already closed, he couldn't get any further away from a smile that had frozen.

He tried to hate again. He wanted to hate again.

But he still felt nothing.

Vile-smelling Smackhead who was just sitting there on his knees and putting all the parts in the right order on his bed, not even hate.

'So . . . you owe me two hundred and fifty grams from before the escape that wasn't like I thought it would be. And for this, a zip gun . . . I want two kilos.'

He held out a metal pipe, some screws.

'I've made nine of these before now. Different prisons and the same result. They work, boy. Most recently, Kumla, a few years ago, the screws, the whole bloody prison service, the journalists . . . they were running around thinking that the gun that was used had been smuggled in. You know . . . from outside. And every time . . . two kilos.'

*Boy.*

The metal door was still as cold, but he looked at the pipe and screws in Smackhead's hands, and then at the other things on the sheet and maybe he wasn't exactly warm, maybe it wasn't that, but he wasn't freezing any more.

'You see . . . I won't do it otherwise, boy. You can hit me as much as you like.'

Out there, through the cell window, the creeping dark, his second evening back at Aspsås already.

Leon took a step closer.

More than a metre between them, but as if they were on top of each other.

'I've emptied Block D, Smackhead. Block G. Block H. Three hundred and fifty grams. There isn't any more.'

'You owe two hundred and fifty. And two kilos for this.'

'*There isn't any more*. Three hundred and fifty now. The rest when you get out.'

The spasms in his face.

The smile.

'How about we say – this has thirteen parts. But I'll make it in seven stages, so it'll be easier for you to calculate.'

Smackhead nodded at the unmade bed and a fifteen-centimetre-long hollow metal pipe, two sawn-off pieces of solid iron piping, a steel spring, a .22 calibre bullet, a bolt, a nut, a washer, a concrete nail, four small screws.

'You give me fifty g, and I'll put together one part. You give me another fifty g, and I'll put together the next part. When it's done, I'll have got three hundred and fifty gs. And I'll get the rest when I'm out. How's that sound?'

Leon took another step forwards.

So close.

He could punch the shit out of him. Maybe even kick the shit.

He didn't do it.

He put ten yellow and white capsules down on one of the pillows on the other end of the unmade bed.

'Ten capsules. Fifty grams.'

Smackhead's arm was shaking when he reached out and his fingers clawed them in and held hard. Then he giggled, not particularly loud, but enough to cut a great hole in Leon's brain.

He could beat him to shit. He could.

---

The skinny hand held up the fifteen-centimetre-long hollow pipe that until this morning had been one of four legs on one of the regular iron chairs in the dining hall, and that he'd drilled two holes in this morning at his workplace in the prison workshop, one at each end, then drilled another three closer to the middle, and then finally, where his finger was resting now, he had sawed a two-centimetre channel.

A pipe with a total of six holes and he ran his fingers up and down between them, a constant grin on his lips that were as tight as the white, clutching fingers and looked at his visitor, expectantly.

He could hit him. Beat the shit out of him.

Leon followed the thin hand, the sawn-off chair leg, met the smile. And put ten yellow and white capsules in the same place he had previously, and when the giggle that cut through his brain was on the way out he'd already decided that it couldn't be heard.

---

Smackhead now lifted up one of the bolts and screwed it into one of the pre-drilled holes on the metal pipe, the one at the very end that would take the force of the whole bolt mechanism, the steel spring.

Ten capsules.

---

One of the pieces of short, solid iron piping, the one that was three centimetres long and a few hours earlier had been part of one of the forklift trucks in the laundry and was now lying close to the head of the bed with a new drill hole from one end to the other, thin fingers holding it, pressing in a concrete nail from the hand towel holder in the shower room and a metal circuit board that had been on the TV cable, a pungent smell of glue between each part.

Ten capsules.

Thin fingers threading the nine-centimetre steel spring from the unit's hair clippers round the nut.

Ten capsules.

Thin fingers holding up the metal piping with the bolt and cement nail and steel spring and nut, the gun's bolt mechanism, feeding it into the long, hollow pipe.

Ten capsules.

Thin fingers picking the last piece of lead piping from the sheet, the one from the laundry's other forklift, four and a half centimetres long, and the gun's barrel, with a drill hole to fit a .22 calibre bullet that he'd collected from Petrovic in Block F at lunch and now carefully inserted.

Ten capsules.

———————

He giggled as he pushed the bolt mechanism into the chair leg until the spring was coiled, then pushed in the barrel, fixed the pieces of metal together with four small screws, giggled again and held out a finished zip gun.

———————

'The Count, that was his name, it was a bloody long time ago, in Hall prison, I think, he was the one who taught me.'

He was holding three hundred and fifty grams of amphetamines in one hand, the pistol in the other.

'Nine. Made *inside* the walls.'

He was almost smiling for real.

'Three unsolved murders. Two escapes from maximum security prisons. One escape from a young offenders' institution. Two for . . . well, debt collection. And one which . . . which I can't say what the fuck it was used for.'

He held the pistol out a bit further.

'The tenth. Who?'

Leon leaned against the metal door that wouldn't go any further back.

'Who are you going to use this on?'

He looked at the piece of metal, at the fucking bastard smile.

'My dad.'

IT WAS DARKER, dusk on its way into late evening, it was no longer possible to see the wall from the cell window. And out there in the corridor, behind his back, the screws preparing for lock-up.

He didn't have much time.

'I asked *who*.'

'And I answered.'

The skinny hand was still holding the pistol it had just made in a firm grip.

'I asked who you were going to use it on?'

'And I answered. *My dad*.'

That fucking smile, even when someone only a few metres from him shook their head.

'That's no fucking answer.'

'It's the only answer you'll get.'

The yellow teeth, the laboured breathing.

'OK. OK, boy.'

He prodded his young visitor in the chest with the pistol.

'Do you want it then?'

'When you've put the trigger on.'

Smackhead was breathing heavily, this was going well, he was the one who decided.

'Oh . . . you want a trigger as well? But that's not so . . . ah yes, that's right . . . your currency, your speed, it ran out, didn't it?'

Leon raised his arm.

Not yet.

Not before it was ready.

'I've paid three hundred and fifty. There *is no more* in here.'

Not before next week.

'Your chain.'

Smackhead giggled again, pointed a yellowed finger at Leon's throat, almost touched it.

'If you take off your gold chain. And put it down there on the bed. Then I might be able to find and attach a trigger.'

Not yet. *Not yet.*

Leon undid the heavy clasp on his chain, weighed it in his hand, threw it down on the disarray of sheets.

'Well done, son. You can do it.'

The skinny body in the middle of the bed, holding the gold chain in both hands, the thickest gold chain in the unit and the last symbol of authority that someone who now reigned would take from someone who until recently had reigned. Trembling fingertips as they fastened the chain round his neck and let the soft metal slip between them, a warm buzz like the one that filled him when he injected Koffazon, anyone who owned a chain like this was really someone and you'd do business with them, they carried the security for every deal round their neck.

'The trigger.'

'In a minute.'

The final piece was lying on the crumpled sheet. One of the bolts. Thin fingers dug it out, screwed it into the last hole on the bolt mechanism leaving a few centimetres free – the head of the bolt had to stand clear, so that the marksman could hold it.

———

He tried to feel something, wanted to feel something.

He felt nothing.

Not even when he turned the pistol on someone who was sitting on a bed giggling with a gold chain round his neck.

'You.'

The chain, it was so nice, fingers holding it tight.

'It's you I'm going to use this on.'

He obviously hadn't heard.

'It's . . .'

'Me?'

'Yes.'

He had heard. But hadn't quite understood yet.

'What the fuck—'

'I said, didn't I? I was going to use it on my dad.'

He wasn't giggling any longer. He sighed, shrugged.

'Listen son, I haven't got any kids.'

Leon tried to meet the eyes that constantly evaded.

'Ana.'

'What?'

'Ana Tomas.'

The bony shoulders shrugged again.

But this time, the shrug of someone who has heard, has maybe even understood and is trying not to show it.

'Who the hell is she?'

'My mum. She was seventeen. She did time in Hinseberg.'

'I don't know what you're talking about.'

A spasm, a shrug again.

'I don't *have* any fucking children.'

'She was in Hinseberg.'

'I've never *had* any fucking children.'

'And I—'

'No kids. *Do you hear me?*'

'—I was born there.'

————

They looked at each other for a long time.

Even when Leon put his finger on the bolt and slowly released the zip gun's trigger.

————

He felt nothing.

———

Not even when he put the pistol to his own forehead and released the bolt completely, when the smile in front of him slowly became blurred, disappeared.

# now

## part six

### (four hours)

WHAT HAD BEEN blue and then turned yellow was now nearly brown. When she let her fingertips gently follow the skin over her face, hip, pelvis, it was still very tender and swollen. He had hit her and kicked her. For the first time. She was the only one left.

Ana had for nearly a week now sat in a soft sofa and watched the news specials on all the channels on TV. A young woman in a blue uniform in a car boot. A middle-aged man blown up in a police station. And then a face, *his* face, a black and white photograph from the Prison Service archives, together with *his* voice on a recording from the car that the young, pale woman had been lying in.

He had been eighteen.

In one month and three days he would have been nineteen.

When he smiled – as he sometimes had – the cleft in his chin had deepened and his upper lip stretched and was narrower than his lower lip. And when he talked he made the emphasis hard – well, only with some vowels, really – so the words were longer. And when he was small, every time he was a bit thirsty, he'd pushed the milk to one side and demanded rosehip soup – she'd known that it wasn't particularly helpful, but had some-times given in and he'd been so happy, balancing the too-big glass in his small hands.

She got up and left without turning off the TV, out into the hall and her coat.

I had a child. I have no children.

She'd followed him as far as she could. She had been a mother who also worked for the authority that was responsible for him until he was fifteen and when the others had gone home, she often stayed sitting at her desk well into the evening and night, with the green and red files on her knees. And she had, when he became criminally responsible and left the desks of the Social Services for those of the Police Authority and Prison Service, met regularly and spoken with José Pereira, and with his help been able to sit and hold other files.

```
Criminal network of young men who have
grown up in different Stockholm suburbs,
with Råby as the hub.
```

Just one of them.

Just one gang of so many in this area alone.

```
Two identified leaders. Leon Jensen.
Gabriel Milton. Both eighteen years old.
Both classified as dangerous.
```

The last time they had met, Pereira had counted seventeen active groups in the southern suburbs of Stockholm that would soon become twenty, twenty-five.

```
Prognosis: continued development in
serious crime, prison, short life
expectancy.
```

And then he'd shown her another file, a joint report by the police and the government about the other five thousand boys from all the other Råbys who right now, today, were being recruited into the criminal networks they had so long yearned to be part of.

Ana listened to the sound of the TV, opened the front door.

Pull down in order to build up.

She started to walk towards someone who was waiting for her.

He had seen a policeman sitting on the floor with his life in his lap and then a woman's beaten body. *Why do you bother putting them out?* He had been reachable, decided to listen. *So your job is to protect Råby, even when the people who live here want it to burn?* For all these years, he had tried to pour water on fires in a world that the young people were trying to burn down as they somehow believed that it was in the way. *You stand there and put out burning mopeds and fences and rubbish bins ten times a day. And still you don't understand? That what's happening will carry on happening until someone makes sure that it won't happen any more.*

Thom followed the asphalt path between the buildings in a neighbourhood he visited several times a day, stopped for a while by a pile of black, sooty metal, which had once been a car and now lacked any colour whatsoever as the paint had quickly burnt off.

Empty holes where the windows had blown out. The hose beside it, cut off. And the text, someone had written in the soot with a finger, *pig bastards.*

He carried on past a container that had been set alight the night before and hid the remains of bulky waste that hadn't actually burnt itself but had carried the flames to the next building – a nursery that normally accommodated seventy children. He wondered where they were now, if they were at home, if they had been squeezed into other already overfull places.

The body of a building with no roof or walls. Toys making splashes of red and yellow in the black.

He stopped again, put down his bag, two mothers and a father with four children between them had arrived and pointed and explained until one of them climbed over the cordons and walked cautiously towards the skeleton of the building, looked for something, bent down and picked it up, put it in a four-year-old hand. Thom stretched up and tried to see but couldn't – something black and sooty that was no longer lost.

He carried on past the moped from yesterday and the rubbish bins from last week and the kiosk that had stood there, half razed, for nearly six months now.

He saw her already from a distance.

She was standing outside the entrance to Råby Allé 12, and it seemed that she had seen him too.

———————

They didn't embrace each other, they weren't that close.

Nor did they take each other by the hand, because for someone who had decided to do what these two were about to do, that distance no longer existed.

They didn't greet each other at all.

They would never again see one another once it was all over.

———————

Thom walked beside her into the stairwell.

Four days ago she had stood naked in front of him and demanded that he look, forced him to see until he couldn't take any more; he had followed her home and listened to a person who didn't want to hurt anyone, only buildings.

They hadn't seen each other since.

They didn't need to, they had decided.

———————

Ana walked past the lift and down the first flight of stairs, stopped and pressed the call button for the lift and then waited until it came, opened the door and held it open while Thom opened the locked door onto an empty lift shaft one floor up, with a key that looked like the one he normally bled the radiators with. One step out onto the roof of the lift, right foot towards the round, red button for emergency stop, then one step back. He closed the door and walked beside her even further down into the depths of the building, the lower cellar.

The square metal key again, and Thom opened the door to the lift shaft. *How many others have you told about this?* He climbed in and down into the one-metre-deep hole. *No one. No one?* What she had shown him in the course of a conversation that had lasted seven hours. *If I talk about it . . . I'm dead. You, of all people, should know that.*

He lifted off the black blankets and took a five-centimetre aluminium pipe with two thin wires, one green, one white, out of a wooden box, and a considerably longer round red stick from a cardboard box. He stood at the bottom of the lift shaft and pressed the detonator into the dynamite stick, screwing in the last part. He was given a mobile phone and a roll of tape and some scissors, checked that the transfer function was working and then taped the telephone to the stick of dynamite and cut the wires at one end of the detonator. He bent down and put the taped package into one of two sacks of bulk industrial explosives, then put the other on top.

'Two sacks. Fifty kilos.'

He put the black blankets back on top to hide what was there.

'An explosion in a lift shaft. One of the load-bearing elements of a building.'

He climbed up and out, closed and locked the door.

'The whole of the ground floor will be lifted and then . . . the building will collapse.'

---

They carried on to Råby Allé 25. To Råby Allé 34. To Råby Allé 57, 76 and 102. Six stairwells in six entrances connected by an underground garage, and a lift shaft in each that contained the same secret. A criminal gang's explosives store.

The same procedure in each place.

The detonator was screwed into a stick of dynamite, the wires cut and a mobile phone taped on, and then each package placed in a large sack. The only thing that made the other five stairs different from the first was that there was only one twenty-five kilo sack, rather than two, which would only half explode the building.

And before he closed and locked every lift door, he checked that the mobile phone's calls were transferred to the next one along.

They hurried together towards the large garage.

Thom calculated as they walked – a total of one hundred and seventy-five kilos of explosives, he guessed from some of the various tunnel construction sites to the south of the city – seven kilos of dynamite, probably from one of the E4's many road-works between Skärholmen and Södertälje – and a couple of thousand detonators, stolen from any large building site.

———

A concrete garage is so different at night, empty of voices, full of cars.

A silence that amplifies every scraping sound, every footstep, runs wild, echoes.

Thom took from his bag a thick roll of white cotton rope, the sort that's used as a wick in paraffin lamps, only a considerably thinner version. First he cut six pieces of equal length, three metres each, and walked towards the car nearest the lift shaft that they had just left. A broad screwdriver to open the tank cap and drop in the cotton wick that then started to soak up the petrol – then he carried on to the next car, forced open the petrol tank cap and dropped in the other end of the cotton rope. The same procedure by the other five entrances where the lift shaft was full of suitably prepared explosives – two cars close to the door, forced petrol caps, a long, white, petrol-drenched cotton wick joining them together.

Then he divided the rest of the cotton rope into six more pieces, shorter this time, a metre or two each, and tied them to the first piece, so that eventually by all six entrances there were two cars joined from tank to tank by a piece of rope with another piece in the middle that just touched the floor, trailing slightly on the grey concrete.

'Now it's your turn.'

Thom came back to the first pair of cars, with a large bottle of transparent liquid in his hand, and gave it to Ana.

'Start to pour out the contents when I go back to the station.'

He pointed to the piece of rope that was trailing on the floor, then towards the middle of garage, and started to walk.

'Pour it in a narrow strip from where the rope touches the ground to about here.'

He stopped about a parking space away from each car.

'Do the same thing six times. Paraffin. That's what you'll be pouring out. From the short rope, all the way here.'

Thom opened the bottle and turned it upside down, two lines like a cross on the floor.

'Six lines of paraffin will meet exactly here.'

He checked his watch.

'And you have to be finished precisely fifteen minutes after I've left.'

A cigarette lighter in his hand.

'You set light to the middle of the cross. And then take it and the bottle with you. No traces.'

He went down on his knees and pointed the lighter at the dust and gravel on the concrete floor.

'Hold it here for at least five seconds and then you'll see a clear blue flame.'

A quick check over the twelve linked cars by six stairwell entrances.

'Thirty metres. That means between fifteen to twenty seconds before the flame reaches each petrol tank.'

Her pale cheeks, heavy breathing. And she was the one who had always been so strong, so sure, so determined.

Now so agitated.

He looked at her.

'A car fire – afterwards no one will see anything apart from just that. We put out burning metal several times a week.'

And he lowered his voice.

'The flames will move towards the petrol tanks, but you will have plenty of time to get out of here and to check that no one else comes in. It's always the petrol fumes that burn first, not the petrol itself, a car has to burn for a long time before the tank really goes up.'

She nodded, the disquiet at once determination again, and he continued.

'And that is when, exactly when, you'll raise the alarm, when you'll ring 112.'

———

*They stood there in the dark garage, on either side of lines that formed a cross of paraffin,*

'I remember, I don't think I'll ever forget him, my first day at work after four years in Hinseberg and then just as long training to be a social worker, the first visit to my office in Botkyrka Social Services. A boy, he sat on one of my new office chairs and was so . . . small, so thin, his mother beside him and a policeman opposite. He was ten years old and after refusing to answer a few questions, he looked at them both long and hard, and then for the first time looked at me and he was so proud and he wanted us to listen, that he'd decided that when he was grown up, he was going to rob CVIT vans.'

'I'll take your call, and ninety seconds later I'll be in the truck. When we leave the fire station, I'll call the police and explain to them that the six stairwells nearest the source of the fire have to be emptied and all the tenants evacuated, that the shared garage is now a powerful blow torch and the lifts are conduits for poisonous smoke.'

*they both knew that they had decided and they probably also talked together,*

'I also remember, around the same time as the boy who was going to be a CVIT robber when he grew up, there was a lot of talk about moving the authorities out to the suburbs, that somehow that would be a way of acknowledging the suburbs, you know, they work here between eight and four and then go home to Täby and Nacka and live their lives there until they come back the next day and carry on talking, and to be fair, they did move a police station out here, and that is perhaps an authority, but the rest, they're still all dotted around the city centre.'

'That's exactly what I'll say, a powerful blow torch and conduits for poisonous smoke, as that's precisely how the fire will behave. And everyone who sees it will assume that it was the heat from the fire that caused it, even though flames don't make explosives explode. It's energy that makes it explode and you need *a lot* of fire and *a lot* of heat to do that, more than this fire will ever produce. Your neighbours will be evacuated in good time. And everyone who saw it will have seen a dangerous fire that caused the explosives stored in six lift shafts to explode.'

*it was hard to tell,*

'I'm thinking about the picture of that young woman, her blue uniform, so still, and that the outside world has been confronted with her over and over again this past week and that what has always been *here* has now for a short while also been *there*. I think that they'll be able to see it now when they come to *our streets* – boys who want to work with CVIT robbery. When it gets like London last summer, and it has been for a long time in the States, and just recently in Copenhagen. I think that if it's there and people outside really see it, then we can also stop it without doing any harm.'

'I want you, and this is the first thing you must do when you've raised the alarm, to run to the doors in every stairwell that we've been to, and open them wide. That is essential. You have to check and make sure. Six metal doors wide open.'

*they at least looked at each other,*

'I'm thinking about a boy who wanted to work in CVIT robbery and all the others who have sat in my office with a mother and a policeman and been him. I'm thinking that if you are exposed to crime and see the benefits, then it's more likely that you will develop criminal tendencies, and if you're *not* exposed and *don't* see the gains, then the probability is smaller. And I'm thinking that if the exposure disappears altogether, if it doesn't exist . . . do you understand me?'

'I will know when all the tenants have been evacuated and then wait until I have confirmation that every flat has been checked. When I've got that . . . we'll detonate them.'

*and they probably listened, before they started to talk again.*

'I live here. I've lived here since I moved away from home. Those colourless square blocks are my home and I sleep in there and drink my morning coffee in there and I'll pull them down to build them up again.'

'I'll see the buildings explode. One after the other. And it won't get any worse, there won't be any more, the aggressive garage fire that we have not yet managed to control will suddenly go out. The explosions, the blast wave after the explosions, will extinguish the fire.'

*They were still standing on either side of the thin lines of paraffin. They were still talking.*
*And it was still difficult to tell, it was, whether they listened before they started to talk again.*

———

'One of the lift shafts is in your building.'

'Yes.'

'That house will also explode and go on fire.'

'Yes.'

———

'I'm going to go back now. To Södertörn fire station. When you've raised the alarm, you'll be taken to Råby school sports hall, in the first instance. When I come there and you see me and I nod to you, you'll know that *everyone* has been evacuated. Then it's your turn again. Then you'll make the phone call.'

He rolled up the left sleeve of his shirt.

'My watch says that it's exactly zero three sixteen. This will be over by . . . zero four thirty, at the latest.'

He looked at her, no hand in hers, not even on her shoulder, they didn't know each other in that way and they were only going to see each other once more, at a distance, in a sports hall full of other people.

SHE HAD JUST closed the door to a flat on the third floor that wasn't very many steps from a lift that was hiding a large store of explosives at the bottom of the shaft. She went down the hall and into the kitchen and had sat down at the table with a big, cold cup of coffee when she heard the first siren. And she did what she had always done, stood up and went over to the window and peered into the dark, looking for the smoke and flames, trying to remember how many times it had been in the last twenty-four hours.

Five fire engines, more than normal.

Ana saw them drive towards the garage and a couple of buildings further down, but one drove straight towards her and stopped outside her entrance.

It appeared that someone had started a fire in the garage, maybe one of the cars, and the flames had spread to several stairwells.

---

She counted the minutes, but still didn't know how long. The time it took to drink a cup of cold coffee. That was when she heard the first footsteps on the stairs.

Someone rang her bell.

She took her time, after all, she was asleep, took off her clothes, put on her nightie, ruffled her hair, now she had just woken up, walked towards the door, opened it.

It smelt of smoke and she thought she could almost see it, not especially thick, but visible.

A policeman and a firefighter, both in uniform, she didn't know either of them, they didn't know her.

It was the policeman who spoke. He was tall and pale and not much older than her own son. Than her own son would have been.

'There's a fire in the garage under the building, under the whole street. It's starting to spread up here. We have to evacuate the building. Please could you get a coat and follow us.'

When she looked out, past the uniforms, more tenants were waiting there, she counted eleven neighbours, the ones she never spoke to, but who lived their separate lives only metres away. She got her red jacket from the hat shelf, it already smelt of the smoke she was now walking through, then a pair of white plimsolls that probably smelt the same, she went out and followed the group down the stairs.

I have done what I can.

For every floor down, the smell of smoke got stronger and more obvious and a rumbling sound that got louder, she knew what it was as it sounded just like she'd had it described to her – the fire getting closer to the lift shaft. When she opened the entrance door to go out, she paused, tried to see two floors down to the bottom of the lift and to what was lying there under a black blanket.

I have done what I can and those who gave up, those who said *this is not our problem, sort it out yourselves, you're the ones doing each other harm*, they will now be forced to come back.

The blue and white police van had nine seats and she had to stand, they weren't going very far.

———

Ana sat on the floor in a corner of Råby sports hall, near to one of the handball goals and a small, dim room with vaulting boxes and high jump frames. It wasn't squashed but there were enough bodies for everyone to have to stand or sit or lie next to someone they didn't know. She'd tried to count, maybe four hundred, a couple of dozen dogs and as many cats, a whole aviary of caged birds and the boy sitting beside her had a small aquarium in his arms.

And yet, so quiet.

They didn't seem to be frightened, more restless, confused bodies that had been asleep and were looking for calm again.

They had no idea what was about to happen.

———

She found herself looking towards the big entrance doors at the other end of the sports hall, more and more often. *When I come there and you see me and I nod to you, you'll know* everyone *has been evacuated. Then it's your turn again. Then you'll make the phone call.* Apart from the clock, there were some scoreboards on the wall next to a basketball basket, fifty-two minutes, there couldn't be many more people to evacuate.

———

She didn't see him at first.

For a moment she had her gaze fixed on the boy's aquarium, one black and one gold fish, crispy flakes from a red tin and the little boy's hand that fed them often and plenty.

Then she saw the tall fireman.

Quietly searching the hall, and she stood up and they looked at each other briefly, it was enough.

She was to ring now.

———

She waved at the boy with the goldfish as she passed and he waved back. She tiptoed between two elderly women who were settling down on the sports hall floor to try and get some sleep, and then took a long step over a man who was already snoring. The small room with the vaults and high jump frames was about as out of the way as she could get in a hall with four hundred tenants and their pets. She sat down on the box for red footballs, the mobile phone in her hand and the number she'd been given when he stood by her front door. She dialled the number and waited.

'Grens. City Police.'

He'd answered immediately. He'd been awake. But his voice was deeper than she remembered, as if he was lying down.

'I want to talk to you.'

'Right.'

She had spoken to him six times in nineteen years.

When he forced her onto the kitchen floor. When he questioned her, watched her son being born, when he delivered him back having acted as a babysitter for a couple of weeks in a flat in Sveavägen. When he had come to her shortly after the escape from Aspsås prison and the day before Leon was arrested, he had come to her again and explained that an eighteen-year-old boy who had once been her son was at risk of dying if he *wasn't* arrested.

Six times.

This would be the seventh.

'Do you have a pen?'

Ana heard the cumbersome body get up, limp a few steps, and then a drawer being opened.

'Yes.'

'I want you to ring me. On this number: 0704244818. In exactly ten minutes.'

He was breathing heavily. He was tired.

'What's it concerning?'

*If you need any help, call me.*

'You'll understand then.'

'If you want me to call, you'll tell me what it's about.'

'You've come to me in the past couple of days. You've wanted to talk to me. Now it's my turn to talk to you. About what we spoke about last time. That only the one who started all this can put a stop to it.'

'If you—'

She hung up.

The mobile phone gave off a faint light in her hand in the dark room.

In ten minutes.

———

She had stood at the back of a hall full of tired people.

They had looked at each other. He had nodded almost imperceptibly and she had nodded equally vaguely back.

Now it was her turn.

Thom had then carried on up the stairs, stopped at the top by the exit to the upper gallery. The large window, the one that opened in, from here he could see the whole of Råby Allé, dark clouds of smoke blanketing the empty concrete blocks.

He looked at his watch.

Four minutes to go until a call was made to a mobile phone that had been transferred.

He leaned out into the September night. He had just ordered all the firefighters who were extinguishing the fire by the first lift shaft to move into the second section of the underground garage in a concerted effort to put out two new fires that had just started after he'd prepped two more cars with cotton rope and paraffin, and then hurried over to Råby school sports hall to give her the all-clear. And the others – who were near the five other lift shafts that would follow the first at ten-second intervals – would in accordance with security instructions run out and away from the buildings when they heard the first explosion.

Two minutes left.

All the tenants had been evacuated. And all the firefighters would be at a safe distance from the six lift shafts.

*If no one is to be harmed.*

Thom leaned out even further, a gentle breeze on his face. He breathed in the faint smell of smoke. And was just about to stretch up a bit more when all of the windows in one of the blocks were blown out at the same time, glass like raindrops to the ground, and the blast wave, a powerful wind that lasted only a moment.

By the time the sound of the explosion reached them, the walls of the building had cracked.

The phone call had been made a bit early, but the effect was the same.

Råby Allé 12, a building with two twenty-five kilo sacks of bulk industrial explosives in one of the lift shafts, was still shaking when the body of the house fell into the load-bearing lift shaft and started to collapse.

Slowly at first, and then, at least so it seemed from one of the open windows at the sports hall, ever faster.

# one day later

THE METRO WAS working again.

One night, one day.

No trains, no carriages, no people.

He was twelve years old and sure that it had never been like that before. Certainly not as long as he'd been around. Maybe not even before that.

Råby without the metro was like his body without a heart. Blood on the way in, on the way out, that needed to be pumped out with vigour and returned tired to be pumped back out again. When he got out of the carriage and stood on the platform, it smelt good, like metros do.

The first night they'd been on mattresses on the floor of Råby school sports hall, some people had slept on the wooden pews in the church beside the petrol station, others in the library at Alby, in the tennis hall at Hallunda, in the caravans by Eriksbergs industrial estate, some had even slept in the corridors of the fire station. He and his mum and Diana were going to move to the house on the outskirts of Norsborg this evening, before tomorrow night, it was to be their home for the next six months until Råby Allé 102 had been rebuilt – he had seen the entrance and lift, just rubble.

Eddie walked down the steps and stopped as he often did by the exit, out of sight of the ticket collector. He counted down out loud, started at sixty and hadn't stood there for more than three minutes when the skinny guy with short hair who sweated so grossly almost ran into him.

'Seven.'

They hadn't even said hello. Eddie held out his hand, waited.

'I want seven.'

'When you've said hello.'

The see-through hand, skin that grated.

'Seven.'

'You know that it's five or ten.'

'Ten.'

'Eight thousand. You got it?'

The guy who was always sweating and shaking dug into his pocket, held out his roll of notes, five thousand six hundred kronor, which would have been just enough for seven grams.

'I said I wanted seven.'

An outstretched boy's hand, on tiptoe when it hit an adult cheek.

'*Eddie's the name. And I sell five or ten.*'

He was twenty-eight, very red on his right cheek and had no idea.

'Five.'

He stuffed one thousand six hundred kronor back into his pocket, held out the rest, waited while the boy in front of him counted the notes.

'Konsum supermarket. Bread section. Under the shelves, a bit to the right.'

It was easy to catch a whiff of him as he disappeared into the shopping centre, heading for the shelves of freshly baked bread, he would soon bend down on his knee on the stone floor, pick loose the package that had recently been taped there. Eddie carried on through the station's dark exit and then it got light, the sun was strong, as it sometimes was. It was easy to see and understand after only a few steps, when all the building that had exploded came into view. His hand through his greased-back hair, gold chain round his neck, he pulled down the zip on his jacket a touch more. He passed the shells of buildings that had been badly damaged and buildings that were whole, and then more that had been badly damaged, and almost liked it – what had exploded and burned in some way belonged to him.

Råby Allé 67.

One of the buildings that was whole, all the tenants had moved back, they'd never stored any explosives in that lift shaft here.

He went into the entrance and into the lift and nodded in the mirror. Every time, it came from inside and he felt it so strongly, he was on his way to Gabriel's flat, to what had been Gabriel's flat; he could see the name SANTOS and he pressed the black bell and after two rings, Bruno opened as Gabriel would have done before and might ask him to stand in the hallway, and they would stand by the shoehorn with the small white pearls and the others would be sitting in there, Jon, Big Ali, they would hear that he'd come and they might say his name.

'In there.'

'In there?'

Bruno had stood in front of him, waiting for the roll of five-hundred-kronor notes in a rubber band, when suddenly he swept his arm between them and pointed in towards the sitting room, even further into their flat.

'Yes. Now.'

In there. No one went in there. Last time they'd put a bullet-proof vest on him and taken out a gun, cocked it and aimed and fired once at his chest and once at his stomach.

He was seldom scared.

He quite simply didn't like the feeling and therefore never was.

This time, he couldn't help it. He swallowed and his heart was pounding.

He looked at Bruno who was still pointing, looked into the room, stumbled a bit on the threshold, regained his balance by putting his hand on the wall.

They were alone.

He didn't stop until he could touch the big sofa and sat down on the edge where he gradually sank down. His fucking fucking heart. He didn't dare look at anything and therefore switched between the TV and the speakers and the pile of films and the spilt beer and the glass table with cigarette stubs in a bowl and peanuts in another.

There were no flowers.

He knew that was a stupid thought but he'd never been in a flat without flowers before, like the window wasn't alive.

Bruno looked at him and sat down as well; he said nothing, just sat there. Eddie looked around the room. No one else. Just Bruno and the window without flowers and a heart that was beating and beating.

That smell. He recognised it.

He relaxed a little. The tin of Rizla papers and leather pouch with tobacco and the small round bottle's three drops of cannabis oil.

Bruno lit it, like Gabriel used to, inhaled.

A half cigarette, Eddie watched the white paper shrink. Until he heard footsteps.

*Until he heard footsteps.*

The kitchen. He was sure of it. Jon. Big Ali. There, through the kitchen door.

The dryness in his mouth.

'Sixteen thousand. Twenty g. And tomorrow . . .'

His heart.

When they looked at him without saying anything and sat down, one on the sofa and one on the chair that was leaning against the wall under the TV.

His fucking fucking heart.

'. . . tomorrow, I'll get the rest, I promise, I . . .'

He held the roll of five-hundred-kronor notes in a rubber band, held it out to Bruno who took it and put it down on the table without counting it.

'It's cool.'

He inhaled again, tobacco, cannabis oil, leaned in closer.

'You do well, every time, for the family. Reliable accounts. No bullshit. Look after our weapons. Stash our hot goods.'

Eddie heard him, he did, but not what he was saying.

'And you haven't talked. You've never talked. Not once. Not even when they questioned us all day.'

Bruno's mouth was moving, Eddie couldn't understand why it was moving.

'And the police station. You kept the bomb. You planted it.'

Eddie left the mouth in favour of the hands, now Bruno's hands were moving, rolling another cigarette, three drops of cannabis oil, lit it and held it out.

'Here.'

Eddie looked at the others who were still sitting there silently, then moved his fingers towards it, round it, a quick puff.

Bruno's hand.

He stretched it out across the table.

'One love, brother.'

Eddie heard it, he did, but he didn't understand.

*One love, brother.*

He looked at Jon. At Big Ali. And back at Bruno and his hand.

Maybe they were smiling.

And now Jon held out his hand.

'One love, brother.'

Big Ali.

'One big love, brother.'

Eddie looked around.

It wasn't Leon. It wasn't Gabriel. Not any more.

*One love, brother.*

It was him. And he was one of them. He had brothers. He had a family. From this evening on, he would have a tattoo on his right thigh.

And he smiled, for the first time in a long time, he smiled and he could feel it way down in his belly, as he sometimes did.

# another day later

IT WAS LIGHT outside.

If he lay down, if he stared hard enough at the blind without blinking either of his eyes, it could for a blurred moment become a blanket that not long ago was red shot with yellow and had a thin white stripe round the edge. He'd never liked that blanket. It hadn't covered the whole dirty window; the sun had forced its way into the room and onto the bed and in between his and Wanda's naked bodies. Now he missed it. Or maybe it was the room he missed. Maybe the days when they lived in the dark and slept through the light and woke again when the evening and night returned.

The blind closed everything in, hid everything outside.

Gabriel blinked and it was clear again.

If he lay on his side, if he looked around the room with a bed and a wardrobe and a basin and a small table and a chair. Cell. But it wasn't, no metal door, no bars in front of the window, but the same emptiness lived here, it stood still, and the same air that he'd breathed in Mariefred prison and Johannisberg secure training unit and Sundbo secure training unit, breath that was black and tasted of dust and was never enough even though he breathed and breathed.

It had been seven days and seven nights now. He was sure of that, because he drew a line with a ballpoint pen on the head of the bed every morning. When he was in hospital he'd been given a piece of paper with four pictures of different houses and a map with four red circles on it and had then been given the choice between a youth hostel some way outside Växjö, one somewhere between Karlstad and Säffle and one between

Hudiksvall and Ljusdal, and then this one that was called Hargebaden, which was quite close to Aksersund. The police-woman had told him that from the same day, Wanda was being held in the women's unit in Kronoberg remand prison and would be charged with serious drug offences and be sentenced to at least four years and a couple of months, and that there was only one possible prison, Hinseberg. This circle on the map had been closest. Eighty-three kilometres. It had been easy to choose and point.

She had been the last one.

On his way from the police headquarters, he had grassed on her too.

But only when he'd understood that she would otherwise give birth and live under constant threat in a Råby that he could never go back to.

The first floor of a yellow wooden house with white frames round every window, door and corner. If he pulled up the blind. Grass and trees and water a hundred metres away, Hargeviken, a big sandy beach; he had walked there once.

Oscar.

Once he'd chosen the youth hostel, he was given another choice, between Oscar, Erik and Carl.

Oscar Hansson.

He couldn't even think it.

He lay on a bed and looked up at the ceiling. He didn't need it. On Tuesdays and Thursdays, the police station in Askersund was open between nine and three and if he wanted to walk along the cobbled streets past the other wooden houses and visit the policeman who was now his contact person, he could. He'd been there a couple of days ago. He probably wouldn't do it again.

He thought about Leon sometimes.

He hadn't understood at first when they sat there talking about him. One of the happy families at the table in the dining room, eating their youth hostel breakfast, as he made his way, thirsty, to the fridge. They were holding the papers and reading out loud to each other about an eighteen-year-old who had escaped and murdered two people and then was himself found dead in a cell in Aspsås prison. Gabriel had heard what they were saying and moved closer to the table and looked at several black and white pictures of Leon's face, but hadn't understood until he got back to his room with the rolled-down blind and lain down on the bed and closed his eyes. He had decided not to feel anything and then lain there all day and all night and occasionally with his fingertips had traced the five round scars from a glowing cigarette pressed against the skin on his face, and could have stayed lying there even longer. Until he couldn't any more. In the morning he'd drawn a line on the head of the bed and breathed in the black and dusty air, and then started to cry silently. Not much, but more than he had done since before the fire and his dad and in a different way from when he'd sat in the car between Råby and Södertälje a couple of weeks ago with a gun loaded with one single bullet and pressed it hard against his temple. He'd sat up on the edge of the bed and forced the fucking tears back down his throat to his chest to his stomach and whispered *I love you, brother* until there was nothing left.

He pulled out the chair by the small table and sat down. Strong sunlight outside, sharp light through the blind fabric. He looked again at the door that wasn't metal, which he could open whenever he wanted and go out. He wouldn't do it today. He'd stay in his room. As he had yesterday. As he would tomorrow. There was nowhere else to go.

That fat fucking pig with the stiff neck and gammy leg had explained that he would live like this. No contact with Råby *meant* no contact with Råby. That someone who first informs on his brothers and then his woman in order to live under a witness protection programme might feel that breathing is black and dusty and give up, relapse, go back.

He wasn't going to do that. He had decided.

He would wait here in an empty house exactly eighty-three kilometres from Hinseberg, close to Wanda who was pregnant and in eight months would give birth to his son in a cell that was much bigger than the others, maybe he would even visit them one day, get to know someone who would get to know him.

# yet another day later

THE BROWN CORDUROY sofa was too soft – especially on the nights when he slept several hours in a row – it was too short – with a stiff left leg that couldn't stretch out – and it was too warm – the fabric was worn and rubbed against his back. But he slept so much better there than anywhere else, he belonged in it in the way that it belonged in the room. It had stood there in the corner, as far from the wardrobe as the window, longer than most people had worked in the building.

Ewert Grens lay down to avoid the piles of paper on the equally ageing coffee table. It didn't move, the letter on top didn't disappear. He'd been standing out in the Homicide corridor, two cups of blackness and an almond slice, when he looked over at his pigeonhole and the note that someone had written encouraging him to empty it. Why do they bother? He'd sighed, gone over, stuffed the pile under his arm and then lain down to open one letter at a time, but he hadn't got any further. The envelope on top – it must have been put there that morning – white, A4, *Prison Service* and *Fridhemsplan Probation* in the right-hand corner. He had looked at it for a long time, chosen to drop it, and had been lying there avoiding it for half an hour now.

He sat up. Fingered it, lifted it up, weighed it in his hand. He went over to the window and the view out to Kronoberg court-yard. Back to the coffee table. It was still there. He lifted it up again, coughed, pulled his index finger from the opening on one side of the envelope to the other side.

A single sheet of paper. Formal formulations that he'd seen before. And at the bottom, a request.

He folded the sheet, walked over to his desk and one of the piles that lay there, went through the files until he found the one he was looking for. Another letter that had been found in a red Adidas bag during a house search, sent from an inmate in Block D at Aspsås prison to a peer in a flat on the second floor of Råby Allé 67.

He held both documents out in front of him, side by side, compared the signature at the bottom of one with that on the other.

It was written by the same hand.

He hurried out into the corridor again, three rooms down, Erik Wilson's office. His boss was sitting hunched in front of the computer screen when Grens crossed the threshold and went in.

'I got a commission from you.'

He held out an envelope, newly opened, *Prison Service* and *Fridhemsplan Probation* in the right-hand corner.

'Because I was *suited*.'

They had stood together in a cell in Hinseberg prison for women. Neither of them had understood then that it was a day that would carry on. It had. This morning in a white envelope.

'I got this today.'

Erik Wilson opened it and read the single sheet inside. Formal formulations that he'd seen before too. And that were always followed by a request. It was remarkable how often criminals, just as they were on their way to being locked up, sat in the remand prison and filled in a form about their probation officer – the person on the other side of the prison wall who would be their contact person and who they had to trust – and wanted the very policeman who had questioned them for days and wrangled with them over the truth, or even the policeman who had pursued them for so long and made sure that they were arrested.

'A request, Ewert . . .'

This form, this request for a probation officer, had been signed by one Leon Jensen.

'. . . that I would have immediately turned down.'

Wilson looked at the detective superintendent in front of him, who somehow managed to make every room feel small, folded the piece of paper and handed it back together with the envelope.

'If it had still been relevant, that is.'

Someone had died. Someone they had both seen being born. They had never talked about it, and they never would.

'Not for his sake. For *your* sake, Ewert.'

A third cup of black coffee in the corridor on the way back. And another almond slice.

He couldn't bear lying down any more, looked at the cassette player and the tapes on the shelf and listened to the silence, then sat down at his desk and randomly pulled something out of the other piles that were there – the explosions three days earlier in six buildings with the same address, Råby Allé. Slowly, and somewhat distracted, he leafed through the thick and until now unread documents. One at a time. Interviews, possible chain of events, more interviews, witness statements, yet more interviews and he'd got to the bottom file – Krantz's technical report. As soon as he read it, he started to get that feeling in his chest that he'd learnt to trust and put it to one side, waited a while, and then decided, when the feeling in his chest didn't let go, to read it again.

The first pages, overexposed and underexposed photos of cut-off electric wires and undetonated explosives, of burnt-out and blasted stairwells and flats, blackened cellar rooms and a garage.

```
Fragments of explosives localised in the
communal lift shafts are highly probably
from the same source as the explosives
previously localised on the kitchen
floor and kitchen table in the flat on
the second floor of Råby Allé 67.
```

Ewert Grens fought to keep down whatever it was in his chest. He couldn't.

*Highly probably.*

In a forensic scientist's world, in Nils Krantz's world, about as close to the absolute truth as you could get.

Index finger over the smooth photographic paper on the last page of the report and pictures from the lift shafts, enlarged fragments of mobile phones and the kind of jute that had once been part of sacks of bulk industrial explosives.

```
When examining the lift shaft in Råby
Allé 12, several pieces of a mobile
phone were found. It is very probable
that the electrical current generated by
the ringing signal caused the first
explosion at 04.34, just as was the case
with the police station.
```

Ewert Grens looked up, took a deep breath, looked down.

*Very probable.*

In a forensic scientist's world they still had a different way of expressing the truth.

```
When examining the other places where an
explosion took place, the lift shafts at
Råby Allé 25, 34, 57, 76, 102, fragments
of a further five mobile phones were
found. The time interval between
explosions favoured by witnesses, eight
to twelve seconds, coincides with the
time it takes for a signal to be
connected, transferred and connected
again. It could be that all the six
```

```
mobile phones were transferred
sequentially. It could be that the
signal to the first mobile telephone was
transferred to the next and to the next,
etc.
```

He got up and went over to the window.

04.34.

That could be true. Eight to twelve seconds. That *could* be true.

Grens left the window and went over to the bookshelf and the tapes and the two photos of someone who calmed him down and took his hand when she sang. He put on a tape, closed his eyes, waited.

*The tears I cry for you could fill an ocean*

That feeling. The one that lingers in your stomach, a bit in your chest.

*But you don't care how many tears I cry*

It didn't let go. Her voice, the words, melodies he knew so well, not even they helped.

It *could* be true.

The car was parked on Bergsgatan and he drove too fast up the hill on Hantverkargatan and through the tunnel on Drottningholmsvägen and the first part of Essingeleden, slowed down around Gröndal and continued at the speed limit in the middle lane. He'd just thought of lying down on the sofa for a while. He hadn't reckoned on two different documents within an hour leading him back to the place he'd thought he would never return to.

Krantz's report, the pictures of what had previously been mobile phones and 04.34 in the morning had linked together restless radio waves and blown up a building every eight seconds. And a white piece of paper in a white envelope sent by the Prison Service, a request to act as probation officer for an inmate called Leon Jensen.

He'd wanted Ewert Grens as his probation officer.

Of all the bloody people, he'd written down the name of the one person who wouldn't be able to answer as he'd ceased to understand what he was feeling a long time ago.

'Where are you?'

The earpiece didn't transmit the sound, so he pulled it out and held the telephone on the steering wheel right in front of him with the loudspeaker function on.

'Can you hear me, Hermansson?'

'I can hear you.'

'Where are you?'

'In my room.'

'On your own?'

She paused.

'What do you want?'

*A request I would have refused. If it had still been valid.*

'How many murders had I investigated?'

'What?'

*Not for his sake. For your sake, Ewert.*

'Which masts did you triangulate those intercepted calls from?'

'What?'

'How many . . .'

'I heard what you said. Both times.'

He'd phoned her, as he usually did, asked about something different as he usually did, and to be sure, had asked her everything again.

He wanted something. And had no idea how to do it.

'What is it that you want, Ewert? Really?'

He was driving. She could hear the constant sound curtain of heavy traffic.

'I don't want anything else. How many . . .'

'Ewert?'

'Yes?'

'What you *really* don't want . . . I think . . . we've talked about it . . . if it's about that, at least . . . you're on your way.'

'Huh?'

'You're on your way, Ewert, don't you understand? I saw it, the anger when you went to tell Pereira's wife that he'd been killed. You thought you were hiding it. I have never seen such anger before. Pereira's wife could feel it, Sven, the children, and it was good for them, for me. It was the kind of anger that goes hand in hand with real grief. *You can feel, Ewert.* In a way that you haven't before . . . as long as I've known you. And if you can feel that anger and manage it, then you can also fall in love, dare to fall in love, maybe feel something that isn't just about you.'

He didn't answer.

The bloody phone, it shouldn't really be on the steering wheel, it wasn't good to have it in view of the traffic. He moved it down to the passenger seat, but then it was difficult to hear what she was saying, so he hung up.

It looked as it had done when he had left two days earlier.

He parked by the blue and white plastic that cordoned off the area around six buildings that housed a total of four hundred and twenty flats. Black, torn buildings that had collapsed and the smell of soot hit him as the wind moved around the burnt-down climbing frame in the playground and the ash from the trees and park benches that had been set out some years earlier to break up the asphalt that now was the only thing left.

He had thought it already.

This is not a crime scene where I have to tread carefully. This is a tragedy. Someone else's everyday.

He counted eight cars from the bomb unit, who had resumed their search after the arrest of Leon Jensen, three cars from

Forensics, who were there to get down on their knees and search for things that no one else could see, and two patrol cars and a van from Södertörn Police with uniformed officers who stood guarding the cordons. If he went up on his toes, he could see the bomb dogs and experts moving between two entrances on the other side of Råby Torg. The three past days equalled fifteen hundred flats in twenty-five buildings, as well as lift shafts, cellar corridors and garage sections, which had all been searched. He pulled the summary that he received regularly from the inner pocket of his jacket. Bomb technicians in protective clothing had now searched a fifth of Råby and found four thousand three hundred and five rifle cartridges, seven hundred and six pistol bullets, two hundred and nine revolver bullets, seven smoke grenades, six fragmentation grenades, five sticks of dynamite, three anti-tank weapons, three stick grenades and a good kilo of military explosives. In the course of their search, they had also seized twenty-five home-made ninja stars, twenty-two sawn-off shotguns, fourteen army knives of various sorts, nine nunchucks, seven bayonets, five AK4 automatic rifles, three Kpist submachine guns and two Kalashnikovs.

Grens looked around.

Another time. And still the bloody same.

He started to walk, his body close to the plastic cordon. He was on his way. She'd said that and he'd had no idea. His anger had been grief. She'd said that as well. He stopped and held on to the blue and white. She'd stood beside him, Sven on the other side, the first funeral he had chosen to go to because he *wanted* to go and he hadn't been ashamed or given himself a hard time afterwards for not having gone to hers. They had stood at a distance and watched as José Pereira's coffin was lowered, he hadn't known that there were still people who did that.

He carried on towards the building that lacked walls in several places, where faces had recently looked out through the windows, and stopped again.

José Pereira. Julia Bozsik. Leon Jensen.

What if a police sergeant called Ewert Grens had not arrested a young woman and taken a young man away nearly twenty years ago? If a boy who had been born had grown up somewhere else?

He looked at all the soot, a deep intake of the acrid smell, the wind was playing with the ash again.

Råby Allé 12.

He got closer. According to Krantz's report and several unanimous witness statements, the building that had exploded first and then collapsed completely.

Pictures from the former Yugoslavia. Or Lebanon. From news programmes with serious voices, houses that had been destroyed by civil war, it looked like that.

*'I want you to ring me . . . In exactly ten minutes.'*

Her voice.

It had been calm and he'd done as she asked.

The mobile phone with the earpiece that wasn't working was in his pocket, he got it out and pulled up the menu for outgoing calls, ran his finger down to three days ago. He had made fourteen calls that day. Four in the morning.

One of them, he'd already realised and now saw, at 04.34.

He carried on. Råby Allé 25. The next stairwell and lift shaft that had exploded and which, according to Krantz, had also hidden fragments of a mobile phone.

*'What's it concerning?'*
*'About what we spoke about last time.'*

Ewert Grens studied more soot. It left nothing untouched. Painted every half wall with its blackness.

He was holding a phone which three nights earlier had made a call to a number he didn't know. He called it again. No reply.

He called directory inquiries. No registered subscriber. He called Nils Krantz.

'The pieces from the mobile phone that detonated the first explosion.'

'Yes?'

'I want you to look at them again. See if you can identify a number on the SIM card.'

'If you come here, we can look together.'

'Here?'

'I'm in one of the Forensic vans. I can see you right now.'

Krantz was on his knees in the middle of the van when Ewert Grens opened the two back doors. The forensic scientist crawled around amongst the black bags and long wires and powerful lamps with different kinds of light, and something else that looked like measuring equipment.

'I've got a picture. Here.'

He pointed at the laptop standing on a foldable basin.

'Can you see it?'

Something black in the enlarged image.

'No.'

'A piece, a few millimetres big, found one and a half metres from the lift shaft. To the left of the picture . . . there. Two digits. The only ones that are still visible. About the middle of the number.'

Grens followed Krantz's finger. He still saw nothing.

'The first one . . . two. The second . . . I'm fairly sure it's a four.'

A two. A four.

He didn't even need to open his phone and check against the list of outgoing calls. But he did, all the same.

0704244818.

Two digits in the middle.

A two and a four.

Nineteen years earlier he had forced a woman down onto her own kitchen floor. He had been responsible for her subsequent arrest, she was detained on remand, convicted by a unanimous court and sent to prison. And for security reasons, she had given birth to a child in a locked cell.

*If you want me to call, you'll tell me what it's about.*
*That only the one who started all this can put a stop to it.*

Ewert Grens gripped the forensic scientist's laptop and looked at the picture of a greatly enlarged part of a mobile phone and noticed that both his hands were shaking. He had phoned the number she'd given, waited until the signal was connected and generated an electric current. And just when the first explosion drowned out all other sounds, the same signal had been transferred and connected to the next phone and the next explosion.

He put down the computer without looking at Krantz and left the van in a rush, started to walk, anywhere.

Six buildings, four hundred and twenty flats.

It was him.

It was her.

And it was as if just at that moment they'd caught up with each other, the restlessness and unease that had hounded him since he'd been given an assignment in the middle of the night a week earlier, as if it was now so close, reached out a hand and prodded him on the back, gave him a push.

He passed Råby Torg and the greengrocer's stalls that hadn't been there for a long time and then the large shopping centre with more dark, closed shops than open ones, he carried on along the asphalt walkway towards the metro station and turned off just before the entrance, walked along the tracks and the sound of a train every ten minutes.

He'd worked in the police in the capital for twenty-seven years and still believed in the same values as he had the day he collected his first uniform as a young trainee. Perhaps it was too obvious, too simple. Maybe it wasn't even particularly deep. *Anyone who aggrieves another party should have balls enough to pay for it afterwards*. That's just the way things were, the only way he could deal with him or her who had given themselves the right always to cause permanent harm.

The sound of a train on his left-hand side blended with that of the E4 and thousands of cars in the distance. He sat down on a park bench with nearly no graffiti, a good place for him. He wanted to see the whole community, as well as the partially bombed houses and two traffic arteries that cut it into equally large chunks.

He hadn't thought about her, about him, about their son, afterwards, not even once.

Why should he?

The following working day their lives had been someone else's.

But then they'd forced their way back in years later, led him back to what he'd left behind so long ago. Three consequences of an arrest that it was not his job to take responsibility for afterwards.

He got up, wiped the back of his jacket free of the kind of dust that builds up layer by layer with every passing train. He started to walk again, back to the car and the high-rise blocks guarded by policemen in front of a blue and white cordon.

His world for a week.

They had smashed a highly dangerous gang and crime in the area would fall for a while until the next gang took over; there was always someone ready to build their reputation. They had taken four fugitives to separate prisons where they would serve out their sentences. And they had removed two gang leaders from the streets they had been part of for so long.

One of them was sitting in a room in a youth hostel close to the green of the forest and the blue of the water and trying to keep himself clean while he waited for his girlfriend, some eighty kilometres away, to give birth to their child.

He had seen the other one being born and he had then carried on and now that he no longer existed he had stopped carrying on.

# much later

SHE'S LYING ON her back, as still as she can, looking at the ugly plastic bag with a tube and a syringe and the transparent drop that slowly gets bigger, she can see it, watches it grow, lose its hold, fall.

Oxytocin.

Yet another millilitre diluted with half a litre of saline solution.

One of the people in green clothes told her that. The one who looks after the infusion pump and had inserted the catheter into a vein on her arm. Fifteen millilitres an hour that leave the plastic bag and are pumped into her body.

It was to speed things up. Some hours ago she had only been one centimetre dilated. The drops opened her more. And the other person in green had inserted a long needle and pressed and pressed until the two membranes broke and the warm water ran out over her thighs and knees, washing her feet.

———

There are more people in the room.

The two green people stay near her the whole time, their hands on her stomach or some of the equipment that ticks and peeps. The others are standing further away. They're wearing long white coats that reach to the floor and sometimes when she turns her head a little, she sees clearly that it's just something to cover their dark trousers and dark shoes.

———

It felt like period pains. The first few times. Now it's stronger. Someone punching her from inside. More often. Longer. She's tried to count, thought one second at a time and it's been slightly less painful, only two minutes between the last three that took forty-two and forty-seven and forty-four seconds to stop.

———————

It's a big cell.

She thinks about the one that Gabriel showed her a picture of, from the prison that's just outside Mariefred, and some others from prisons without walls that she can't remember the names of. She thinks about the one that Leon once described when she brought him a delivery in the visitors' room in Aspsås, and the ones that Reza and Uros were in when she delivered to them at Österåker prison and Storboda prison. Their cells had been much smaller. A pregnant inmate who, for security reasons, is not given permission to give birth in Örebro hospital or the one in Karlskoga, needed to have one that was big enough to accommodate a metal bed in the middle and all the equipment that ticks and peeps and six people in green and white overalls who are working or waiting.

If she stretches up a bit, turns her head slightly to the other side, she can see the barred window, through it. It's evening, quite cold even though it's spring, and the trees nearby are sporting young green leaves. An ambulance is waiting just outside the window, facing the prison gate. Behind it, another car that looks new, red, shiny.

She counts again. Not even a minute in between now. And then the pain that presses from inside – exactly fifty-one seconds.

———————

She recognises the two of them by the door. The big one without hair, who she thinks is the one Gabriel phoned. And the one who's a bit younger, who questioned her along with the woman five times before the trial, before she left Kronoberg remand prison.

She'll ask them afterwards.

They had been sitting on the floor at the top of the stairs, he was in pain, like she is now, and he'd gone to Råby police station to ask for help again and had then just disappeared.

She'll ask them if they know where Gabriel is, if he's alive.

———

She can't count the intervals any more. She knows that it won't be long now.

She spoke to the woman in Social Services right at the start, it had only been a few weeks and the sesame seed wasn't even half a centimetre long, the woman she knew was Leon's mother, even though you weren't allowed to talk about it, and during their conversation the woman had looked at her belly, it hadn't even started to show, and asked if she was pregnant. She hadn't answered. And the woman hadn't asked again. But said that if that was the case, if she was to get pregnant and have a child, it would probably feel the same as it had for her. Like waves. Like fire. As if something inside her body was punching and pushing and she had no control over it.

It felt exactly like that.

———

She often thought about that day.

Already in the morning, in bed beside Gabriel, with the blanket letting in the sharp sunlight, her breasts had been swollen and on those days it always felt like a fever rushing through her, ovulation, she'd known it, she always did.

She'd never got undressed in front of anyone else before, not before Gabriel. And every time she felt like this, her breasts, the fever, she'd tried to avoid him and when that wasn't possible and he made his demands, she had always managed to get to the toilet and a pessary, and crossed her fingers until the next period.

It was one of the days she was going to deliver. So that day she hadn't even needed to avoid him. A plastic bag that weighed exactly two hundred grams and the smell of acetone had been in the way.

Despite all that.

The day she got pregnant.

She had lain down on the hard stone floor at the Shell station by the Täby exit, had dipped what she needed to push up in baby oil and held it inside until the smell of acetone would penetrate into her vagina and labia, and then pulled it out again, stood up, dropped it down into the toilet.

She was to put it in, dump it, smell, be noticed by the prison dogs, body searched, let in. She was to be empty when she visited Leon.

She'd sat opposite him in the ugly, depressing room and reported on the robberies in the jewellers' shops in Solna and Huddinge and the newsagent by Slussen, and the collection of a debt in Sundbyberg. She'd confirmed that his mobile phone was bugged. She had *You still live there?* several times *Still, all the time?* answered *Still, in Gabriel's room?* the questions he always asked. And then, and this is what she had thought of so often, he'd leaned in close to her and whispered that she had done well, that she had to stay the whole hour this time too so the visit would be like any other, that Gabriel was his brother and wouldn't mind sharing, that she should get undressed and lie down on the bunk beside his equally naked body while they waited, to pass the time.

———

Your dad was born here.

You will soon be born here.

THIS IS THE same cell. At least, he thinks it is.

Nineteen years have passed.

The girl lying there is called Wanda. The one who lay there before was called Ana.

Two different young women and another time, but it felt like it was happening in parallel all the same – after a while Ewert Grens was forced to glance to the side where Erik Wilson had stood before and Sven Sundkvist was standing now, run his hand over his head and check that he had no hair, over his stomach that is big in a way that it hasn't always been, and just to be on the safe side, to stretch a stiff leg that didn't hurt back then.

Another time.

He hears her scream. And then another.

A ribcage passing down the narrow birth canal, being squeezed, and pressing out the water and a head and mouth that's already out and fills the lungs with air.

The first intake of breath.

————

He moves a step closer.

*Every intervention by a police officer has consequences.*

The tiny thing lies on her stomach.

*It's not his job to assess them, weigh them up, to try to understand how long the consequences will carry on.*

The hair is matted, wet. The head is oval, it has been pressed together, a swelling that would soon disappear.

*Not even now.*

*Not even in front of a face he almost recognises.*

----------

And yet.

He wonders, he can't help it, who will be *your* Julia Bozsik, *your* José Pereira.

----------

The two others, who are also wearing white coats – a man and a woman – leave their places by the door and walk past him on either side, four hands lift up what has been lying warm and safe on her stomach, open a briefcase, fill in a sheet of white A4 paper, hurry out to the red, shiny car that is standing behind the ambulance, waiting, and a portable incubator is placed on the back seat.

----------

He stays where he is. Silence. The couple in the red car have driven off towards the prison gate and the family unit in Botkyrka, the two who were wearing green overalls are sitting in an ambulance on their way to Örebro hospital, Sven is waiting further down the corridor – Ewert Grens hears female voices behind the locked metal doors, alternating between *pig bastard* and *pig cunt* – and he just stands there, searching for words.

'I think . . .'

He remembers a question. *Did you see?* He wasn't prepared then. *See what?* Sometimes it's the first time. *If it was a boy or a girl?* It's easier the next time.

'. . . that I saw.'

'What?'

'Just now. The baby on your stomach.'

Her eyes, it's difficult to make contact, she's so tired, she doesn't want to.

'What . . . are you talking about?'

He tries to follow her gaze, but can't, it isn't there, and he turns slightly, looks higher up, further away, through the barred window.

'I saw that it was a boy.'

# from the authors

With our great thanks to

R, S, R and B for trusting us and inviting us in – for some years we have been a part of your world.

*Johan Åkerlund*, Section Against Gang Crime, for essential knowledge about the day-to-day reality of a police officer working with gang crime.

*Bertil Ahlgren*, Leading Firefighter, for essential knowledge about the day-to-day reality of a firefighter who is constantly under threat.

*Reine Adolfsson*, for his expertise in explosives, *Peter Blomqvist* for his expertise in forensics, *Henrik Druid* for his expertise in forensic medicine, *Lasse Lagergen* for his expertise in medicine, *Mikael Gilliusson* for his expertise in dealing with the wounded, *Leif Nordeén* for his expertise in young people in detention, and *Mikael Madenteg* for his expertise in young criminals at large.

# CELL 8

## Roslund & Hellström

### ONE CELL

A convicted murderer dies awaiting execution

on Ohio's death row.

### ONE CRIMINAL

Six years later, the same man walks into a Stockholm

police station.

### ONE CONSPIRACY

He's defeated death. He's played the unplayable system. And now

Detective Superintendent Ewert Grens must discover how.

'Astonishing . . . Passionate . . . Taut with suspense'

Sunday Times

OUT NOW IN PAPERBACK AND EBOOK

## Quercus

www.quercusbooks.co.uk